THE STRONGBOW SAGA

THE STRONGBOW SAGA, BOOK FOUR:
THE LONG HUNT

Cover design:
Luc Reid

Interior artwork:
Judson Roberts and Luc Reid

Editors:
Jeanette Roberts, Laura Beyers, Luc Reid, Alexa Linden

Copy edit:
Layla Milholen

For Jeanette,

without whom this book
would not have happened.

CONTENTS

List of Characters

ALF   A pilot who guides ships to Birka.

ARINBJORN   The Danish jarl who rules over the island of Mon.

ASBJORN   One of Hastein's warriors who sometimes fights as an archer.

ASTRID   A female thrall on the estate of the deceased chieftain Hrorik, Halfdan's father, who served as Sigrid's maid.

BAUG   A carl on the estate of the deceased chieftain Hrorik, Halfdan's father; the brother of Floki.

BJORGOLF   One of Hastein's warriors. He and his identical twin brother, Bryngolf, are known as the Ravens.

BJORN   Bjorn Ironsides, a 9th century Viking chieftain and one of the sons of Ragnar Logbrod.

BRAM   A young man who lives in the village near the estate of the deceased chieftain Hrorik, Halfdan's father.

I

BRYNGOLF	One of Hastein's warriors. He and his identical twin brother, Bjorgolf, are known as the Ravens.
CULLAIN	A former Irish monk, skilled in the treatment of wounds and illnesses, who is now a slave owned by Hastein, and who serves as the cook aboard Hastein's longship, the *Gull*.
EINAR	A warrior from the village on the Limfjord in Jutland who is Halfdan's closest friend.
FASTI	A thrall on the estate of the deceased chieftain Hrorik, Halfdan's father.
FLOKI	A carl on the estate of the deceased chieftain Hrorik, Halfdan's father; the brother of Baug.
GENEVIEVE	A young Frankish noblewoman who was captured by Halfdan during the campaign in Frankia, and with whom he became romantically involved.

GUDROD	A carl on the estate of the deceased chieftain Hrorik, Halfdan's father, nicknamed Gudrod the Carpenter because he was in charge of woodworking chores on the estate.
GUDFRED	A carl on the estate of the deceased chieftain Hrorik, Halfdan's father.
GUNHILD	The widow of the deceased chieftain Hrorik, Halfdan's father, and the mother of Toke.
HALFDAN	The son of Hrorik, a Danish chieftain, and Derdriu, an Irish-born slave owned by Hrorik; the warrior who has come to be known as Strongbow.
HALLBJORN	One of Hastein's warriors who sometimes fights as an archer.
HARALD	Halfdan's half-brother, and Sigrid's twin.
HASTEIN	A Danish jarl who befriends Halfdan.
HERIGAR	The commander of the king's garrison at Birka.

HROALD   The headman of the village near the
          estate of the deceased chieftain Hrorik,
          Halfdan's father.

HRODGAR   The headman of the village on the
          Limfjord in Jutland located near the
          farm where Harald, Halfdan's brother,
          was killed by Toke.

IVAR   Ivar the Boneless, a 9th century Viking
          chieftain and one of the sons of Ragnar
          Logbrod.

NORI   A village headman on the island of
          Oeland.

OSTEN   A village headman on the island of
          Oeland, whose wife was stolen by
          pirates and died in captivity.

RAGNAR   Ragnar Logbrod, a famous 9th century
          Viking chieftain; the father of Bjorn
          Ironsides, Ivar the Boneless, and
          Sigurd Snake-in-the-Eye, and the war-
          king who led the Danish army that
          captured Paris.

RAGNVALD A chieftain who serves King Horik of
          the Danes.

RAUNA	A young Sami woman.
REGIN	A member of the crew of the longship the *Serpent*, who serves as the ship's cook.
ROBERT	The Frankish count who ruled over Paris; Genevieve's father.
SERCK	A villager on the island of Oeland, whose daughter was stolen by pirates and died in captivity.
SIGRID	Halfdan's half-sister.
SIGTRYGG	A captain who serves Jarl Arinbjorn.
SIGURD	Sigurd Snake-in-the-Eye, a son of Ragnar Logbrod.
SIGVALD	The chieftain who leads the pirate band.
SKJOLD	One of Toke's men, who was captured by Sigvald's pirate band and joined it.
SKULI	A young man who lives in the village near the estate of the deceased chieftain Hrorik, Halfdan's father.

SNORRE   A chieftain who served Toke, and who was killed by Halfdan in a duel in Paris.

STIG   A chieftain who serves Jarl Hastein.

STOROLF   One of Hastein's warriors who sometimes fights as an archer.

TOKE   The son by a previous marriage of Gunhild, the widow of Hrorik, Halfdan's father; the Danish chieftain who murdered Harald, Halfdan's half-brother.

TORE   The captain of the archers who serve Hastein.

TORVALD   Hastein's second-in-command; a warrior of unusual tallness and strength.

UBBE   The foreman on the estate of the deceased chieftain Hrorik, Halfdan's father.

1

A Good Plan

Soon it would be done. Soon Toke would be dead, and Harald avenged. For we had a plan.

"I have been giving this matter much thought," Hastein had told me, after we'd reached Danish waters on our voyage home from Frankia. "You wish to bring a case under the law against Toke at a Thing, charging him with murder. And I would of course support you in such a case, as would Hrodgar. Having the jarl ruling over the Limfjord district and the chieftain of the village closest to where the killings occurred join you in the case would almost certainly guarantee success. But the greatest sentence a Thing can pass is outlawry. Toke would forfeit any lands he now holds here—lands which rightfully belong to you, anyway—and would be banished from the kingdom of the Danes. But there is a way Toke could contest a Thing-court's decision. He would have the right to challenge his accuser to a duel...."

I knew what Hastein had left unsaid. I was greatly changed from the boy who had sworn an oath of vengeance against Toke. I had gained much experience as a warrior in Frankia, and I had killed men—many men, counting all those my arrows had felled in battle. I had even killed Snorre, Toke's second-in-command, in a formal duel. But Toke was different. I did not want to face Toke one on one. He was as strong as a bear and

1

nearly as large as one, and very quick and light on his feet. And I was afraid of him. I had always been afraid of him, for as far back as I could remember. I did not believe I could best him in such a fight.

"No, we must surprise and trap him with overwhelming force. Then, as jarl over the Limfjord district, I will call upon him to surrender. I will tell him I will take him to King Horik, to answer the charge that he wrongfully killed Harald and his men, and I will give him my oath that he will come to no harm on the journey there. Ivar and Bjorn will join with me, also—it will be no small thing, to a man like Toke, that two sons of Ragnar Logbrod are urging him to come peacefully and appear before the king.

"Toke is of noble birth. He is the grandson of a jarl. He will not believe the king will do more than outlaw him, if that." Hastein smiled a grim smile. "Had he only killed Harald and his men, he would probably be right. These things happen. His mistake was killing everyone—the women, the children, even the thralls. And he killed them after giving his oath that they would be safe. It was the worst kind of niddingsvaark. King Horik is a man who greatly values honor. He has no use for a Nithing. He will hang Toke. I feel sure of it. It is a good plan."

My own plan differed slightly from Hastein's. I knew Toke. He would never surrender. He would fight us, even if he knew he could not win. He would rather die with a sword in his hand, killing as many of his enemies as he could, than allow himself to be taken without a fight. He would fight us, and when he did, I

2

would put an arrow through his eye.

Soon it would be done.

We had landed at dusk a short distance up the coast from the estate that had once belonged to Hrorik, my father, and after him to my brother, Harald. Ivar and Bjorn had indeed come with us. They wanted to see the end of the tale Hastein had told the entire army at the feast that last night in Paris, the night before our fleet had left Frankia and sailed for home with the ransom and plunder we'd won. Hrodgar and the men from the village on the Limfjord had come, too, although some of them had grumbled at the prospect of further delay in returning to their homes, once they were so close.

"It is our duty," Hrodgar had chided them. "It was we who discovered the slaughter at Hrorik's farm. It was to us that Toke spun his web of lies, to cover his own misdeeds. We allowed him to escape, and even sent two of our own to help hunt Halfdan, believing Toke's tale that he was a bandit. Toke must know, when he is brought to justice, that we are no longer his fools."

We planned to surround the longhouse in the last hours before dawn while the household still slept, trapping Toke and his men inside. Hastein and Ivar and most of their warriors were with me now, hiding in the edge of the woodlands that bordered the cleared lands of the estate. I'd led them there in the dark, through the forest I'd hunted in so often as a boy. At first light, Bjorn, Hrodgar, and the rest of the men would bring the ships around to block any chance of escape by sea.

"It is time," Hastein whispered, touching my arm from where he was sitting nearby, his back against the

3

trunk of a tree. When we'd arrived, he'd been but an indistinct shadow. Now I could make out his outline, and see the looming shape of Torvald sitting beyond him. "The sky will begin to lighten soon," he continued. "We should be in place before anyone ventures outside."

I seated my helm on my head, twisting it back and forth with my hands until it felt comfortable, then tied the strap under my chin. I stood, braced my bow against my right foot, and strung it. Beside me, Tore did the same.

"Do you think he might fight?" he asked me. "This Toke? Against great chieftains like Jarl Hastein, and Ivar, and Bjorn? It would be madness. But Torvald says he is a berserker, and with them, you never know."

I shrugged my shoulders in answer, and slipped the strap of my quiver over my head, so that it hung at my right hip with the arrows ready to draw. I searched through them and selected one I knew shot true. It had a heavy oak shaft, and was tipped with a short iron head with a square cross-section that tapered to a sharp point. I called such heads mail-breakers. I'd found a barrel full of them in a storeroom in the island fort that had been the home of Count Robert of Paris before we'd taken it and the town. I'd stowed a sack of the heads in my sea chest, and had mounted two dozen on my heaviest arrows during the long voyage back from Frankia.

I touched my finger to the tip, feeling its sharpness, and for a brief moment my thoughts took me back to Paris. Where was Genevieve now? What was she doing? I remembered the last words she had spoken to me. She'd brushed my cheek with her hand, and whispered,

4

"I will pray every day to my God to watch over you and protect you. I will pray to Him to shelter my love from wind and wave on your long journey back to your land." Then she had turned and walked away without looking back.

I shook my head, trying to clear it of thoughts of her. I could not afford to be distracted by memories of the happiness we'd shared so briefly then lost. I had a man to kill. Perhaps many. All of my thoughts must be on that for now.

I led our force of warriors from the forest's edge that lay just below the crest of the low hill overlooking the longhouse down on the shore. It was atop this hill where the bodies of my mother and Hrorik had been burned and sent upon their death voyage. Harald had found me here, the morning after their funeral pyre. The burial mound within the standing stones that formed the outline of their death ship had grown a lush cover of tall grass since I had last been here.

In the great feast hall of the gods, did my mother know what I had become? Did she think it was worth the sacrifice she had made? And what did Hrorik think now of his slave son? When Harald had reached Valhalla, he would have told them of how he'd trained me, and of my first battle—the one that had cost him his life. But much had happened since then. Did my family know these things, where they dwelled now in the distant land of the gods?

Morning fog shrouded the hilltop. We spread out into a long line, Hastein at its center. Torvald, Tore and I, with the rest of the warriors from the *Gull* save the skeleton crew who were sailing it round from where we'd landed yester-night, aligned ourselves to his right. Ivar and his men formed to Hastein's left. Hastein's two captains, Stig and Svein, and their warriors anchored the two ends of the line, barely visible now in the thick mist.

Hastein drew his sword, waved it overhead, then pointed it toward the longhouse. We moved forward slowly across the hilltop and down its slopes, the fog muffling the sound of our advance as it blurred our shapes. From the longhouse below—had anyone been watching—we would have looked like an army of ghosts gliding silently through the mist.

When we reached the base of the hill, Stig and Svein and their men trotted ahead, curving the ends of the line forward to encircle the longhouse within a wall of armed men that touched the shore at either end. The trap was closed, and those inside were now surrounded. No one would be able to escape.

Ivar raised his horn to his lips and blew a long, challenging peal. After a moment, he blew it again. From out over the water, we heard another horn give answer. The ships, which had rounded the point and were waiting for the signal, would pull for the shore below us now that they knew we were in position.

The door to the longhouse opened, and a head peered out. Seeing us, it jerked quickly back inside and the door slammed shut.

I thought it lax of Toke that no sentries stood guard outside during the night. Even though the estate lay in the heart of the lands of the Danes, he was a man with enemies.

Hastein called out in a strong, clear voice, "You, inside the longhouse. Hear this! My name is Hastein. I am jarl over the Limfjord district. I have business with Toke. I come in peace, so long as violence is not offered to me and my men. On that, I give my word. But those inside must come out now, bearing no weapons. You are surrounded. If you do not come out and meet with us in peace, blood will be shed."

For a long while, there was only silence. I spent the time recalling in my mind images of the longhouse. If we had to breach its walls with a ram, where would be the best place to attack? Hastein was not Toke, nor was I. We would not burn the building with innocents inside.

Finally the door opened, and a voice from within shouted, "We are coming out. We bear no arms."

Gunhild lead the procession that filed out of the longhouse door. That I had not expected. As much as I hated her, I could not deny that she showed courage in doing so. Behind her, one by one, peering fearfully at us as they left the safety of the longhouse, came the estate's carls, their wives and children, and the thralls who lived and worked on the estate where most of my life had been spent.

Toke and his warriors were not among them.

"Does anyone remain inside the longhouse?" Hastein shouted. "If you are not truthful, it will go hard on you."

Gunhild shook her head. "There is no one left inside."

Hastein murmured to Torvald, "See if she speaks the truth. Take Halfdan and Tore. Be careful."

The three of us strode toward the open door of the longhouse. Tore and I had our shields slung across our backs and our bows raised and at ready. Torvald, advancing between us, held his shield angled in front of him, covering his chest and neck, and carried a spear cocked back, ready to throw. The moment when he entered the doorway would be the most dangerous. Tore and I would cover him as best we could.

Something nagged at the back of my mind. I stared at the faces of the frightened folk huddled behind Gunhild and realized that Toke and his men were not the only ones missing.

"Wait," I said to Torvald and Tore in a low voice, then turned toward Gunhild and snapped at her in a louder one, "Where is Sigrid? Where is Ubbe?"

She'd looked pale before, but at my questions, the blood remaining in her face drained from it.

"Who are you to know those names?"

It was not surprising she did not recognize me. The light was still dim—it would be a while yet before the sun rose—and the mail curtain hanging from the sides and back of the helm I was wearing partially obscured my features. Also, I was not the boy she had last seen. I was a warrior now. The boy who'd left here was now a man, wearing a shirt of Frankish mail, and a Frankish helm, with a fine sword hanging at his hip. I'd grown taller in the months since I'd left, and the beginnings of a beard lined my jaw. Around my right arm was the torque of solid gold—a treasure such as a king or jarl might wear—that Ragnar Logbrod himself had given me. I wore it now because I wished to make a strong impression when I first reappeared at my former home. I was no longer Halfdan, the former slave. I was a warrior.

"I am called Strongbow," I replied. "Answer me. Where are Sigrid and Ubbe?"

Someone said, "I know that voice," and a man in a shabby, soiled tunic pushed his way to the front of the crowd.

"Get behind me, thrall," Gunhild snapped, but he ignored her.

"Is it you?" he asked in a quavering voice. "Is it Halfdan?"

I had not counted on this. I loosened the strap under my chin and pulled my helm from my head. "Fasti," I answered. "It is. I have returned."

Gunhild staggered back. She would have fallen had those behind not supported her. "But you are dead!" she gasped.

"It would seem I am not." To Fasti, I added, "Quickly. You must tell me. Where is Toke? Are he and his men still inside? Where are Sigrid and Ubbe?"

The expression of wonder that had filled his face a moment before was replaced by a look of pain and fear.

"Toke is gone. He and all of his men. He killed Ubbe, and took Sigrid with him."

2

Niddingsvaark

After our ships landed, Hastein sent parties of warriors out to the edges of the fields to stand watch in case a force came from the nearby village, or from the forest as we had done. "Toke may be gone from here now, but he and his men could still be nearby. We must take no chances," he said.

The rest of our men lounged at ease around the yard outside the longhouse, while the leaders of our party gathered inside to hold counsel. In the center of the longhouse, near the hearth, Hastein and I sat Fasti down on the long bench against the wall and were questioning him, trying to learn more about what had happened. Hrodgar, Ivar, Bjorn, Stig, and Svein were seated at the high table nearby, listening. Torvald was with them, too.

It was proving difficult to get clear answers from Fasti, for he was distracted. The assemblage of chieftains and warriors who had taken possession of the estate, seemingly with hostile intent based on their warlike appearance, clearly unnerved him. It did not help matters, either, that Gunhild was hovering nearby, scowling at him.

"I need to know more, Fasti," I told him. "You must tell me everything that happened."

"It was after the ship came," he said.

"Ship? What ship?" Hastein asked. With a sinking feeling, I felt certain I already knew.

"The *Sea Steed*," Gunhild volunteered.

I had feared we were tarrying too long on our voyage home from Frankia. The night of the duel in Paris, after I'd killed Snorre, some of our sentries had reported to Ragnar that a ship had left its mooring and was headed downriver in the dark. It had not taken long to determine that it was the *Sea Steed*. Snorre's crew had slunk away to their ship and fled. No doubt most of them had been with Toke and Snorre up on the Limfjord, among the party that had burned the longhouse there and killed my brother Harald and his men. Perhaps they'd feared, after Hastein had exposed the treachery of their attack, that they, too, might be in danger. I'd urged Hastein to pursue them, but he had not wished to leave Frankia ahead of the main fleet.

"What happened when the ship came?" I asked.

"I do not know what news it brought, but Toke was very upset," Fasti answered. I glanced at Gunhild. She added nothing, but glared back at me defiantly. She had regained some of her composure and was acting more like herself now.

"And then?" I prompted.

"Toke was very upset," Fasti repeated. "Many of us felt his wrath."

I turned to Gunhild. "Do you know what news the ship brought?"

She did not answer. "Do you know where the ship had been?" I asked. I knew the answer, of course, but I wondered how much she knew. Still she remained silent.

Hastein stepped forward until he loomed over her. Although he'd removed his helm, he was still wearing

11

his mail brynie and his sword, slung by its baldric over his shoulder. His left hand was resting lightly now on its hilt at his hip. He snapped, "Speak, woman! You are wasting our time."

Gunhild flinched. An angry jarl, dressed for war, is admittedly an intimidating sight. "I know that the ship had been raiding in Frankia. With the fleet that sailed against the Franks last spring. Its captain was a man named Snorre. He was one of Toke's most trusted men." She paused for a moment, then added, "He did not return with the ship."

At that, I smiled a grim smile. Hastein continued questioning Gunhild.

"What news did the ship from Frankia bring? Did Toke tell you?"

Gunhild shook her head. "I do not know. I swear it. Toke insisted on speaking with its crew in private. He sent everyone out of the longhouse while he did. Even me. But whatever news they brought him, as the thrall said, Toke was very upset by it."

I could well imagine. I asked Gunhild, "Do you know what happened to the ship's captain, Snorre?"

"Only that he died in Frankia."

"*I* killed him, Gunhild," I told her. Her eyes widened. "I cut his throat," I added. She looked at Hastein, alarmed.

He shrugged. "It was in a fair fight. A duel. With witnesses. Many witnesses. I was among them. As were all the men here with us this day."

There was a question I had long wanted an answer to.

"What do you know of how Harald died, Gunhild? He and his men?"

The change of subject took Gunhild by surprise, and obviously disturbed her. Again she glanced at Hastein, as if looking for support, but she found none in his cold gaze.

"I...I know nothing," she stammered.

"Nothing?"

"Only what Toke told us. That the farm up on the Limfjord where Harald had gone was attacked by bandits, and all its folk, including Harald and his men, were slain."

"All of Harald's men were slain? Including me?"

"That is what Toke said." Gunhild looked confused. And worried.

"How did Toke say he knew this?" I asked her.

"He said he'd been sailing through the Limfjord, heading back to Ireland, and by chance happened to be camped for the night not far from the farm when it was attacked. He told us the longhouse had been burned by the bandits in the attack, and he and his men saw the flames and went to investigate. He said he was able to catch and kill most of the attackers, and avenge Harald's death."

I'd wondered how, when he'd returned to the estate, Toke would have explained his presence at the site of the attack. Certainly Sigrid and Ubbe, knowing the ill will Toke had long felt toward Harald, and of the recent conflict between them, should have been suspicious. So he'd claimed he was on the Limfjord because he was heading back to Ireland. That was a twist

I had not expected. It even sounded plausible. Toke was a clever liar.

I turned my head and spat upon the floor of the longhouse to show my disgust with the story, and with Gunhild for believing it. Hastein scowled at me disapprovingly. In truth, it was ill-mannered of me, but I did not care.

Gunhild looked indignant. "How dare you! Toke himself was wounded when he sought to avenge Harald's death, and many of his men were slain in the fighting."

"Wounded?" Hastein asked. "How?"

"He was struck by an arrow in his chest, when he and his men attacked the bandits. It pierced his mail."

Toke the hero, wounded while fighting those who'd caused Harald's death. Winning honor for himself by claiming to avenge murders that, in truth, he himself had committed. I turned my head and spat on the floor again. "Halfdan!" Hastein snapped.

"Do you not wonder, Gunhild, that I am still alive? That I am here, standing before you this day?" I asked her.

"I do not understand it," she admitted.

"There were no bandits. It was Toke and his warriors who attacked the farm on the Limfjord. It was they who killed Harald and his men. And they killed every woman, child, and thrall on the farm, as well. Only I escaped."

"I do not believe you! You are lying. You have always hated Toke. He is a great chieftain and you are...you were...but a thrall."

"That still troubles me," Ivar remarked to Bjorn. "How can one who was a slave for almost his entire life fight so well now? It should not be possible. I find it worrisome."

I ignored him. "There were no bandits," I said again. "It was my arrow that wounded Toke. I wish it had killed him."

Hrodgar stepped forward and spoke to Gunhild. "You do not remember me, but we have met before. I am the headman of the village on the Limfjord that lies just down from the farm that was attacked. We met when Hrorik brought you north to visit his lands there, after the two of you wed. What Halfdan says is true. My men and I reached the farm not long after the attack against it had ended. The longhouse had been burned to the ground, and all of its people had been slain. Toke and his men were there. He told us, too, that there were bandits. He told us Harald and some of his men had been at the longhouse—we had not known that—and that they had been slain by the bandits. But it was all lies. One of his own warriors later confessed to the truth of what happened. Niddingsvaark was done that night on the Limfjord by Toke and his men."

My anger had fanned the flames of Gunhild's own in return, but Hrodgar's quiet voice drained it from her, and his words seemed to suck the very life from her eyes. She covered her face with her hands, and, murmuring, "Toke, Toke, what have you done?" turned and staggered away from us. When she reached a bed-closet—the one that once had been my mother's, and briefly mine—she pulled its door open and collapsed

15

inside.

We still did not know what had happened here, at the estate. Turning back to Fasti, I asked, "How long ago did Toke leave?"

"Two days. No, no, three. It was three days ago."

"That is unfortunate," Ivar said to Bjorn. "We laid over for three days at Hastein's estate, resting and feasting after the voyage from Frankia. If we had not...."

"What happened with Sigrid and Ubbe?" I asked Fasti.

"I did not see it. I was out in the fields at the time. Most of the menfolk of the household, free and thrall, were there, too. We were harvesting hay. But I know that it started with Astrid."

"Who is this Astrid?" Hastein asked him. In his voice I could hear the same growing impatience with Fasti that I, too, was feeling.

I answered. "She is Sigrid's maid-servant. She is a thrall."

From the high table, Bjorn called out. "And who is Sigrid?"

I turned toward him. "She is my brother Harald's sister. They were born together. She is his twin. She is my half-sister."

Bjorn looked exasperated. "What does she have to do with anything?" he grumbled to Ivar. "What has Hastein dragged us into?"

I was growing weary of trying to pry information out of Fasti. Perhaps Astrid could tell a clearer story.

The folk of the estate were huddled down at the end of the main hall that was closest to the animals' byre,

16

seated together on the long benches lining the side walls, with Tore and another of our warriors watching over them. Once we had searched the longhouse and made certain that Toke and his men were truly gone, Hastein had ordered them to go there and wait. "I will fetch Astrid," I told Hastein, and strode down the hall toward them.

"I am looking for Astrid," I called out, as I approached. "I need to speak with her."

The faces of those along the benches all turned toward me, but at first no one among them responded. Finally a sturdily built man with brown hair and beard stood up and walked down to where a woman was seated, almost at the end of the hall. She hung her head and cowered as he drew near.

"It is all right, girl," he told her. "These men mean you no harm." Turning to me, he said, "She is here."

I walked over to them. The man stared at me curiously.

"You really are the boy, aren't you?" he said. Seeing me scowl, he added, "I mean no offense. You're clearly a boy no longer. But you are the one who was Hrorik's son, by the Irish woman, the thrall. The one he freed and acknowledged just before he died."

He did not even know my mother's name. She had been just a slave to him. As I had been, until Hrorik had freed me.

He continued. "My name is Gudfred. I was with Hrorik and Harald on their last voyage to England."

"Yes," I said. "I remember you." It was somewhat of an exaggeration. His face was vaguely familiar—I

17

knew he was one of the carls who lived and worked on the estate, and had served Hrorik as one of his warriors—but I had not remembered his name. After I was freed and Harald had taken me under his care, he'd made a point of trying to teaching me the names of all of the free folk who lived on the estate. Before then—when I was still a slave—there were many, including this man Gudfred, whose names I had never known, as they, no doubt, had not known mine. Gudfred had been one of Hrorik's followers, one of his housecarls, for years. For most of my life, that was all he'd been to me, as I had been just a slave, one of the estate's thralls, to him.

"Toke said you were dead," he continued. "He said you'd been killed with Harald, and Ulf, and Rolf, and the others. Up on the Limfjord, in the attack by the bandits."

"Toke lied."

Gudfred grunted. "About you, at least, so it would seem. And Harald?"

"There were no bandits. Toke and his warriors attacked the longhouse in the night. They burned it. They killed Harald and his men, and all the folk of the farm, too. I alone escaped."

"Gods! And he was here, living among us all these months. After Snorre left for Frankia with most of his men, he would have been at our mercy. If only we had known."

"We—the chieftains who have come here, and I—need to know what happened here, and where Toke has gone," I told him. "I was told Astrid was involved."

"Aye," Gudfred answered. "She was. But getting the tale from her will not be easy. She has not spoken

18

much these last few days. I saw it all. I can tell you."

I looked more closely at Astrid. She was still huddled over, her head averted, her long hair hanging loose and hiding her face.

"Astrid?" I said. "I am Halfdan. Don't you remember me?"

She slowly straightened up and looked at me. Had I not been told who she was, I would not have recognized her. Her face looked gaunt, with deep, dark hollows under her eyes, one of which was swollen almost shut. A dark bruise covered that side of her face. Her gaze was unfocused. "Is Harald here?" she whispered. "Has he returned?"

I shook my head. "No, Astrid. He is not here. He is gone."

She hung her head again.

"Come, then," I said to Gudfred, and we walked in silence back to where Hastein and the others were waiting.

Gudfred began his tale at its beginning, back when Toke had first returned to the estate from the Limfjord.

"There were none of us among the carls living here who much liked him," he explained. "We'd all followed Hrorik for many years, and had known Toke as he was growing up. We all knew what he could be like. We remembered why Hrorik had thrown him out. And we'd all been here when he'd come back earlier this year, when the ill will between him and Harald had almost caused blood to be spilled. Had we come to blows on that night, I, for one, would gladly have stuck a spear in Toke myself.

"We live here because we followed Hrorik. We were his men. And we were glad to follow Harald, too— he was a brave man, and a fine warrior. But when Toke came back, and told us Harald was dead...."

Gudfred was silent for a few moments. He shook his head and started again. "Toke was the only heir, then, you see? This estate, these lands, became his. We could choose to stay on the land, if he agreed, and if we were willing to follow him. Or we could choose to go. When Toke first came back and told us the estate was now his, more than a few of us—I among them—were seriously considering leaving. It would have been hard on our families, though.

"But Toke seemed a changed man. He clearly wanted us to stay, and to accept him as our chieftain, and he worked at earning our good will and respect. Some of his crew were a rough lot, and there were minor troubles at first between us and a few of them— arguments, mostly, but once or twice men came to blows. But Toke made it clear to his men from the start that he considered us their equals in every way, and he showed them no special favors or treatment.

"His man Snorre was a hard one to like—he seemed to enjoy stirring up trouble—but after he left to join the big raid on Frankia, and took most of Toke's men with him, things here settled down. Only a few of Toke's men stayed here. Most that did had been wounded, like Toke had, fighting the bandits up on the Limfjord."

"There were no bandits," I said. "I have already told you. I shot the arrow that wounded Toke."

Gudfred shrugged. "We did not know."

"We want to know where Toke is," Ivar said. He sounded impatient. "Where did he go? Back to Ireland?"

Gudfred shook his head. "East. To Birka. That is where he said he was going."

"Why did he leave here?" Hastein asked. "What happened?"

"His ship, the *Sea Steed*, returned from Frankia. Its captain, his man Snorre, wasn't on it. Toke went aboard and spoke briefly with the crew as soon as the ship made land. I'd gone down to the shore to meet the ship, as had a number of our folk. Toke started cursing almost as soon as he went on board. Then he ordered everyone out of the longhouse, and he and the *Sea Steed*'s crew went inside. They stayed there, and spoke in private, until almost dusk. When the rest of us were finally allowed back in to go about our business, Toke was well on his way to being drunk, and was in a foul temper."

"What happened with Sigrid, and with Ubbe?" I asked.

"It started over the girl, Astrid," Gudfred replied. "When Toke had first come back to the estate, he had tried to take her to his bed. She was afraid of him, and didn't want to go. He and Sigrid had argued then about it. He said he was the master of the estate now, and had the right to bed any of its thralls. But Sigrid stood up to him, told him Astrid was her slave, not his, and Toke backed down. He didn't want trouble, back then. He wanted us, all of us, to accept him. And besides, there were other female thralls.

"But that night, the night the *Sea Steed* returned, Toke changed. He was in one of his black moods, like the old Toke again. After the meal, he walked over to the hearth, grabbed Astrid by the arm, and started dragging her to his bed chamber. Sigrid ran in front of them—she has courage, that's for certain—and told him to let the girl go. But Toke just shouted at her to get out of his way. He told her if she didn't, it would be worse for the girl, and for her. He said something more, too, but in a lower voice so the rest of us couldn't hear. Sigrid stepped aside then and let them pass. I saw her face just afterward. She looked afraid.

"The girl had a rough night of it. We could hear her screams all through the longhouse. Sigrid begged us— the carls who were Hrorik's former men, and Ubbe—to do something. But with the crew of the *Sea Steed* back again, Toke had as many of his own men to back him as there were of us."

"And it wasn't worth fighting over a thrall," I said bitterly.

Gudfred shrugged. "It's true. None of us liked that he was hurting her, but she *was* just a slave. Ubbe told us to stay calm, and bide our time.

"In the morning, Toke ordered us and his men to ready both ships for a voyage. To load them with provisions and water, and have them ready to sail by noon."

"Both ships?" Hastein asked.

"Toke's ship, the *Sea Steed*, and Hrorik's, the *Red Eagle*. Ubbe asked him where he was going, so late in the season. That's when Toke said he was sailing to Birka. When Ubbe asked him why, all Toke would say was that he had business there.

22

"'You cannot expect the men to make a voyage and not know its purpose,' Ubbe told him."

Gudfred paused and shook his head again. "All those months when he was trying to win us over to him, he threw them away with just a few words. 'I do not want these farmers with me,' he told Ubbe. 'I sail with my men alone.'"

"Did he have enough men to crew both ships?" Hastein asked.

"Just barely. Light crews in each. Enough to sail both ships easy enough, but if they have much need for rowing, they'll have slow, hard going, for certain.

"Our men backed off after that. We kept to ourselves and our own business—most of us went out to work in the fields, for there was hay to be cut—and left Toke and his men to prepare the ships on their own. When they were ready to sail, Toke and fifteen of his warriors marched back up to the longhouse. They were all wearing armor, with shields, helms, full kit, and were fully armed. Most had spears, and the rest had their swords drawn.

"As I said, most of our men had gone out to work in the fields, but those of us near the longhouse—I was one of the few who happened to be—ran for our own shields and weapons, and warned our families and the folk inside to run for safety, out through the byre. We didn't know what to expect.

"Toke and his men charged inside. Sigrid, Gunhild, and few of the kitchen thralls were at the hearth. Ubbe was there, too. On Toke's orders, two of his men grabbed Sigrid, threw her face down on the main table, and began tying her hands behind her back, and her feet together.

"Sigrid was screaming. All of the women were, even Gunhild. Ubbe grabbed one of the men holding Sigrid, trying to pull him off of her. Toke stepped forward, spun Ubbe around, and swung his fist back-handed into the side of Ubbe's face, knocking him to the ground. He should have stayed down. He had no weapon. But Ubbe was Ubbe. He was an old man, and crippled, but still a warrior in his heart. As he started to get back up, Toke drew his sword and swung it at him, hard, in an over-handed cut. He hit him here," Gudfred said, touching the edge of his hand to where his left shoulder joined his neck, "and split him down almost to his breastbone. Ubbe was dead before his body hit the floor."

"What about the rest of you?" Ivar asked. "Did no one help?"

"There were only five or six of us in the longhouse, and none of us was wearing armor. Toke's men formed a line, shoulder to shoulder, spears out, between us and the hearth. There was nothing we could do. When Toke's two men finished binding Sigrid, one of them hoisted her over his shoulder, and they all retreated back to their ships.

"Ase, Ubbe's wife, had been in the byre when Toke and his men had burst in. There was a sickly calf she had been tending to. Just as Toke and his men were leaving, she came into the longhouse—no doubt she'd heard the women screaming. She ran to where Ubbe was lying in a pool of blood, but he was already gone. She grabbed a spear off the wall and headed out the door, after Toke and his men, screaming, 'Murderers!'

"Two of Toke's men launched their spears at her as she drew near, and knocked her down. By then I and the few men with me were coming out through the longhouse door, and others of our men were running in from the fields. Ase was already dead by the time we reached her. More spears flew back and forth, from both sides, but no one else was killed. They boarded their ships—Toke and Sigrid were on the *Red Eagle*—backed them away from the shore, raised sail, and were gone."

3

A Blood Debt

We held a feast of sorts that night. Enough food for a feast was prepared and served, at any rate. I ordered that two young steers be slaughtered and roasted, to provide a meal of beef such as a king might serve, to feed the chieftains and warriors who had come to help capture Toke. I felt it was the least I could do. They'd come, of course, for Hastein—not for me. I had no illusions about that. But they'd come to help hunt Toke, and for that, I wished to thank them.

Gunhild protested the extravagance, and she was correct—the estate did not have so many cattle that two could lightly be consumed at a single feast. But I boldly told her that these were my lands now, and my cattle— although in truth, my claims were more bluster than words I truly believed. I told her the men here were my guests, that they were mighty chieftains and seasoned warriors, and that they would be fed and honored properly. She glared at me, but did not argue further— perhaps she, too, was not sure where my rights lay—but she gave the necessary orders and began the preparations for the meal.

That evening, when the food was ready, the chieftains—Hastein, Ivar, Bjorn, Hrodgar, Svein, and Stig—all took places at the head table, closest to the long, raised central hearth, as was their due. I had expected Hastein to take his place in the center, as he was the highest ranking among them, so I told the women-folk working at the cook-fires to serve him first, and serve him there. But when he heard what I told the women, he just stood beside the table, staring at me, with an amused look on his face. The rest of the men in the hall stood, too, waiting for Hastein to sit. After a moment, he spoke.

"This is your hall now, is it not? This is your feast. Are you offering me the high seat this night?"

I had told Gunhild these were my lands now. But coming back here, I felt I was still viewed by the folk of this estate as a thrall, or at best a former thrall. How could a slave, even a freed slave, claim such a rich holding? I was Hrorik's bastard, nothing more. Did that make me now the heir to all of his lands?

I felt my face turning red, as Hastein waited for my answer. Had I already made a fool of myself? I searched my memory, trying to recall feasts Hrorik had held in this hall. Had he ever offered the high seat to any guests? I could not remember.

"Yes," I finally said. "I wish you to have the high seat this night."

"Hail, Hastein," Ivar smirked. "In a chieftain's longhouse, such an honor is usually bestowed only upon the king." After a moment, he added, "When it is offered by the chieftain."

If my face had blushed red before, no doubt it was crimson now.

Hastein ignored Ivar and spoke to me, nodding his head. "Then I thank you for the honor you show me. You will, of course, sit here beside me, at my right hand," he added. I appreciated his kindness, as well as the hint, though I would have felt more comfortable slinking away and hiding in a dark corner.

As a feast—the first I had ever hosted, in a longhouse hall I'd had the presumption to claim as my own—the evening was not a success. There was none of the mirth of a feast. No tales were told, no poems recited, no songs sung. The mood in the hall was subdued. The men ate and drank and talked quietly among themselves. After the food was finished, few lingered long at the tables, even though ale was still available. Most retired early to where they would make their beds for the night—either in the ships' tents which had been pitched on the grounds around the longhouse, or on the long wall benches and the floor inside the hall. Eventually, even those at the high table bade me and each other a good night and retired, leaving me alone.

I sat there, in my seat at the high table, late into the night, long after the only sound within the hall was the low rumble of many men snoring. I felt restless and uncomfortable, and knew I could not sleep. For so many months I had dreamed of being able to return here, of coming home, but now that my dream had become real, I found I did not feel at home. This was where I had grown up, the place where I had lived for most of my life. But none of those who had made it a home for me— my mother, Harald, Sigrid, even old Ubbe—were here. They were all gone, and I was changed.

Finally, I arose from the table, stiff and sore from sitting for so long, and stumbled toward the door to relieve the discomfort that had been building in my bladder from the feast-ale I had drunk. Afterward, I wandered aimlessly through the great hall, lit now only by the flickering remnants of the fire burning on the central hearth, until I reached the small, enclosed private sleeping chamber that had once belonged to Hrorik and Gunhild. Toke had apparently taken it over, forcing his mother to move out to a bed-closet. Ironically, she'd taken the one that had been where my mother, Derdriu, had slept, the one Hrorik had given her, a mere thrall, scandalizing the household and enraging Gunhild. I found it somehow fitting that she had ended up there. But now that Toke was gone, no one was using the sleeping chamber. I decided that if I was claiming the longhouse to be mine, I should sleep there.

When I pushed open the door, the sleeping chamber was pitch black inside. I remembered that Hrorik had kept a small clay lamp, filled with seal oil, in a niche just inside, next to the door. Feeling blindly for it in the dark, I discovered that it was still there. Making my way carefully back across the darkened hall, I lit the wick with an ember from the central hearth, then returned to the sleeping chamber, holding the lamp in front of me to light my way.

The furs that once had covered the floor of the chamber had been pulled up and thrown in a heap in one corner, and the earthen floor beneath was now pitted with holes and littered with piles of loose dirt dug from them. Toke must have believed Hrorik or Harald had buried their wealth there. Perhaps they had. I recalled that Harald had spoken of how he, Sigrid, and Gunhild had each taken a share of Hrorik's treasure as their inheritance after his death, though I had never seen it, nor known where it was kept. Had Toke taken Harald's share of Hrorik's treasure, and Sigrid's too, when he had fled?

I tossed several of the largest furs into a heap along one wall, and lay down upon them. I had no desire to sleep in the bed that had once been shared by Hrorik and Gunhild, and more recently in which Toke had slept. I closed my eyes and tried to sleep, but found my thoughts filled with memories, and peopled by the faces and voices of too many who were now dead. Eventually, though, even the ghosts from my past could no longer overcome the exhaustion I felt, and I slept.

I was awakened by a hand tapping me lightly on the shoulder. With difficulty I opened my eyes. It was still dark within the sleeping chamber, but through its open door I could see, out in the main hall, sunlight streaming down through the smoke-hole in the roof. I had slept late into the morning.

"Master Halfdan? The jarl is asking for you."

Fasti was kneeling beside my makeshift bed, watching me anxiously.

"I am not your master, Fasti," I told him, as I sat up.

"But Master Hrorik is dead, and Master Harald, too," he replied. "With Toke gone, are you not now the master?" A look of alarm crossed his face. "Do you not intend to stay? Are you leaving again?"

Fasti asked questions to which I did not know the answers. My imagined homecoming had not included this day. I had thought we would catch and kill Toke here. That was as far into the future as my dreams had ventured. I did not know what to do now, for Toke was gone, he had escaped. And worse, he had taken Sigrid. How would I—how could I—find him now?

"Master Halfdan?"

I shook my head, trying to clear the fog from it. This, too, I had not foreseen. With Sigrid gone, was this estate now mine, and mine alone? If so, then its thralls were now my slaves, my property, and I their master.

"Do not call me that," I said gruffly.

At the tone of my voice, Fasti recoiled as if he feared I might strike him. *You are much changed, Fasti,* I thought.

"What has happened here, Fasti?" I asked. "Since Harald and I sailed for the Limfjord. After we did not return." *You are a thrall,* I thought. *I know what it means to be a slave, for I, too, was one. But you were not so broken then.*

He hung his head, but said nothing.

"Fasti?"

"There were beatings. Many of them."

Of course there had been. Neither Hrorik nor Harald had been harsh masters. Though they considered the estate's thralls to be their property, they did not treat them cruelly. A thrall who angered Hrorik or Harald might expect a tongue lashing, but rarely worse. In some ways, the female thralls who worked in the household had it harder, for Gunhild had a hot temper, and would often slap a thrall who angered her, or sometimes even whip her with a switch. My mother had often been the recipient of Gunhild's anger.

But Toke had always been free with his fists, even when he'd still lived on the estate, before Hrorik had disinherited and banished him. I could well imagine

31

how he would have treated the thralls without Hrorik or Harald to intervene. For certain Gunhild would not have stopped him.

"By Toke?" I asked.

Fasti shrugged, then nodded. "He angers easily. And some of his men, too. It took little for them to find fault, or take offense. The big one, with one eye, was almost as cruel as Toke. And after a while..." Fasti paused, as if hesitant to continue.

"After a while?" I asked.

"Even a few of the carls here. Some of them would laugh at the beatings. Some of them joined in."

"Things are changed now, Fasti," I told him. "The one-eyed man is dead. *I* killed him. And Toke will not be coming back here. I will see to it."

Fasti was silent for a long time. Finally he raised his eyes to mine, and spoke again.

"Do you remember Huginn?"

In truth, at first I did not—I did not even understand what Fasti was asking. Huginn was the name of one of the two ravens who serve All-Father Odin. What should I remember about him? But it was plain that Fasti believed the name should have some meaning to me. I searched my memory from the time before I was free, when I was still a thrall, like Fasti.

"Do you mean the chicken? The black one?" I asked.

Fasti nodded, and he smiled.

The chickens roosted in a corner of the byre. Fasti was in charge of caring for all the beasts, and seeing to their needs. Each morning, before he cleaned out the stalls, he would collect the eggs from the hens, and bring them scraps and leavings from the kitchen. When I did not have other duties, I would join him and help him clean the byre.

Whenever Fasti entered the byre, the hens would run up to him, eager for more of the treats he sometimes brought. We would laugh together at the way they competed for the scraps—they loved to steal from each other. It was a rare happy memory from that time, for there is little humor in a thrall's life. And there had been one black hen who grew especially attached to Fasti, and would follow him around the byre as he worked, flying up onto the edges of the stalls and perching there, chattering away at him in her funny voice—*brr, brrr-brrr-brrp*—as if he understood.

"*This is my Huginn, Halfdan,*" Fasti would say. "*She tells me all that has happened in the byre, just as Odin's ravens tell him what is happening across the wide world.*" Sometimes he would pick her up—she was tame enough to allow it—and hold her close to his chest, stroking her breast for a few moments, while murmuring, "*How is my girl today? Did you give me an egg?*"

"I remember her," I told him. Fasti seemed pleased that I did.

"One day I was in the byre, bringing the chickens the scraps from the kitchen. I was kneeling, feeding Huginn out of my hand. I did not know Toke had come into the byre, or that he had been watching, until suddenly he was there, standing over me.

"'The black hen,' he told me, 'Give her to me.'"

"I was frightened. I did not want to anger Toke.

33

Huginn let me pick her up." Fasti closed his eyes and sighed. "I gave her to him. She trusted me."

"You had to," I told him. Fasti continued.

"He held her for a moment, and looked at me. He smiled at me. Then he grabbed one of her wings, and ripped it off of her body.

"Did you know, Halfdan, that chickens can scream? Huginn screamed. I can hear her still."

There were tears streaming down Fasti's cheeks now. He honored the chicken he had loved with his tears. I had not grieved so openly when my mother had died. I felt shamed by his grief.

When he continued, his voice was barely more than a whisper. "He grabbed her head in his fist, and twisted and pulled until he ripped it off her neck. Then he handed her back to me. 'Pluck this bird,' he told me. 'I will eat it this night.'"

Ivar and Bjorn were the first to decide to leave. That morning, not long after I'd awakened, they told Hastein they were going.

"My men have been away for months in Frankia," Ivar said. "They have lost many of their comrades. They wish, now, to spend time with own folk, to be in their own homes."

"Do you really intend to carry on with this?" Bjorn asked Hastein.

"I do not like to leave unfinished what I have begun," he responded. It struck me that his answer did not necessarily mean "yes."

"Without question, this Toke is a man who

deserves to die," Ivar continued. "But this is not our fight. Winter approaches, and with it the storm season on the sea. And I cannot see how there is likely to be any profit for my men from continuing with this. I will not ask them to do it."

Hastein said nothing in reply. What was there to say? Ivar was right. It was not his fight, nor was it Bjorn's. In truth, it was not Hastein's, either.

Ivar continued. "In the spring, I plan to sail for Ireland. As well you know, there is much promise there for our people, many rich lands for the taking. Give this matter up, Hastein, and come with me. I have unfinished business there, and I could use your support."

Again Hastein said nothing. Ivar seemed to take his silence as agreement. To my surprise, he turned and spoke next to me. "In Ireland, we could use a warrior like you. Come with us. Come with Hastein and me."

I looked at Hastein, searching his face for a sign. Was Ivar correct? Was Hastein abandoning the hunt for Toke? His expression gave me no answer. He merely raised his eyebrows as he stared back at me, as if he awaited my answer.

Feeling numb, I nodded my head to Ivar, indicating my thanks. "You do me honor. But I swore an oath to avenge my brother's death. I will not dishonor myself or Harald's memory. I have a man I must hunt and kill."

Ivar nodded his head to me in return. "Then good hunting to you, Strongbow. And good fortune." To Hastein he said, "Bjorn and I will ready our ships today and sail on the morrow. Will you be coming?"

Hastein let out a long sigh. "I do not like to leave

unfinished what I have begun," he said again. He was silent for a time, then added, "I will not sail with you tomorrow."

"And Ireland? In the spring? Will you join me then?"

"Much could happen between now and the spring. We will see."

After they'd left the longhouse, Hastein pulled me aside. "There are more than just Ivar and Bjorn and their men who do not wish to continue on. It is unfortunate that we did not catch Toke unawares here."

Was Hastein telling me that he, too, would be leaving? "I understand," I said. "It is my fight, and no one else's." Though in truth I did not see how I could carry on, how I could hope to find Toke and defeat him, on my own.

Hastein shook his head. "It is not your fight alone. I have chosen to make it mine, too. I have told you I would help bring Toke to justice for the slayings of Harald and the others, up on the Limfjord. I did not make such a promise lightly, and once made, I will not break it." He sighed and shook his head. "Not if there is a way. But even among my own followers there are many who feel as do Ivar's and Bjorn's men. They have already been long away from their homes and families. And we do not know how long the pursuit of Toke will be, or where it will lead us." He sighed again. "I will speak with Svein and Stig and the men. There are some of the warriors I know I can count on to follow me anywhere. But I will force no man to undertake this journey who does not wish to, and I fear there may be many who will not want to take this road."

While Hastein met with his captains and men, I wandered the grounds of the estate. As I passed the work sheds, Gudrod the Carpenter came out of the one where he kept his tools.

"I have been waiting for a chance to speak with you," he said. "I confess I did not recognize you at first yesterday, even after you removed your helm and spoke to Gunhild." He smiled. "You have changed greatly from the boy—and the thrall—who used to help me here in the carpentry shed."

Gudrod looked much older than I remembered. His head had for many years been bare on top of any hair, but the long fringe hanging to his shoulders around the sides and back, which I recalled being brown, was now almost entirely gray. Had he aged so much during this one year, or was my memory playing tricks on me? At least seeing *him* brought back memories of my former life here that were not painful. He had always treated me kindly. He'd valued the skill my hands possessed with tools and wood, and by doing so, he had made me feel more than just a piece of Hrorik's property. And most importantly, he had taught me how to make and shoot a bow.

"It is good to see you again," I told him.

"Gudfred has told us—we carls of the estate—what you told him yesterday. How it was Toke and his men who killed Harald, up on the Limfjord." He shook his head. "I never cared for Toke, even when he was just a boy. He always had a meanness in him. But I would not have guessed he could be so treacherous. And then to come back here, and live among us, Hrorik's and Harald's own men. Gods, but I wish we'd known.

"And some of the jarl's men told us, last night at the feast, about the war in Frankia. So that is where you have been. From what they said, our warriors won a great victory there. They told us about you, also. That you are one of the jarl's chosen warriors now, and a member of the crew of his own longship. They even said you saved the life of Ragnar Logbrod himself during a battle with the Franks." He paused and ran his fingers through the hair hanging from the back of his head. "I did not realize old Logbrod still lived. And to think that you, Halfdan, who was once a thrall here on this estate, have met him, have fought beside him, and even saved his life. The Norns are weaving a strange and twisted fate for you, that is for certain."

I agreed with Gudrod about that.

"The jarl's men said Ragnar gave you a name—Strongbow—after that battle," Gudrod continued. "Strongbow," he repeated. "It has a good sound."

Just then, Einar came out of the longhouse. Seeing us, he walked over to where Gudrod and I were standing.

"Jarl Hastein is inside," he said, nodding back over his shoulder in the direction from whence he'd come, "talking with all of the warriors who came here with us," It was something I already knew. "He says you and he wish to pursue Toke. He is asking who is willing to join him on the voyage."

"And how goes it?" I asked.

Einar shrugged. "It was a long and hard campaign we fought down in Frankia. I do not know about the jarl's men, but the men of my village all wish to return home. They will not be joining you."

I did not blame them. This was not their fight, and they had been too long away from their homes and families. At least in Frankia, they had won treasure to bring back with them. But as Ivar had said, there was not likely to be any profit won on this voyage.

"I, of course, am coming with you," Einar continued. "You are as true and brave a man as I have ever known, and a fine comrade." He grinned. "Besides, this is my fight, too. Toke and his men killed my kinsman, Ulf."

Einar's words touched my heart. I had never had such a friend in my life. "Thank you," I said.

Gudrod had been watching our exchange in silence. "So you know Halfdan well?" he asked. "I knew him as a boy, but he is much changed since I last saw him."

"Aye, I know him well," Einar answered. "He is a rare killer, to be sure."

Einar's words embarrassed me, and jarred my memory, too. He had called me that the first time we met. Then, it had troubled me. And even in Frankia, the faces of men I had killed had sometimes haunted my dreams, and disturbed my sleep. But now? The dead were dead. The faces of those I had killed no longer visited me when I slept. I did not think myself as particularly "rare"—none of Hastein's warriors were hesitant to kill, if the need arose—but it was certain a killer I had become. The fate the Norns had woven for me had seen to that.

Einar, loquacious as ever, was still talking. "There was one time, down in Frankia, when our army needed to cross a river at night without the Franks realizing we were moving. The Franks had placed sentries to watch us from the forest along the river's banks. Halfdan and I went into the woods alone to clear them, but there was one we could not get close to. He saw us, and tried to flee. It was nighttime, mind you, almost pitch black in the shadows under the trees."

Einar paused and tapped his finger against the center of his forehead. "Halfdan put an arrow right here. One shot, in the dark, and put him down."

.I felt embarrassed for certain, now. Gudrod looked impressed, though.

The day was beginning to fade when I finally returned to the longhouse. I'd left Einar and Gudrod hours before, although they'd hardly noticed my leaving. Gudrod had been eager to hear more about the campaign down in Frankia, and Einar was more than happy to oblige a willing listener. I'd walked up the hill to visit the grave mound where the ashes of my mother and Hrorik were buried, and from there had wandered into the forest. These woodlands had been my refuge when I was a boy, and still a thrall. Only here had I felt free. They still felt peaceful to me now. Unlike in Frankia, here I did not have to worry that enemies might be lurking behind every tree. Wandering aimlessly through the trees and sunlit clearings, I lost track of time.

Hastein was seated at the main table when I

entered the longhouse. Torvald and the other chieftains were with him. As soon as he saw me, Hastein stood and waved for me to come over.

"I have been looking for you," he told me. "No one knew where you had gone."

"I was walking," I said. "And thinking."

"It is worse than I feared. Many of the men wish to return to their homes. Those who serve on the *Gull* are all my housecarls. If I go, they of course are willing to continue on, although even some of them are less than eager. But most of the rest of my war-band—those who crew Stig's and Svein's ships—live on small farms near my estate, and they want to return to them. Winter is fast approaching, and they do not wish to be away from their farms and families during its long months."

Stig spoke up. "There are some of my men, and a handful of Svein's, who either have no families, or if they do, have little wish to spend the winter with them. They're the sort who enjoy a good fight as much as a warm fire and soft bed. I myself am willing to keep up this hunt, and if Hastein and I go, these men will come with us. But..." he shrugged his shoulders.

Hastein explained. "The problem is that they are too few. On the *Gull*, we are badly under manned. We lost many good men in Frankia. Even with the men from Stig's and Svein's crews who are willing to continue on, we would have only enough to fully man the *Gull*, plus a few extra. Toke is a dangerous man, and it is clear, now, that we will not take him without a fight. If we must fight him, I want the odds to be strongly in our favor. Pursuing Toke with just a single ship, a single crew, is

41

too risky. I do not wish to lose more of my men. Not for this. Not for a fight that is not theirs, and which—as Ivar has said—will bring them no profit. I am grateful to those men who are willing to continue on, and I will not forget that they were. But I will not subject them to unnecessary risk."

My heart sank as I listened to Hastein. So Toke would escape. There was no way I could pursue him alone.

"Would you be willing if you had more men?"

The question had been shouted from the doorway of the longhouse. Gudfred was standing there. Another man, whom I did not immediately recognize, was standing beside him. The two of them strode toward us. More men streamed through the door and followed them.

Gudfred and the other man stopped in front of Hastein. The men following arrayed themselves behind them.

"This is Hroald," Gudfred said, indicating the man at his side. He had brown hair and a beard that were heavily streaked with gray, and he was wearing a tunic and trousers of coarse undyed wool. "He is headman of the village that lies just beyond this estate. These men with him are from the village, too."

"Most of the warriors in our village have sailed with Hrorik before, some many times. He was our godi—our chieftain, and our priest," Hroald said. "These men who are here with me now sailed with him and Harald on their last voyage to England that cost Hrorik his life. Hrorik was a good and brave man, and Harald was, too."

Hroald paused and took a deep breath. Speaking in front of so many great chieftains clearly made him nervous. He swallowed and continued. "Harald's killing, by his own foster brother, was niddingsvaark. It is a fine thing that a mighty chieftain such as yourself—a jarl, a man of power and authority—is willing to right this great wrong. I have seven men here with me. The eight of us are all willing to join you, and help hunt Toke down."

"And all of the housecarls here on the estate wish to join you, too," Gudfred added. "Harald was our leader, and the men who died with him were our comrades. Toke betrayed them, and lied to us, telling us he had slain those who'd murdered Harald. He owes us all a blood debt. If you will accept us, Jarl Hastein, we will help you catch and kill him. It is our duty. We owe it to Harald and those who died with him."

Hastein looked over at me and a smile spread slowly across his face.

"It seems the Norns intend to continue weaving the threads of our fates together," he said. "Well then. The hunt is on."

4

The Hay

Unfortunately, it proved to be not as simple as that. Hastein turned to Torvald and immediately began listing what must be done to ready the ships for a quick departure. Torvald scowled as he listened, and Hroald's expression looked increasingly alarmed. He rocked from side to side nervously and cleared his throat several times, as if he wished to speak but was afraid to interrupt. Finally he blurted out, "But there is the matter of the hay."

There was a long silence, while Hastein appeared to be weighing what Hroald had said, and attempting—apparently without success, for a confused frown grew upon his brow—to discern what it meant. Finally he conceded defeat and asked, "The hay?"

Hroald nodded vigorously. "Yes, the hay. For the winter feed, for our cattle. We have cut it, but it is still drying out in the fields. We must finish drying it and bring it in before we can leave with you."

Ivar and Bjorn exchanged incredulous glances and rolled their eyes.

Gudfred chimed in. "Aye, it is so with us, too. We've not even finished cutting all of ours. It must be done before we can leave. We must bring in enough hay to feed the beasts we do not slaughter. Winter is coming, and we cannot know how long we will be away. If the beasts starve, the folk will, too. This must be done."

Ignoring Gudfred's and Hroald's remarks, Torvald leaned over, placing his head close to Hastein's ear, and spoke in a whisper that unfortunately was loud enough for all nearby to hear. "Hastein, we cannot just sail away with these men! We do not know their mettle. They are untested. They do not know our ways, nor we theirs. We expect to have to fight, if we pursue this hunt for Toke."

Gudfred bristled, and spoke angrily to Torvald. "Do not disdain us because we do not serve a great jarl, as you do. Do not think, because we cut hay with scythes tomorrow, that we cannot also harvest men with different blades. Hrorik, our chieftain, was no bench warmer. We raided with him every summer. We are all experienced warriors."

"I do not doubt it," Hastein told him, speaking quickly before Torvald could respond. "Hrorik Strong-Axe was a doughty warrior, and as you say, you all have sailed and fought with him. I have no doubt that you have courage, and can wield the tools of war. But there is some truth in what Torvald has said. In battle, in a shield wall, we must all fight as one. We should train together, at least briefly. If you would sail with us, on our ships, you must learn our ways."

He sighed. I thought it a restrained response. It was all I could do not to groan aloud.

"And the hay?" Hroald asked. Ivar sniggered.

"Ah, yes...the hay. How many days will it take to bring it in?" Hastein asked Gudfred and Hroald.

Gudfred glanced over at Hroald, who shrugged his shoulders, and said, "Ours is all cut, and has been drying. If the morrow is warm and sunny, our hay might be dry enough to gather by evening. If clouds hide the sun, maybe two more days to dry. But if it rains...." He shrugged his shoulders again.

"And you?" Hastein asked Gudfred.

"That we've already cut has been drying for several days now. It can be brought in tomorrow. Cutting the rest, then drying it and bringing it in?" I felt my heart sink. He, too, shrugged his shoulders, as Hroald had done. There seemed to be much of that these days. "It would go faster with help," he suggested.

Ivar snorted. "When did you last cut hay, Hastein? Or have you ever?"

Hastein ignored him. To Gudfred and Hroald, he said, "You will cut your hay, and gather it, and we will help you. And we will train together, also. We must do all of these things as quickly as we can. Toke's trail grows colder every day that we delay our departure."

The following morning Ivar and Bjorn sailed. Before they departed, Ivar pulled Hastein aside. They obviously did not realize that I was near enough to hear their words. "You should come with us," Ivar said. "Give up this folly. This is not your fight. You do not owe Halfdan anything. He was nothing when you met. He was just an untested boy, and a former slave, besides. It is enough that you gave him the chance you did, that you took him into your crew. It is he who owes you a debt, not otherwise. And this Toke is dangerous. It would be unwise, and would put yourself and the rest of your men at risk unnecessarily, to pursue him with a ship full of farmers as your war-band and crew."

46

"If there is a debt between Halfdan and me, it runs both ways," Hastein replied. "In the battle with the Franks and Bretons, our line was breaking. Had it failed, many who are alive this day would have died. I might well have been among them."

"But our line did not fail," Ivar said.

"Had Halfdan not been there—had he not rallied the archers..." Hastein countered. "There, and at Ruda, too, he saved my life. The Norns have woven our fates together. I do not understand it, but I believe it is so."

It was a day for partings. Later that morning Svein sailed, taking with him on the *Sea Wolf* those of Hastein's followers who were not continuing on. "Fare-well," Svein told Hastein, clasping wrists with him before he turned to board his ship. "May you find Toke quickly, and finish this thing before winter settles on the land and sea. I will hope that we celebrate the Jul feast together."

The ship from the village up on the Limfjord departed, too. To my surprise, Hrodgar did not leave on it.

"I had a dream last night," he told Hastein. "My wife, Brynhil, came to me during the night. She was a good woman, and a good wife. She has been dead for ten years, now.

"She told me that great danger lies to the east. She said that many who sail with you on this voyage will not return, and if I sail with you on it, I will be among those who do not."

Hrodgar's words caused a shiver to run up my spine. Though living men cannot see into the future, the eyes of the dead are not so blinded.

Hastein looked troubled, too. "This is not a good omen," he said. "Sometimes a dream is just a dream, but when the dead appear and speak to you, when they bring a message from the other side...."

"Do you believe it was truly the spirit of your wife?" Torvald, who was standing nearby, asked. "Perhaps you just drank too much ale last night."

Hrodgar shook his head at Torvald's suggestion. "It was her," he answered. "She was wearing the same dress, the same brooches and necklace, that we dressed her in before burning her body."

"Then why do you choose to come with us?" Torvald asked. I was wondering the same thing.

"She also told me that I am an old man now, and I shouldn't pretend that I am not. She said I am too old for long sea voyages, and should stay at home, in the village where I belong, and let our daughter care for me in my old age." He snorted. "Although a good wife, she was always a nag. I was not too old to sail with the fleet to Frankia, and blood my spear there."

"But what if she spoke the truth?" I asked. I did not think that messages from the dead should be disregarded lightly.

Hrodgar shrugged. "You are too young to understand. She is right. I *am* an old man. I feel age-worn and weary. I no longer have the strength in me that I had when I was young, or even five years ago. One way or another, I shall die, for no one lives forever. But I would rather my life end while I still have the strength to hold a sword in my hand, than to finish my days sick and weak in bed from a fever—or even worse, to suffer the slow, wasting rotting that befalls those who do not have the good sense to know when it is time to die. And besides," he added. "Killing Toke is a thing that needs doing, and I wish to be a part of it."

Hrodgar said his wife had told him that many would not return from our pursuit of Toke. I wondered if she'd named to him any of the others who were fated to die. What if she'd named my comrade Einar, or Torvald, or Hastein? What if she'd named me? I almost asked him, but then decided I would rather not know.

Gudfred and the other men of the household, carls and thralls, had headed out to the fields early that morning. The departures, the exchange of fare-wells among comrades who were parting ways, were not their concern. The hay—the cutting, the spreading, and the drying—was. After the partings were spoken and the ships had sailed, I headed out to the fields to join them. The sooner the hay was harvested, the sooner our pursuit of Toke could begin.

The long rows of hay which had previously been cut, though still a faded green in color, had dried enough to be gathered and hauled to the byre for storage. Thralls using wooden rakes were rolling up each row from either end into two loose stacks at the row's center. As each row was completed, Fasti led a large two-wheeled cart, drawn by a single ox, to the stacked hay, and the thralls heaved it aboard with their rakes.

Beyond, a row of carls was advancing slowly through the unmowed portion of the field, swinging long-handled scythes. The slow, steady rhythm of their movements—swing, step, swing, step—and the *chuff, chuff* of the long blades slicing through the tall grass called a memory of my brother Harald to my mind.

Harald had never cared for the work of the estate—the growing and harvesting of the crops and beasts necessary to feed the folk who lived here. While Hrorik was alive, he'd had to assist, for Hrorik did not tolerate sloth. Could Harald have had his way, however, he would have devoted his life entirely to fighting and raiding, and in between to training to perfect his fighting skills. I think he had welcomed the need to train me in no small part because it gave him a reason to ignore the labors of farming.

The one exception was scything hay. "There is a skill to using a scythe, Halfdan," he'd told me one day, when trying to explain how my use of a sword was still lacking. "You do not just chop at the hay. You do not just hack it. The edge of the blade should slide across the grass, and slice through it. It is the same with a sword. Draw the blade across what you are striking as you swing through. You should slice, not hack. Your blade will cause a far deeper wound, with less effort, if you learn how to do this."

At the time, I had not found his comparison between scything and sword-work helpful. He'd forgotten that slaves were not allowed to use the big, sharp blades. Carls cut the hay; thralls followed behind with wooden rakes and spread it into neat rows for drying.

When I reached the field I found some extra tools

lying in a pile at the edge, waiting for more workers to arrive and use them. I would have liked to have tried my hand with a scythe this day, but there were no scythes among them, only rakes. I took one and headed out into the field.

The scythers were moving across the field in a staggered line, each man far enough behind the one to his right so he could safely swing his long, cutting stroke to overlap the edge of the swath cut by the man ahead. Einar, who had come to assist in the harvest, was the fourth man over. He appeared to be the only worker who was not from the estate. None of Hastein's men had come out to assist.

Thralls trailed behind several of the scythers, pulling the cut hay into neat rows with their rakes. I recognized Ing behind the man cutting to Einar's right, and beside him, Hrut. For now, no one followed Einar. I suppose I will be Einar's thrall this day, I thought, and I began raking the irregular trail of hay he had cut. This was not the homecoming I had dreamed of.

I had been working for some time, raking the scattered, cut hay into a neater row for drying, when the carl mowing to Einar's right happened to glance back and saw me. He laid his scythe down and walked back to where I stood.

"Do you remember me?" he asked. I did remember him, though not his name. He had light brown hair, cut off so it hung just below his shoulders, and a beard which he kept trimmed and shaped to a sharp point. He was not as tall as Harald had been, but had a stockier, more heavily muscled build. He had been one of the carls Harald had recruited to help when he'd trained me to fight in formation, in a shield-wall.

"My name is Floki," he continued, when I gave no answer. "My brother, Baug"—when he spoke the name, he nodded his head back toward the carl scything to the right of where he had been—"and I were close comrades of Harald's."

I remembered that now, after he said it. The two of them, more so than any of the other carls on the estate, had been Harald's drinking companions in the evenings.

"Gudfred has told us, of course, that it was Toke and his men, not bandits, who killed Harald, up on the Limfjord," Floki said. "Had we known, Toke would be dead now. We plan to avenge Harald, and the others— Rolf, Ulf, Odd, and Lodver—too. They were all good men, and our comrades.

"But Baug and I have been talking, and thinking, about this tale you told Gudfred. About Toke's attack. And there is one thing we do not understand. How is it that everyone else—Harald, Rolf and the others, and even all of the folk of the estate up there—was killed, but you survived? Harald was the finest swordsman I have ever known, and Ulf a very skilled and experienced warrior. Yet they were killed, and you escaped unharmed. How did that happen?"

Floki's words took me by surprise. I had not expected them, nor the tone of his voice, or the scorn visible in his eyes. I could feel my face getting hot and flushed, and my feelings swirled in a confused mix of anger and shame, as I realized Floki believed—and was all but accusing me to my face—that I was a coward.

52

All but. And then, when I said nothing, he did.

"Did you run from the fight?" he asked, sneering. "Did you flee, and leave the others behind to die?"

Had this been Frankia, had this been a member of our army there, and I the warrior Strongbow, I would have killed Floki for his insult, or died trying. But this was my home, or so I had considered it. Here I was just Halfdan, not Strongbow. I had believed this man was one of my people, and I one of his.

Many moments passed in silence, as I struggled to gain control of my emotions while Floki stared at me with a disdainful expression. Finally, I answered, speaking in a low voice.

"Yes, I did run. In the end, we all did—all who were left alive. We beat back their first attack, giving better than we got. But we did not realize, in the confusion and dark, that those who'd surrounded the longhouse were Toke and his men. Harald thought they were the kinfolk of a man he'd killed in a duel, up on the Limfjord. In the lull after the first attack, he bargained with the attackers, seeking safe passage for the women, children, and thralls before the fighting resumed. The leader of the attackers—Toke, who was hiding his features and muffling his voice with a cloak—gave Harald his word that they could leave safely. As soon as they were clear of the longhouse and far enough away that they could not make it back to its safety, Toke and his men slaughtered them, in full view as we watched, helpless to intervene. Or so Toke thought. I did manage to hit him with an arrow, though it was only a superficial wound."

Floki's eyebrows rose at that. I suppose it did not fit well with what he'd believed had occurred.

I continued. "After that, Toke and his men set fire to the longhouse, and we were forced to flee into the open. We tried to stay together at first, using some of the beasts from the longhouse byre as shields from the missile fire Toke's men were raining down upon us, but we did not make it far before the beasts were all slain.

"Our only chance of survival was to reach the shelter of the woods. But it was at best the slimmest of hopes, for we were greatly outnumbered and surrounded. So yes, we ran from the fight, in the end. We all ran. Harald told me, as we made that last attempt to escape, that when he gave me the word, I must go, and leave him and the others behind. He died cutting a path clear for me to escape. I will never forget his words that night. 'Someone must survive to avenge us,' he told me. 'If you reach the forest, they will never take you. None can match you there. You must do this thing for me. For all of us. Survive and avenge us.' I did survive, and I will avenge Harald."

I said no more. Floki was quiet for a long time, pondering my words. Finally, begrudgingly, he nodded his head. "I can see this," he said. "It is what Harald would have done." He took a deep breath, and blew it out slowly. "But you should know this," he added. "Baug, me, Gudfred, and the others, we go on this voyage for one reason: to kill Toke. We will join with Jarl Hastein, and we will follow him on this voyage, because we must, to avenge Harald and the others. You should understand that we follow the jarl, not you. You may be

Harald's half-brother, and Hrorik's son. You may be a warrior to the jarl and his men. But *we* know who you are. We know *what* you are. You are not a chieftain—especially not *our* chieftain, and you never will be. We are not *your* men."

5

The Omen

We—the men-folk of the estate, and those few of us, like Einar and me, who'd traveled here with Hastein and deigned to help—finished cutting the hay that same day. Two days later, we brought it into the byre. Gudfred and Floki and some of the other carls protested that it was too soon, that the hay was still too green. Hastein countered that if they thought so, those who remained behind could continue turning it in the byre, to ensure it did not grow mold and spoil.

Hastein and Torvald began the training during the days while the hay lay drying out in the fields. It did not go well. The disagreement that had begun over the hay continued during the training, and grew into discord. Hastein and Torvald insisted that the men of the estate and village adopt their ways, their commands, their style of working together in a shield-wall. In truth, the differences between what Hastein demanded and what Hrorik's men were used to were minor. But some of Hastein's crew rolled their eyes and sniggered into their sleeves at the newcomers' initial awkwardness with moves and commands they did not know, and the men-folk of the estate and village seethed at the disrespect they felt was being shown them. In the few practice skirmishes that were fought, blows that should have been pulled were at times struck, and more than once tempers flared.

After three days of training—the last occurring after the practice was interrupted for a full day while the hay in the fields was gathered and hauled to the byre—Hastein declared that he was satisfied. Clearly he was not, but he must have felt that sailing with a crew not yet melded was the better alternative to sailing with one whose members were in a state of open hostility. He told Torvald to supervise the loading of provisions and fresh water aboard the ships, and have them ready to sail in the morn.

I had my own preparations to make. I had won considerable wealth during the campaign in Frankia. I felt it unwise to continue carrying it with me in my sea chest everywhere I traveled. Ships—even those commanded by the best of captains—sometimes sink.

During the days we'd been at the estate, I had continued to use the small enclosed sleeping chamber that formerly had been Hrorik's and Gunhild's as my own. It pleased me that by doing so, Gunhild was forced to continue sleeping in the bed-closet that had once belonged to my mother. I wished for her rest every night to be disturbed by the memory of how Hrorik had given it to my mother. It had infuriated Gunhild at the time. I hoped it angered her still.

After the first night, I had moved my sea chest from the *Gull* to the sleeping chamber. I opened it now and surveyed its contents. Some of them—my arms and armor, for certain, the blacksmith's tools I'd purchased in Hedeby, my spare clothing, the simple but sturdy pottery cup and bowl and wooden spoon that served as my mess kit, and at least some part of my considerable hoard of Frankish silver coins—I would carry with me on the coming voyage.

But I had won ten whole pounds of silver coins for Genevieve's ransom, paid reluctantly by her father, Count Robert. And added to that already significant sum was my share of the silver paid by the Franks' King Charles to ransom the city of Paris and buy the retreat of our army from his kingdom. Of the seven thousand pounds of silver—most, like Genevieve's ransom, paid in Frankish deniers—the four commanders of the army, Ragnar, Hastein, Ivar, and Bjorn, had each claimed one hundred pounds as their due. The rest had been divided equally among the one hundred and twenty ships of the fleet, to be further divided among each crew according to their felag.

In the *Gull*'s crew, Hastein, as captain, was entitled to five shares under the felag. Given the huge sum he'd won as a commander of the army, he'd graciously relinquished those shares, so a greater amount could be divided among the rest of us. The shares of our fifteen dead had been set aside, to be given to their families. My portion, including my extra half share for serving as the ship's blacksmith, added almost two more pounds of silver coins to the profit I'd won on the campaign.

Many of the *Gull*'s crew—and for that matter, most of the warriors of the army—had won far more wealth in Frankia from looting than from their share of the final ransom. I had not. Other than the fine sword and armor I had stripped from the body of Leonidas, Genevieve's cousin whom I'd slain, and the long spear that had belonged to a Frankish cavalryman I'd killed, I had acquired only a few items of value by theft. All of them—two silver candlesticks and an ornate silver cup, the kind the Christians called a chalice—I had taken from an altar in a small room I'd happened upon in the Abbey of Saint Genevieve, in Paris on the day I had led a party of warriors there to secure it. I had not, of course, told Genevieve, after we'd later become reacquainted, that I had taken these things. I felt certain she would have thought less of me for stealing from her convent, and her God.

The coins paid for Genevieve's ransom had conveniently been transferred to my possession in two sturdy leather sacks. I pulled them now from the sea chest and set them on the bed, then dumped the rest of my silver—loose coins, cup, and candlesticks—out of the chest and onto the bed beside them.

How much to take, and how much to leave behind? What might this voyage bring—what needs that would require silver?

I had acquired the habit of carrying at least ten or so coins in the small pouch I always wore on my belt, in which I kept my flint and steel, a small whetstone, and the comb my mother gave me. That clearly was not enough for a voyage of unknown duration. Searching through my sea chest, I came upon the small leather bag I'd filled with iron arrowheads that I'd found in a storeroom in Count Robert's island fortress in the middle of the Seine River in Paris. I dumped the arrowheads out, rolled them up in a piece of sheepskin I cut from one of the hides that had been used to cover the sleeping chamber's floor, and tucked them back into the chest. I decided that I would take with me as many silver coins as the bag would hold, and would leave the rest behind, in a safe hiding place.

I was filling the leather sack with coins from among the loose coins I'd dumped on the bed, when a shadow darkened the entrance to the chamber. I glanced up and saw Astrid standing there, holding a wooden chest in her arms. Several pieces of folded clothing were on top of it. Her face was still discolored by the bruises from the blows Toke had struck, but over the past few days she had otherwise recovered somewhat from the attack, and no longer seemed in a daze, or cowered whenever someone approached her.

"This is for you," she said, and held out the chest and clothes.

"What is it?" I asked, not understanding how she could have anything for me.

"These were Sigrid's. She saved the feast clothes she made you, for Hrorik's funeral feast. And some of Harald's things are here, too. Sigrid kept them. She did not wish any of Toke's men to end up with them. I am certain she would want you to have them."

I took the chest and clothes from Astrid's hands and set them on the bed, beside the pile of silver. I saw her eyes widen when she saw the mound of coins.

The chest was small—less than a third the size of my sea chest—but of much finer quality. The wood was a dark, lustrous walnut, and the hinges and catch—which included a lock, from which a key protruded—were of bronze, cast in an ornate design that included a serpent coiled around each piece. I opened it and began removing its contents, one by one.

As Astrid had said, among them were the feast clothes Sigrid and my mother had made for me by altering some of Harald's clothing, while he and I had labored to build the death ship in which the bodies of Hrorik and my mother would be burned. The white linen tunic, with embroidery around the sleeves and neck, I folded and added to my sea chest. It would make a comfortable under-tunic to wear beneath a wool one. The green wool trousers I added to my sea chest, too. They were in good condition, and looked much finer now than the brown ones—also made for me by Sigrid— I was currently wearing, which over the past months had acquired a number of stains and showed considerable wear.

The short cloak I'd worn at the funeral feast I folded and placed on the bed. It was a garment designed more for appearance than usefulness, and would provide little protection from wind and rain on a sea voyage. The fancy silver brooch I'd worn to secure it at the feast I added to my pile of silver coins and treasure that I intended to leave here. I preferred to fasten my cloak with the much simpler ring brooch I had been using ever since my journey north to the Limfjord with Harald.

The next item my hands pulled from the chest caused me to suck in my breath in surprise when I realized what it was: a small sealskin pouch, containing the scroll whose writings, about the White Christ, my mother had used to teach me Latin. I'd thought it long lost.

"Sigrid kept it, to remember Derdriu by," Astrid

said.

It was all I had left now of my mother's, besides the small comb she had given me. I was glad the scroll had not been lost. I was glad Sigrid had kept it.

The rest of the chest's contents had belonged to Harald. There was much less than I would have expected: a small knife, a comb made from walrus ivory, and a pair of short but sturdy leather boots. I tried them on. They were a little large, but if I wrapped my feet with rags or stuffed dried grass in the toes to fill the space, they would do, and would provide far greater protection from winter weather than my own well-worn shoes. I added them to my sea chest.

When I picked up the knife to examine it, Astrid volunteered, "Sigrid gave that to Harald, as a gift." Its blade was short—no longer than my forefinger—and its handle was formed from a piece of deer antler. A dark brown leather scabbard encased the blade and half of the handle. I remembered that Harald had sometimes used this knife to cut his meat with, at meals. It was a handy size. The dagger I wore at my belt—a gift from Harald, given to me on the night he had died—had a long blade that could be unwieldy for delicate work. I added the knife, too, to the contents of my sea chest.

"Is this all?" I asked. I remembered a silver cup Harald had often used. Where was it? For that matter, what of Harald's inheritance, his share of Hrorik's treasure? And what had happened to Sigrid's share? Was their treasure what Toke had dug up the floor of this chamber looking for? Had he found it?

"Sigrid gave most of Harald's things to his closest

comrades, after we learned of his death. She kept just a few to remember him by." Astrid answered.

I looked at her. "Do you have anything that belonged to him—to Harald?" She had shared his bed, and although as a thrall she'd had no hope he would marry her, she'd still visibly cared for him.

Astrid shook her head.

"Take this," I said, and gave her the comb. "To remember Harald by. I am sure he would have wanted you to have it."

She held the comb in the palm of her hand, saying nothing, just staring at it. I could not see her expression—her head was hanging down, and her braids hid her face—but after a few moments she sniffed, wiped at her eyes with the back of her hand, and tucked the comb into the small pouch on her belt.

The folded clothes Astrid had stacked on top of the chest had all belonged to Harald. Sigrid had, I supposed, not yet found appropriate recipients for them. One of the pieces she'd kept was the fine linen tunic, dyed a deep crimson color, that Harald had worn for the somber feast when he'd addressed the folk of the estate and the village, that first night after he and Hrorik and the others had returned from their ill-fated voyage to England. It was his feast tunic, and was a fine one. Its color was remarkable. No doubt the dye for it had been costly. Harald had worn the tunic on the night of Hrorik's funeral feast, also. Saying nothing, I folded it and placed it in my sea chest. It would be my feast tunic, now. I would think of Harald whenever I wore it.

There was also a gray tunic of especially thick,

heavy woolen cloth. I recognized it as Harald's winter tunic that he wore when venturing out in harsh weather in the coldest months. As a slave, I'd often admired it. It, too, I folded and added to my sea chest. It would be useful in the coming winter.

There was still another tunic, and a pair of trousers. They were more clothes than I could use. Even if I'd wanted them, my sea chest was almost full already.

"Give these to Fasti," I told her. "Tell him they were Harald's. Tell him they are a gift from me."

As she turned to go, she said, "You must find her. Sigrid—you must save her. You must save her from Toke," and then she hurried away.

After Astrid left, I returned to my preparations for the coming voyage. I finished filling the leather sack with coins, knotted the cord around its neck, and tucked it in the bottom of my sea chest. The other, smaller chest—the one than had belonged to Sigrid—I filled with the remainder of my treasure: the two bags containing Genevieve's ransom, the loose coins, and the silver chalice, candlesticks, and brooch. The latter pieces I wrapped in the short cloak. I weighed adding my gold torque and the fine, silver-trimmed drinking horn which Hastein had given me to the little chest, and leaving them behind, too. But they both could be useful in making an impression. They were the kind of items a high-born noble or a renowned warrior might have. They made me feel more than a former slave. I decided I would keep them with me.

I had earlier found, in the boathouse down on the shore, a number of large sacks sewn from sealskin. Such were useful aboard a ship, because they kept their contents protected from water and the elements. I had taken one, and used it now to wrap Sigrid's chest in. Then I heaved it up onto one shoulder, and strode through the longhouse and out to one of the small work sheds, where tools were kept. Taking a wooden spade from inside, I turned and headed toward the hill that rose behind the longhouse.

As I began climbing the hill, Tore saw me and called out, "Where are you going? We must ready the *Gull* for departure."

"I will be back soon," I told him, and kept going— up the hill, past the stone death ship that held the ashes of my mother and father, and into the woods beyond.

There was a place I was searching for, a place I remembered from when I had been a boy. During a storm one winter, a huge, old oak had fallen over. It had been weakened already, its core partially rotted out, and the storm's high winds, coupled with the weight of a heavy load of thick, wet snow that had filled the old tree's branches had brought the aging giant crashing down, dragging several smaller, surrounding trees with it as it fell.

As a boy, I'd found a secret hideaway up against the old tree's trunk, a small open area within the tangle of branches, broken and whole, that surrounded it. It had been a place I would escape to whenever I could, a place where I could hide from Gunhild's wrath, or Toke's torments. It had been a place where I could be alone, and where I would sometimes dream an impossible dream, that someday I would no longer be a thrall.

My memory of the woods did not fail me. I found the fallen tree, and within its branches, against the trunk, the hidden open area that had been my hideaway. Although much smaller than I remembered, it was big enough. I dug a hole there, against the trunk, and buried the sealskin-wrapped chest in it. As I refilled the hole, scattering the loose dirt that would not fit back in it, and spread loose leaves over all to hide that the earth had been disturbed, I wondered if I would ever return here.

Like the training, the task of preparing the two ships, the *Gull* and the *Serpent*, for the morrow's voyage did not go smoothly. The problem was that most sea voyages are planned weeks, if not months, in advance, so there is time to gather provisions for the journey, time to slaughter beasts and salt their meat to preserve it, and the like. Because the pursuit of Toke was being launched on such short notice, in order to provision their ships, Hastein and Stig had no choice but to draw upon the estate's stores. And even though they stocked the ships with less food than they felt comfortable with, not knowing how long this voyage might last—each ship was loaded from the estate's reserves with only a single small barrel of dried, salted pork, three barrels filled with barley, and a single barrel of storage vegetables: cabbages, carrots, parsnips, and rutabagas packed in hay—a number of the folk of the estate expressed concern that if the coming winter proved a long one, they might face shortages and hunger before spring arrived.

Gunhild was the most vocal of these. She even

suggested that Hastein and Stig should pay for the stores they took—a proposal that came close to causing Hastein to lose control of his temper.

"We should pay for these meager stores we are taking?" he asked incredulously. "Will they not be eaten in part by warriors from this estate, who sail with us? And do we not sail to bring to justice one who has murdered a number of your own people, including your chieftain, Harald? While you stay here, we sail into danger, both from your treacherous son whom we hunt, and from the rapidly approaching winter, with its dangerous weather. We do this to help your own men-folk avenge losses that, if not redressed, might stain their honor in the eyes of others. And *you* complain that if the winter should be a long one, your belly might not be as full as you would wish?"

Those of Hastein's men who were near enough to hear the exchange growled their approval of his words. Gunhild blanched and hurried away to the hearth, where she kept her head averted, and avoided looking toward Hastein while she assisted in the evening meal's preparation. But several of the carls from the estate murmured angrily, too. From bits and pieces of their speech I happened to overhear, it seemed Hastein's words had offended their already prickly pride. I heard Floki mutter, "Does he think we are not men enough to avenge Harald without his help?"

Afterward, Hastein approached me. "This is a troubled household," he said. "It is not at peace. It is unfortunate that you must leave again so soon after returning. These folk need a guiding hand—someone other than that woman."

At least in part, I agreed with what Hastein said. The folk of the estate did need someone to lead them, to guide them. Someone other than Gunhild. But I did not believe now that it could be me.

That evening, as dusk was falling and all were gathering in the longhouse in anticipation of the evening meal, I called all of the folk of the estate to come together in the open center of the longhouse, around the hearth. Hastein, Torvald, Tore, and several others of the crew came also, no doubt curious about what I intended to do.

Stepping up onto the edge of the hearth so all could see and hear me, I addressed them. It felt strange to do so. It was like something that Hrorik or Harald would have done. But now they were both gone, and there was only me.

"I have some things to tell you," I began. "By now, all of you have heard that it was Toke and his men who killed Harald, up on the Limfjord."

When I said that, many of the carls, and some of their wives, turned and stared at Gunhild. She glowered back at them. I continued. "In the morning, at first light, I am leaving with Jarl Hastein and his men. We sail in pursuit of Toke. Many of the carls of this household, plus men from the village, are joining us on our hunt. I am grateful to all who are coming with us."

"And I am grateful that you and your high and mighty companions will be leaving," Gunhild muttered, loud enough for all to hear. "You have left those of us who stay behind sparse fare to make it through the winter."

I could feel that all eyes were on me, that all the folk of the estate were wondering what I would say to Gunhild, what I would do. I chose to ignore her. We would have words later, she and I. But now, I needed to speak to those who would come with us, and those who would stay behind.

"Ubbe, who was foreman here for many years, is dead. Someone who is remaining behind must take his place, must see to the running of the estate, and be in charge," I said, turning back and forth, scanning the upturned faces before me, as if trying to decide, although in truth, I had made the decision earlier that day.

"I have always managed this estate, whenever Hrorik was away," Gunhild protested.

This time I did answer her. "Aye," I said. "But now things are greatly changed here. And I want someone other than you—someone I know I can trust—in charge."

"Who are you to decide? Who are you to give orders?"

The voice came from the back of those who stood gathered in front of me. I did not see who uttered the words, but I recognized the voice: Floki.

"I am Hrorik's son, acknowledged by him before he died," I answered, in a voice that sounded more filled with confidence and authority than I felt. "I am, by right and law, now the heir to these lands."

More than a few of the carls of the estate standing before me shook their heads and muttered under their breath. It would seem that some of the folk here did not agree. This was not going well.

"Do you think your claim is stronger than Toke's?" demanded Gunhild, ignoring the fact that most of the warriors present in the longhouse would be sailing on the morrow with the intention of finding and killing him. "You are a bastard. Bastards cannot inherit."

"I was acknowledged by Hrorik as his son. And Toke has no claim. He was disinherited by Hrorik," I replied. "As you well know. As all here know," I added, hoping my words might cause at least some to feel shame, because they had accepted him as the heir. I could feel an anger growing inside me at these folk.

"As to who will manage the estate while I am gone, I have made my decision. Gudrod," I called, "come up here and stand beside me."

He stood motionless for a long moment, a startled expression on his face, then Gudrod pushed through the crowd and made his way toward the hearth. When he reached it, I held my arm out, locked wrists with his, and pulled him up beside me. Under his breath, he murmured to me, "Is this wise? I am just a carpenter. I do not know how to run this estate." I murmured back, "You will learn. You have lived here your whole life. You know how this estate, this farm, works. You need only keep things the same as they have always been." *And I know I can trust you*, I thought, *and that is what matters most*.

"Gudrod will be the new foreman of the estate," I said in a loud voice, for all to hear. Gunhild rolled her eyes and shook her head.

"There is one other thing I have to tell you," I continued. *And you will like this even less*, I thought. "Now that this estate is mine, there are going to be changes. All who live and labor here will be free. I will not have slaves on this estate."

"You are selling the thralls?" Gunhild exclaimed.

"No," I said. "I am freeing them."

A long silence followed. The carls of the estate and their women-folk looked at each other with stunned expressions. Torvald and Tore, standing to my right, close to the hearth, glanced at each other with raised eyebrows. Even the thralls looked taken aback.

Hastein stepped up onto the hearth beside me and leaned close to whisper in my ear. "They are your property now, of course. It is your right. But do you think this wise?"

In truth, I thought it probably was not. But I did not care. I did not know if I would return from the pursuit of Toke. And even if I did, I did not know if the carls who had known me as a slave would ever accept me as their chieftain. Those were all threads that the Norns had not yet woven into the pattern of the great tapestry of fate. But whatever might happen in days to come, it was in my power, here and now, to free the thralls of this estate. It was in my power to allow them to escape a life of slavery, as I had.

As the surprise from my words wore off, those standing before me found their voices, and a clamor of questions and angry exclamations was shouted at me. Most were some variation of "Who will do the work?" Fasti—whom I noticed was wearing his new tunic and trousers—cried out, "Where will we go? How will we live?"

I held up my hands for silence, but was ignored. Finally Torvald roared out, "Let him speak," and stepped out in front of me, glowering this way and that, as if daring anyone to disobey. An angry giant is a daunting sight. The hall quickly fell silent.

"Things here will not be greatly changed by this," I explained. "All of you here, free and thrall, have always done the work of this estate together. But from this day forward, this estate will be governed by two rules. No one may live here on these lands, no one may have the shelter of this roof over their head, unless they share in the work of the estate. And all who do live and work here shall be free. The thralls will continue to live here, so long as they do their share of the work. But they— you," I said, looking Fasti in the eyes, "will live and work here as slaves no longer. You are now free."

And the carls? I did not say what I was thinking about them. When I returned—if I returned—at some point, there would have to be a reckoning. Those like Floki who refused to accept me would have to leave.

"It will not be as simple as that," Hastein said to me, in a quiet voice. "Free men will not so easily accept slaves as their equals. There will be strife."

I sighed. I was certain there would be. "Well," I replied. "As you have said, this is a troubled household."

We sailed the following morning, after the rising sun had burned the morning fog off of the sea. All of the folk of the estate who were remaining behind came down to the shore to watch us depart, and to say their fare-wells and safe voyages. Only two had any words for me.

Gudrod approached me as I was walking from the longhouse down to the shore, carrying my sea chest on my shoulder and my bow in my free hand.

"I suspect you may find a use for this," he said, and held out a bundle of arrows, bound together by a narrow cord wrapped several times around them. "These are all the finished arrows I had stored in my work shed, plus a dozen bare shafts that I have fletched and put heads on over the past few days. And this," he said, "is a sealskin case I have made for your bow. It will protect it aboard ship."

I lowered my chest to the ground, opened it, and lay the arrows inside. There barely was room for them. I unrolled the sealskin case and slid my bow into it. It was a useful gift which I greatly appreciated. The constant dampness of wave and weather aboard ship can be hard on a bow. "I thank you," I said. "Very much."

Straightening up, I held out my right arm to clasp wrists with him. He took it, then pulled me close and embraced me. I was too startled to react.

After a moment, he stepped back and held me at arm's length, his hands gripping my shoulders. His eyes looked moist.

"You have grown into a fine man," he said. "Your father and Harald would be very proud of you. If you find Toke, be careful. Take no chances with him—kill him as quickly as you can, and be done with it. Then get back here without delay and help me with this hornets' nest you have stirred up and left me to deal with. I am no foreman. I am just a simple carpenter." Dropping his hands and stepping back, Gudrod turned and hurried away, before I could gather my wits enough to answer.

Fasti was standing off to the side, watching. After Gudrod left, he stepped forward and said, haltingly, "M...Master Halfdan?"

"I am not your master, Fasti," I told him. "You are free now."

He stood there, just nodding his head up and down, as his eyes grew moist, too. I felt uncomfortable, and again I could not think of appropriate words to say. I was not used to having anyone care whether I stayed or left. After a long moment he said, in a choked voice, "Thank you. Thank you. May the gods guard you on your voyage, and bring you back to us."

He paused, then extended his clenched right hand out to me, and opened it. Something covered with black feathers was in his palm.

"This is Huginn's wing," he said. "The wing that Toke tore off of her. I kept it to remember her by."

I stared at it, but did not know what I was supposed to say or do.

"The feathers. Use them for an arrow," Fasti said. "Huginn will make it shoot true. Kill Toke with it."

Chicken feathers made poor fletching for an arrow. The wing feathers of a goose are longer and stiffer, and better suited. But Fasti did not know that, and I did not tell him. I took the black wing from him. He said nothing more, but nodded his head in thanks, then turned and hurried away.

At the shore, the *Gull* and the *Serpent*, which were tied up along either side of the narrow wooden pier that jutted out into the water, were in the final stages of loading, as the crew members who had, like me, been sleeping ashore, carried their gear to the ships. Near the pier's end, Hastein was wrestling a ram down to the water's edge with the help of Torvald and Stig. I stowed my sea chest and bow aboard the *Gull* and hurried back to where the two crews' members were gathering around them.

By now Hastein was standing in the shallows, the waters of the inlet lapping around his ankles, the ram at his left side. Torvald, standing on the sheep's other side, had a horn in each of his big hands, immobilizing its head. Stig stood behind Torvald, both hands buried in the wool on the ram's back, holding its body steady so it could not buck or rear.

Hastein raised both arms overhead—his golden godi ring around his upper left arm, and a knife in his right hand—and shouted up at the sky.

"All-Father Odin, mighty, hear us! We ask for your blessing and protection on the voyage we are about to take.

"We pray to you, mighty Thor, as god of oaths and honor. We go to hunt an oath-breaker, a Nithing who has no honor.

"We pray to you, wise Odin, as god of vengeance and death. We go to avenge foul treachery and murder. Help us bring death upon those whom we hunt.

"Brave Thor, master of rain and storm, lord of thunder, grant us fair weather. Accept this blood-offering we give you now. Let the sea drink the blood of this ram, and spare ours. Let its hunger be sated, and spare our ships from wind and wave."

As he finished speaking, Hastein reached down and with a single swift motion, pulled his knife's blade from left to right across the ram's neck, just below its jaw. Blood spurted from the gaping wound out into the water. The ram gave several sharp, convulsive jerks, but Torvald and Stig held it secure.

"The sea drinks our blood-offering," Hastein cried, and the folk gathered along the shore nodded their heads and murmured in approval.

Hastein turned and gestured to Tore, who was standing at the water's edge, holding a shallow copper basin and a short branch freshly cut from a spruce tree. Tore hurried forward, holding them out to Hastein, who swished his knife's blade in the sea, wiped it dry on his trouser leg, and sheathed it. As Hastein extended his hands to take the bowl and branch, Tore's foot slipped on a slick rock in the shallow water, and he went down on one knee. He would have fallen face-forward into the water had he not dropped the branch and put his arm down to catch himself and stop his fall.

The crowd on the shore gasped. Tore looked up at Hastein, a frightened expression on his face, and said, "I am sorry, my Jarl."

Hastein took the copper bowl in one hand, and with his other seized Tore by the upper arm and hoisted him to his feet. Then he bent down, retrieved the spruce branch, and shook the water from it. "It is of no consequence," he said, but I thought his face looked grave.

The ram was beginning to sag in Torvald's and

Stig's grasp, as the flow of blood from the wound in its neck slowed to a steady draining instead of pumping out in spurts. Hastein held the basin under its neck and let it fill. Carrying it out onto the narrow pier, he used the spruce branch to paint the prows of the *Gull* and *Serpent*, below their carved, brightly painted dragon's heads, with the sacrificial blood as he chanted, "Let breakers spare thee, and waves not harm thee. Turn aside from rocks that lurk beneath the surface, and fly before the wind like a bird."

I was not among those in the two crews who pushed forward, after Hastein returned to the shore, seeking to be anointed with the blood. I did not believe that a few drops of blood from a slain sheep held any power to protect me from death or harm. I could not help but recall a similar scene, up on the Limfjord at Hastein's estate, when a blood-sacrifice had been made before our fleet had sailed for Frankia. Many who had sought the protection of the blood then, at that sacrifice, had not returned from that campaign. The threads of all our lives were in the hands of the Norns, the weavers of fate. When the three sisters decided to cut those threads, nothing could turn the blades of their scissors aside.

Torvald had carried the carcass of the now-dead ram onto the *Gull*. At least this night our ration of barley and vegetable stew would be flavored with mutton, instead of salted pork. The rest of the members of the two crews were filing down the narrow dock and boarding the two ships. We would be leaving soon.

I had one last thing to do. I searched the faces of the folk of the estate, still standing along the shore waiting to watch us depart, until I saw Gunhild. Pushing through the crowd, I made my way to where she was standing.

"It is my hope," I told her, "that you will not be here when I return. Your father is a jarl. There will be room for you in his household."

"Hrorik was my husband," she replied, in a haughty voice. "As his wife, I am entitled to live on these lands. More so than you are. You are a bastard, and not entitled to inherit."

"Hrorik acknowledged me before witnesses," I snapped. "You were there. And he gave me one inheritance—the farm up on the Limfjord. I am an heir. The only one, unless Sigrid returns, with any claim to this estate."

Gunhild said nothing, but glared angrily at me. Had I been a thrall, I had no doubt she would have struck me.

"You filled my mother's life with misery," I told her, glaring back. "Do you not think I will do the same to you? I do not deny your right to live here, as Hrorik's widow. But you will not be welcome here, nor will your life be a happy one. Go to your father. Perhaps he will find you a new husband."

"*You* cannot drive me away. And I do not expect you to return. I know my son. Toke will kill you. He will kill you all."

"Halfdan!" Torvald called, from the *Gull*. "It is time."

As I turned and made my way to the ship, Gunhild called after me, in a louder voice this time, that all could hear. "You saw the omen. We all did. The sacrifice was rejected. You are all doomed—you are cursed. You are all going to die."

6

The Eyes of the Realm

Our company numbered eighty-one warriors and one thrall: Cullain, Hastein's Irish slave, who served as cook on the *Gull*. Forty fighting men sailed on the *Serpent*, and forty-one on the *Gull*. Fifty-six of our total war-band were warriors who had long followed the two captains, Hastein and Stig. Thirteen carls from the estate and eight warriors from the nearby village also sailed with us, divided between the two ships. Hrodgar, the headman of the village up on the Limfjord, and my comrade Einar—both of whom sailed aboard the *Gull*—completed our hunting party.

At my urging, Einar had placed his sea chest across from me, rowing the oar that once had been manned by Odd, in the stern at the second position. Torvald had assigned two men from the village to row the third pair of oars, in the positions behind Einar and me. He and Hastein had made a point of scattering the newcomers throughout the ship, interspersed among Hastein's own men.

While the lines securing the two ships to either side of the narrow pier were being untied and coiled, Hastein, who was standing on the *Gull's* small raised stern deck, called across to the *Serpent*. "Stig! Let us row for a bit."

Torvald, who was standing beside Hastein, his hands resting on the carved handle of the steer-board, grunted. "Why?" he said. "There is enough of a breeze to fill the sail."

Ignoring him, Hastein dug his hand into the pouch on his belt, pulled out something, and held it aloft. It was a silver coin. "And Stig—I will wager you this denier that the *Gull* will reach the chop line, where the mouth of the fjord meets the open sea, before the *Serpent* does."

Stig grinned and called out to the *Serpent's* crew, who were readying the ship to get underway. "What say you? Shall I take the Jarl's wager? And his Frankish silver?" When they roared out their approval, he turned back toward Hastein and shouted, "Let us make it two deniers, if the winner is ahead by a full ship's length or more."

Hastein turned to Torvald. "What are you waiting for? Get us underway. I do not want to lose."

Torvald sputtered indignantly. Hastein grinned and strode off toward the bow, making his way through the men milling around on the ship's deck, positioning their sea chests and securing their shields and other loose gear. As he passed near where I was standing, he paused, rested his hand on the shoulder of a warrior named Asbjorn, who kept his sea chest in the stern area and traded off rowing with those of us who rowed the back three pairs of oars.

"Do not row," he said, in a low voice. "I want every new man on an oar for now." To the two men from the village who were standing nearby he said, "You two will be rowing the third pair from the stern, yes?" They bobbed their heads up and down in reply.

"My comrades," Torvald's voice boomed out. All

save Hastein turned and looked toward him. "The *Gull* is a fine ship, but she cannot row herself. The jarl has issued a challenge to the *Serpent*. It is his silver that has been wagered, but it is we who shall win or lose this race. What do you wait for? Oarsmen, draw your oars!"

Hastein continued on toward the bow. I saw him pause and speak briefly to others among the crew—some his own men, presumably telling them the same thing he'd said to Asbjorn, but also to the warriors from the estate and the village, on occasion pointing to a rowing position as he did.

"Our oars are on the high rack," I told Einar. "All of the *Gull's* longer oars, for the stern and bow positions, are kept there. The side racks are for the center oars that are all the same length."

The two men from the village—one, who looked vaguely familiar, appeared to be no older than me—followed us. When we reached the overhead rack, I reached up, grabbed the end of an oar, and slid it down. Examining its shaft, I turned and called back toward the stern, where Tore was still lashing his shield against the ship's side.

"Tore," I said, "this one is yours." He straightened up, nodded, and headed toward us. I handed the oar to Einar, who extended it to Tore. As he did, another of Hastein's housecarls, a warrior named Storolf, joined us at the rack. One of Hastein's warriors who'd remained behind during the Frankia campaign to guard the jarl's estate up on the Limfjord, he'd joined the *Gull's* crew when we'd returned, replacing a warrior who'd been badly wounded in Frankia. Storolf rowed the other oar in the first pair, opposite Tore.

I pulled another oar down. "You can tell by the notches," I explained to the villagers, and pointed to where two small cuts had been made in the oar's shaft, just beyond where a rower's hands would grip it. "This one is for the second position from the stern, where Einar"—as I spoke his name I nodded my head in his direction, to indicate of whom I spoke—"and I are rowing. The two of you will need the oars with three notches."

"Oarsmen, take your positions," Torvald shouted. Hurrying, I handed the oar in my hand to Einar, and slid another down. It had three notches. I handed it to the younger of the two villagers—again wondering why he seemed familiar—and pulled down another, and another, until all six of us rowing the back three pairs had our oars.

"Quickly, take your positions," Torvald called. "The *Serpent* is already pushing free of the dock. Will you let them beat us?"

Four men were standing amidships, using their oars to push the *Gull* clear of the dock, while up and down the length of the deck, the rest of the crew who were manning the *Gull's* thirty oars were positioning themselves on their sea chests, and resting the long shafts of their oars across their thighs. I pushed my sea chest into position and did the same, then reached over to my oar hole in the ship's side, untied the cord that secured its wooden cover, and swiveled it down out of the way.

"Oars out," Torvald ordered. I fed the wide blade

of my oar through the cut extending above the oar hole, slid the shaft out until the oar was fully extended, then leaned forward, arms stretched straight out in front of me, holding the long oar level, poised above the water, and stared at Torvald, waiting for his command.

"Ready…pull!" he shouted.

I dropped the blade of my oar into the water, bracing my feet against the deck, and heaved back on it, pulling with my back and shoulders.

"Pull!"

The first strokes were always the hardest. The *Gull* barely moved each time the banks of oars dipped and bit into the water, and as I strained to drag my oar through each stroke it felt as if the entire weight of the sea was hanging on its blade.

"Pull! Pull!"

Gradually the *Gull* gained speed, at first moving forward in uneven surges with each stroke but slowing in between, as the rowers raised and returned their oars to ready, until we finally reached that magic moment when she suddenly seemed to come alive and to take flight like the sea bird that was her namesake, skimming swiftly across the surface of the sea, while our oars dipped and flashed in unison.

"Pull, pull, pull!" Hastein was chanting the cadence now in unison with Torvald, as he paced up and down the center of the deck, between the rowers.

In front of me, Tore's broad back rocked back and forth with each stroke. "Ha!" he exclaimed. "We are pulling ahead!"

I glanced sideways as I rowed, and saw that it was

true. Although the *Serpent* had gotten underway before us, now—bit by bit—the *Gull* was edging ahead. Aboard the *Serpent*, Stig had changed his own cadence chant from "pull, pull" to "harder, harder." But it was to no avail. The *Gull* was a very fast ship—faster than the *Serpent*. And I could see, glancing over my shoulder, that we were almost abreast of the headland that marked the mouth of the fjord.

From behind me, somewhere amidships by the sound of his voice, Hastein called, while Torvald still chanted the cadence, "Rowers...ready...." Then in unison, he and Torvald gave the order: "Raise oars!"

As I pushed the handle of my oar down, holding its blade well above the surface of the water, I could feel the *Gull's* hull flex and twist as she sliced through the low swells that marked the beginning of the open sea.

"Well done! Well done, my brothers," Hastein exclaimed.

A ragged cheer rose from the crew, as the *Serpent* glided up beside us. Stig, standing in the stern at her steer-board, shook his head. "For certain, the *Gull* deserves her name," he said. Pulling a coin from the pouch at his belt, he flipped it across the space between the two ships.

Hastein grinned as he reached up and caught it. "It was a close race," he answered. "Rowers, stow your oars. Let us spread the *Gull's* wings, so she can ride the wind."

While the crew members who had not been rowing readied and raised the sail, the rest of us returned our oars to their racks. As he slid his oar into place, the younger of the two villagers said to me, "My name is

Bram. And this"— he indicated his comrade—"is Skuli. We are from the village near Hrorik's estate. We both sailed with him to England, in the early spring of this year."

It was apparent that neither of them recognized who I was. They thought me just one of Jarl Hastein's men, nothing more. In truth, there was no reason they should have known me. If either of these two had ever visited Hrorik's estate during the years I was a slave, I did not remember seeing them, and they certainly would not have noticed or remembered a young thrall. And during the brief time when I had lived as a free man on the estate—the weeks between Hrorik's funeral and the ill-fated voyage up to the farm on the Limfjord—there had been little contact between the folk of the estate and those of the village.

"Welcome to the crew of the *Gull*," I answered. "My name is Halfdan."

Watching their faces, I could see that at first my name meant nothing to them. I could also see, after a few moments, when it did. The young one, Bram, realized first.

"You are... you are Hrorik's...."he stammered, searching for the correct words.

"Hrorik's bastard? I am."

His companion, Skuli, sniggered, but Bram looked embarrassed and turned his face away for a moment, saying nothing. The gesture made me realize why he'd looked familiar to me. I'd seen him do the same, once before.

"Your father and brother also sailed on the voyage

with Hrorik to England, did they not?" I asked.

Bram looked surprised. "Yes," he said, nodding his head.

"But they did not return."

"My father, Krok, was killed in the battle with the English. My brother was wounded. He died on the voyage home."

I remembered how his mother had wailed when she had learned of their deaths. Why did you join this voyage? I wondered. Toke is not *your* enemy. Why do you not stay with your family?

The wind held steady out of the northwest all day, leaving most of us aboard the *Gull* with little to do. We sailed south after leaving the coast of Jutland, and by late morning the island of Samso came into view off the bow. At first Torvald closely skirted its coastline, keeping the low profile of the land visible off our steer-board side, bearing south and east along it, until the shoreline of the island began to gradually fall away toward the west, and we headed due south again.

At noon, Hastein took over the steer-board to give Torvald a chance to sit and rest his legs. Torvald, Tore, Storolf, and Asbjorn pulled their sea chests into a loose circle and sat on them, passing the time by rolling dice to see whose luck was the stronger. I pulled my own chest close and sat on it, watching. Torvald threw the highest roll the most often. He was lucky with dice. Tore, on the other hand was not, at least not this day. He rolled the lowest more than any of the others, and after a time it made him morose.

"Do you think it is true?" he suddenly asked. "What that woman said? Was the sacrifice rejected by the gods?"

"Our sacrifice was not rejected," Hastein said, from where he stood back on the stern deck.

"There was nothing wrong with the sacrifice." Torvald agreed. "You were just clumsy, but that is nothing new. If your clumsiness so angered the gods that they would kill us all for it, we would be long dead."

Tore glared at him. Turning to me, he asked, "You know that woman, Halfdan. Does she see things before they happen? Does she have the second sight? Or is she a witch? Did she curse us?"

My mother had possessed the sight. She sometimes saw things that had not yet happened in our world. She had known of Hrorik's return from England, and that he was dying, before his ship had reached the estate. But that had nothing to do with Tore's question.

I shook my head. "Gunhild is just a bitter and angry woman. She wishes ill on others, and hopes to see it happen. But she has no power to make it so."

"But what if it *was* an omen?" Tore persisted. "What if the woman spoke the truth about that? What if we are all going to die?"

"Of course she spoke the truth," Torvald said. "We *are* all going to die. It is the only sure thing in our lives, from the day we are born."

Storolf and Asbjorn began laughing. Even Hastein, up on the stern deck, smiled.

"You are mocking me," Tore snapped, and pushing

his sea chest aside, he strode angrily toward the bow of the ship.

Torvald shook his head, watching him go. "Tore is much changed since Odd died. He has lost his laughter, and sees signs and portents everywhere."

Signs and portents. The words caused a shiver to run down my spine. Harald had spoken those same words, the first night of our voyage up to the Limfjord. We had seen a star fall from the sky, and he had said that some believed such events foretold the death of a great man. A few nights later he was dead, slain by Toke and his men.

"Do you not believe that sometimes there truly are signs to see?" I asked. "That sometimes there are warnings of things to come?"

Torvald shrugged. "Perhaps. Perhaps not. What does it matter? I myself would not wish to see such signs. It would be a great woe to know in advance of your own death. Every man must die, and no one can avoid death when his time is come. It is all in the hands of the Norns. It does no good to worry what the morrow will bring. What will be will be."

By midafternoon we left the southern tip of Samso astern, and as Hastein swung the *Gull* to head due east, we hauled on the braces and sheets, pivoting the sail to keep the wind behind it. The *Gull* tended to heel over with the wind blowing from more directly off her side, so we slid our sea chests to her high side, and stood or sat there to help balance her. But the sea remained calm, and still we made good time.

We made landfall—a narrow promontory jutting out from the western coast of Sjaelland—in the late afternoon.

"We have made good progress this day," Hastein said. "We will break our voyage here tonight, and on the morrow, if we have fair wind again, we should be able to make our way down the great belt, and hopefully beyond."

Sjaelland—the island of the Danish kings. I had been here once before, when Hastein had sailed from Hedeby to hold council with King Horik and other great chieftains of the realm, including Ragnar Logbrod. It was then that the decision had been reached to carry war to the Franks. Was it truly just earlier this same year?

The tip of the promontory ahead of us loomed over the sea, higher than the mast of the *Gull*, its sides falling off sharply down to a narrow, rocky beach below. When we drew closer, I could see a small building atop the point, and beside it, what looked to be a large pile of brush and wood. As I watched, three men came out of the building and pointed in our direction.

"Watchers," Torvald said. "King Horik's men." He turned toward the stern, where Hastein was standing, also staring at the men. "Hastein?" he asked.

Hastein nodded. "Aye," he said. "Show the peace-shields. Though I do not think they would light the beacon for just two ships."

Torvald went forward and unfastened two shields, each painted solid white, from where they had been secured in the peak of the bow, below the carved, brightly painted dragon's head that topped the *Gull's* front stem post. He lashed one on either side of the dragon's head, covering its fierce visage and showing that we came in peace.

Hastein steered the *Gull* closer to shore as we passed below the watch-post. Torvald pulled the tall standard pole down from the overhead rack, stripped off its cover, and— stepping back to the stern deck to stand beside Hastein— raised the standard so that Hastein's gull banner rippled back and forth in the breeze above him. Up on the cliff, one of the guards raised his arm overhead, waving in acknowledgement and greeting, and Hastein did the same in reply.

The finger of land we were passing formed the north side of a broad bay. Hastein steered the *Gull* south now across its mouth, toward a second peninsula that jutted out from the big island's mainland, framing the bay on its south side.

"Where will we stop for the night?" Tore asked him.

"The north shore here is steep and its beach rocky, but there is a spot along the south shore of the bay, near its mouth, where the bottom is smooth and shallow enough for a good anchorage close to the beach," Hastein replied. After we'd sailed on for a short time, crossing most of the distance across to the far side of the bay, he called out, in a louder voice, "Prepare to lower sail. Oarsmen, draw your oars."

We rowed a short way along the south shore of the bay, near its mouth, until we found the shallows Hastein was searching for, and anchored the two ships close in and parallel to the shore. With their gangplanks extended from amidships, it was only a short wade through ankle deep water to dry land. Hastein and Stig dispatched four men to stand watch from the heights overlooking our anchorage, while the rest of the members of the *Gull's* and *Serpent's* crews set about the tasks of preparing to camp for the night. Some used the sail and awnings to pitch tent-like covers over the ships' decks, for shelter to sleep under. Others scattered ashore, searching for firewood. I elected to help Hastein's thrall, Cullain, prepare the evening meal, as did Tore, Storolf, and Gudfred from the estate.

Cullain and the cook for the *Serpent's* crew, a stocky, balding carl named Regin, set up their tripods on the beach and hung large iron cook-pots, half-filled with fresh water, from them. As our scavengers began piling the wood they found nearby, Tore and Gudfred used small-axes to chop up the larger branches and stacked the cut pieces beside the tripods, while Storolf and Regin laid fires beneath the cauldrons and lit the tender with sparks from their flint and steel.

I helped Cullain butcher the ram that had served as our sacrificial offering that morning, while nearby Regin began chopping carrots, parsnips, and rutabagas on a slab of wood. As he filled up the surface of the board with diced vegetables, he would sweep them into the two pots, then grab another handful and begin chopping again.

Cullain had gutted the ram early in the day, to keep the meat from spoiling. Most of the offal he'd tossed overboard as we were sailing, but he'd reserved the heart and liver. We laid the ram on its back on the beach—its body had stiffened, making it somewhat awkward to work with—then with Cullain working on one side, and I the other, we slit the skin down the neck and chest and along each leg, and began working the hide loose from the body. Spreading the flayed hide out on the ground, bloody side up, we used it as a working surface to cut the carcass into sections on.

By now both ships were tented. Most of the crew members who'd help set the shelters came ashore, and having nothing better to do, several gathered around where we were working, to watch. Torvald was among them, as were two brothers named Bjorgolf and Bryngolf, who rowed in the *Gull's* bow. Hastein's men called them the ravens, perhaps because both had coal-black hair and beards, or possibly because they were twins, and looked so much alike it was difficult to tell them apart. Like Storolf, they had remained behind in Jutland to guard Hastein's lands during the Frankia campaign, and had only joined the *Gull's* crew on our return to Denmark, to replace men lost fighting the Franks.

"I want all of the meat cut off of the bones," Cullain told me. "All that we can. We will cut it into small pieces, like this," he added, making a circle with his thumb and finger to show me. "We are starting this stew late in the day, and will need it to cook as quickly as possible."

We had already cut all of the muscles off of the neck, and had separated the front and rear legs from the carcass. Storolf and Tore began cutting the large sections of muscle from the neck into small chunks, as Cullain had instructed, adding them by handfuls to the cauldrons.

Cullain was using a knife to separate the sections of muscle from one of the rear legs and free them from the bone, tossing the bloody pieces of meat into a heap on a clear area of the hide as he cut them free. I had skinned and butchered many beasts while a thrall, and had come to think of myself as more adept than most at the task. But watching the speed with which Cullain turned the carcass of the ram into cleanly trimmed portions of meat, with quick cuts of the small, sharp knife he wielded and no wasted motion made me feel clumsy and unskilled.

I began using my small-axe to cut along the spine on either side, chopping the ribs loose. "Those," Cullain told me, "the ribs—we will have to just cut them into sections, and throw them into the pot bones and all."

"What will you do with the backbone?" Bjorgolf asked.

Cullain glanced up at him. "I have no plans for it."

Bjorgolf glanced at his brother, who nodded. "May we have it?" he said. "We'll dig a trench on the beach, in the shallows, and leave the backbone in the bottom. Perhaps it will catch us some crabs, or maybe even a halibut."

Cullain shrugged. I had finished chopping through the ribs. Taking his shrug as a yes, I held up the bloody backbone, the ram's head still attached.

"Not the head," Torvald told me. "Cut it off and give it to me. This ram was a sacrifice. It belongs to the gods. It is fitting that we honor the ram and the sacrifice by eating its meat. But to use its head as bait for crabs might offend the gods."

I used the edge of my small-axe to slice around the spine, between two bones in the neck, then twisted the head, breaking it free.

"What will you do with it?" I asked, as I passed the ram's head to Torvald.

"I will make a cairn of stones at the water's edge and place the head upon it, and leave it there for the gods."

"And crabs will still eat it, but we will not catch the crabs," Bjorgolf muttered.

I was surprised. Torvald had never struck me as a religious man. Had the earlier talk of omens and death unnerved him, too, despite his show of bravado?

Darkness fell while the stew was cooking. Once the vegetables began to show signs of softening, Cullain and Regin had added handfuls of barley to the pots, to thicken the contents and add heartiness. While we waited, Hastein, Hrodgar and Stig spread out a thick bearskin on the beach to sit on, and built a small fire in front of it. They poured cups of wine from a small cask Hastein had brought ashore and tapped, and after Cullain brought them a pottery bowl filled with the ram's liver, which he had sliced into thin strips, they skewered pieces on sticks and roasted them over the flames of their fire, as the members of the two crews watched hungrily.

In anticipation of the coming meal, Torvald, Tore, and I had waded back out to the *Gull's* gangplank and had fetched our bowls and cups from our sea chests aboard ship. Torvald's stomach was growling by now with hunger, and when he saw Cullain deliver the bowl of sheep's liver to Hastein and Stig, he let out a loud sigh, then walked over to the bearskin and sat down.

"I will join you. Thank you," he said. Hastein looked at him with his eyebrows raised, but said nothing. Their years together and their friendship allowed Torvald certain liberties with the jarl that no other man would dare assert.

Torvald held the small cask upright while he pulled the stopper from the bung hole, then he tilted it and poured himself a cup of wine. He took a long draught, sighed with pleasure, and refilled his cup. "Ale is good, very good, and well-brewed mead has a strength to it that no other drink can match. But wine...ah, wine!"

"I suppose you will want some of the liver, too?" Hastein said.

Torvald nodded his head and smiled. "Why, yes. I thank you." Turning to me, he said, "Halfdan, I need a skewer. Will you find me a slender branch from the firewood pile?"

Stig rolled his eyes. Hastein shook his head, grinning, then to my surprise, said, "Bring two skewers, Halfdan, and join us."

"Fill your cup," Hastein said, after I'd sat myself down on the bearskin. Torvald held out his hand, took my cup, and filled it for me. As I took it back, Hastein began.

"I have been wanting to speak with you about this. I think that what you did— freeing the slaves—was very unwise. I cannot understand why you did it. Admittedly

96

you can be rash at times, but normally I do not consider you a fool."

I had not thought that Hastein would approve. In his eyes, no doubt it seemed I was giving up valuable property for no reason. But to call me a fool, as he seemed to be doing, was harsh. I had not expected such bluntness, and was taken aback by it.

"Are you saying that you think me a fool?" I asked him.

"Until now, I have not," he replied. "I am hoping you can persuade me that in this instance, you were not."

I was silent for a long time, searching my mind for what to say, while Hastein stared at me expectantly. Finally, because I could think of nothing better to say, I told him simply, "I do not expect you to understand."

"That is your answer? It is certain I will not, if you do not even attempt to explain."

How do you make a man who has known only privilege his entire life understand how it feels to be the property of another?

"What would be the most bitter thing that could befall you?" I asked him.

Hastein thought briefly, then answered, "To lose my honor. A man without honor is not a man at all."

Stig nodded in agreement. "Aye," he said. "I would rather lose my life than my honor."

"Does a sheep on the farm have any honor?" I asked. "Does a pig?"

"That is a foolish question," Hastein snapped. "They are not men. They are beasts."

"And what, then, is a slave? Surely not a man, with honor. For he is just property, is he not? Nothing more than another beast on the farm."

Torvald nodded his head in agreement, and poured himself another cup of wine. Hastein began stroking his beard with one hand, and his eyes narrowed as he stared at me. "What you say is true, and yet it also is not," he said.

Stig frowned. "How so?"

"A thrall may be property, but he is more than a beast. Halfdan was a slave. Yet he clearly is a man who possesses a strong sense of honor. Was his honor suddenly born in him after he was set free, or was it there all along?" Hastein replied.

"Perhaps Halfdan is different, and that is why the Norns chose to weave his fate in such a way that he became free," Torvald suggested. "Perhaps he was not supposed to be a slave. Perhaps he is different."

"Perhaps I am not," I said.

Just then, a shout came from the hill above us, where the sentries were posted. "Jarl Hastein! I see torches. Riders are approaching."

We all scrambled to our feet. Hastein and Stig picked up their swords, which had been lying on the bearskin beside them, and slipped their baldrics over their shoulders.

"We will speak more of this later," Hastein said to me. "I can see where you are leading me. I still do not understand why you did what you did, but your words are clever. They certainly are not those of a fool."

A party of riders appeared above us on the edge of

the hill overlooking the beach. Six of them were armored with mail brynies and helms, and had shields slung across their backs. They were carrying torches to light their way, for the sky was cloudy and the night dark. The seventh, their leader, wore no armor and was unarmed save for a sword he wore, carried like Hastein's and Stig's by a baldric slung over his right shoulder, that held the blade in its scabbard suspended at his left hip. While his guard sat upon their horses watching, lined across the hill crest, he guided his mount down the slope to the beach, then walked it over to where we were gathered.

"My name is Ragnvald," he said. "I serve Horik, King of the Danes. I am one of his captains who stand watch over the lands of Sjaelland. My men reported to me that your two ships made camp here, and that they look to be carrying no cargo save warriors. I would know your purpose."

"I am a Dane," Hastein replied. "My name is Hastein. I am jarl over the lands around the Limfjord, in the north of Jutland, and I rule them for the king."

Ragnvald nodded. "My guards described the banner you flew as you approached their post. I thank you for that courtesy. What they described sounded to me like the gull banner of Jarl Hastein. I had thought they must be mistaken, but it appears it is I who was." He swung his right leg up over his horse's neck, and slid to the ground. Extending his right arm toward Hastein, he said, "Welcome, Jarl Hastein, to Sjaelland."

Hastein extended his own arm and the two men clasped wrists. "I thank you," he said. "Cullain, fetch another cup for our guest." To Ragnvald, he added, "We are drinking wine from Frankia. You must join us. And although we have but simple fare to dine on this evening, you and your men are welcome to share it."

Cullain reached into the plain wooden chest in which he kept his cooking gear and withdrew a pottery cup from it. After filling it from the small cask, which Torvald held for him, he handed the cup of wine to Hastein, who presented it in turn to Ragnvald.

After taking a drink, Ragnvald said, "It is good. I thank you. We do not often get wine out here. As for the meal, I thank you for your offer, but will decline. My lands and longhouse are located at the head of this bay, and our womenfolk have food cooking for us there. We had no time to prepare for unexpected guests. But tomorrow, I would honor so illustrious a visitor to these lands with a feast, if you and your men will join us. It is my understanding that you have just recently returned from western Frankia. We would enjoy hearing more about the campaign there. So far we have heard just bits and pieces, related by a messenger from the king who was at the feasts held when Ragnar visited."

I was surprised to hear that Ragnar had already visited King Horik. Although his sons, Ivar and Bjorn, had stayed at Hastein's estate up on the Limfjord for our entire three day layover upon returning from Frankia, and had accompanied us from there down to Hrorik's estate, Ragnar had left Hastein's lands after only a single night, saying he had urgent business to attend to. Torvald nudged me in the ribs with his elbow, and leaning over, whispered—in a voice loud enough that all who were near could hear— "Ragnar wastes no time spreading tales of his own successes." Hastein turned and scowled at him, then turned back to Ragnvald.

"Alas," Hastein responded, "I thank you for your generous offer of hospitality, but I fear we will not be able to feast with you. We must sail on tomorrow, at first light."

"If I may ask," Ragnvald said, "What brings you here? King Horik will want to know, when he hears that you have passed this way. The winter approaches, and the raiding season is over. And from what Ragnar has told the king of the campaign in Frankia, all who fought there should have little need to seek further success this season."

"The gods did in truth grant us a great victory in Frankia," Hastein said. It was an answer leaving much unanswered.

When Hastein did not seem inclined to say more, Ragnvald prodded, "May I convey any message from you to the king?"

Hastein shook his head. "No, thank you," he said.

Ragnvald said nothing further, but stared at Hastein expectantly. After a time, the silence grew awkward.

"We are seeking some men," Hastein finally said. "They were traveling in two ships. They may have passed this way." It surprised me that he was being so unforthcoming.

"Many ships pass this way," Ragnvald responded. "Many pause their voyage here, in this bay, either before sailing down through the great belt, or upon leaving it when coming up from the south. As to two particular ships, it would be hard to say without knowing more."

Turning to me, Hastein said, "Describe them for him."

"Both are longships. One has a dragon's head carved like the head of an eagle, painted red, with a golden beak. She has sixteen pairs of oars. The other ship is smaller, fourteen pairs, and her dragon's head is gilded, and carved like the head of a fierce fighting stallion."

Ragnvald shrugged, but said nothing.

"Both ships would have been manned by very light crews," Hastein added.

Ragnvald shrugged again. "As I have said, many ships pass this way. Were these men friends of yours?" Now it was he who was offering little with his words. I suspected he had taken offence at Hastein's reticence.

"If they passed this way, it would have been roughly ten days ago." Hastein added. He seemed determined to convey as little information as possible. I did not understand why. It would be very helpful to know if Toke had sailed this way.

"The larger ship's captain is a very big man—tall, and strongly built," I volunteered. "His hair and beard are black, and he wears them long. He often wears a sleeveless outer tunic made of bearskin. And there was—there may have been—a woman aboard his ship. She is tall and slender, with long hair the color of pale gold."

"You seem to know much about these folk," Ragnvald said to me. "More, perhaps, than the jarl himself. Your name is…?"

I was about to tell him that my name was Halfdan, when Hastein interjected. "He is one of my housecarls. He is called Strongbow."

To my surprise, Ragnvald said, "I may have heard of him. The recent messenger from King Horik is a skald. He is composing a lay about Ragnar and his campaign against the Franks. He recited it to us—as much as he has composed so far. There was a Strongbow in it, who with his arrows saved Ragnar from a Frankish champion in a great battle. How did those verses go?"

We fed the wolves and ravens with our enemy's dead.
On the Frankish plain our shield wall strong,
Held again and again against the charging steeds and iron-clad men.
The sea-king's axe split shields and clove helms,
The green field of battle was painted red with blood.

We fed the wolves and ravens with our enemy's dead.
Surrounded by foes great Ragnar stood.
Like wheat before the scythe a Frankish champion cut down
All around him; the raven banner nearly fell.
But swift and sure did fly the deadly shafts of Strongbow,
The sea-king lived to fight again.

"Yes, I think that is how it went," Ragnvald said. "There was much more, of course, but I remember the Frankish champion falling from the swift and sure shafts. I thought it clever phrasing. So this is the warrior, the Strongbow who shot them and saved Ragnar?"

Hastein nodded. "He is the same."

Ragnvald looked at me appraisingly, and said, with surprise in his voice, "You are very young." He pursed his lips and was silent for a few moments, as if weighing what further to say. Then, turning back to Hastein, he spoke.

"It is clear to me that there is much unsaid here, and that you do not wish to say it. But you are known throughout the lands of the Danes as a man of great honor. I must trust that you have your reasons— although King Horik will not be pleased with me that I did not learn them. The ships you seek, lightly manned and commanded by the man he has described" he said, nodding at me, "did pass this way. It *was* ten days ago. I remember the captain well, for he, like you, had little to say about his business."

"He spoke his name to you?" Hastein asked.

"He said his name was Harald, though I had reason to doubt it. The warriors standing with him, when I rode down to the shore where they were cooking their evening meal, looked surprised when he spoke the name, and two laughed aloud. I found him a somewhat ill-mannered man," Ragnvald added.

It was evil humor on Toke's part to use Harald's name. "Did you see the woman I described?" I asked.

"I did not. But the ships were tented for the night

by the time I arrived. They were anchored offshore, as you are, and I did not go aboard."

"I thank you for this information," Hastein said.

Ragnvald nodded, then drained his cup of wine and handed it to Cullain. "I do not know why you are pursuing these men, although I suspect the woman is at least a part of it. But ten days is a long lead."

Later that evening, after Ragnvald had left, I asked Hastein why he had not just told him we were pursuing Toke, and why.

"We do not yet know for certain where Toke has gone. He told Ubbe, the slain foreman, that he was sailing for Birka. But we do not know if that was the truth or a lie. All we know as yet is that he stopped for the night here, in this bay on the coast of Sjaelland, ten days ago. And from here, he almost certainly sailed down the great belt. There would be no other reason for him to pass this way. So thus far all we can be sure of— but it is no small thing—is that he did not sail north, for Norway, or beyond, to England or Ireland.

"But beyond the great belt, he could just as well have continued on south to Hedeby, instead of east into the Austmarr, toward Birka. Or he could still be nearby, in Danish waters, seeking allies. His mother's father is jarl on the island of Fyn, is he not?" I nodded, and Hastein continued. "And even if Toke did sail east, there are many places other than Birka, within the Austmarr, he could be heading for."

Hastein made it sound hopeless. My face must have reflected how discouraged I felt, hearing his words.

"Then what will we do?" I asked.

"For now, we must continue on toward Birka. It is all we have to go on, and if he came this way on the first leg of his journey, Toke could in truth be bound there."

"But why did you not tell Ragnvald it was Toke we are hunting?" It was a question Hastein had still not answered.

"Because Ragnvald would be bound to tell King Horik, and it would quickly become common knowledge—and the source of much talk and speculation—within the king's longhouse. Many folk pass through there. Who knows to whom or where word of our quest might spread to? Our only advantage, at this time, is that Toke does not know for certain that he is being pursued, or if so, by how many."

"I wonder why Toke would be sailing to Birka," I murmured, more to myself than to Hastein.

Hastein stared at me silently for a few moments, then asked, "Why do you think he stole your sister Sigrid, and took her away with him?"

It was a question that, in truth, I had tried not to think of. Toke had twice raped Astrid, Sigrid's maid, and had tried to rape my mother—the act that had led to his banishment by Hrorik. And he had murdered Harald, his own foster brother. If he would do all of that, I could not imagine he would feel constrained by the fact that Sigrid was his foster sister. And I could well believe that, in Toke's twisted mind, hurting her, dishonoring her, would be a way to further express his hatred of Harald and Hrorik, and to strike out at me. But what then?

"I fear..." I hated putting my fears into words, as if

speaking them aloud might make them more real. "I fear he took her to dishonor her. And because Ragnvald did not see her, I fear he may have killed her afterwards. I fear she may already be dead."

Hastein considered my words for a time, as if weighing the possibility that they could be true. He took a deep breath and blew it out, then said, "Perhaps, but perhaps not. Such actions would not explain why Toke would be sailing for Birka—if, in truth, he is. I believe he could have taken her for another reason. There is a great slave market there."

At first I did not understand. And then I did. "But Sigrid is not a slave," I protested. "She is a Dane, and of noble blood. Surely the Sveas would not allow such as her to be sold into slavery in their markets!" Even as I said the words, in my heart I did not believe them.

"Some buyers who purchase slaves in Birka travel from there down the eastern road and trade with the Araby kingdoms. Slavers who buy for the Arab markets pay high prices for comely slave girls. Those who are especially fair, and have red or golden hair, are particularly prized by the Arabs. Women of beauty such as that are rarely born into slavery."

When I did not answer, Hastein added. "We do not know that this was Toke's plan. But if the Norns have woven this fate for her..." he shrugged. "No one can escape their fate. It is the way of things."

After I'd finished my evening meal, rinsed my bowl, cup and spoon, and had stowed them once more in my sea chest aboard the *Gull*, I returned to the shore and climbed the slope that rose above it to relieve my comrade Einar, who was one of the four sentries standing watch.

"I am not due to be relieved yet," he told me, "and someone has already been ordered to relieve me later."

"It does not matter. Go and get some food, while it is still warm. And tell the man who was to relieve you that I will stand his watch, too. I have much on my mind, and do not feel I can sleep. I would rather be sleepless up here than in my bed."

I passed the long hours of the night pacing back and forth along the crest of the slope over the beach, wrapped tightly in my cloak. It was a good thing that we were camped for the night in a land where there was no threat of attack, for my mind was not on my duty. I could not drive from my thoughts the image of Sigrid being sold into slavery. She had told me once that she could not wed a man she did not love. Did she now face a far worse fate—becoming the property of a foreigner in some distant land who would use her however and whenever he wished? Such a life would be far worse than the slavery I had endured. I wondered whether, for a woman such as Sigrid, death might become preferable.

Eventually weariness overcame even such troubling thoughts, and when four warriors climbed up from the beach in the last hours before dawn to stand the final watch, I stumbled down the slope past them, eager to snatch a few hours of sleep aboard the *Gull*. Because I had been farthest out along the hillside, the other three sentries who'd been relieved were well ahead of me by the time I reached the beach, and were already climbing their ships' gangplanks.

As I approached the water's edge I heard a sound, a rattling of stones, off to my right along the shore. There should not have been anyone there.

Swinging my shield around in front of me—I had been carrying it slung by its long leather strap across my back—I grasped the wooden rod that spanned its back side and formed its grip, and held my spear more tightly in my right hand, extending its blade out ahead of me.

"Is someone there?" I called, in a low voice. There was no response. Then, after a moment, I heard the sound again: as if two rocks were scraping against each other, followed by the sound of a stone falling and hitting others, not far ahead.

I dropped into a crouch, so that my shield covered more of my body, and crept forward, peering into the dark above its top edge. A low shape appeared out of the darkness to my left. As I drew closer, I realized it was the cairn of stones that Torvald had stacked at the water's edge. With a start I realized that the ram's head he had placed atop it was gone. An involuntary shiver ran down my spine.

From somewhere close ahead, I heard a soft crunching in the sand, as if someone—or something— was moving quietly, carefully, across the beach, trying to not be heard.

"Who is there?" I hissed. The sound stopped. I edged forward one step, then another. Suddenly I realized that there was a shape in the darkness ahead of me. It looked very large—larger than a man.

"*Unnnnhh. Unh! Unh!*"

The sound, coming from the dark shape ahead, was not human. Was there a god, or some kind of servant of the gods, on the beach ahead of me, come to claim the sacrifice? Or could it be a draugr, one of the walking dead who rose from their graves in the night? Either way, I did not want to find out. Fear overcame me, and I turned and ran for the *Gull's* gangplank.

The morning dawned as dark as my mood. Rain had begun to fall just before daybreak—a steady, mist-like curtain of rain so light that it made no noise striking the tented shelter above the *Gull's* deck. It was enough, though, to saturate the awnings and sail until they dripped through on those sleeping below, enough to make the pile of firewood stacked on shore too wet to burn, when Cullain tried to boil barley for a simple porridge to break the night's fast before we took ship. It was enough to soak into our cloaks and tunics and trousers and leave them sodden and cold.

And the rain killed the wind, too. "Oarsmen, draw your oars," Hastein ordered. "It appears we will do some rowing this day."

I was standing at the high center rack with the others who rowed in the stern when Tore nudged me in the ribs with his elbow and said excitedly, "Look, Halfdan! The cairn of stones on the shore. The ram's head is gone from it. The gods must have taken it."

What he said was true. I felt a shiver run down my spine.

Torvald, who was walking past headed for the stern, paused and said, "You see, Tore. It is as the jarl and I told you. The sacrifice was not rejected by the gods."

Tore nodded. "No, no, it was not," he agreed, sounding relieved. Drawing his oar, he turned and hurried back toward his rowing position.

Torvald watched him go, then shook his head and grinned. "Tore is a good man to have at your side in battle, but somewhat simpleminded."

"Something took the ram's head," I murmured, as I reached up and pulled my oar from the rack. I was not about to volunteer what I had seen.

"Indeed," Torvald answered.

I was turning to head back to my rowing position in the stern when I heard, from where Torvald was standing behind me, "*Unnnnhh!*"

For a brief moment, the fear I had felt last night returned, and I froze. Then, as my face turned bright red from anger and embarrassment, I scowled back over my shoulder at him.

Torvald held a finger to his lips and said, "Shhh." In a low voice, he added, "I am glad you did not throw your spear in the darkness and skewer me."

Under power of our oars, we headed out of the mouth of the bay and turned south, into the broad channel between the islands of Sjaelland and Fyn known as the great belt. All day we rowed, trading turns at the oars with our extra crew members, for the wind did not return. The coastline of Sjaelland curved away from us until it was only a low smudge barely visible off to the east. Out on the open sea there was no way to measure our progress, or even to feel that we were truly moving forward at all. It was just endlessly dip, pull, raise the blade from the water and rock forward, and then do it all again, over and over and over, while the constant mist of rain fell. At least the labor at the oars kept us warm.

We rowed and rowed until finally, as dusk was falling, we reached a short, broad peninsula jutting out from the western coast of Sjaelland. We beached the prows of our ships on the sandy, gently sloping shore, near its tip, and made camp for the night. The land inland was low and flat, with large stretches of marsh. It did not look inviting.

"We made slow progress this day," Hastein said, shaking his head as we gathered on shore, stretching our legs and swatting at the tiny flying bugs that had swarmed out from the marshes, as we waited for Cullain to bring a simple meal of boiled barley porridge to completion. "Very slow. We have not even cleared the great belt. I have never seen an entire day with no wind at all in these waters."

Hrodgar and Stig, who were standing nearby, both nodded in agreement. "It was a strange day," Hrodgar said. "The belt was as slick and still as a pond. But at least the rain has finally stopped."

The wind returned with the dawn, a gentle but steady breeze blowing out of the northeast. By mid-morning we cleared the southern end of the belt, and after sailing through a narrow channel between two small islands off the southwest corner of Sjaelland, we turned our course toward the southeast, following the southern coastline of the island of the kings. Almost as if to make up for its absence the day before, the wind shifted soon after and began blowing harder and from the northwest, pushing our ships along at such a pace that the *Gull* seemed to almost skim across the surface of the sea.

We broke our voyage earlier than yester-day, after reaching the island of Falster, south of Sjaelland, in the late afternoon. "We have not had a decent meal since the first night of our journey," Hastein explained. "I, for one, am hungry, and have no wish to eat boiled barley again. Cullain will fix us another stew." To Torvald, he added, "It is why—one of the reasons— I have stopped our journey early this day. It will take Cullain some time to boil the salted pork enough to make it edible."

"One of the reasons?" Torvald asked. I, too, wondered what others there might be.

The wizened little Irish thrall, who usually went about his business in silence, interrupted. "As you wish," Cullain said to Hastein. "But you should know that already our store of vegetables is getting low. We brought but one barrel-full aboard the *Gull*, and there are many mouths to feed."

"I am aware," Hastein answered. To Torvald, he said, "I plan for us to stop tomorrow on the isle of Mon. It will be but a half-day's sail from here, if the wind is as steady as it was this day. A jarl named Arinbjorn rules there is, and I wish to speak with him. The passages between Mon and Sjaelland to the north, and Mon and Falster to the west, are both narrow. They are the gateways leading from the Austmarr into Danish waters. Arinbjorn keeps close watch over all who pass through them, for the Vends often try to raid up into our southern islands."

Cullain looked confused, and frowned. "The vegetables...?" he asked, interrupting again.

"When we stop at Mon, I will purchase more stores," Hastein told him. "I have planned for this. There is a large village on the north side of the island, not far from the jarl's lands. The folk there will have food to sell to us. They often trade with passing ships, for it is not uncommon for those preparing to sail across the Austmarr to stop at Mon seeking provisions. "

Turning to me, Hastein added, "If Toke's ships passed this way, Arinbjorn will know. That is the other reason we are stopping at Mon."

Hastein had not exaggerated when he'd said that Jarl Arinbjorn kept a close watch over all who passed through the waters around the island of Mon. We had not been sailing long up the channel that separated Mon from the southern shoreline of Sjaelland when we reached a point where the channel narrowed considerably due to a headland that jutted out from the smaller island. As we passed the headland, two longships that had been lying in wait behind it raised their sails and headed out into the channel on a course to intercept us. The two ships were smaller than either the *Gull* or the *Serpent*, but they were very fast, and as they drew closer, I could see that their decks bristled with armed men.

"Do you see those pennants flying from the tops of their masts?" Hastein said, pointing at the approaching longships. He was on the small raised rear deck, standing beside Torvald, who was manning the steer-board. Like several others of the crew, I had walked to the *Gull's* steer-board side to watch the approaching vessels.

Each of the two longships had a long, narrow banner, pointed on the end, flying from its mast-top. I could not make out the design upon them.

"It is a serpent—or perhaps a dragon," Torvald said, squinting.

"It is a dragon, with its tail entwined around its body," Hastein told him. "The same design is on Arinbjorn's standard. His ships fly those pennants in these waters, so all will know they are being approached by his men."

"Shall we lower our sail?" Torvald asked.

Hastein shook his head. "We do not need to stop completely. We will reef it, though, and slow the *Gull*, so they can sail alongside us with ease."

At Hastein's command we lowered the boom and shortened the sail, bunching the mid-section and tying it up with its reefing lines, then hauled the boom and the reefed sail fully aloft again. By the time we'd finished, one of the Mon ships had pulled along our steer-board side, less than an oar's length away, and was shortening its own sail to hold our pace, while the other had passed behind the *Gull* and was now sailing between her and the *Serpent*.

I studied the closer ship as it sailed beside us. It was shorter in length than the *Gull*—upon close inspection, I could see it had but twelve pairs of oars. But I found

115

another difference between it and our ship more notable. As was typical on a sailing voyage of any length, the *Gull's* deck, along her center line, was filled with such cargo as we carried: the barrels holding our rapidly diminishing supplies of provisions, a large cask situated in front of the mast filled with our store of fresh water, and the sea chests of our crew members, pushed out of the way into the center of the deck when not being used for seating or as rowing benches. By contrast, this ship clearly was fitted out only for patrolling through local waters. The empty space aboard her deck made possible by carrying no cargo or supplies allowed her to be manned by a crew far greater than a ship her size could normally bear on a sea voyage. There looked to be close to forty warriors aboard her, all fully armed. Several were holding strung bows, and most of the rest spears. These ships and the warriors aboard them were ready for battle, should the need arise.

A tall warrior standing in her stern, wearing a brynie and helm with a nasal bar that obscured his features, called out to us. "These waters belong to the isle and folk of Mon. We guard them on behalf of the Jarl of Mon. If you would sail through these waters, you do so only by his leave."

"And do we have leave of Jarl Arinbjorn to sail this way?" Hastein responded. I was surprised by his reply. I thought the other ship's captain had sounded arrogant and overbearing, and Hastein tended to be a proud man.

"Who are you? Where are you from, and where are you bound?"

"My name is Hastein. I am jarl over the lands

around the Limfjord, in Jutland. We have sailed from those lands, and are bound for Mon, for I have business with Jarl Arinbjorn."

"Your pardon, Jarl Hastein." The Mon captain's voice sound far more respectful now than when he had first spoken. "Your ship displays no banner, and I did not know to whom I spoke. Of course you are free to pass." He turned his head and spoke to his steers-man, and the ship began to veer away from us.

"It is probably a good thing that when they wish to question the right of honest sailors to pass through these waters, they do so with two ships filled with armed men," Torvald muttered. "Otherwise, I suspect that many might wish to prove their right to pass with steel."

Beyond the headland behind which the two guard ships had lain in wait stretched an enormous bay. In the very center of its long, curving shoreline, a short channel led to a nor in the middle of the island. A small fortress, with earthen walls topped by a wooden stockade, guarded the mouth of the channel, and three longships similar in size to the two that had challenged us were anchored near it, their prows against the sandy beach.

The nor itself, though not nearly as large or long as that on which Hedeby was located, nevertheless was sizable. A village sprawled along its shore a short distance from the channel. I was surprised to see that no wall or ditch protected it, but perhaps the folk of the village felt the nearby fort and its garrison provided protection enough.

Numerous small boats were pulled up along the shorefront of the village. Behind them, fishing nets had been hung out to dry across wooden frames. A strong smell of fish, mingled with smoke, hung in the air. The smoke was coming from a row of squat, windowless sheds beyond the nets.

Torvald wrinkled his nose. "The problem with fishing villages," he said, "is that they always smell like fish."

"Do not turn your nose up at the smell, or the fish," Hastein told him, as we rowed the *Gull* past the beached boats, heading for an area of the shoreline further down where a number of narrow piers jutted out from the shore. "We will be eating much of them in the days to come. Great schools of herring swim out in the bay. The folk here brine and smoke them, and pack them in barrels for trade. They keep well once smoked, and unlike salted pork, do not need to be boiled before they can be eaten."

"Huh," Torvald grunted, noncommittally. He did not look convinced that smoked herring was preferable to dried, salted pork.

"I am putting you in charge of provisioning the *Gull*," Hastein continued. He walked over to one of his two sea chests, lifted a leather sack from it, and counted out a handful of silver coins. He paused for a moment, then counted out some more. "This will be more than enough to buy what we need for both the *Gull* and the *Serpent*. Buy four barrels of smoked herring for each ship. Take Cullain with you, and let him select such vegetables as are available, and have them packed in straw, in barrels. And I want three more barrels of barley per ship, as well. Take Tore and some of the others with

118

you, to help carry what you purchase back to the ships."

"And ale?" Torvald asked hopefully. "If they have any to sell, shall I buy some casks of ale, also?"

Hastein nodded, and counted out more coins.

"Where will you be?" Torvald asked.

"I go to meet with Jarl Arinbjorn," Hastein replied. "I will take Stig with me, and Halfdan, as well."

I was surprised that Hastein chose me. My face must have showed it.

"I have undertaken this voyage because I feel a need to bring Toke to justice," he explained. "He has killed too many folk in lands that are my responsibility to protect. And the warriors sailing with us who are from your brother Harald's estate" — I noticed he did not call it mine — "have reason to seek Toke's death, also. But this voyage for vengeance we are on — this hunt we have undertaken — is yours, more than anyone else's. So in any matters that concern our search for Toke, on *this* journey you are more than just one of my men."

He looked at me, pursed his lips, and frowned. "You should put on a better tunic. A clean one, and clean trousers, too."

I was wearing the gray woolen tunic Sigrid had made for me, what seemed now like so long ago. It was well-worn and somewhat stained, but was warm and comfortable. But though well-suited to wear on a sea voyage, apparently it would not do to meet with Jarl Arinbjorn. "You should wear your sword," Hastein said. He frowned again, studied me, then after a moment added, "And bring your bow, also."

I felt puzzled by Hastein's detailed instructions as

to what I should wear and what weapons I should bring, but went to my sea chest so I could fulfill them. I removed the trousers and tunic I'd been wearing, and replaced them with the green wool trousers and blue linen tunic which had been a gift from Hastein, before we had sailed for Frankia. He'd said at the time they were for me to wear on occasions such as at feasts or councils, so my appearance would reflect well on him. Apparently our meeting with Jarl Arinbjorn was such an occasion.

I added the short leather boots that had once been Harald's—if the clothing I had been wearing looked too shabby, no doubt my worn, patched shoes did, also—and after I slung my sword's baldric over my shoulder, I draped my best cloak over my back, too, and used the silver ring brooch to secure it at my shoulder. The air was somewhat cool, and the tunic I had put on, though much finer looking than the one I had removed, was made of linen rather than wool, so it was not as warm. Last, I took the better of my two quivers from my sea chest, and pulled my bow from its sealskin case Gudrod had given me, then presented myself to Hastein.

He, too, had put on finer clothes—the tunic he had changed into was made of brightly colored silk. Hastein was the only person I had ever seen to wear entire garments made of the rare and expensive fabric. He glanced at me briefly and nodded.

The two black-haired brothers called the ravens were standing with him. "Bjorgolf and Bryngolf will be coming with us, also," he said. I wondered if their purpose—and to some extent mine, also—was to give

Hastein a retinue of warriors when going to meet with another jarl. Their identical appearance certainly made them striking to see.

By now the *Gull* and *Serpent* had been tied to either side of a narrow wooden pier that extended out into the brackish waters of the nor. As other members of the *Gull's* crew secured their oars and Torvald assembled the party who would assist him with the re-provisioning of the ships, I followed Hastein down the pier and into the village.

Jarl Arinbjorn's estate was some distance away, at the end of a long, narrow finger of the nor. It was not overly far—from the village we could see the longhouse and outbuildings in the distance—but Hastein announced that he did not intend to walk there, that we would ride. For a time it appeared his desire to do so would be thwarted, for there was no one in the village who even possessed five horses, much less would have been willing to hire them out to total strangers. But fortunately the captain in charge of the nearby fort had walked the short distance over to the village with several of his men in order to determine who was aboard the two ships that had docked there. He was more than willing, after meeting Hastein and learning who he was, to loan us the necessary mounts.

We had ridden but a short distance from the village when Hastein, who was riding in the lead with Stig beside him, turned in the saddle and motioned for me to come up and ride by his side. As I did, Stig dropped back and rode behind us, with Bjorgolf and Bryngolf.

"There is another reason—besides Toke—that I

121

wished you to come with me to meet Jarl Arinbjorn," he said. "And it is why I wished you to look more presentable.

"I have been thinking," he continued, "about the estate in Jutland, the lands that were your father's, and your brother Harald's after him. You do have a lawful claim to them. No one else has a stronger one. It *might* be possible—I suppose—to work the lands successfully with only the slaves you freed, if they do not all run off. But it is a chieftain's estate. A man who holds such lands, if he wishes to keep them, must surely have some followers who are more than former thralls. He must have housecarls, warriors, who can fight to protect the estate and its folk, if necessary."

I thought it ironic that Hastein was ignoring the fact that I was a freed slave, yet was capable of fighting, but I said nothing.

"It is clear to me," he said. "To take that estate as your own, you must become a chieftain. The folk of the estate must accept that you are one. So you must learn how to act like a chieftain. In part you must learn how to command men, and how to make them wish to follow you. But there is more to it than that. You must conduct yourself in all things as if you believe you are as good as any man, and better than most. So I have decided—it is I who must teach you these things. There is no one else who can. You have no one else—your father and brother are both dead."

I was speechless. This was totally unexpected.

"Well?" Hastein asked. He clearly expected some response.

"I...I do not know what to say." In truth, I was not at all certain this was something I wanted. When we had been at the estate, I had asserted that I had a claim of right to it. But Hastein was correct: it was a chieftain's estate. And I was not chieftain, and did not believe I could ever be. To the folk of that estate, I would surely always be just Hrorik's bastard son and a former slave. But I could not tell Hastein that—especially not now. "I thank you," I finally said.

Hastein nodded his head, apparently taking my response as an acceptance of his plan. "I have said before that I believe the Norns have woven the threads of our fates together for a reason," he said. "I believe this may be part of it."

I found the whole idea of fate, of some great pattern the Norns were weaving from the lives of all men, very confusing. And I could not imagine—could not believe— that *my* life could matter in any grand plan of the Norns.

"In truth," I said hesitantly, "I have never felt that my life was guided by the Norns. And I do not understand fate, or how my life could matter in any pattern the Norns are weaving."

"Surely you do believe that the Norns exist, and that they are the weavers of fate?"

I did not like to think about such things. I could not understand how three ancient sisters, sitting at the roots of the world-tree, could weave something, anything, out of the lives of men. How could the lives we lived be threads in their hands, to be woven on some great loom? But I did not wish to voice my doubts aloud. If the Norns did exist, if they truly were the weavers of fate and controlled the threads of all men's lives, I did not want to anger them.

"Of course I do," I lied.

"It is good that you believe," Hastein said. "Do not be concerned that you do not understand. You should not expect to be able to. That to the Norns, our lives are but threads to be woven, is a thing beyond the understanding of mere mortal men. It is not for us to comprehend—it is enough if we believe, and trust that our lives, and all that befalls us, is for a purpose, is part of a great plan that we cannot know." Hastein nodded his head. "It is good that you believe," he said again. "There are many men who are unable to believe what they cannot understand. Torvald is one. I do not think he believes in fate or the gods."

"But why would *my* life be of any concern to the Norns? Why would they bother to have linked it to yours?"

Hastein shrugged. "I do not know. But the Norns do everything with a purpose. And when I awoke this morning, I found myself wondering 'What if it is part of the Norns' design that Halfdan become a chieftain? What if it is their wish that someday he will be a great leader of men?' It was then that I realized that if that is your destiny, if for some reason that is the plan the Norns have for your life, then I must help you achieve it. That must be part of my purpose."

I appreciated Hastein's desire to help me. I truly did. But I still could not believe that his doing so—or that my becoming a chieftain—could be part of some grand plan.

"So that is why I told you to change your shabby clothes," he continued. " If you wish men to believe that you are a person of note, a chieftain or at least someone who might someday become one, you must look and act like one. It is also why I wished to ride to Jarl Arinbjorn's estate, rather than walk there. From now on, you must always be aware of the impression you make when others meet you—particularly important men, such as Arinbjorn. And it is also why I told you to bring your bow. You have already gained some renown as a warrior, in no small part due to your unusual skill with your bow. A renowned war-king, Ragnar Logbrod, has named you Strongbow, in front of an entire army. That is an honor that few achieve. Do not let others—and particularly do not *ever* let the carls of your estate— forget that. Many a great man *is* great to a large extent because others believe he is."

What Hastein wished of me would not be easy. How could I convince others that I was worthy of becoming a chieftain, if I myself did not believe it?

"Do you truly believe that the path of my life has already been set by the Norns? That the paths of every man's life has been?"

Hastein shook his head. "Oh, no. Not at all. It is not like that. It is not that simple. I have given much thought to this matter—the nature of fate—and I believe that I perhaps may understand it better than most.

"You mentioned the path of your life. It is useful to think of life that way. Each of us, as we travel through our lives, regularly come to places where the path forks—where there are different directions our life may

125

take, depending on some decision we must make. In your life for example, what would have happened if, after Toke slaughtered your brother Harald, and his men and the folk of the farm up on the Limfjord, you had not sworn to avenge their deaths? What if you had just fled, caring only for your own safety, and had become a homeless wanderer? For certain, if I had met you under such circumstances, I would not have been moved to offer you a place in the crew of the *Gull*. And had that not happened, you would not have been with me and my men in Frankia, and would not have been in a position to save the life of Ragnar Logbrod. And had *that* not happened, you would not have been honored by him before an entire army as 'Strongbow,' a warrior of renown. Do you see how it works? How so much has flowed from that one decision you made? How your life could so easily have gone a different way?"

The more Hastein tried to explain it, the more confused I felt.

"If it was part of the Norns' plan that I seek to avenge Harald and kill Toke, could I have decided anything else?"

"Oh, yes," Hastein said. "It was your decision to make, or not to. The path of a man's life is not like runes carved into stone, which cannot be changed."

"But if, as you suggest, the path my life has taken thus far is part of a great pattern of fate being woven by the Norns, had I not sworn vengeance—had I just fled from Toke—would the pattern not have been altered?"

"Ah!" Hastein said. "That is a good question!" He clearly was enjoying this discussion far more than I was.

"What makes fate so very hard to grasp is its vastness. That is why mortal men do not have the ability to truly comprehend it."

That, among other things, I thought.

"To the Norns," he continued, "every man's life is no more than a few threads—and short threads, at that. You have seen cloth woven, have you not?"

I nodded. When growing up I had watched my mother and the other women of Hrorik's household seated at the big looms, weaving the threads they'd spun from sheep's wool into cloth.

"Think of it this way. Many, many threads are woven into a single bolt of cloth. And to make something as large as a longship's sail, many bolts of cloth must be woven, and sewn together. If a single weaver were to fail to weave a few short lengths of thread in their proper place and order into a single bolt of cloth, it would not change the sail in any way you could notice, would it?"

I shook my head.

"Fate—the fate of the whole world, which the Norns are weaving, is far, far vaster than a longship's sail. Unlike mortal men, the Norns can see, as they weave, that which has not yet come to pass. As they hold the threads of each man's life in their fingers, they can see a path our lives could follow that would best serve the pattern they are weaving. We are, each of us, given the chance to follow that path which the Norns wish us to take. But if any man, through his own decisions and actions, turns aside from that path..." Hastein shrugged. "He is but one man, and his life but a few threads. There are other lives, other threads, which can be woven instead to achieve the final pattern. No single man's life can change the course of fate itself."

I tried to picture it. I tried to think of the decisions I had made, the things I had done, that could have changed the path of my life. But I quickly realized it was much more than just me. What of every other person whose path of life my own had crossed—of the decisions they had made, too? What of all the men I had fought and killed? What if they had decided not to fight me? What if they had not died? And for that matter, what if I had not met Genevieve? Was it all part of some great pattern of fate the Norns were weaving? It was too much to grasp. Thinking about it made my head hurt.

Hastein laughed. "You look very confused," he said.

I nodded. "I am."

"Do not try to understand it. You will not be able to. As I have told you, no mere mortal man can."

"Then why have you given it so much thought?" I asked.

"That, too, is a good question. I do not try to understand the great pattern the Norns are weaving, for that is beyond the ken of any man. But I do believe it can be possible, at times, for a man to discern the path the Norns would have *him* travel—to sense which choices will make his life fit smoothly into their plan, and further it. It is not so unlike your own skill at reading signs, which allows you to track men or beasts in the forest. There are times, when I am weighing a choice to make, that I feel I can almost see the fork I have come upon in the path of my life. At such times, I weigh the decisions I make very carefully, for I seek always to live my life as the Norns would wish it to be."

"Why do you try so hard to serve the Norns?" Many believed in fate, but I had never before heard of anyone who tried to serve it.

"In truth, because I believe it often profits me to do so. I believe the Norns caused your path and mine to cross for a reason. I believed, when we met and I learned what had befallen you, that the Norns wished me to take you into the crew of the *Gull*, and to aid you in your quest for vengeance. But aiding you has certainly brought benefit to me, as well. You saved my life more than once in Frankia. I could have died there, but instead I came away from Frankia a much wealthier man."

"So you believe that by aiding me—by furthering what you believe is the Norns' plan for my life—you will benefit as well?" That somehow made me feel better.

"I believe that if any of our lives no longer furthers the pattern the Norns are weaving, we will be of no use to them, and then the risk grows that they will choose to cut the threads of our lives."

By now we were approaching Jarl Arinbjorn's estate. I was glad for an excuse to end our discussion of the Norns and fate.

Arinbjorn's longhouse was the largest I had ever seen. It was far larger than Hrorik's, in which I had grown up, and bigger even than Hastein's, on his estate up on the Limfjord. The land around it contained numerous other buildings, as well: three boathouses on the shore of the nor, various work-sheds, a separate byre for livestock, and even what looked to be a second, much more modestly-sized longhouse.

Unfortunately, Jarl Arinbjorn was not at home. He had ridden, we were told by some of his retainers as we approached the great longhouse, to the cliffs along the eastern edge of the island, to inspect the watch stations there. They did not know when he was expected to return.

I had hoped Hastein might be able to speak briefly with Jarl Arinbjorn, learn whether his men had seen Toke's two ships, and we could be on our way. It was an unrealistic wish, of course. When one jarl called upon another, the occasion required at least a modest feast. But how much longer would we be delayed here now, since Arinbjorn was away?

An old man came out of the longhouse. He had white hair and a long white beard. His back was crooked with age, and he leaned on a staff for support as he stared at us, squinting.

"By the gods!" Hastein exclaimed. He swung himself down from his horse's back and approached the old man, studying him. "Aki? Is that you?"

"Do I know you?" the old man said.

"I am Hastein. I am the younger son of Jarl Eirik."

"There's a name I have not heard in many years. Jarl Eirik. Drowned, did he not? And you say you are his son? I thought he drowned too."

"That was my brother Hallstein. I am Hastein. I spent a summer here, many years ago. You were the foreman of the estate then."

The old man—Aki—pulled his crooked body

upright and jutted his chin out. "And I still am," he asserted. "I may be old, but I have not gone too simple in the head to keep this place in order. Hastein, son of Eirik. I know who you are now. Arinbjorn told me the tale of your father's and brother's deaths when it happened, but that has been some years ago. And there was some trouble after your father died, as I recall, but in the end you became the jarl. You say you spent a summer here?" He scratched his head and squinted at Hastein again, studying his face, then a look of recognition slowly came over his face.

"I see it," he said. "You are a man now, and much changed. But I see it now." He grinned. "You are *that* boy. I had forgotten. Where are the rest of your men?" he asked.

When he learned there were two ships and their crews, currently docked down at the village, Aki insisted that Hastein and all of his company must be guests of the estate for the night, if not longer. Bryngolf was dispatched, leading the rest of our mounts to return them to the fort, with instructions that the *Gull* and the *Serpent* should be rowed down the nor to the jarl's estate as soon as their re-provisioning was complete. "And I will send a rider up to the cliffs, to fetch Arinbjorn," Aki said.

It would be dusk, Aki told us, before Jarl Arinbjorn could return, even though the messenger was instructed to ride hard. "You and your men are welcome to use the bathhouse," Aki offered. "It is always good to wash the salt off, after a sea voyage."

After ale was poured for us to drink, while water

131

for the baths was being heated, Aki hobbled off to give orders for the preparations for the night's feast.

"So you know Jarl Arinbjorn?" I asked Hastein. "You have met him before?"

"Oh, yes," Hastein replied, nodding. "He is one of King Horik's most trusted councilors, and because Mon is so close to Sjaelland, the king often consults with him, even when he does not call a broader council. I saw him most recently at the meeting of the council when the decision was made to carry war to the Franks.

"But I also know him from many years ago. Arinbjorn is an old man now, and rarely leaves Mon except to cross the strait to Sjaelland, to visit with the king. But as a young man he was a great warrior, and he and my father sometimes raided together, in the Austmarr. As a boy, I spent a summer here on Mon—it was the year before I was fostered in Halland, in the household of Thorfinn, a chieftain there who was a comrade and ally of my father. I stayed here, in Arinbjorn's household, while he and my father went raiding for the summer."

As he spoke, Hastein's eyes took on a far-away look, and his mouth a faint hint of a smile. I wondered if the summer on Mon had been a happy time for him.

"What did Aki mean when he said you were *that* boy?" Hastein frowned at me, as if he thought me impertinent to ask.

Stig nodded. "Aye, I wondered that, too."

"It was of no consequence," Hastein said. After a few moments, when we kept staring at him expectantly, he added, "There was a girl."

Stig grinned. "Aye, there would have been," he said.

Jarl Arinbjorn was, as Hastein had said, now an old man, but he wore his years lightly. His carriage was erect—age had not bowed him, as it had Aki—and he looked still fit enough to wield a sword or spear, and bear the weight of mail brynie, helm, and shield. His hair and beard were a yellowish-white in color, but they looked well-groomed—the beard trimmed close around the line of his jaw, and his hair, which still fully covered the top of his head, was straight and tangle-free, and had been cut so that it hung just above the top of his shoulders.

He seemed genuinely glad to see Hastein. "I was pleased to hear that you came safely through the campaign in Frankia, and won much silver from the Franks, besides. Though a great victory, it sounded as though the battle fought with their army was won at the cost of many lives."

"You have already heard about the campaign?" Hastein asked, sounding surprised.

Arinbjorn nodded. "At Horik's court. It is fortunate you did not arrive sooner. We only returned to Mon four days ago."

Arinbjorn turned and waved his hand at a young man standing behind him, indicating he should come forward. "This is Sigurd. He is Ragnar's youngest son. He is fostered here with me. When Ragnar arrived at Horik's estate, upon returning to Denmark from Frankia, the king summoned us to come to the feasts he held to

133

honor Ragnar, and to celebrate the victory over the Franks. And there was another matter he wished to discuss with me, as well. Concerning the Sveas."

I was surprised to learn that Ragnar had a son so young. Though nearing manhood, Sigurd looked to be younger than me. His two brothers, Ivar and Bjorn, who had helped command the army on the Frankia campaign, were many years older than he. Sigurd's hair was a light, yellowish tan, the color of sand, as was Ivar's, and he had Ivar's lean build, too, rather than Bjorn's stockiness. There was something strange about his right eye, though I could not make out what it was.

"This is Stig, one of my captains," Hastein said, as Stig stepped forward and nodded to Arinbjorn and Sigurd. To Arinbjorn, Hastein added, "You may have met Stig when he was with me at the meeting of the council on Sjaelland in the spring." Arinbjorn and Sigurd nodded back to Stig.

"And this is one of my warriors, Halfdan son of Hrorik," Hastein continued. "If you have already heard tales of the campaign in Frankia, you may have heard of him. He is also known as Strongbow."

Arinbjorn looked at me appraisingly. "Ah, so you are the one who with his mighty bow saved Ragnar the Raven-king."

"Raven-king?" Hastein asked.

"It is the name they were calling Ragnar, at the feasts," Arinbjorn explained. "I believe it was coined by one of Horik's skalds, in a poem he is composing about the campaign. Something to do with Ragnar's victory as war-king in Frankia, and how he fed the ravens with the dead of our enemies, and perhaps it has to do with that bird of his, as well. In truth, it sounds better than Hairy-breeches."

I felt embarrassed by Hastein's introduction of me, and of the tales that apparently were being told about me, but tried not to show it. If Hastein wished to present me as a potential chieftain, I must try to play my part, even if I did not believe it.

"It is an honor to meet you, Jarl Arinbjorn," I said, nodding to him.

"What brings you to Mon?" Arinbjorn asked Hastein.

"We are hunting a man whose life carries a heavy blood debt. I was hoping that if he passed by Mon, you or your men might know."

Arinbjorn shrugged. "Perhaps," he said. "We do keep watch over the straits. It is the scot King Horik asks of me: to be the eyes of the realm in the south. Primarily we watch for Vendish raiders—they have been growing bolder in recent years. I have sufficient warriors here on Mon, and ships, to turn back small raids, or to kill the raiders if they are not wise enough to flee. Thus far the Vends have never attacked in great force, but if they should, we have great bonfires laid atop the cliffs to light as warning beacons. The cliffs are high enough for the fires to be seen in Sjaelland, and on Falster, and beacons there would be lit to spread the warning to the west and north."

"I had noticed that your war-band seems quite large," Hastein said.

"Some of the warriors and ships are provided by

135

King Horik. He considers it to his advantage to stop any raiders from the south here at Mon, at the edge of his kingdom."

"Two of your ships approached mine when we entered the waters around Mon. Do they examine every ship that passes so closely?"

"It depends on which of the captains are out in the straits. Some are more inquisitive than others. But they do so more often than they do not. This man you are seeking—how was he traveling?"

Hastein turned to me and nodded.

"He sails with two longships," I said. "One has a dragon's head carved like the head of an eagle, painted red with a golden beak. She has sixteen pairs of oars. The other is smaller, just fourteen pairs, and her dragon's head is gilded, and carved like the head of a stallion. Both ships would have been manned by very light crews."

"That last is a thing that would draw notice," Arinbjorn said, nodding. "This man is a chieftain, then? These are his ships?"

"They are."

"And his name?" Arinbjorn asked.

Hastein answered him. "His name is Toke. He does not yet know for certain that we are pursuing him. We would keep that unknown to him as long as possible."

"I will send word out to all of my captains, asking if any have seen these two ships. They do not need to know why I am asking. If any do recall seeing them, I will ask that they come here, to my hall, so you may question them. We will know by mid-day tomorrow.

"And tonight," he added, "we will feast together."

7

A Feast and a Contest

To my great surprise, at the feast I was invited by Jarl Arinbjorn to sit at the high table. It was the first of several surprises that night.

Two of his captains, plus Hastein, Stig, Hrodgar, and I joined Arinbjorn and his wife at the high table. Women from the jarl's household—all comely, and save Arinbjorn's wife all young—were paired with each of us. As the guest of honor, Hastein was given the place to Arinbjorn's right. The jarl's wife sat at her husband's left side, with young Sigurd beside her. I was seated to the left of Sigurd.

"My name is Asny," a young woman said who sat down on the bench beside me. She was holding a drinking horn whose silver rim around its mouth was carved with the design of a long dragon, its tail entwined around its body. I recognized the design as similar to that on the banners flown by the two ships we'd encountered approaching Mon. The horn was filled almost to the brim with dark brown ale. "I am your horn partner for the feast."

I did not know how to respond. In part, I was startled by having this young woman suddenly appear at my side, and sit herself beside me. The fact that she was very comely did not help my confusion. I found myself staring at her features, admiring them, when I should have been coming up with some courteous reply.

"Horn partner?" I finally managed to say.

Asny smiled, barely suppressing a laugh. "You are not familiar with the custom?" she asked.

I shook my head. "My name is Halfdan," I belatedly added. "I am pleased to meet you."

"Are you the son of Jarl Hastein?" she asked. I was confused by her question and could not understand why she might think so.

"No," I replied. "I am just one of his warriors."

Now she looked confused. "You seem very..."

"Young, to be seated at the high table?" I suggested. She blushed and nodded.

Sigurd leaned over across the body of the young woman who had taken the seat by his side. She did not seem to mind. "He is called Strongbow," he told Asny. "He won much honor in the recent campaign down in Frankia." He sat back and placed his arm around the shoulder of his horn partner. "This is Saeunn," he said, introducing her to me. I nodded in greeting to her. She had red hair, hanging in two long braids down her chest, and very striking green eyes. She looked to be several years older than Sigurd. "I requested that you sit with me this night," he told me.

That, I thought, at least explains why I am at the high table.

Just then Jarl Arinbjorn stood up. The great feast hall gradually grew silent, as its occupants realized he was standing.

"We welcome honored guests this night, and hold this feast to celebrate their visit to Mon," he announced, in a deep, strong voice that carried throughout the hall.

"This is Jarl Hastein of the Limfjord district. He is the son of an old and cherished comrade of mine, Jarl Eirik. His father and I bloodied our swords together many times. Jarl Hastein helped command our victorious army in Frankia. Hopefully he will share tales of that campaign with us this night." Raising high the drinking horn he held in his right hand, Arinbjorn continued. "Stand, and join me now in a toast to Jarl Hastein."

All in the feast hall rose to their feet. Beside me, Asny held out the drinking horn for me to take.

"To Jarl Hastein," Arinbjorn called out. "To Jarl Hastein," all the menfolk in the hall echoed, then like Arinbjorn took a drink of ale.

"Now give the horn back to me," Asny instructed. At Arinbjorn's side, his wife—a dignified looking woman who looked to be close in age to him—raised the horn she now held and repeated, "To Jarl Hastein." In unison with the rest of the women at the high table, and others scattered throughout the hall at other tables, Asny said, "To Jarl Hastein," then took a drink from the horn. Turning to me, she smiled and said, "You see? That is how it is done."

Hastein, of course, responded with a toast to honor Jarl Arinbjorn, and the process was repeated. Then, to my relief, Arinbjorn sat down, and the women-folk and thralls working at the central hearth began serving the meal.

I quickly realized that one advantage of being seated at the high table was that its occupants were served first. In so large a hall, those sitting at one of the outer tables would have a long wait for their food.

It was a very fine meal. We were given wooden platters, pottery bowls, and spoons. The serving thralls brought around great pots filled with a hearty soup made with cabbage, carrots, and turnips, then came again with large platters on which were arrayed large sections of roasted leg of mutton. The servers held the platters steady at each place, so the diners could use their eating knives to carve off as much as they wished.

There is a thing about drinking horns. Hastein had given me one, a very fine one, at the funeral feast in Frankia after our victory over the Frankish army. I had not used it since that night, preferring to use a cup instead. A horn filled with ale or other drink cannot be set down. While impressive looking and useful, perhaps, for drinking bouts where many toasts are to be made, a horn is not convenient when one wishes to eat, also.

After carving off a slab of mutton for myself, I had to serve Asny as well, for she could not manage the task while holding the drinking horn. It was apparent that she would not be able to slice her own meat, either.

"Do we pass the horn between us, and take turns eating?" I asked her. I hoped I would not have to feed her, too.

"That could be done," she said. "But in truth, it is not the custom. I will give the horn to you, so you will not have to delay satisfying your thirst whenever you wish. And I will cut your meat for you."

It was a strange way to eat a meal, so dependent on another like that, but after a bit, I found it not at all unpleasant. In order to attend to my needs, Asny had to sit close beside me on the bench, her thigh touching

141

mine. She had a scent that reminded me of freshly cut summer hay.

It was obvious that Sigurd and his companion, Saeunn, had been horn partners before. They seemed very familiar with each other, laughing and talking as they ate, and feeding each other bites of food. I wished I could have as free and confident a manner as Sigurd did. Although I was feeling more at ease than at first, and was enjoying Asny's company, I did not find it easy to make casual conversation with someone I did not know. And I sensed that to Asny, being my horn partner for the feast was more a duty than a pleasure. Although unfailingly courteous, when she smiled, she did so only with her mouth— her eyes rarely joined in. She was, I learned, a daughter of one of Jarl Arinbjorn's captains. Perhaps she felt it beneath her to be paired with a mere warrior, and such a young one, besides.

Glancing out across the hall, my eyes happened to meet those of Floki, from the estate. He and his brother, Baug, were seated near the end of a table in the second row out from the center of the hall. What do you think of me sitting here, at the high table, I wondered? Does it gall you to see me thus honored? Holding his gaze, I raised the horn to him and took a drink. After a few moments, he raised his cup back to me in response and drank, then looked away.

"Who is that man?" Asny asked.

"He was one of my brother's housecarls."

"Was?"

"My brother is dead."

"Whom does he follow now?" she asked.

"On this voyage, Jarl Hastein."

After the eating was finished, the tale-telling began. Jarl Arinbjorn asked Hastein to tell the gathering a story about the campaign in Frankia. "Tell us about the great battle that was fought with the Franks," he requested. "I have heard some stories of it while at King Horik's court, but many here have not. And I would enjoy hearing your account of what happened."

I soon learned another custom that was practiced in Arinbjorn's feast-hall, in addition to that of horn-partners at the high table. Tales were punctuated frequently with toasts.

Hastein was a skilled speaker, and told the story well. To my embarrassment, he began with the night crossing before the battle, and told the gathered host how two lone warriors had swum the cold river in the dark, and had hunted through the forest along the shore, silencing the Franks' sentries so that the Danish army could cross undetected.

"I have not heard this part of the story before," Arinbjorn, who was enjoying the tale greatly, exclaimed. "Who were the two warriors who did this?"

"One was a skilled woodsman from up on the Limfjord," Hastein replied. "His name is Einar." Looking out across the hall, he called, "Stand, Einar, and be recognized."

When Einar stood, Jarl Arinbjorn stood, too, and said, "Well done. I salute you. To Einar," and he raised his horn and drank. The hall echoed with the shouted responses, "To Einar," first by the menfolk, and then by the women.

"And the other?" Arinbjorn asked Hastein.

"He is here at the high table: Halfdan, son of Hrorik."

I had no choice but to stand, and try to keep my face from turning too bright a shade of red as the toasts were drunk to me.

It got worse. Hastein proceeded to tell the tale, spread by Einar, of how the last sentry had been hidden from us in a spot where we could not get close enough to kill him with our knives. "But Halfdan here has, without question, the greatest skill with a bow that I have ever seen," Hastein continued. "When it proved impossible to kill this final sentry with a blade, he, in the dark of night, amid the deep shadows of the forest, shot an arrow into the center of the Frank's head"—Hastein touched his forefinger to his forehead as he spoke—"killing the man instantly."

An awed-sounding murmur spread across the hall. Asny was staring at me now as if she'd suddenly found herself seated beside someone entirely different.

"How did you do that?" Arinbjorn asked me. "How did you make such a shot in the dark?"

Unable to think of a better answer, I told the truth. "It was not skill on my part," I replied. "It was an accident. I was aiming for the Frank's chest. But at the moment I released my arrow, he tripped and fell backwards. It was luck, not skill, that I hit him at all."

There was silence for a long moment, then the hall erupted with laughter. I could feel my face turning red. Arinbjorn raised his horn, chuckling, and toasted, "To your luck, then. Sometimes that is better to have than skill."

After the toast was drunk, echoed, and drunk again, one of Arinbjorn's captains, who was among those sitting at the high table, suggested, "Surely there were two sets of luck at play there. Halfdan's good luck, and the Frank's bad." Again the feast-hall erupted with laughter.

Hastein's narration of the battle itself was skillful, and by the time he reached the place in the tale where the Franks were breaking through our line, and his own standard and that of Ragnar were at risk, the listeners in the hall were hanging on his every word.

"At that moment," he said, in a muted voice, "I have no doubt that the Norns were holding the threads of my life in their hands—mine, and many others among our army— weighing whether the time had come to cut them. But it was not my fate to die that day, on that field of battle deep in Frankia. For Halfdan—he who is also known as Strongbow—positioned himself on the hillside behind the two standards. And with his bow, he struck down the Franks who had broken through the shield wall in front of me, and he slew the Frankish warrior who had driven Ragnar to the ground and was hacking at his Raven banner. The arrows of Odin himself are no more deadly than those shot by Strongbow that day."

Cheers rang through the hall, followed by many toasts—to me, to my bow and its arrows, to Hastein, to Ragnar, to the Raven banner. Asny had to refill the horn with ale several times. I was thankful we were not drinking mead.

Sigurd leaned across Saeunn—she stroked her

fingers through his hair as he did so—and asked me, "In the battle—how many men did you kill?"

It was a question I could not answer. It was not just the amount of ale I had consumed that night, nor even that on the day of the battle, during the charges by the Frankish cavalry against our line, I did not know how many of the Bretons I'd hit had died. In truth, I could not even remember now how many I had hit. But it was more than that. It was what had happened after Ivar had launched his attack on the Frankish army's flank and their warriors had become caught between his force and our main army. We had all closed in around them and had held them trapped, pinned against each other. By then I had long ago run out of arrows and had left my bow up on the hillside. I remember pushing forward with the rest of our warriors against the horses, which were pressed together so tightly they could not move, all the while stabbing, stabbing, and hacking with my sword. When the mounts directly in front of us had all been cleared of their riders, we hacked and cut at them, too, until poor beasts collapsed, while others of our warriors, impatient to kill, clambered across their backs to get at the remaining Franks beyond. All of us—Danes, Franks, and horses—had drenched in blood, and the ground beneath our feet had grown sodden and slippery from it.

"I do not know," I answered. The feast hall faded, and in my mind I saw and smelled the blood again, and heard the screams. "I do not know."

"Was it more than ten? More than twenty?"

I truly did not know. The butchering had gone on

for a long time. "Perhaps. Probably," I replied.

"I have never killed a man," Sigurd said. He sounded disappointed. "You killed a man in a duel, also, did you not? In Frankia?"

I nodded my head. "Yes. I did."

By now Hastein was finishing his tale of the great battle. Arinbjorn stood, wobbling a bit as he did, and addressed the hall, many of whose occupants were by now looking bleary-eyed from the many toasts that had been drunk.

"We all thank Jarl Hastein for his fine telling of the great victory of our Danish warriors over the Franks. It would be good to hear more tales of the campaign, but the hour grows late, and the ale has been freely flowing. Let us all away to our beds. The feast is ended."

I, for one, was glad. As the evening had worn on, I had tried to pace my drinking, taking only modest swallows for many of the toasts, but nevertheless I felt unsteady on my feet as I stood up from the bench. Asny, too, seemed affected by the quantity of ale we had shared, and rocked backward when she stood. Fearing she might lose her balance and fall, I reached out and grabbed her arm above the elbow, pulling her upright and toward me to steady her.

Sigurd, who clearly had not paced himself at all during the toasting, misjudged my action.

"No, Halfdan," he slurred. "She is well-born and marriageable. That is why her father encourages her to be a horn partner at Arinbjorn's feasts. If you want a woman for your bed this night, I will send a thrall to you."

Asny's face turned a deep shade of red. "I am sorry," she murmured to me. "I know you did not intend…"

"It is of no consequence," I told her. "I am glad I did not give you offence. And I thank you for your company this evening."

As she hurried away, I turned to Sigurd. He was leaning on Saeunn, one arm draped over her shoulders, one of her arms around his waist. "Well?" he asked. "Shall I?"

If I were to say yes, would you even know the name of the girl you sent to my bed, I wondered? Would you care at all how she might feel, being ordered to submit to the pleasures of a man she had never seen before? I found myself suddenly intensely disliking Sigurd.

With difficulty, I reminded myself what Hastein expected of me. I must at all times act like a man who could be a chieftain, a leader of men. That surely included wearing a lying face, to avoid making an enemy of the son of a rich and powerful man.

"I thank you," I told him. "You are very kind. But I am very weary, and this night I wish to find nothing more in my bed than sleep."

"In the morning," Sigurd called, as I was walking away, "perhaps we will shoot bows together."

The day meal served the next morning in Arinbjorn's hall was a simple, informal affair. Two large pots of hot barley porridge were suspended by chains over glowing coals at one end of the large central hearth, tended by a stout woman with graying hair. As the folk of the estate and the guests awoke, they stumbled outside to the privies, relieved themselves, washed, and made their way to the hearth. There a thrall handed out pottery bowls and wooden spoons, and the gray-haired cook filled the bowls with porridge. Thick slices of dense rye bread were available, too, and a soft cheese to spread on them.

Despite the night's sleep, my mind still did not feel completely clear from the effects of too many toasts. I felt thankful again that Jarl Arinbjorn had not chosen to serve mead at his feast to honor Hastein's visit. At least my head, though foggy, did not throb.

I had taken my food back to the location where I had slept last night on one of the longhouse's long wall-benches, using my cloak as bedding. The porridge was having a soothing effect on my stomach. I found the bread somewhat dry, but I'd spread enough of the soft, runny cheese on it to make it easier to swallow. I was completely absorbed by the meal—enjoying thinking about nothing more than the taste and feel of the food in my mouth and belly, and ignoring the sights and sounds of the hall around me—when a voice broke through my reverie.

"Ah! There you are. I have been looking for you."

It was Sigurd. He looked surprisingly fresh and alert, considering his condition when I had last seen him. He was holding a bow in his left hand and a quiver of arrows in his right. The sight of them brought back to me his parting words the night before.

"Do you have your bow with you, or is it on your

jarl's ship?"

Thanks to Hastein's insistence the day before, I had it with me. I jerked my hand with its thumb extended back over my shoulder, indicating where my bow, quiver, and sword were lying along the wall, at the back edge of the bench. "It is there," I said, after managing to swallow the mouthful of bread and cheese filling my mouth.

I had no wish to shoot with Sigurd. In truth, I had no wish to spend any further time at all in his company. He struck me as spoiled and arrogant, and completely unlike the two men who were his brothers. But I could see no way to courteously decline.

"Where do you shoot?" I asked.

"There is a large butt of rolled hay which we use for a target," he replied. "It is not very far from the longhouse."

Perhaps this was not a bad thing after all. I had had little opportunity of late to shoot my bow. Since the capture of Paris, I had shot it in practice only once, briefly, with Tore at Hastein's estate during our layover there. A longbow is not a weapon that can be shot both infrequently and well.

Sigurd sat down beside me on the wall-bench while I hurriedly finished my porridge and bread. "Do you know my brothers, Ivar and Bjorn?" he asked.

I nodded. "We have met."

The brevity of my answer seemed to leave Sigurd momentarily at a loss for words. He overcame it.

"I had two other brothers," he said. "Eric and Agnar. They were born to Father's first wife, Thora. She

150

died. Eric and Agnar are dead now, too. They tried to conquer the Svear kingdom and take its throne, but King Eystein defeated and killed them."

This seemed a strange thing to volunteer to someone almost a stranger. "I did not know that," I replied, for lack of a better response. A desire to acquire a kingdom seemed to run in this family. It was certainly a hunger that afflicted Ragnar. I glanced sideways at Sigurd, wondering if he, too, wished to someday become a king. When I did, I noticed again that there was something strange about his right eye.

"You are staring at my eye," Sigurd said.

"What is wrong with it?" I asked.

"Nothing. It is the sign of the serpent. I am called Sigurd Snake-in-the-Eye because of it. My mother, Kraka, says it means that I have the spirit of a dragon within me, and that I am marked for greatness."

It sounded like something a mother might say. There was a red line, sort of a wiggle, across the bottom of the colored center of his eye, but I would not have thought it to be a serpent.

"I am finished," I said. I stood and slung the long strap of my quiver over my left shoulder so that its arrows hung at my right hip. Draping my cloak over my arm, and picking up my sword and bow, I told Sigurd, "Take me to the butt."

It was a warm day, and a number of the folk of the household, as well as many of the members of our two crews, were standing or seated around the yard outside of the longhouse, enjoying the sunshine. Hastein and Arinbjorn were there, too, speaking together, and

Torvald, Hrodgar, and Stig were standing nearby. As we passed them, Hastein called out to me, "Do not go far. One of Arinbjorn's captains did see the two ships we are seeking. He will be here soon."

Before I could answer, Sigurd announced in a loud voice, "We are just going to the archery butt. Halfdan and I are going to shoot bows together."

"I would like to see that," Arinbjorn told Hastein. "From what you have said, his skill is remarkable."

Unfortunately, the prospect of entertainment when there was nothing else to do prompted most of those who were out in front of the longhouse to follow as well. I noticed that Gudfred, Floki, and Baug from the estate were among them.

I had just hoped to get in a little practice with my bow. Having an audience to watch me shoot was bad enough. Torvald found a way to make it worse.

"Jarl Arinbjorn," he said. "Are any of your men especially skilled with the bow? Perhaps they could shoot against Halfdan."

I knew what Torvald was doing. He was hoping that there might be a contest which I would win, and he wanted to wager on it.

"Sigtrygg is the most skilled archer among my men," Arinbjorn answered. "He is quite good." He turned to a man walking nearby—it proved to be a captain who'd sat at the high table the night before, the one who had made the jest about the Frankish sentry's bad luck—and asked him, "Will you shoot?"

"With pleasure," he replied. "I will fetch my bow."

The butt, made of rolled hay that had been bound

around with cord, stood roughly as high as my shoulder. A small square of white cloth, about the size of the center boss of a shield, had been pinned to its center to make a target. As we approached, two of Arinbjorn's men, wearing helms and brynies and holding shields as if armed for battle, were practicing casting spears at it. Seeing the crowd approaching with their chieftain, Arinbjorn, in the forefront, they retrieved their spears from the target and stepped off to one side.

The butt had been placed in a location that would allow the practicing of long shots, but Sigurd continued forward until we were only a spear cast away.

"I do not have great skill with a bow," he said, apologetically.

"One must learn to shoot well at closer distances first," I told him, "before attempting longer shots. This is a good distance to practice from."

"What was the longest shot you have made, when you killed a man?" he asked.

He seemed fascinated with killing. I thought about his question. It took a while—there had been so many times. But in truth, only during the great battle in Frankia, and that night on the Limfjord when Toke and his men had attacked, had I attempted shots at any great distance to speak of, and I suspected most of those had probably missed. The times I knew for certain I had killed a man with my bow—like when I had slain Stenkil's comrade, Sigvid, in Ruda—he had for the most part been fairly close.

"Most I shot at about this distance, sometimes less," I told him. Sigurd looked surprised.

I laid my sword, in its scabbard, on my cloak on the ground. Straightening up, I began rubbing my hands up and down along the limbs of my bow.

"What are you doing?" Sigurd asked.

"It has been some time since I have shot my bow. When not used, its limbs get stiff. I am warming them, so they will be easier to bend and string."

Bracing the tip of the bottom limb against the instep of my right foot, I grasped the bow's leather-wrapped grip with my right hand, and as I pulled back on it, I pushed my left hand hard against the upper limb, sliding the loop of the bowstring up along it with my thumb and forefinger as the bow bent, until I could slip the loop into the notch cut in the horn tip.

Pulling my leather bracer out of my quiver, I slid it over my left forearm and tightened its laces, then slipped my fingers through the loops on the tab of thick hide I wore now to protect my fingers from the bowstring. I had only recently begun using it. Tore had given me the tab after the battle with the Franks. That day I had shot my bow so many times that even though they were thickly calloused, the tips of the fingers I pulled the string back with had become raw and bloody. "This was Odd's," he'd told me, when he gave me the tab. "He would be glad to know that it will be yours now. He thought highly of you."

Sigtrygg approached from the longhouse carrying a bow and quiver. He looked to be a man who spent much thought and care on his appearance. He wore his beard trimmed close to his jaw—prudent in one who shoots a bow regularly. His hair—a gold so fair it looked almost white—he wore longer than most men do. It hung loose and gleaming down his back now, halfway to his waist, and admittedly looked very striking. I realized he had changed tunics while fetching his bow. Before, he'd been wearing a dull gray one, but now the tunic he wore was deep blue. Several women, including Asny and Saeunn, were walking with him, laughing at something he was saying.

When he reached us, he made a show of looking back and forth several times from the butt to the ground at our feet, then proclaimed, "This is not a very challenging distance to shoot from."

Sigurd blushed. When he did, it made him look very young. "I chose that we would shoot from here," he said, sounding embarrassed.

I noticed that both Sigurd's and Sigtrygg's bows had flattened limbs. Such bows were easier to make—when old Gudrod had first taught me to craft a bow, it was a flat-bow we'd made together. But though far easier to carve from a stave, such bows could not be made to be as powerful as a well-wrought longbow, with its long, slender, rounded limbs. Sigurd's bow, in particular, looked as though it probably had a light draw.

"Shall I shoot first?" Sigtrygg asked Arinbjorn. The jarl glanced at me, and when I shrugged, he nodded.

Sigtrygg handed his quiver to Asny, who looked as if she felt very pleased that he had. Selecting an arrow from it and nocking it on his bowstring, he turned sideways to the butt, planted his feet, and came slowly to full draw. He held there for what seemed a very long time, while staring intently at the target, before he released.

The shot was very good. His arrow embedded itself in the exact center of the square of white cloth which formed the target.

Sigurd stepped up to shoot next. He had not exaggerated when he'd said he did not have great skill with a bow. When he drew his arrow, he did so entirely with his right arm, not using his back at all, while holding the bow clutched tightly out in front of him in his fully extended left arm. And he held it high, trying to sight along the arrow toward the target, rather than keeping his arms and the arrow down level with his shoulders. A powerful bow could not be drawn so. Sigurd held his draw long as he aimed, as if mimicking Sigtrygg. His arrow, when he finally released it, struck off to the left, just inside the edge of the cloth target.

"Not bad, lad, not bad," Sigtrygg said. Sigurd blushed again and glared at him.

The night before, at the feast, I had taken a dislike to Sigurd. He'd struck me as a spoiled and arrogant young man who held a high place in the world—or at least in Arinbjorn's household—solely due to his renowned father, rather than for any qualities he himself possessed. This morning, though, he seemed much more a boy than a man, and it struck me that by the airs he affected, he was perhaps merely trying to live up to being the son of Ragnar, and the brother of Ivar and Bjorn. It made him seem, if not likeable, at least a little less unpleasant.

"I believe it is your turn to shoot," Sigtrygg said to

me. He had a slight smirk on his face. His shot would be impossible to better, and he knew it. I found myself badly wanting to do so, though.

I selected an arrow from my quiver, nocked it on my bowstring, and positioned myself. If I can hit his arrow, I thought. It would be an almost impossible shot, but if I could....

I wanted it too much. I tried too hard. I pulled to full draw and held there, while trying to focus my gaze tighter and tighter on the end of Sigtrygg's arrow, silhouetted dark against the white patch of the target. But I was too aware of the crowd around me, watching. And the longer I held, trying to aim, the more I could feel my muscles straining against the power of my bow. When I finally released, I could tell instantly that I had jerked the string rather than letting it slide off my fingers as I eased them open.

It was a bad shot. Worse, even, than Sigurd's. I missed the cloth target altogether.

There was moment of silence, then laughter rippled across the gathered onlookers. Hastein looked embarrassed.

"Well," Sigtrygg said. "It is fortunate that Ragnar Logbrod's life, and the safety of the Raven banner, did not depend on *that* shot."

His remark provoked great hilarity. Arinbjorn's folk were laughing the loudest. No doubt they were pleased that their champion had so thoroughly defeated the challenger whose skill with a bow had been praised by Jarl Hastein, and who had even been honored in verse by the king's skalds. I noticed Floki and Baug were guffawing loudly, too, and even my own shipmates who had fought in Frankia with me seemed very amused.

All except Torvald. He strode forward, scowling, and pulled me aside.

"You are much better than that! What are you doing? I was planning on proposing a wager."

I shrugged his hand off my shoulder and walked to the butt to retrieve my arrow. Torvald followed. "What happened?" he persisted. "You have embarrassed us all in front of Jarl Arinbjorn and his men. And look at Sigtrygg! He is prancing back and forth now in front of the women like a rooster. It is a good thing I did not bet on you."

I glared at him, then snapped, "I am not used to shooting at the butts." As soon as I said it, I realized how foolish my words sounded.

"What?" he asked, incredulously.

It was too complicated to explain. I had been taught to shoot a bow in the woods by Gudrod the Carpenter, after he'd taken a liking to me. We could not shoot at the butts on Hrorik's estate, because a slave was not allowed to handle a bow or any other weapon. So I had first learned to shoot at targets such as pine cones lying on the ground, and as soon as I could hit those regularly, I had progressed to shooting at squirrels, birds, and other small creatures which would not stay still for long to allow careful aiming.

My gaze happened to fall upon a woman standing among the crowd who must have stopped to watch while making her way back to the longhouse from the nearby fields, for she was carrying several cabbages in a large basket.

"Shall we shoot again?" Sigtrygg called. "We can move closer to the butt, if you would prefer." Again laughter rippled across the crowd.

"Jarl Hastein, Jarl Arinbjorn," I said, in a voice loud enough to carry over the laughter. "I apologize for my poor showing. In truth, I am not used to this kind of shooting—at the butts. With your permission, may we try a different sort of target?"

"What do you propose?" Arinbjorn asked.

"Help me with this," I murmured to Torvald, and walked over to the woman holding the cabbages. "I need two of these," I said.

She looked at Arinbjorn, who told her, "Give them to him."

Glancing around, I spied the two warriors who had been practicing with spears. "May I borrow two of those?" I asked them. "Just for a short time?"

"Are you going to throw spears instead of shooting your bow?" Torvald asked, frowning.

"Follow me," I told him, and walked back to the butt. Once in front of it, I handed Torvald a spear plus one of the cabbages, then impaled the other on the point of the spear I'd kept. Holding the spear's shaft at shoulder level, I pushed its butt end deeply into the big roll of hay, so that the cabbage was suspended upon the spear in front of the butt.

"Ah," Torvald said, as I took the other spear and cabbage from him, and repeated the process.

"You said you are not used to shooting your bow at the butts?" Sigtrygg asked loudly. "Did you learn to

159

shoot it in a cabbage patch instead?"

"Keep crowing, cock," I muttered through clenched teeth.

"Good," Torvald said. "You are getting angry."

I trotted back over to the two warriors whose spears I had taken. "Your helms," I said, "may I borrow those, too?"

They looked at each other, grinned, and handed me their helms. By now the crowd had stopped laughing and was watching with interest.

I returned to the butt and seated the helms firmly on the cabbages, leaving only half of each still exposed. Then I returned to where Sigtrygg was standing, with Torvald trailing behind me.

"These targets are not unlike warrior's heads, would you agree?" I asked him. "In size, and the way a helm covers them? Here is what I propose. We will shoot at the same time—you at the head on the right, I at the one on the left. We will each nock an arrow on the string, but we will not raise our bows and shoot until Jarl Arinbjorn gives the signal. He whose arrow strikes home first wins."

"This is a foolish game," Sigtrygg sputtered.

"We can move closer to the butt if you would like," I told him. His face turned red.

"What say you, Sigtrygg?" Arinbjorn asked him. "I think it seems a clever contest."

Having made such a show earlier, he had no choice now. "Very well," he said.

"A moment, Jarl Arinbjorn, a moment," Torvald asked. "Perhaps some of your men might wish to support their comrade's skill with a wager that he will win? I will be glad to match them."

Arinbjorn waved to him to proceed, and Torvald turned to the onlookers and called, "I'll wager two silver pennies that Halfdan will win, against all who will take my bet. Will anyone risk their silver, and match their pennies against mine?" Several men crowded forward to take the wager.

I pulled an arrow from my quiver and stuck its tip lightly in the ground in front of me, then pulled a second out and nocked it on my bowstring.

"Two arrows?" Sigtrygg asked.

"The way I am shooting this day, I may miss with the first," I told him.

The bettors having concluded their negotiations, Arinbjorn called out, "Archers, are you ready?"

I was holding my bow down at my waist, both arms flexed, with the nocked arrow pointed at the ground. I turned so that my left foot and shoulder were toward the target, then looked over at Arinbjorn and nodded.

"I am ready," Sigtrygg said. His left arm, holding his bow, was hanging down fully extended and he was leaning forward slightly, his right arm cocked over the string.

Arinbjorn raised his right hand. "When I drop my hand, you may shoot," he said, then let his hand fall.

I swung my bow up, simultaneously pushing my left arm and the bow out and pulling my right arm and the string back as I did. I did not look at my bow at all as it rose into position—my eyes were on the cabbage which was my target, staring tightly just to the right of the helm's nasal bar. As my thumb, extended up above my right hand, brushed against my ear, I opened my fingers and released the string.

Sigtrygg had raised his bow arm level and was just reaching full draw as my arrow flashed forward off my bow. The sight startled him, and he jerked off his own shot in response. His arrow hit the rim of the helm on his target with a ringing sound and glanced off to the side, sticking in the edge of the straw butt.

As soon as I had released my first arrow, I turned my gaze down to the arrow stuck in the ground in front of me, swinging my bow back down and flexing my arms again as I did. Snatching the arrow with my right hand, I nocked it on the string and swung my bow up again in one fluid motion as my eyes found the second cabbage. Again I released as soon as my right thumb brushed my ear. As I did, Sigtrygg exclaimed loudly, "Your shot missed, too! It is not even in the butt."

My second arrow smacked into the second cabbage. The force of its impact caused the helm, already knocked askew by Sigtrygg's shot, to tumble to the ground.

Turning to Sigtrygg, I told him, "You are mistaken. I did not miss."

Sigurd ran forward to the butt. Sigtrygg stared at me for a moment and then trotted after him.

"It is true," Sigurd called out. "Halfdan's first arrow struck his cabbage and passed clean through. It is in the butt behind. He has shot both cabbages, and Sigtrygg hit none!"

I did not anticipate the discord that my actions

would cause. When Torvald attempted to collect on the wagers that Arinbjorn's men had placed with him, they angrily protested that they had been dishonorably tricked—that I had shot my first arrow badly on purpose to lure them into betting that Sigtrygg would defeat me. Instead of attempting to persuade them that such was not the case, Torvald inflamed the losers further by asserting that even if their accusation was true, they could not expect to be allowed to back out of a wager merely because they had been foolishly gullible.

The matter would likely have resulted in blows being exchanged at that point, but for Torvald's imposing size and obvious great strength. Nevertheless, Arinbjorn's men continued to shout angrily, shaking their fists at Torvald and me, and refused to pay. Tore, the two ravens, and several others of our crew were crowding in by now, and Torvald was proclaiming loudly that men who did not pay their debts were no better than thieves, when Hastein and Arinbjorn pushed their way between the two sides and ordered all to be silent.

Arinbjorn ordered his men to pay the wagers they had lost to Torvald. "Whether you were tricked or no, you placed wagers with this man and lost them, and they are now debts you owe. You will not dishonor yourselves and me by refusing to pay them. Although in truth," he added, "if there was trickery involved, by one who was treated as an honored guest at my high table in my longhouse at last night's feast, then there is another whose honor is called into question by this matter."

"Jarl Arinbjorn," I told him, "I assure you, there

was no trickery on my part. My first shot was a very poor one, but honestly so. I did not shoot so badly on purpose."

"To shoot beneath the rim of a helm as you did and strike an enemy's face—or a cabbage—is not an easy thing to do," he replied. "To do so twice, as quickly as you did, was a mark of great skill with a bow. I confess I cannot understand how one so skilled could take his time shooting at a much easier target and miss it altogether."

I did not blame him for not believing me. My protests sounded implausible even to my own ears.

"I do not know how to explain it," I told him, "other than to say I am unused to shooting at a butt. I am used to shooting at a target that is only briefly seen, or is moving. I am used to shooting in order to kill."

Thankfully, Hastein intervened. "I, too, am surprised by how poorly Halfdan shot his first arrow, given his skill with a bow. And I will admit to you that my steersman, Torvald, is overly fond of jests and of wagering, and I could well suspect that trickery might be involved due to his role in this matter. But I know Halfdan to be a man of unwavering honor. He would not lie about this. If he says there was no trickery on his part—if he says his first arrow was just a poor shot, and nothing more—then I must believe him, no matter how unlikely the truth would seem to be."

Hrodgar also spoke up. "I agree with Jarl Hastein. In my own dealings with Halfdan, I have found him to be more honest and desirous of doing what is right than are most men. I do not believe he would lie to you."

Arinbjorn was silent for a long moment, his eyes with a faraway look in them and his right hand absent-mindedly stroking his beard, as he was weighing all that had occurred and had been said. Finally he spoke, directing his words first to Hastein. "I cannot doubt your word or your honor, for I know the man you are." Turning to me, he added, "Therefore it seems that I cannot doubt your word, either. There was no trickery involved. I accept that as the truth. This matter is over—we will put it behind us."

He turned and strode off in the direction of the longhouse. Hastein accompanied him. Gradually the rest of the folk began to drift away in that direction, as well.

Sigurd came up to me. "How do you do it?" he asked. "How did you learn to shoot your bow so well? I would like to become as skilled as you."

How did I learn to shoot my bow so well? I could not tell him the true answer. When I was a thrall, the times when I could slip away into the forest with my bow were the only times I could feel free. If I had not produced meat for Ubbe when he had allowed me to leave my other chores behind, if I had not managed to find and kill game when I was allowed to take my bow into the forest, I would quickly have lost that privilege. The hunger for freedom is a great motivator.

"Do you wish to learn to shoot a bow in war?" I asked him. Many men did not. While they might occasionally pick up a bow to try their hand at hunting, most warriors preferred to fight with spear and sword. My brother Harald had been such, and my father, Hrorik, as well.

Sigurd nodded. "I do," he assured me.

"You must practice often," I told him. "Not because you must, but because you wish to. And you should learn to shoot a much more powerful bow—one capable of shooting a great distance, and pushing its arrows through armor. There are also some things you must do differently." I took his bow from him, and handed him mine to hold.

"The way you draw and shoot your bow will prevent you from ever being able to shoot a powerful bow. You must change how you do them. You draw your bow like this," I said, and held his bow in my extended left arm, while I drew the string back with my right. I had been correct—Sigurd's bow was a weak one. "You draw the bow only with your right arm. You cannot do that with a truly powerful bow."

I lowered his bow and held it pointing down, at the level of my waist, with both arms flexed. "You must learn to use the strength of your back and chest, and both arms together, when you draw," I explained. "Like this," I added, as I raised his bow, pushing it out with my left arm at the same time as I pulled the string back with my right.

Holding his bow at full draw, I raised my arms up and tilted my head down until I was looking along the arrow. "And you try to aim your bow like this," I told him. "Looking along the arrow. It does no good to do so—the arrow will not shoot where you are looking, unless you are very, very close to the target—and again, by drawing a bow in this position, you will never be able to shoot one that is powerful." I lowered the drawn bow until my left arm, holding it, was extended out level from my shoulder. "This is where you should hold the bow when you draw it," I told him. "And do you see my thumb, on the hand with which I draw the string? Do you see how it is extended up?"

Sigurd nodded.

"I always draw my string back until my thumb just touches my ear. That way I know I am always drawing the same."

"But how do you aim your arrow?" he asked.

"I do not look at the bow, or at the arrow. I look where I wish to hit. If you practice enough, and learn to draw the way I have told you, in time you and the bow will learn to work together as one, and it will do your bidding."

"That is all I need to do?" Sigurd asked. He did not sound convinced.

Learning to shoot a bow well required much practice—more than I suspected Sigurd would ever be willing to do. "That is all *I* can teach you," I answered.

The captain who had seen Toke's ships was named Bard. "I only just happened to see them," he told us. "They were abroad very early—just past dawn. I had taken my ship out from the nor at first light. We were headed for the northern opening of the channel between Mon and Sjaelland, to watch for ships entering from the Austmarr. We had just rounded Nyord—the small island that lies close to Mon's northern cape—when we saw them: two ships up ahead, heading out into the Austmarr under sail. I remember thinking that these were men who did not wish to be seen."

"Why did you think that?" Hastein asked.

"The channel between Sjaelland and Mon is quite narrow in places, and it is a winding path to follow. Yet to have reached its eastern end by daybreak, these ships had to have traveled it in the dark. It would have been far safer for them to have waited for daylight to sail it."

"Did you stop them? Did you speak to them?"

Bard nodded his head. "They were hugging the Sjaelland side of the channel, and were already well ahead of us—almost beyond Nyord—when we spotted them. Although we were supposed to remain in the channel to watch for any ships heading into our waters from the open sea, I was curious, so we gave chase. We were eventually able to draw close enough for me to get a look at them, and see that they were two longships, one whose dragon's head was painted red and carved like the head of an eagle, the other a gilded stallion's head. And both ships were lightly manned. At first, they did not slow at all when they saw us. If anything, they seemed to be trying to pull away from my ship. I thought perhaps they feared that we planned to attack them, so we mounted our peace shields on our dragon's head. When we did, although they did not stop, they reefed their sails and slowed, allowing us to pull alongside."

"Did they tell you where they were bound?" Hastein asked him.

Bard shook his head. "I asked. But their leader—he was big man, heavily built, with long black hair and beard—told me that he was not accustomed to sharing his private business with men he did not know."

"Did you see a woman with them?" I asked anxiously.

"Aye," Bard answered, nodding his head. "I did. She was on the ship their leader was on—the one with the eagle's head. I could not see much of her, for she had a cloak wrapped around her, and pulled up to cover her head, as well. It was cold out on the sea that morning. But I could tell it was a woman."

"Does this help you?" Arinbjorn asked Hastein. "It is unfortunate Bard could not learn where they were bound."

"I am almost certain that wherever they were heading, they planned to sail along the northern coast of the Austmarr," Bard volunteered.

"Why do you say that?" Hastein asked.

"As we were preparing to break away and head back to Mon, I called out to their leader that if they planned to sail near Oeland, they should be careful of the pirates there. He became very interested then in what I had to say. He wanted to know all I could tell him about them."

"Pirates?" Hastein asked.

Arinbjorn answered. "We have been told by a number of travelers that a pirate fleet has been hunting the waters off the island of Oeland all summer. They demand tribute from any ships that would pass, if they think them too weak to defend themselves."

"I do not think my warning would have concerned the black-haired one, had he not planned to sail that way," Bard added.

169

"I thank you," Hastein told Bard. Arinbjorn nodded to him and said, "You may go." To Hastein, again he asked, "Is this of help to you?"

"It is better to know something than nothing," Hastein replied. After a moment, he added, "There is a good chance that the men we pursue are headed for Birka."

"It could be," Arinbjorn said. "If so, following the northern coastline is the most likely route they would take. Have you sailed the Austmarr before?"

Hastein shook his head. "My voyages have all taken me to the west."

"Birka is a goodly distance away. I do not think it can be reached from here—from the western end of the Austmarr—in less than ten days, if you break your journey each night, and that would be with ideal winds. More likely than not it could take you somewhat longer.

"The course you will need to follow will lead you, like those you pursue, along the northern shore of the sea. For the first part of your journey, you will bear east along the southern shores of Skane. There, you will still be in Danish waters. Then the shoreline and your course will turn to the north, and you will pass a long stretch of coast which lies below the southern reaches of the kingdom of the Oster-Gotars, and is sparsely settled. Their folk live mostly inland, well away from the sea. Beyond that lie the lands of the Gotars, then the kingdom of the Sveas. Birka is there, but it is not on the coast. It is a ways inland, located on an island in the midst of a great lake."

"How do we reach that lake? I thought Birka was a

port town?"

"It can be reached from the sea," Arinbjorn replied. "Not long after you pass Oeland—the island where the pirates are — the nature of the coastline will change and you will begin to pass many fjords, plus many small islands along the shore. You will be bearing almost due north when this first happens. After the shoreline turns and runs toward the northeast, you will be drawing near. You must watch for the mouth of a channel that looks from the sea to be a wide bay or the end of a fjord. It drains from the inland lake. Follow it. For most of the channel's length you will be bearing due north, and it narrows toward its end, but after it opens into the great lake, the island on which Birka lies will be in sight, straight ahead of you."

"Are there any particular dangers we should watch for?" Hastein asked.

"It is a great distance, and many years have passed since I have sailed that way," Arinbjorn responded. "This time of year, there is always a risk of bad weather, of course." He paused, and scratched the side of his head. "But the only unusual dangers we have heard of, from ships that have sailed back from that way—to Denmark from Birka, or beyond—are the pirates at Oeland."

I wondered what might lay beyond Birka, and who would venture there, and why.

"Tell me more about these pirates," Hastein said.

"Oeland is a long island that lies a short distance off-shore from the coastline of Gotarland. It is roughly halfway between here and Birka. From what we have

171

heard, there are several ships of the pirates, and they have made a base on or near the island. I should think it unlikely they will trouble you, because of the strength of your war-band you are traveling with. I expect that they seek easier prey. But the men you pursue…" Arinbjorn shrugged. "Two longships, with only light crews to defend them, would make a tempting prize."

My heart sank at Arinbjorn's words. I knew Toke. If pirates had attacked his ships, he would not surrender to them— he would fight. And if he were badly outnumbered, he would almost certainly lose, and likely be killed. If so, my quest for vengeance might be ended. That, at least, would be a good thing. But what of Sigrid? What would happen to her, if the pirates took her?

8

The Austmarr

We departed Mon before mid-day. As was customary, Hastein and Jarl Arinbjorn exchanged gifts at their parting. Hastein gave our host an ornate helm covered with engravings and inlaid with gold, which he had found in Count Robert's quarters in the island fortress in Paris. It was obviously intended more for show than war, but it made a fine gift. In return, Arinbjorn gave Hastein a very thick, long cloak that was dyed a deep blue and decorated with red and gold embroidery along all of its edges. He also gave him a spear with a fine pattern-welded blade, wide and sharp for stabbing and cutting, and a thick, sturdy shaft. It was a spear made more for hewing with rather than throwing.

"With winter approaching, it will be cold out upon the open sea. This cloak will keep you warm," he said. "It was woven by my youngest daughter, Ingirid. She is quite skilled at the loom." His daughter, who had accompanied him to the shore to see us off, looked demurely at the ground when her father complimented her, then raised her gaze and smiled warmly at Hastein.

Torvald chuckled and whispered, "I think Arinbjorn hopes Hastein will be the one who will take the last of his daughters off his hands. He paired her with Hastein at the feast, as his horn partner. The girl is certainly fair, and it *would* be a good alliance for both sides."

To my surprise, Sigurd came up to me as we were boarding the *Gull* and said, "I have a parting gift for you." He twisted a ring off of one of his fingers, and handed it to me. It was silver and had been cast in the shape of a serpent, wound round and round the wearer's finger.

"It is a serpent," he explained unnecessarily, and pointed at his eye. "It is my sign."

"I thank you," I said. I felt awkward, for a gift in return was expected, but I did not know what to give him. I had not planned for this.

Reaching into my quiver, I pulled out an arrow and gave it to Sigurd. "This is the arrow with which I felled the Frankish warrior who almost killed your father, Ragnar, in the great battle in Frankia. May it bring you luck, and whenever you shoot it, always fly true."

In truth, I did not know if the arrow I gave him was the same one I had slain that Frank with. I had many arrows whose feathers were lashed to the shaft with the same color of thread. But Sigurd did not know that, and although an arrow seemed a poor exchange for a silver ring, he looked pleased with the gift.

It was a clear day and we had fair winds. After exiting the mouth of the channel between Mon and Sjaelland, Torvald, who was manning the *Gull*'s steerboard, set a course bearing to the east and slightly north. Ahead of us I could see only the endless rippling waves of the open sea. Behind, the high white cliffs along Mon's eastern coastline remained visible long after the rest of that island, and Sjaelland to the north, had sunk from view as though swallowed up by the wide waters of the Austmarr, the Eastern Sea.

The brief layover on Mon, and the generous feast provided by Jarl Arinbjorn the night before, had left all aboard the *Gull*—even those still feeling the effects of too much ale—in good spirits. For the first time since we had begun our voyage, those aboard the ship seemed to be a single company, rather than three separate groups of warriors: Hastein's men, the carls from the estate, and those from the village. Tore announced loudly for all to hear than while Ragnar Logbrod himself might have given me the name Strongbow while we were fighting down in the land of the Franks, to him I could only be known from this day on as Halfdan Cabbage-Slayer. Everyone—even the brothers Floki and Baug, from the estate—laughed and shouted, "Hail, Cabbage-Slayer!"

Dusk had fallen by the time we approached land again. The coastline of Skane showed as a low shadow against the darkening sky. The old moon had died, and a new moon had not yet grown in the night's womb, leaving only the dim light provided by the stars to cut the blackness. We rowed the ships toward shore slowly and cautiously, as lookouts in the bows threw out weighted lines to test the water's depth and tried to see what dangers might lie ahead, concealed by the darkness.

From the *Serpent*, Stig called out, "Hastein! It is no good. We cannot see a thing."

By now we were close enough to the shore for the water to be no deeper than Torvald was tall, but we still could not tell whether the shore ahead was rocky or a

175

sandy beach. "You are right, Stig," Hastein replied. "It is too dangerous. We will anchor here for the night."

We set anchors from the *Gull's* bow and stern while the crew of the *Serpent*, lying nearby, did the same, then we rigged tent-like shelters over the two ships' decks with their sails and awnings. Due to the lateness of the hour and the fact that Cullain could not build a fire ashore to cook on, our night meal was a cold, meager one: smoked herring and pieces of hard, dry bread from the new stores Cullain and Torvald had acquired from the village on Mon.

Neither the bow nor the stern were covered by the tenting, and most of the crew gathered in those two areas to eat in the open, under the canopy of stars that filled the night sky overhead. I pushed my sea chest against the ship's side to make room for others, and sat on the deck beside it, my back resting against the strakes of the hull.

Hrodgar walked past carrying his dinner, heading toward the small raised deck in the stern where Hastein and Torvald were sitting. When he saw me he paused, then asked, "May I join you?"

"Of course," I answered.

"I will sit on your sea chest, if you do not mind." After he had settled himself there, he said, "I am glad I finally had the opportunity to see you shoot your bow this morning. I have heard tales about it from Einar, of course." He chuckled. "Cabbage-Slayer. That was a good jest. But the speed and accuracy with which you shot was a fine thing to see. Your father, Hrorik, would have been proud of the warrior you have become. It is a shame he did not live to see it."

"If he had lived, I would not be a warrior," I replied. "I would still be one of his thralls."

Hrodgar was silent for a long time. In the dark, I could not make out the expression on his face. Finally he let out a long sigh, and said, "Ah. Yes. I had forgotten about that."

What Hrodgar had said to me was kind. I hoped my reply had not sounded churlish. "It is difficult for me to think of Hrorik as a father," I told him, trying to soften my earlier words, "for I never knew him as such." After a few moments, I added. "I thank you for speaking for me this morning to Jarl Arinbjorn."

"Hunh," he replied. "It was clear that he believed you had tried to trick his men so Torvald could win their silver. His feelings were understandable, but unjust. That is not a thing you would do. A man who believed that honor and fairness required him to pay me for killing my hounds, although I had sent them to help hunt him down, would not engage in the kind of petty trickery Arinbjorn suspected."

I was surprised that Hrodgar placed such import on my regret for having killed his hounds. He had been deceived by Toke into offering them to help track a man whom he believed had aided in the massacre up on the Limfjord. I had not blamed him for helping Toke's men hunt me, and had not wished him to suffer loss because of it.

"Have you ever sailed across the Austmarr?" I asked him.

Hrodgar shook his head. "I have not traveled

widely. Some men are strongly called by the Viking life. They desire the wealth and adventure that raiding—successful raiding—can bring, and have little use for a life of peace. Jarl Hastein is such a man. But going i-viking was never a hunger in me. I find more pleasure in my family, my home, my village, than in the thought of stealing someone else's silver. I have no need for that kind of wealth, or to sail to distant lands. I prefer to see the changing seasons upon the Limfjord, and the rewards each brings. Seeing new lambs born to my ewes in the spring, hearing the wild geese sing as they cross the sky in the evening, such things are my wealth. I will fight if need be, and my spear has drunk blood more than once, but the life of a warrior has not been mine, and I do not regret it."

"Then why did you join in the attack against the Franks? Why do you sail on this voyage?"

"There are things a man must sometimes do even if he has no desire to do them. King Horik sent out the war arrow, calling upon all Danes to join in the attack against the Franks, our enemies. It is a scot that our kings rarely demand, but when they do, it is the duty of all free men to respond. It has happened two times before, that I am aware of. My father answered the war arrow when the Franks' King Louis attacked our lands, but was driven off by the bravery of our warriors. And in the time of my father's father, King Godfred called the Danes to rally in the south of Jutland to repair and strengthen the Danevirke, and defend it and our lands from a mighty Frankish army led by their King Charles, who was a great killer of men. The Saxons who lived to the south of

Jutland fell to his armies after a long and bloody war, and now their folk are scattered or enslaved and their lands belong to the Franks. But we are Danes, and no foreign king will ever take our freedom or our lands. It is a lesson it seems we must teach the Franks and their kings time and again."

"What of this voyage? Why have you left your home behind for it?" What I truly wondered, but did not ask, was, *Why did you choose to follow this path when your wife returned from the land of the dead to warn you it will cost you your life?*

"You father, Hrorik, was a fine man. Although I saw him only rarely after he moved to his great estate far to the south of the Limfjord, when we were younger men we were comrades. And his son, Harald—your brother—was a fine man, too. I would not have Harald's murder and the slaughter of the folk of the farm up on the Limfjord go unavenged. I feel I owe a blood debt to Hrorik's line, and do not wish to leave it unpaid. But for the courage of Hrorik's older brother, my village might have fallen to Gotar and Svear raiders, and my wife and children might have been carried off and ended their lives in slavery."

I nodded. "Einar told me about the attack."

"My body is aging and grows weaker with each passing year. There are not many winters left in it. This thing—helping you find Toke, and kill him—will repay my debt, and is a good way to use whatever time is left to me. I have lived a long life and I am satisfied with it. All I wish for now is a good death."

Hrodgar took a deep breath and let it out slowly.

"Your own life, though brief so far, has been a strange one. I have never known, nor even heard of, any man who was born a thrall but went on to become a warrior, and a very fine one, at that." He paused for a few moments, then continued. "I have never owned thralls. No one in my village has. We are simple folk. May I ask…does it anger you that you were a slave?"

His question startled me, and at first I was taken aback by it. But I knew Hrodgar meant no offense.

"When I was still a slave, it angered me greatly," I replied.

"You did not think it was your fate and accept it?"

"I gave no thought to things like fate, and the Norns, when I was a slave. The carls of the estate, and especially Hrorik—the man who sired me, but was never my father—were no different from me, but they were free, and could live whatever lives they chose, whereas I was merely property. The free women could choose whom they would wed, but my mother, who once was a princess in Ireland, had no right to refuse Hrorik whenever he wished to enter her bed and use her for his pleasure. She, too, was merely his property, and had no rights. Would such things not anger you?"

Hrodgar did not answer my question. Instead, he said, "The past is the past, and cannot be changed. Your own past—including that you were once a thrall—is part of what has shaped you into the man you have become. Iron must be beaten with the hammer and burned in the fire to become steel. You have grown into a fierce warrior and a fine man. I hope your past will not always anger you."

*

We sailed due east all of the next day, following the coastline of Skane. By day's end, we reached the point Arinbjorn had told us of where the land fell away to the north. From here on, we would be beyond Danish waters.

It turned out that Stig had sailed this way many years before, when he was a young man. "I was in the crew of a ship on a trading voyage," he told Hastein. "Our captain had never sailed the Austmarr before, so he followed the shoreline, as we have been doing. I remember this part of the voyage—I remember that after leaving Skane behind, the shoreline turned to the north. We eventually discovered that the shoreline gradually curved around and formed a huge bay, beyond which it turned north again. On our return voyage, instead of following the shore we sailed straight across the mouth of the bay and saved considerable time."

"How long will it take, sailing straight across?" Hastein asked.

"Just one day. With any decent winds at all, if we make an early start we will make land on the far side by evening."

"What course would we need to follow to sail straight across?" Torvald asked.

"North by east."

What Stig remembered proved true. As evening approached the following day, we reached a cluster of islands lying off the mainland and made camp for the night on the outermost one. A marshy inlet lay a short distance down from where we pulled the prows of the *Gull* and the *Serpent* up onto the beach. From the honking we could hear coming from it, it was apparent that many wild geese were nesting there. Einar and I looked at each other, grinned, and headed that way with our bows.

Tore saw us leaving and hurried after, carrying his bow, too. "Wait for me," he cried. "I am coming."

An extra bow might help us harvest more meat, but with Tore behind it, it might have the opposite effect. Though a good man to fight beside in battle, he was not a skilled hunter and tended to be clumsy and loud in the woods. "You will have to be very quiet," I told him, when he caught up with us. "And do only what I tell you to do." To my surprise, he did not protest.

"Spread out," I whispered to Tore and Einar, as we neared the edge of the inlet. To Tore, I added, "Try to pick a spot where there are several geese close together, and have extra arrows out and ready. Watch me. When I rise up, we will all shoot together. You must shoot as swiftly as you can. For a few moments they may not realize what is happening, but it will not take them long to become frightened and take flight."

I moved down along the shore of the inlet, keeping low behind the fringe of tall grass and reeds that lined the water's edge, until I happened to see the long necks of two pairs of geese raising and lowering above the level of the reeds. Always one in a pair would keep watch, while the other fed.

I glanced back down the shoreline. Einar was squatting, watching me. Beyond him, Tore was doing the same. I pulled three arrows out of my quiver—each with wide, sharp hunting heads—and stuck their points in the sandy soil so that they stood upright in a line in front of me, then laid a fourth arrow across my bow, its shaft resting against the top of my bow hand, and nocked it on the string.

I nodded to Einar, and when he nodded back I stood up swiftly, drawing my bow as I did. The two watchers—from their size, they both looked to be the males of their pairs—swiveled their heads in unison toward me, but did not sound any alarm. I focused my gaze on a spot on the breast of the farther of the two watchers just in front of the edge of its wing, opened the cupped fingers of my right hand releasing the bowstring, and reached down for another arrow.

The twang of my bowstring and soft whoosh of the arrow through the air did not startle them. Clearly, these geese had never been hunted by men. My arrow hit the goose where I had aimed and passed clear through it. The big bird flopped over, dead by the time it hit the ground. Its mate honked in alarm, and both of the other pair turned and looked in its direction.

My second arrow hit the female in the second pair while she and her mate were looking away. She was the closer of the two to me. The arrow's impact as it passed through her body knocked her forward to the ground. Hearing the sound, her mate turned back around and honked in alarm, then waddled over to her, trying to discern what had happened. Meanwhile the female in the first pair, realizing her mate was dead, raised her wings in preparation to fly. I snapped off a quick shot that hit her, but not cleanly. She fell on her side, then staggered back to her feet, honking loudly, and headed off down the shore, dragging a wing that had obviously been broken by my arrow.

By now the last goose had reached its fallen mate and was standing over it, honking loudly in distress. All across the shore of the inlet other geese, heeding the sounds of alarm, were taking flight. I pulled my final arrow to full draw and sent it into the center of the grieving male's breast, then trotted in pursuit of the wounded female.

Einar also took four geese. He killed all of his birds cleanly, and he laughed as he watched me chase my wounded goose back and forth along the shore trying to catch her, until I finally gave up and shot her again. Even Tore managed to take three. As he walked up carrying two clutched in one hand, hanging by their legs, with the third and his bow in his other hand, his face beamed with a huge smile.

"Look!" he exclaimed. "Three geese! I have never before had such a day hunting. We must hunt together more often."

I did not relish the thought of Tore becoming a hunting partner. But he had not looked happy since Odd's death down in Frankia. It was good to see him with something other than a glum frown on his face. Tore had his faults, but he was a true comrade nevertheless. I smiled back and said, "But now the real work begins. Now we must pluck them."

Fortunately several others from the *Gull*'s crew, including Gudfred from the estate and Bram and Skuli from the village, volunteered to help us pluck and clean the geese. By the time we finished, the beach was covered with tufts of wind-blown down.

Though it was a good harvest, eleven geese could not come close to filling the bellies of eighty-one men. While the big birds roasted on spits above two long fires built in shallow pits dug on the shore, Cullain and Regin prepared large pots of barley and vegetable stew, as the men of the two crews staved off their hunger by gnawing on some of the smoked herring we'd purchased on Mon. The smell of the roasting geese made for a festive air to our evening, and Hastein authorized a cask of ale to be broached and shared among the men while we waited for the birds to cook.

"If my memory is correct, it will take us less than a full day's sailing to reach the southern end of the island of Oeland on the morrow," Stig told Hastein. "What of the pirates that Arinbjorn said might be there? What shall we do about them?"

Just then, Einar called me over to the cook-fires to consult on whether I thought the geese were done, so I did not hear Hastein's response. But a short time later he walked over to where Cullain was tending the stew, closed the lid of the wooden chest in which the little Irishman stored his cooking gear, and stepped up on it. Cullain frowned but said nothing.

"Gather round," Hastein called. "There are matters I need to tell you about."

The men of the two crews, who had been milling about on the beach or resting aboard ship while the meal was being cooked, came and stood expectantly before him. When all had arrived, Hastein continued.

"Before we left Mon, Jarl Arinbjorn warned me that in recent months, a fleet of pirates has been hunting the waters off a large island called Oeland. On the morrow, the course we follow will take us past Oeland. It is a long island, and it will take us more than one day to pass it by.

"Stig sailed this way many years ago. He tells me that the center portion of the island lies close to the mainland and the passage between them becomes a narrow strait there. He thinks that if pirates are hunting, that is where they will likely be lying in wait.

"I do not know the strength of these pirates—how many ships and men they number, or even if they are still in these waters. If they are, I think it unlikely they would wish to attack two longships filled with fighting men. But we would be foolish to be unprepared. For the next two days, you must all keep your weapons with you rather than stowed in your sea chests. If they need sharpening, see to it this night. Those who possess brynies or other armor should wear it, and keep your helms and shields close at hand."

The next morning, after we had broken the night's fast with the day meal, I opened my sea chest and began pulling out what I would need to arm myself. I sorted through my arrows, putting the best ones in my favorite quiver, and filling the extra quiver with the rest.

I had stored my mail brynie rolled up in the padded jerkin I wore under it. Taking them out of the chest, I unrolled them, pulled the jerkin on over my head and shoulders, then did the same with the brynie. I now normally wore the small knife that had once been Harald's. It was poorly suited for fighting, though, so I slipped its scabbard off of my belt and dropped it into my sea chest, threaded the belt through the loops of my dagger's scabbard, and strapped it around my waist.

While the *Gull* was at sea I kept my bow in its sealskin case lashed with my spear against the side of the ship, by the position where I normally rowed, near the stern. My shield was there, too. I placed my sword, its baldric wrapped around the scabbard, the two quivers, and my small-axe on the deck against the side with them. If we encountered pirates at all this day, it was likely to be only after many hours of sailing. There was no point encumbering myself with my weapons until there was an actual need. Last, I pulled my Frankish helm—which I had taken, like my brynie, shield, and sword, from the body of Leonidas, the young Frankish cavalry officer I had killed—from the sea chest and added it to the pile of weapons. The mail curtain attached to its back and sides made it somewhat heavy but did protect my neck. More importantly, the fact that it had no nasal bar, unlike my other helm, was less distracting to my aim when I shot my bow, although it did leave my face more exposed.

Bram, the young man from the village, walked up and opened his own sea chest as I was finishing. "That is a fine looking helm," he said.

I nodded. "It is Frankish," I told him.

His own preparations were far simpler than mine. He was already wearing a large seax in its scabbard on his belt. He pulled a small-axe from his chest and stuck its handle under his belt, in the small of his back. He, too, kept his spear and shield secured to the ship's side near the stern.

"Do you not have a helm? Or armor?" I asked. The latter was not surprising. Mail armor was expensive and somewhat rare. Mostly just wealthy men owned it, or those who, like me, had stripped it from the body of a slain enemy. But since Bram had gone raiding before with my father, Hrorik, I would have expected him to at least own a helm.

He looked embarrassed by my question, and shook his head. "I had a helm," he answered, "but I lost it on the voyage to England with your father. In the battle with the English, when we were running for the ship."

I lifted the lid of my sea chest again. "I have an extra one," I told him. "And I have this heavy leather jerkin, too. You may use them if you wish."

Bram's face lit up and he took them eagerly. "I thank you," he said.

The morning winds, though of modest strength, blew in a favorable direction and we forged our way steadily north, hugging the shoreline of the mainland. That had been Stig's suggestion. "If there *are* pirates ahead, it's possible they may have lookouts along the shore of Oeland," he'd told Hastein. "If we sail close to the mainland, we will be able to travel undetected for a considerable distance along the length of the island, before the channel narrows enough to be seen across from one side to the other."

By mid-day, Stig estimated that we had probably traveled far enough to be opposite the southern tip of Oeland, although as yet nothing could be seen of it. Hastein took over the *Gull's* steer-board, and sent Torvald up to the bow to keep watch, reckoning that with his height and keen eyesight, he would be able to see the island before anyone else. Torvald placed two sea chests side by side on the small raised bow deck and stood atop them, one hand grasping the neck of the ship's carved dragon head, scanning the sea to the north and east.

The afternoon was half gone before Torvald sent word back to Hastein that he could see land off to the east, just at the horizon. Hastein ordered the sail reefed and the boom lowered so that the shortened sail hung just above the central oar rack. Without her full expanse of sail stretched out above her, the *Gull* would sail more slowly, but would be far more difficult to spot from a distance.

The crew of the *Serpent* did the same with her sail, and Stig steered her close alongside.

Hastein called across to him. "Torvald has seen the island. The channel is narrowing, as you said it would."

Stig shaded his eyes with one hand and stared toward the east for a time, then shook his head. "Torvald's eyes are far sharper than mine," he said.

"Aye, than mine, too, plus he looks from higher above the sea than we do. Can you guess how much longer it will take us to reach the narrow strait where the mainland and island are closest?"

Stig shook his head. "I know there is still a ways to

travel, though I am not certain how far. It has been too many years. But once within it, we will travel a considerable distance before the channel widens again. We cannot clear the narrows this day, for certain. Night is too near."

"Then we will break our voyage as soon as we find a suitable place to land and make camp," Hastein decided. "I do not wish to pass the night so close to where the pirates may be that our cook-fires might be seen by watchers. I do not want to risk being snuck up on in the dark."

I slept poorly, and the night seemed to drag on forever. The chance that we might fight on the morrow was always on the edge of my thoughts. All in the two crews seemed more subdued than usual, and Tore asked me again whether Gunhild had ever shown any signs of possessing the second sight.

The next morning when I armed myself again, I did not leave my weapons in a pile upon the deck as I had before. I slung my the strap of my quiver and my sword's baldric over my shoulders, crisscrossed over my chest with the sword's hilt hanging at my left hip and my quiver at my right. Like Bram had done the day before, I stuck my small-axe through my belt so that it rested in the small of my back. Last, I pulled my bow from its case. Only my helm did I not put on. It was too hot and heavy to wear until it was needed.

Around me, the other members of the *Gull*'s crew did much the same. We were a warlike looking company. Surely, even if there were pirates ahead, they would not trouble us.

The weather had changed overnight. Yesterday's blue sky, dotted with high tufts of white cloud, was gone, replaced by a dull gray cover of clouds so thick and solid that the sun's position could not be seen through them. A cold wind blew steadily from the north, whipping the surface of the sea into choppy waves, and filling the air with spray blown from their crests.

"We can make some headway under sail for a bit longer," Stig told Hastein. "But when we reach the strait itself, where the channel is narrowest, we will be heading almost directly into the wind, with limited room to tack. I fear it will be a slow passage with hard rowing before we see the far side of Oeland."

It proved as Stig had said. For a time, we had room to steer back and forth across the channel, catching the wind at enough of an angle to move the ships ahead, though our forward progress was slow. But the farther we advanced, the closer the shore drew on either side and the shorter our tacks. Finally Hastein gave the order to lower and secure the sail, and draw out our oars. On the *Serpent*, Stig did the same.

We made slow headway, rowing against the wind. I could see Oeland clearly now off to my left. Its shoreline was straight, and behind a narrow beach and gently sloping grasslands beyond the land rose steeply up to a ridge running along the center of the island. To my right, on the other side of the channel, the mainland was low and heavily wooded for as far as I could see, and its shoreline was dotted with numerous small islands.

It was mid-afternoon, after we had been in the

narrow strait for some time, when Torvald, who was manning the steer-board, called out to Hastein, who had gone forward and was keeping watch from the bow.

"Hastein! A ship is following us."

Hastein hurried back to the raised stern deck and stood there looking back in the direction the *Gull* had come from. From where I was seated, rowing my oar, the up-curved stern blocked my view to the rear, but I listened as Torvald and Hastein talked.

"When did you first see it?" Hastein asked.

"Just before I called out to you. It cannot have been there long. I have been checking the sea behind us regularly."

"Hunh," Hastein said. "It must have been lying in wait, behind one of the small islands we passed. I cannot tell its size from this distance, but there are many oars flashing. For certain it is a longship, not a knarr."

"They are making no effort to catch up to us," Torvald observed.

"No," Hastein agreed.

Like me, Tore had been listening to them speak. "Is it the pirates?" he asked.

Hastein did not answer him directly. But he turned and called to two of the crew standing nearby who were not rowing. "Harek, Solvi. Come back here. I need you to take over Tore and Halfdan's oars." To us he said, as he picked up his shield from where it was leaning against the side of the ship, "Fetch your bows and stay close to me. I am going back to the bow."

By the time Tore and I had retrieved our helms and bows and made our way to the front of the ship, the

192

Serpent had pulled even with the *Gull* and was plowing through the choppy sea so close to us that the tips of the two ships' banks of oars were almost touching as they churned back and forth. Stig had handed off the steer-board to one of his men and was, like Hastein, now standing on the raised fore-deck of his ship.

Ahead of us, an island just off the mainland's shore—much larger than any others we had passed since entering the narrow channel—extended so far out into the strait that the channel between Oeland and the mainland was reduced by half.

"That is where it will be," Hastein muttered. "If I was hunting here, that is where I would set a trap."

As if on cue, a longship, its oars flashing, pulled into view from behind a spur of land jutting out from the island. Moments later a second followed it, and then a third.

I seated my helm on my head and tightened its strap. As I did, Hrodgar stepped up onto the fore-deck beside Hastein. "Will you try to push on past them?" he asked.

Hastein shook his head. "If they will not give way—if they will not give us clear passage—then we will have to fight. I will not flee like a deer pursued by a pack of wolves. It would be too dangerous if our two ships became separated.

"Stig," Hastein called. "If it comes to a fight, we will lash the *Gull* and *Serpent* together."

Stig nodded, and turned to a man standing on the deck behind him. "Pull out grapples and ropes, and have them ready."

By now the three longships had rowed to where they formed a line across the center of the channel ahead of us. As we watched, in unison they raised their oars, holding them at ready out over the water, while the ships slid forward through the gray, choppy sea, slowing. When their forward progress had nearly stopped, the two on either end of their line dipped their oars into the sea and held them steady, bringing the ships fully to a halt, still broadside to us across our path, less than a long bow-shot away.

As the other two stopped, the ship in the center turned sharply in place, its rowers on one side backing their oars while the other side pulled. When its bow had swung around to face us, it began moving forward slowly.

"*Gull!*" Hastein shouted. "Raise...oars!" On the *Serpent*, Stig gave the same command, and our two ships gradually coasted to a stop.

I turned and looked back toward the stern. The ship that had been following us had drawn much closer, till it was barely a spear throw behind us, but now it, too, had ceased its forward progress.

The center longship ahead continued to draw closer to the *Gull* and *Serpent*, though at a slow pace. A tall, broad-shouldered man stood in her prow, one hand resting on the neck of her dragon's head, which was carved to look like a snarling wolf. What was visible of his body was covered by a mail brynie, and he wore a helm that protected his face well, with hinged metal cheek flaps on each side and a long nasal bar in the center. He had a long, bright red beard that hung down

194

over his chest. Other men, also armored, were crowded behind him in the prow of the ship.

Hastein glanced over his shoulder at Tore and me and said, "Ready arrows on your bows, and stand behind me on either side, where you can be seen." Turning back toward the approaching longship, he shouted loudly across the water, "Hold! Draw no nearer."

The red-bearded man held up one hand and said something over his shoulder to those behind him. The rowers on his ship raised their oars. The wolf-headed ship drifted to a stop with its bow little more than an oar's length away from that of the *Gull*, squarely in her path.

"You are blocking our passage," Hastein shouted. "Give way."

"That is an ill-mannered greeting to give a stranger," the other ship's captain—for so the red-bearded man clearly was—replied. "My name is Sigvald. I am called Ship-Taker. With whom do I speak?"

"My name is Hastein. I am jarl over the lands of the Danes around the Limfjord, in the north of Jutland. Now we know each other's names. Again I say to you, give way, and let us pass."

"Hastein. And a jarl of the Danes, from the Limfjord in the north of Jutland," Sigvald repeated, a mocking tone in his voice. "Now that is a very fine thing. Strangely enough, I have just days ago heard of you.

"I myself am but the captain of this small company you see. Although in truth, it would seem that this day at least, I have more warriors in my band than do you. But

195

though I am not a jarl, nor even a great chieftain, I do consider these waters around Oeland to be mine. Those who wish to pass through them must pay a toll to do so."

"The sea belongs to no man," Hastein replied. "I will not pay for the right to travel upon it."

"Those sound like the words of a greedy man," Sigvald said, in the same mocking tone. "Surely a great jarl like yourself can afford to share some of his wealth with those less fortunate than he? You have recently returned from Frankia, have you not? I have heard that you won a great victory there, and much silver. I am asking only that you and your men share a bit of that new-won wealth with this less fortunate band of sailors."

How, I wondered, could this pirate know that? How could he know of Hastein, and Frankia, and our victory there?

"Make ready," Hastein murmured to Toke and me. "When I give the word, shoot your arrows into this arrogant dog's face."

In a louder voice, Hastein called out, "I will ask you just once more: Give way. If you do not, you will not see our silver, but you will taste our steel."

"It is a fool who chooses to lose all to save a little," the red-bearded man answered. "I have never had the pleasure of killing a jarl. It seems a good day..."

"Now!" Hastein said. As one, Tore and I raised our bows, pulling them to full draw as we did, and shot.

The pirate captain must have been expecting that we might try to kill him, for he ducked behind his ship's stem even as we released our arrows. The men standing behind him were not so well prepared. My arrow struck the side of a warrior's helm and glanced off, but sent him staggering backward. Tore's arrow caught another man square in the face and put him down.

"Ship oars!" Hastein cried. "Prepare for battle!"

As the rowers in the crews of the *Gull* and *Serpent* hurriedly pulled their oars in, two men on Stig's ship tossed grappling hooks with sturdy ropes tied to them across to the deck of the *Gull*. Two of our men carried them to either end of the mast-fish, the heavy wooden brace that supported the *Gull*'s mast, and hooked them over it. As soon as the hooks were in place, Stig's crew hauled on the ropes, drawing our two ships together until their hulls were touching amidships.

On the pirate ship, its captain, Sigvald, was shouting, "Pull, pull!" The ship's rowers heaved on their oars, propelling it forward into the space between the bows of the *Serpent* and the *Gull*. It was a bold move, but a risky one. Until the other pirate ships arrived, Sigvald's ship and crew would be outnumbered.

"To the bow! To the bow!" Hastein shouted. "Do not let them board!"

Our warriors in the front of the *Gull* surged forward in answer to Hastein's call, the two brothers Bryngolf and Bjorgolf in the lead, jostling past Tore and me.

"Halfdan," Tore cried. "With me!" He turned and ran back to where the *Gull*'s main water cask, as big around as the wheel of a wagon and as tall as a man's waist, sat on her deck in front of the mast. "Up here," he said, and clambered on top of it, then reached his hand down. We grasped each other's wrists and he pulled me up, too. Our height above the deck gave us a view into the enemy's ship, looking over the backs of our own men crowding forward into the fight.

Warriors in the bow of the pirate ship swung grappling hooks around their heads then flung them, trailing ropes behind, onto the prows of the *Gull* and the *Serpent*. From further back on the pirate ship's deck, other warriors arced spears over their shipmates' heads onto our ships.

"Torvald!" Hastein called. "To the fore-deck! To me!" Turning to Hrodgar, he said, "Take command of the stern. Do not allow those on the ship behind to board us."

I felt, more than heard, a thud as the hull of the pirate captain's ship butted up against the *Gull*. A pirate in her bow, standing to the side of the raised stem post, was pulling with both hands on a rope attached to a grapple hooked over the *Gull*'s side. His chest was exposed above the ship's side. I put an arrow into it.

Bryngolf, Bjorgolf, and another of Hastein's men named Thorstein were up on the fore-deck now beside the jarl. They held spears in both hands, the points aimed out over the edge of the *Gull*'s prow, their shields slung across their backs. Hastein, who was armed with only his sword, held his shield in front of him.

A warrior climbed up onto the rail of the pirate ship, trying to jump down onto the *Gull*. Bjorgolf and Thorstein pushed the points of their spears against his mail-covered chest, holding him fast. As he beat at the spear shafts with his sword, trying to knock them aside, Tore shot an arrow into his face.

"Like shooting cabbages," he said, grinning.

Another pirate tried to cross, using his shield to sweep the spear points facing him aside as he climbed up onto the ship's rail. Hastein swung a lunging cut with his sword and severed the man's leg below his knee. He screamed, flailing his arms wide, and Bjorgolf stuck his spear point through his throat.

By now the other two pirate ships that had been blocking the channel to our front had reached us. One took a position lying a short way off the front half of the *Gull*, on our steer-board side. She did not try to grapple us, but instead her crew lined her rail and shot arrows and hurled spears at our warriors in the *Gull*'s bow. I saw arrows strike the shields slung across Bryngolf's and Bjorgolf's backs, and one glanced off Bryngolf's helm. A spear sailed past Hastein and hit Thorstein in the side. He staggered and fell backward off of the fore-deck, landing sprawled just behind it. After a few moments he sat up, pulled the spear out with his right hand, then crawled on his hands and knees past us toward the stern, leaving a trail of blood on the wooden planks of the *Gull*'s deck, as other warriors stepped up to fill his place.

"We must protect them," Tore shouted.

Men shooting bows without shield bearers to protect them make exposed targets. There were five men shooting bows from along the second pirate ship's rail, while others hurled throwing spears. I picked a man who was just beginning to draw his bow and hit him high in the back, just below his shoulder. Tore shot a warrior laying an arrow across his bow, standing upright and picking a target on the *Gull*'s fore-deck with no

199

thought that he himself might be in danger. Both men went down, but others pressed forward to take their places. We shot as fast as we could pull arrows from our quivers and killed six more, including all of the men at the ship's rail armed with bows, before the pirates realized where the deadly fire was coming from. Some turned in our direction and hurled their spears, while others snatched up the bows of their fallen comrades. Now it was Tore and I who were exposed without shield bearers, and we leapt down from the water cask and took cover behind it as arrows and spears whizzed overhead or thudded into the deck around us.

The third pirate ship slid alongside the pirate chieftain's wolf-headed longship, nosing up against the far side of the *Serpent*'s bow. While some of its crew hurled grapples to pull their ship tight to the *Serpent*, others used long spears to stab across at the warriors who were on the *Serpent*'s fore-deck, fending off those who were trying to board from the first attacker.

Behind us, the pirates' fourth ship had swung around so that she faced broadside across the sterns of the *Gull* and the *Serpent*. Her crew lined her rails, exchanging missile fire with the warriors in our rear who were fighting under Hrodgar's command. I glimpsed Einar standing at Hrodgar's side, shooting steadily with his bow.

After losing several more men who tried to clamber up over the bow rails onto the *Gull* and the *Serpent*, the pirates had given up their attempts to board. The battle in the bows had stalled—for now at least—as on both sides the warriors jammed onto their ships' fore-decks stood shoulder to shoulder, as if in a shield wall, stabbing across at each other with their spears.

Accompanied by Torvald, who had only moments before reached the bow, Hastein scurried back and took cover with Tore and me behind the water cask. Torvald was shaking his head, a grim expression on his face.

"There are too many, Hastein. They are all around us. We cannot win this fight, and we cannot escape."

His words caused my stomach to twist on itself with fear, and my mind for a moment carried me back to the night on the Limfjord when we had been surrounded by Toke's men, and Harald and so many others had been slain. There, at least, we could try to reach the safety of the forest. Here there was nowhere we could flee to.

An arrow thudded into the mast nearby. Hastein instinctively ducked his head, then cautiously raised it again and peered over the top of the water cask, turning this way and that, studying our ships and the attackers around them. "I fear you may be right," he said to Torvald, after a few moments. "Perhaps we cannot win. But we must not lose. If we can just hold them off—if we can make the price of winning too costly for them—we may yet persuade them to withdraw and let us pass, and manage to come out of this alive."

Turning to me he said. "Go to the *Serpent* and fetch Stig. Be careful. Stay low, and do not make yourself a target. And tell Hrodgar to join us here also."

I handed my bow and quiver to Tore. "Keep these for me until I return," I told him.

"Where is your shield?" Hastein asked.

"Back in the stern."

"Take mine," he said. "I will not need it while we bide here."

Most of the crews of both the *Gull* and the *Serpent* were in the front third of the ships, where the greatest threat lay, although enough were in the stern of each to respond to an attack if the pirate ship there should close in and her crew try to board. The center of the *Gull's* deck felt strangely deserted. Keeping low, with Hastein's shield slung across my back for protection from stray spears or arrows, I scrabbled like a crab to mid-ship where the rails of the *Gull* and *Serpent* were touching and clambered across.

Stig was in the prow of the *Serpent*, just behind the front rank of warriors there. The ship's sides, which curved up to meet the bow's stem post upon which the dragon's head was mounted, protected his men from their waists down as if they were fighting from behind a low stockade, and they held their shields high, completely covering their chests, barely looking over the shields' top rims while they stabbed and pushed with their spears at the pirates, who were fighting from only a few feet away, similarly protected behind their own ships' sides. Occasionally a warrior on either side might take a glancing cut to the face if he was slow to block with his shield, or a spear point might pierce or cut an arm reaching out to strike, but in truth, it would take either bad luck or great carelessness for a man to receive a fatal wound in the fight in the bows if it stayed like this. Perhaps we were not doomed, after all.

"Stig," I said, touching his shoulder to get his attention. "Hastein wants you on the *Gull*, to confer." He nodded, told the warrior beside him where he would be and left him in command, then followed me, running in a low crouch, back to mid-ship where we crossed over to the *Gull*. As he scuttled forward to where Hastein and Torvald were waiting, I ran, crouched low, back to the stern and summoned Hrodgar, fetching my shield, extra quiver, and spear while I was there.

"What are your losses so far?" Hastein asked Stig and Hrodgar, after we all arrived back at the water cask.

"None dead aboard the *Serpent*," Stig answered. "A few wounded, but nothing that will not heal if we get out of this."

"Two with minor wounds in the stern," Hrodgar said.

Hastein nodded. "It is much same in the *Gull*'s bow. Thorstein took a spear in his side, but it was a light throwing spear and his brynie stopped it from piercing too deeply. Cullain is binding the wound now. He will not swing a sword with much force for a time, but he will live. A few more have wounds, but they can still fight."

"What is your plan?" Stig asked. "If the two ships now standing off should also close with us and try to board we will have to defend from several sides at once, and will be stretched thin. I fear too thin."

"We must make their leader, Sigvald, believe that he will lose too many men if he presses this fight. He has already taken heavier losses than we have, when they first tried to board. I saw at least four fall that I recall."

"I killed one for certain," Tore volunteered, "when he climbed up onto the rail. And together Halfdan and I shot down eight men, all armed with bows, on that ship off there," he added, pointing at the pirate ship off the *Gull*'s steer-board bow. "They were attacking our men on the fore-deck with bows and spears, and did not see us shooting from atop the water cask back here."

"Perhaps that can be our way out of this," Hastein said. "We will hold them off for now in the bows and in the stern, while all of our archers concentrate their fire on that ship, off our steer-board side, and further weaken its crew so they dare not try to board. If we can keep it and the other ship behind us from closing, so the fight is just in the bows, two ships against two, we will see who are the better men. How many have we between our two crews who are armed with bows?"

It took some time to find out, and more still to pull those who were up in the ranks of the shield-walls out and have them gather their bows and quivers and meet mid-ship on the *Gull*, beside her mast. In all, there were thirteen archers between the two crews: six from the *Serpent*, and seven on the *Gull*: Tore, me, and three others of Hastein's men—Asbjorn, Hallbjorn, and Storolf—plus Einar and, to my surprise, Gudfred from the estate.

"I wish Odd was here," Tore said.

By now, the volume of missile fire from the pirate ships had slackened considerably, no doubt because their stores of arrows and throwing spears were becoming depleted. Hastein had spread the word among our own warriors that none should cast a weapon back unless he was certain of a hit, and several men had been tasked with collecting the spears and arrows shot at us that had not passed over the side into the sea.

Up in the bows, the pirates behind their shield-walls had begun to lob stones over their front ranks onto our fore-decks. I saw one strike a man's helm with a loud clang and knock him to his knees.

"They have opened up their deck and are throwing their ballast stones at us," Torvald said.

The pirate ship lying off the steer-board side of the *Gull* had now begun to gradually edge further down along our hull—eight of her crew using the ship's back four pairs of oars to maneuver—in order to give the warriors shooting from her bow a better angle of fire at the backs of our men fighting on the *Gull*'s fore-deck. They, too, had also begun hurling stones as missiles, as well as shooting arrows and—though now only rarely—throwing spears. In the *Gull's* bow, our warriors behind the front rank turned and raised their shields to protect themselves and their comrades from the flanking fire.

I nudged Hastein and pointed at the ship. "They are drawing closer. They do not know we have gathered so many archers here. Our fire will be most effective if it is unexpected and concentrated," I told him. "If our archers can reach the rail of the *Gull* unseen, just opposite the bow of their ship, and rise up and fire as one, we can deal them a heavy blow."

Hastein studied the pirate ship for a moment, then a grim smile crossed his face.

"Perhaps we can do even more than that," he said. "We shall do as you say. But once your archers rise up and fire, they must keep shooting. Keep the ship's bow clear of all warriors. If you can do that, we will hook her and pull her in."

I turned and looked at Tore. He nodded. "It is a good plan," he said.

While Hastein, Torvald, and Stig prepared ropes with grappling hooks, Tore and I spoke to our small band of archers. "We will crawl flat on our bellies from here to the side there, just opposite that ship," I told them, pointing to where we would take our firing positions. "We must stay low. They must not see us."

"We will rise up and shoot together, all as one, on my signal," Tore added. "Pick your targets and shoot carefully. Some of you have but a few arrows. Make all of them count. We will keep shooting until the bow of their ship is cleared, so Jarl Hastein can board her."

"We are ready," Hastein said. He was holding a coil of rope in his left hand and a grappling hook, tied to the end of the rope, in his right. His shield was slung across his back, and a spear—the hewing spear that had been a gift from Arinbjorn—lay on the deck at his side. Behind him, Torvald and Stig also crouched concealed behind the water cask, each holding coiled ropes and grapples. Five more warriors were hiding nearby, on the deck of the *Serpent* behind her rail, ready to cross over and join the fight.

Tore and I crawled, staying low on our bellies like wriggling snakes, from where we'd been hiding behind the barrels of provisions stacked along the center of the deck over to the *Gull's* steer-board side rail. Tore, in the lead, positioned himself a short way down from the *Gull's* fore-deck. I moved into place beside him, and Einar took position next to me. It felt good to have him fighting by my side. The rest of our archers followed us to the *Gull*'s side, lining up along her rail.

Each man got to his knees, keeping concealed below the level of the top strake, and readied an arrow across his bow. "Good hunting," Einar whispered to me, and winked. Tore looked back at Hastein and nodded. Hastein nodded back.

"Archers! Now!" Tore shouted, and stood, drawing his bow back as he did. The rest of us did the same, while hurriedly scanning the ship across from us, searching for a target.

Because they had been receiving so little return fire from the *Gull*'s bow—only an occasional spear thrown back at them—and none at all from elsewhere on our ship, the warriors launching missile fire from along the pirate ship's rail were standing tall, exposed to our quarter as they searched for targets among the warriors crowded on our fore-deck. Their ship had pulled so close by now that I could have reached out and touched its side with a fully extended spear.

Directly across from me a warrior with a long brown beard plaited into two braids was drawing back his bow while staring intently at our warriors in the *Gull*'s bow. He was so close I could see his eyes widen as he glimpsed me suddenly rising up into view, and he tried to turn and aim his arrow at me. He was too slow— I put my arrow into the middle of his face and sent him flopping backward. The man just to his left, who was holding a large stone cupped in his right hand, swung around to watch in surprise as his crew-mate fell. Einar shot him in the neck, the arrow passing clean through, and he staggered away from the ship's side, blood spouting from the wound and from his mouth.

Our archers' first round of fire, so unexpected and from such close range, proved deadly. All along the pirate ship's rail men dropped. "Keep firing! Keep firing!" Tore shouted, as he launched another arrow.

Aboard the pirate ship, those along her side who were not slain by the first volley and our scattered follow-up shots dropped to her deck, out of sight and danger. Only seven men in the front half of the ship had survived our deadly attack. "Do not waste arrows," I cried, as they took cover.

Hastein and Torvald rushed from cover to the *Gull*'s rail and heaved their grappling hooks across the short gap between the two ships. The iron grapples thudded onto the pirate ship's now empty fore-deck, and Hastein and Torvald heaved on the ropes, setting the hooks against the ship's side. Torvald braced both feet against the top strake of the *Gull*'s rail and heaved himself backward, holding the rope with both hands and straining against it to pull the ships together.

"Quickly—to us! To the ropes," Hastein cried. The five warriors hiding aboard the *Serpent* scrambled over the rail and rushed to help pull on the ropes. Four of our archers dropped their bows and also joined them.

Slowly our men dragged the dead weight of the pirate ship closer. Realizing the danger, three of her warriors who had taken cover to avoid our arrow fire scuttled on their hands and knees toward her bow and the ropes. The man in the lead rose up just enough, as he neared the fore-deck and raised a sword to chop at one of the ropes, to expose his back. He was not wearing a brynie. Tore and I both shot arrows into him.

The other two men heading toward the bow dropped flat again, hidden from our sight. A few moments later, one of the ropes—obviously cut through—suddenly gave way, and our men pulling on it, including Hastein, fell backward onto the *Gull*'s deck in a heap.

Stig rushed forward and heaved the third line across, hooking the pirate ship again. "Tore! Halfdan!" Hastein shouted as he scrambled back to his feet. "Protect the ropes!"

"I cannot see them," Tore cried. "I have no shot."

"Hold my belt," I told him. "Do not let me fall." Pulling three arrows from my quiver and gripping them in my left hand together with my bow, I put one foot up on the top edge of the rail. Tore and Einar both hooked their fingers under the back of my belt and as they heaved I stepped up onto the top strake of the hull's side. As I stood swaying atop the rail, trying to gain my balance while they held fast to my belt to keep me from falling, I selected one of the arrows and nocked it on my bowstring.

In the bow of the pirate ship one of the two warriors was sawing at Torvald's rope with a knife. I drew and fired, but my unsteadiness threw my aim off and the arrow thudded harmlessly into the ship's side above the man's head. The pirate ducked, startled, and turned to see where the shot had come from. I nocked another arrow and began to draw it back as he spotted me, but before I could fire he rolled against his ship's near side, out of my sight.

The pirate ship's bow was now only a few feet from the side of the *Gull*. Drawing his sword from its scabbard, Hastein swung his shield around in front of him and ran at the *Gull's* side. He leaped up, his right foot landing on the top of her rail and in the same motion pushing off again, and soared across the narrow space between the two ships, landing on the pirate ship's deck just beyond her fore-deck. His momentum carried him forward and he staggered against the ship's side, off balance.

The second of the two pirates—the one I had not yet seen—raised up, cocking a small-axe back to throw at Hastein. At almost point-blank range, I drew and shot an arrow into his back, hitting him between his shoulder blades. The impact knocked him face-forward onto the deck. Hastein pushed himself upright and lunged across the deck, stabbing with his sword at the pirate I had shot at moments earlier and missed. He was still hidden from my sight by his ship's rail, but I heard him scream, and when Hastein pulled back his sword its tip was bloody.

The pirate ship's bow bumped against the side of the *Gull's* hull. Had Tore and Einar not been holding onto me, the impact would have caused me to fall.

Torvald dropped the rope he'd been pulling on, bent down, and picked up Hastein's spear from where he'd left it lying on the deck. "Stig," he cried, "Secure the ropes. The rest of you...follow me!"

While Torvald, the five warriors from the *Serpent*, and the four archers who'd been helping pull on the ropes clambered across the two ships' rails and dropped down onto the deck of the pirate ship, drawing their weapons as they did, Stig wrapped one of the grappling lines around the *Gull*'s mast and secured it on a cleat.

"Let go of me," I said to Tore and Einar. When they released my belt, I jumped down onto the pirate ship's deck and nocked another arrow on my bowstring. "I am coming too," Tore cried, and he and Einar climbed across after me.

Of the original group of warriors who had been firing at the *Gull* from the pirate ship's bow when our archers had first attacked, only four now remained. They had retreated to just in front of their ship's mast and were bunched together there, crouching low behind their shields. Beyond them, in the ship's stern, eight warriors were still seated at the last four pairs of oars. Their backs toward the bow, they did not realize their ship had been boarded. Two more—one, who was manning the steer-board, presumably the ship's captain—stood on the raised stern deck.

Hastein was running at the four warriors before the mast, roaring like a wild beast. Torvald and the rest of our men raced after him, a few steps behind. One of the four pirates turned and fled toward the stern. I drew and fired, hitting him low in the right side of his back. As he stumbled forward onto his hands and knees, Hastein crashed into one of the remaining three warriors—the one standing on the left side of their short line— smashing shield against shield. The impact knocked the pirate off his feet. As he fell, Hastein dropped into a low crouch and swung his sword in a downward cut to his right, hitting the man beside him in the leg, severing it just below the knee. The third pirate turned toward

Hastein, but by now Torvald had reached the fight and lunged forward with the hewing spear, stabbing its long blade through the side of the man's neck, then wrenched the spear sideways and hurled him down.

Hastein raced on toward the stern, Torvald and our other warriors close behind him. One—it was Gudfred, from the estate—paused by the man Hastein had knocked down and hacked at him with his sword.

The pirate captain was shouting now and pointing toward the front of the ship, trying to warn the men at the oars of their danger. Tore and I both launched arrows at him but he swung his shield up and blocked them. Einar drew and fired and hit one of the rowers in the back, as he was just turning his head to look over his shoulder. He fell sideways off his sea chest. I pulled another arrow from my quiver, nocked and drew it, and hit the man rowing in front of him.

Then Hastein and the rest of our men reached the stern. The remaining six rowers were quickly overwhelmed, cut down as they tried to draw their weapons or pull their shields from the racks along the ship's rail. The pirate ship's captain and the warrior at his side attempted to fight, but too many weapons were hacking and stabbing at them to be able to block them all. Within moments they, too, lay dead upon the deck, bleeding from numerous wounds.

Beside me, Tore gave a loud whoop. "We have cleared her," he shouted. "She is ours."

While Gudfred and several others of our men began methodically checking the fallen pirates, finishing off any that still lived, Hastein and Torvald trotted back to where Tore and I were standing. Stig, who by now had climbed across to the pirate ship, too, met them there.

"Well done," he said, grinning broadly. "Well fought."

Still panting from the exertion of the fast-moving fight, Hastein bent over for a few moments, his hands braced on his thighs, and drew in several deep breaths. He was splattered with blood, but none of it was his.

"It is a beginning," he said, straightening up. "We must not waste the advantage we have gained. Tore, Halfdan, gather your archers. From the stern of this ship you should have a clear line of fire at the warriors fighting in the bow of the pirate chieftain's ship. If you can harry them hard enough from the rear, we may be able to cross the bows and drive them back. If we can get to their captain, Sigvald, and slay him, this battle will be ours. Hold your fire until my signal. I will blow a horn three times when we are ready."

Turning to Torvald and Stig, he told them, "Torvald, you and I will go to join our men on the *Gull*'s fore-deck. Stig, return to the *Serpent*. On my signal, we will all attack the bow of the pirate chieftain's ship from both of ours, while our archers here fire from behind on them. If we set some sea-chests on our fore-decks to step up on, we can cross over the rails more easily. Come—let us show these dogs how ships are taken."

The curved bow of the pirate ship we were on was now lashed tight with the two grappling lines against the side of the *Gull*'s hull, amidships opposite her mast. As a result, the hull of the pirate ship was angled out from the

213

Gull's side. Hastein had been correct. From the ship's stern we would have an unobstructed line of fire, shooting toward the bow of the pirate chieftain's ship, that would allow us to shoot into the back ranks of the warriors fighting there. But we would not be shooting at point blank range, as we had been when attacking this ship. It was unlikely our fire would be nearly as effective.

While Hastein, Torvald, Stig, and the five warriors who had crossed over from the *Serpent* returned to the *Gull*, Tore explained the plan to our men. The four who'd left their bows aboard the *Gull* went to retrieve them, and at my request brought me my shield and spear when they did. Then we all began the grim task of searching for and retrieving our arrows from the bodies of the men we'd shot. At least none were still alive. "Be quick about it," Tore warned. "We must be ready when Hastein signals."

I was standing over the body of the first warrior I had killed in our close volley—the man with the plaited beard—when Einar approached. My arrow had entered the man's face below his right eye, and its iron head plus a finger's length of the shaft were now jutting out the back of his skull. I gave the shaft a tug, but the bone it had pierced was holding it tight. That was the problem with shooting for the head: a hit was almost always a kill, but reclaiming your arrows unbroken was difficult.

"Look," Einar said, pointing. "That ship is moving."

What he said was true. The crew of the fourth pirate ship, the one that had been lying off the sterns of the *Gull* and *Serpent*, had manned their oars. But they were seated facing toward the front of their ship, rather than the rear. They were backing her up, slowly moving her over toward the side of the *Gull* we were on.

Tore, Gudfred, and several others of our archers joined us. "They are going to come for us," Einar said. "They are going to try to retake this ship."

I heard a dull *whump*. A warrior named Storolf, one of Hastein's housecarls who had been with us in Frankia, was standing beside Tore. He gasped, then gave a choking cough. As he sank to his knees, blood began to trickle from the edge of his mouth. An arrow was sticking out of his back.

I dropped into a low crouch, pulling Einar down beside me as I did. Another arrow whistled through the air over our heads. It had been shot from somewhere on the pirate chieftain's ship. As the rest of our archers ducked low and ran for the cover of the ship's side, three long peals of a horn sounded from the front of the *Gull*.

"The attack is starting," Tore cried. "Up! Up! We must support them." He stood and was laying an arrow across his bow when an arrow skimmed just above the edge of the ship's top strake and smacked into the quiver hanging at his right hip, piercing its thick leather and the skirt of his mail brynie beneath. Tore roared in pain and dropped his bow, clutching with both hands at the arrow now embedded in his hip.

I reached up and pulled him down, just as another arrow whistled through the air overhead. "Gods," Tore said. "That one would have killed me. Whoever is shooting that bow is very good."

215

"How badly are you hurt?" I asked.

"I cannot tell. Help me. My quiver is pinned to me by this shaft."

I grasped the shaft of the arrow with both hands, just above where it pierced Tore's quiver. He nodded, and I snapped the shaft in two between my hands. Tore gasped in pain as the arrow moved.

I eased the quiver up over the broken stub of the wooden shaft. Inside it, several arrows had been broken by the missile cutting through them. I slid the skirt of the mail brynie, and the padded jerkin underneath it, over the end of the broken shaft, too.

Beside me, Einar, who was peering cautiously over the edge of the rail, said, "I see him. He is hiding behind the mast. And he has a shield bearer who protects him when he steps out to shoot." He laid an arrow across his bow and nocked it on the string, then stood, drawing as he did. He held at full draw for a brief moment then released, dropping back down below the cover of the ship's side as soon as he did. An arrow sliced through the air where he had been standing.

"I missed him. Gods but he is fast. Very fast, and very good."

"We must support Hastein," Tore said through gritted teeth.

"We will have to kill this man first, or very shortly the jarl will have no archers," Einar replied.

Blood had soaked the bottom of Tore's tunic and his trousers around where the arrow was embedded in the side of his hip. But I could see, showing above the edges of the wound, the end of the iron socket of the arrowhead where it encased the tip of the wooden shaft. At least the head had not pierced too deeply. Striking the quiver and brynie must have broken its force somewhat.

"I will deal with this," Tore said. He drew his knife from its scabbard on his belt and began slitting the fabric of his tunic and trousers, cutting them away from the arrow to expose the wound. "You must take charge of our archers."

I raised my head just enough to peer over the edge of the top strake. In the bow of the pirate chieftain's ship, warriors were pressing forward in response to Hastein's attack. Beyond them, in the bow of the *Gull*, I could see two warriors battering at the pirates' front rank with long-handled great-axes, while around them others jabbed with spears, trying to push the defenders back. So far our men had not managed to cross over the rails and board the enemy ship. Glancing back along the pirate ship, I could see a man behind its mast, his head leaning out on the right side as he watched for a target to appear. Another man was crouching low beside him, holding a shield in front of his own chest.

Again three horn blasts sounded.

"Jarl Hastein needs us," Tore said. "Do not fail him."

Along the side of the ship, our archers were crouched below the cover of the rail, watching me.

"Spread out," I cried. "The man who is shooting at us is very dangerous. He is shooting from behind the pirate ship's mast. Four of us—Einar, Asbjorn, Gudfred, and I—will shoot at him. The rest of you, shoot at the pirates fighting in the bow. We must weaken their defense. On my word, we will all stand and shoot at once, then take cover again."

I drew an arrow and nocked it on my string. When the others were ready, I shouted, "Now!" and stood, drawing my bow as I did.

As Einar had said, the enemy archer was very quick and very good. As soon as he saw our archers beginning to rise up, he stepped just to the side of the mast while drawing his bow. The shield bearer rose beside him, standing close and ready.

I shoot my bow quickly, not lingering over my aim, but by the time I released my bowstring, the enemy archer's arrow was already launched and on its way. It sped across the open water between the two ships and hit one of our archers standing further down the side, a man from the *Serpent*'s crew whose face was familiar but whose name I did not know. The arrow struck him in the shoulder and spun him around. One of his comrades pulled him down into cover behind the ship's side.

Of the four arrows we'd launched at the enemy archer, three were caught by the shield bearer, who stepped forward as soon as his man shot and held his shield in front of him, blocking the arrows that should have struck him. The fourth arrow thudded into the mast.

We were now down to ten archers. We had to support Hastein's attack, but we could not afford to keep losing men at this rate. I glanced back to see where the fourth pirate ship was. It had backed fully clear of the *Gull*'s stern and had swung around so its bow was pointed toward the ship we were on. Its rowers had

218

turned so they were facing their ship's stern, and were heaving on their oars. Slowly but steadily, the ship was heading for us.

I turned back and cautiously raised my head to look over the top of the ship's rail. The pirate archer must have seen me do the same before, because he was ready this time, his bow already at full draw, and he launched an arrow at my face. Quickly I jerked my head back down, and the arrow sailed overhead and thudded into the ship's far side.

Our archers had been watching me, arrows ready on their bows, waiting for my next command. When they saw the arrow pass over me, Asbjorn and Hallbjorn rose up and launched quick shots toward the warriors in the pirate ship's bow, then dropped back down into cover.

The fourth pirate ship was picking up speed and drawing near. She was a small ship, with only ten pairs of oars. In her bow, I could see two men standing holding coiled ropes and grappling irons.

We were trapped unless we could kill the pirate archer.

Beside me, Tore had pulled the arrow out of his hip, and was now holding a wad of cloth he'd cut from the bottom of his tunic against the wound, trying to staunch the flow of blood from it. "Very soon now, this is going to be a bad place for us to be," he said, through gritted teeth.

My shield was lying nearby, where I'd laid it beside my spear. I picked it up and slid it down the deck to Hallbjorn.

"I need you to draw the enemy's fire," I told him. "At my signal, stand up with your bow visible in your left hand, as if you are looking for a target in the front of the pirate ship. But hold my shield in your right, out of sight below the rail, and be ready to swing it up to cover yourself. Be careful—he will shoot very quickly. As soon as you see him release, shout 'now' so we will know."

Turning to Asbjorn and Gudfred, I told them, "You two and Einar must be ready, and when Hallbjorn tells us the enemy has shot, rise up and launch your arrows at his shield bearer. Kill him, or at least make him protect himself. I will rise with you, and hope for a shot at the archer."

Behind us, I heard a *thunk, thunk,* as the two grappling hooks landed on our deck.

"Look," Einar said. "It is Hrodgar. He is coming to help us."

But there was no time to look. I nodded to Hallbjorn. "Go!" I cried.

He stood, and a moment later, began to swing the shield up. "Now!" he shouted.

The four of us—Gudfred, Asbjorn, Einar, and I—rose up from behind the rail, drawing our bows back as we did. The thumb on my right hand brushed against the side of my jaw and touched the bottom my ear as I reached full draw. On the pirate chieftain's ship, the shield bearer was beginning to step forward as the archer stood staring out across his bow, watching his arrow's flight.

From the corner of my eye, I saw a flash as the enemy's arrow streaked over our ship's side and smacked into the shield Hallbjorn was holding. At the same time, I heard two *twangs* off to my side as Asbjorn and Gudfred released their arrows. A moment later Einar released his. I forced myself to focus my gaze on the archer, to focus my aim on where I knew his chest was, even though it was now hidden behind the shield.

The three arrows arced across the water and struck. One hit the shield low, near its bottom rim, and the second skimmed below it, grazing the shield bearer's thigh. The third arrow—Einar's—clanged into his helm and glanced off. Startled, the man staggered back a step and swung his shield up to cover his face. As he did, I opened the curled fingers of my right hand, releasing the bowstring and my arrow.

My arrow's flight, arcing across the water between the two ships, seemed to take forever. I feared the enemy archer would realize his danger and duck behind the mast. But he turned to glance at his comrade, perhaps to see if he had been wounded. It was just long enough. My arrow struck, and he went down.

I drew another arrow from my quiver, glancing back at the danger behind us as I did. Warriors from the fourth pirate ship were already boarding us, but as Einar had said, Hrodgar had brought our men from the *Gull's* stern to defend against them. Men were stabbing and hacking at each other in a confused, swirling melee along the ship's side where the two pirate ships were grappled and lashed together, and several were already down, their bodies on the deck beneath the feet of those fighting.

A third time, Hastein sounded the signal on his

horn.

Turning back to our archers, I pointed toward the bow of the pirate chieftain's ship. It did not look as though any of the warriors from the *Gull* had yet managed to beat back the defenders and board. "Rise up!" I cried, "Jarl Hastein needs us to support his attack."

They stood and readied arrows on their bows. Gudfred began to draw.

"No," I said. "We will all draw and shoot as one, on my command. We will rain our arrows upon them in volleys, like death falling from the sky.

"Draw!" I ordered. "Choose your targets. Loose! Draw...Loose! Draw...Loose!"

Five times we launched our arrows as one. The fore-deck and bow area of a longship is not so large a place. Fifty arrows, raining down among men crowded tightly into such a space are a fearsome thing to experience.

After our fourth volley, I saw Torvald rise behind the front rank of warriors in the bow of the *Gull*, holding a barrel up over his head in both hands. He heaved it onto the enemy warriors crowded on the fore-deck of the pirate ship, crushing several beneath it and scattering the rest, just as our fifth volley landed among them. Warriors from the *Gull* and *Serpent* scrambled over the bow rails of their ships onto the pirate ship's bow and fell upon the suddenly disarrayed defenders there, stabbing and hacking.

We could no longer shoot without endangering our own men. Dropping my bow and quiver upon the deck,

I retrieved my shield and spear and turned to face the growing danger upon the ship we were on.

On the edge of the fight, I spotted Bram, the young man from the village, backing away from a pirate who was swinging his sword back and forth with rapid cross strokes, each one chopping a piece out of the top edge of Bram's raised shield. I ran toward them and as I drew near, hurled my spear. I missed—in truth, I have little skill throwing a spear—but when the spear flashed past him the pirate looked to see who had thrown it and saw me running toward him, drawing my sword as I came.

He swung a final slashing cut at Bram then turned to face me. I raised my shield and drew back my sword to strike, but when I tried to slow my speed and plant my feet, they landed in a large pool of blood and slipped out from under me.

I landed hard, flat on my back. As the pirate lunged forward and chopped down at me, I frantically swung my shield across my body to cover it and blocked his blade. Behind him, Bram moved forward and stabbed his spear at the pirate's back. Snarling, he spun around, swatting at the spear shaft with his blade and knocking it aside. As he did, I rose up into a sitting position and swung my sword from right to left in a slashing cut that hit the pirate's back leg just below the knee. My blow did not have enough force to cut through the bone, but the wound caused the pirate to topple sideways onto the deck. I crawled onto his chest and stabbed my blade into his throat.

As I was rising to my feet, someone—I did not see who—struck a blow that rang hard against my helm and momentarily stunned me, dropping me down onto my hands and knees. As my senses cleared, I realized I was straddling a body. It was Hrodgar. There was an arrow in his back—it must have been one of the last ones shot by the archer on the pirate chieftain's ship—and his neck had a gaping wound that had almost severed his head from his body. His eyes were open, and his once-white beard was now stained red. His body was surrounded by a large, spreading pool of blood—the blood that I had slipped in.

I felt a wave of rage wash over me. In truth, I do not know exactly what happened after that. The next thing I knew, I was in the stern of the fourth pirate ship, standing over a man's body, swinging my sword down into it, over and over.

Someone grabbed my shoulder. I turned on him, raising my sword to strike, but another man reached from my other side and grabbed my sword arm.

The first man spoke. It was Gudfred. "It is enough. He is dead," he said.

The man holding my sword arm was Einar. "They are all dead," he told me. "We have cleared the ship. It is ours."

9

Oeland

Though the tide had turned in our favor, the battle was far from won. We had cleared two of the pirates' ships, and aboard the ship of their chieftain our warriors, led by Hastein and Torvald, had pushed its defenders down the length of the hull as far as the mast.

I shook my head, trying to clear my mind of the red killing rage that seemed to have clouded it, and looked around me. The bodies of fallen warriors were strewn along the pirate ship's deck from its bow to its stern. We had driven them off the ship we had been on and had followed them onto theirs, fighting a running battle back to the stern, where the last of them had died. I had no recollection of any of it. It troubled me.

Our warriors—the ten remaining archers, all of whom had survived the fight, plus another ten or so men from the crews of the *Gull* and *Serpent* who had come across with Hrodgar—stood gathered around in the stern, staring at me, watching me, as if awaiting orders.

"How many men did we lose?" I asked.

Gudfred answered. "Four dead. Skuli and Kari from the village, old Hrodgar from the Limfjord, and one of our own men—Grimar. All fell during the first of the fighting, on the other ship. We lost none after we pushed them back onto this one."

For a moment my mind struggled to understand what Gudfred had meant when he'd called the man

Grimar one of "our "men. They were all our men, all from the crew of the *Gull*. Then I recognized the name, and realized that Grimar had been one of my father's and brother's men, one of the housecarls from the estate.

"We should go," Einar murmured quietly, so the others could not hear.

He was right. The fight was not over. "Archers," I said. "Retrieve your bows. The rest of you, come with us. There are enemies yet to kill."

We trotted the length of the cleared pirate ship back to its bow and climbed over the rail onto the deck of the first ship we'd captured, the one which was now lashed tight against the hull of the *Gull*. I stopped when I reached Hrodgar's body, where it lay in the pool of his own blood. Einar came up behind me.

"He was a good man. I shall miss him," he said, then added, "It was here that we broke them. It was you that did so, you know."

I looked at him and frowned. Gudfred paused beside us and nodded his head. "Aye," he agreed. "It is true."

"From across the ship I saw you down on your hands and knees on the deck, here by Hrodgar's body," Einar continued. "I thought you were wounded, and was running to help you, for two pirates were closing in. But suddenly you were up on your feet, and had stuck the blade of your sword through the neck of that one." He pointed to the nearby body of a warrior sprawled on his back, his throat ripped open. "Then, almost quicker than I could see, you whipped your blade sideways and cut clean through this other one's neck." He pointed at

226

another body, this one headless. Einar grinned. "I think it was the sight of his head sailing through the air that unnerved the rest, for the pirates closest to you backed away as fast as they could, and they all broke when the rest of us pressed forward against them."

Gudfred turned his head to the side and spit upon the deck in disgust. "It is always a bad idea to turn and run," he said. "Many of their slain have their death-wounds in their backs. It is a poor way to die."

I stared at them blankly. Einar squinted and studied my face. "You do not remember it, do you?" He and Gudfred exchanged quick glances.

I did not answer. "We must not tarry here," I said, and trotted away to where I had left my bow and quiver. Tore was still there, leaning back against the side of the ship, his eyes closed. His breathing was so shallow that for a moment I feared he was dead. When he heard me approach he opened his eyes and looked around, seeming confused.

"How goes the battle?" he asked. He was very pale, and the leg of his trousers was soaked with blood.

"Help me lift him," I said, turning to Einar. "We must take him to the *Gull*, to Cullain. Perhaps he can stop the bleeding."

Tore groaned as Einar and I pulled him up and draped his arms across our shoulders. "Do not leave my bow," he panted.

Gudfred bent down and picked up Tore's and my bows and quivers. "I will bring these," he said.

"Get Storolf's quiver, too," I told him. "Divide his and Tore's arrows among the archers."

Aboard the *Gull*, the wounded who were strong enough to walk or crawl away from the fighting had gathered aft of the mast, and were seated or lying on the deck there. Cullain was moving among them, checking and binding their wounds. He was helping the archer from the *Serpent* who had been hit in the shoulder with an arrow remove his tunic when Einar and I arrived with Tore. He was no longer even trying to walk between us—his feet were dragging across the deck, the right one leaving a trail of blood behind it.

Seeing him, Cullain hurried over. "Where is he wounded?" he asked.

"In his hip. It was an arrow."

After we laid Tore on his back on the deck, I straightened up and took my bow and quiver from Gudfred. "We must go," I told Cullain, who was removing the makeshift bandage Tore had tried to staunch the bleeding with. The strips of cloth were so soaked that blood was dripping from them onto the deck. "Can you save him?"

"His life is in God's hands, but I will do what I can."

The battle was now being fought primarily on the wolf-headed longship of the pirate captain, Sigvald. Its bow was still wedged between and lashed to the bows of both the *Gull* and the *Serpent*, and the sounds of fighting—men shouting, cursing, sometimes screaming in pain, and the clash of weapons striking shields and helms—carried from it back onto the deck of the *Gull*, where I paused just forward of her mast to survey the scene. The front half of the *Gull* was completely deserted—all of her crew, save Cullain, the wounded, and the warriors who were with me, had boarded Sigvald's ship with Hastein.

Most of the *Serpent*'s crew, including Stig, had also joined the boarding party, climbing from the right side of the *Serpent*'s prow onto the pirate vessel, though a handful of men still manned the *Serpent*'s fore-deck to guard it against attack from the pirates' other longship, which had grappled the left side of the *Serpent*'s prow early in the battle and was still lashed bow to bow with her. The pirates aboard it had also grappled and tied their ship side by side with Sigvald's, and most of them had by now joined in the battle to repel Hastein and his men. Some had crossed over to Sigvald's ship to fight with his men, while others lined their own ship's side and launched missile fire at Hastein's flank. Seeing that most of the *Serpent*'s warriors had boarded Sigvald's ship, the pirates had left only a few men on their ship's fore-deck to guard against any attempt to board from the *Serpent*.

As I studied the scene before me, I realized with a shock that the gilded dragon's head mounted on the stem post in the bow of the last pirate ship was carved in the likeness of the head of a fighting horse. It was the *Sea Steed*—the ship Snorre had captained in Frankia, and one of the two ships Toke had fled from Jutland with.

Einar and Gudfred were standing beside me, with the rest of our archers and the men whom Hrodgar had led gathered close behind.

"Look," I said to Gudfred, and pointed at the pirate ship. "It is the *Sea Steed*."

He stared at it for a few moments, frowning, then grunted. "Hunh. So it is."

"What are your orders?" Einar asked. It was strange to hear those words coming from him. We were comrades. I considered us equals.

How could we best help Hastein? Our small force was the only reserve of warriors on either side that was not already committed to the battle.

"We will clear the fore-deck of that ship," I said, pointing at the *Sea Steed*. "Einar, Asbjorn, Hallbjorn—you come with me. Gudfred, take the rest of the men to the *Serpent*'s fore-deck. I want you, with Stig's men who are already there, to cross the bows and board her."

"And you?" Gudfred asked.

"When you begin your attack, the three of us will shoot them from behind."

Only six pirates had been left to guard the bow of the *Sea Steed*. When they saw Gudfred and the warriors with him clamber from the *Gull* onto the *Serpent* and race toward them, they cried out in alarm to their comrades farther down their ship, calling for help, then raised their shields and spears and pressed forward to stand against the bow rail, to try and fend off the attackers' attempts to climb across onto their ship.

The fore-deck of Sigvald's ship was deserted like that of the *Gull*, save for the bodies of those killed during Hastein's attack, for the fight had by now moved further down the hull. Einar, Asbjorn, Hallbjorn, and I climbed from the bow of the *Gull* over the butted rails of the two ships, dropped down onto the deck of the pirate vessel, and moved down along it until we had a clear line of fire at the bow of the *Sea Steed*.

The six pirates desperately trying to defend the *Sea Steed*'s bow from being boarded by Gudfred's much larger force were little more than the length of a spear shaft away from where we stood. I nocked an arrow, drew it, and shot it into the back of the head of one of them. Shooting beside me, Einar, Asbjorn, and Hallbjorn each killed a man, too. At such short range, it would have been difficult to miss. One of the two remaining pirates swung around to face the new danger. A spear thrust by one of Gudfred's men from the fore-deck of the *Serpent* pierced his back. The last man tried to flee, but Einar and I each put an arrow into him and brought him down.

As Gudfred and the warriors with him began climbing across the bow rails onto the fore-deck of the *Sea Steed*, the rest of the pirates aboard her who had been lining her left rail, firing on Hastein and his men, cried warnings to each other and hurriedly swung around to form a line across their ship's deck. There were only ten of them. The rest of her crew—besides the six we had just killed—must have crossed over to Sigvald's ship.

"For once in this fight the odds favor us," Einar said. Including the members of the *Serpent*'s crew who had been guarding her fore-deck, our warriors who were now boarding the *Sea Steed*'s bow numbered twenty-one.

A warrior in the center of the pirates' shield wall, a big man almost a full head taller than his fellows, was exhorting his comrades to close up and tighten their line. His attention was solely on Gudfred and his men—he was unaware that four enemy archers were standing in the bow of Sigvald's ship, alongside. I nocked another arrow, drew, and fired. My arrow hit him in his left eye. The odds were even better now.

"Gudfred!" I cried. "Line your archers across the fore-deck, and the rest of your men on the main deck in front of them in a shield wall, to protect them. We will all shoot together, on my command."

It is a hard thing to stand and watch a man, not thirty paces away, draw a bow and aim it at you. It takes much courage to keep watching until the arrow is released, and great quickness to evade or block the shot. It is far, far worse when there are ten men shooting at you from two different directions.

Our first volley felled three men. Our second, four more. Then our shield wall charged and cut down the rest, and the ship was ours. Our men aboard the *Sea Steed* standing over their enemies' bodies waved their bloody weapons overhead and let out a ragged cheer.

On the pirate chieftain's ship, the main battle was still being fought amidships. The pirates had arrayed their shield wall in a wedge rather than a straight line. Its peak was held by Sigvald and two other men, one on either side of him, each of whom was armed with shield and spear. Behind them the line slanted back on either side until it reached the ship's sides. The remainder of the pirates were massed inside the wedge, ready to step forward and take the place of any warrior who fell.

Sigvald was armored, in addition to his helm, in a brynie with long sleeves that came to his wrists, and a skirt that reached below his knees. I had never seen such a mail shirt—it left little exposed on him to strike at. He had slung his shield across his back, and was using both hands to wield a weapon that was also unlike anything I had seen before—a long-handled axe with a spear point for stabbing mounted above its blade on the end of the shaft. He was using it to both strike with and to parry blows aimed at him. His position at the peak of the wedge meant he faced the brunt of our shield wall's attacks, but also allowed him to swing great blows with his weapon. The bodies of four of our warriors, crumpled on the deck in front of him, attested to his ferocity and skill.

Hastein and Torvald opposed him in the center of our line. Their shields were badly hacked and looked as though they'd taken several hard blows from Sigvald's weapon. When the cheer by our warriors rang out from the deck of the *Sea Steed*, Hastein glanced quickly in that direction, then cried out, "Fall back! With me—fall back."

As our shield wall disengaged from the pirates and slowly backed away from them, on the *Sea Steed* Gudfred arrayed his men along that ship's left side. He and the five archers with him lined up opposite the right side of the pirates' wedge formation, two warriors with shields and spears guarding each archer, and began to launch arrows into the pirates' ranks at point blank range, steadily drawing and firing.

By now our shield wall aboard Sigvald's ship had pulled back far enough from the pirates' line to be safe from anything except a thrown weapon. At Hastein's command, they stopped and stood facing the pirates' wedge, their line bristling with spears held at the ready.

233

Hastein switched his spear to his left hand, holding it together with the handle of his shield, raised his horn to his lips and blew one long peal upon it. At the sound, the warriors aboard the *Sea Steed* turned and looked in his direction. "Hold your fire!" he cried to them. "Hold your fire!"

Torvald, who because of his height could see above the heads of our warriors crowded in the back ranks of our shield wall, glanced behind him toward the pirate ship's bow. Spotting me and the three archers standing beside me back on the fore-deck, he leaned down and spoke to Hastein, then waved his arm, signaling us to come forward.

When I pushed through our men and reached him, Hastein asked, "Where is Tore? I do not see him aboard that other ship."

"He was hit by an arrow."

"Is he dead?"

I shook my head. "He still lived when I left him with Cullain. But he is in a bad way. And Hrodgar is dead."

Hastein shook his head. "Stig is down, too. He fell when we were crossing over the bow rails. I do not know if he still lives."

Stig had fallen? I must have passed his body in the bow. I had not bothered to look closely at the dead there.

"Who commands those warriors aboard that ship?" Hastein asked.

"Gudfred. He was one of my brother Harald's men."

"Hunh," Hastein said. "Clearing that ship was well

done. He must be a good man. What of the fourth ship?"

"It has been cleared as well," I answered.

He turned and stared at the pirates' line. They were staring back, but for now showed no inclination to attack.

"They have lost their stomach for this fight," Torvald said. At some point during the battle he had armed himself with a long-handled war axe. The edge of its big, curved blade was wet with blood. "Let us finish them now."

"We are closely matched in numbers," Hastein said. "And now it is they who must fight on more than one front. But I would end this without losing any more of our men. Halfdan, you and Einar come here, and stand beside me on my right. Asbjorn, Hallbjorn, on my left. Ready your bows. On my signal, shoot together. Kill their leader."

I nocked an arrow and held my bow at ready down in front of me, my bow arm flexed, the first three fingers of my right hand curled around the string, ready to draw. Beside me, Einar did the same.

In a loud voice that carried the length of the ship, Hastein called out, "Put down your weapons and surrender. You cannot win. You are surrounded. Your other ships have all been cleared. All of your comrades aboard them are dead. Put down your weapons, and we will let you live."

Sigvald raised his weapon over his head, brandishing it with both hands, and roared, "We will never...."

"Kill him!" Hastein shouted.

Einar and I swung our bows up together, drawing them as we did. Asbjorn and Hallbjorn did the same. I was staring at Sigvald's eyes, at his right eye, and saw it widen in fear and surprise. At such close range, he had no time to try to escape his doom. All four of our arrows slammed into his face, snapping his head back, and he flopped down onto the deck.

"Like shooting cabbages," Einar said. "Eh, Halfdan?" I remembered that Tore had said the same to me, early in the battle. I wondered if he still lived.

"Put down your weapons," Hastein cried again. "Surrender, and I give you my word, my men will not kill you."

One of the two warriors who had been standing beside Sigvald glanced down at his captain's lifeless body, then slowly bent down and laid his spear and shield upon the deck. Behind him, others began to do the same.

Over the course of the battle, the wind, which had been blowing from the north all day, had gradually pushed our ungainly raft of lashed-together ships toward Oeland's shore. By the time we'd finished disarming the pirates who surrendered—there were more than a score of them—we had drifted close enough to the island to be able to see that its beach was rocky.

"We need to free the *Gull* and *Serpent* from these ships and from each other," Torvald warned Hastein. "We must be able to steer if we are to keep them clear of the rocks."

Hastein stared at the shore, as if trying to gauge

how much time we had before the ships were blown against it.

"We will cut away all but this ship—their captain's ship," he finally said. "It is the finest of them, and the richest prize. I do not like letting the others go, but you are right—we have no time to try and save them all. We must send men to each of the other ships to retrieve any of our dead or wounded who are aboard them. And they should quickly search each ship, and take all weapons and anything else of value they find on board before they cut them loose." He glanced around, scanning the faces of the men nearby, then spoke to the two brothers called the Ravens, who had been listening. "Bjorgolf, Bryngolf, take five men each and do this quickly. As soon as you have searched each ship, cut it loose and push it off from us."

Turning to Torvald, he said, "I will need you to take command of the *Serpent*. Once they are done and we separate our two ships, we will head back down the channel, and look for a safe anchorage along the mainland shore."

"What of the prisoners?" Torvald asked.

"We will leave them aboard this ship, under guard, and tow it behind us. Halfdan," he said, turning to me, "you will stay aboard here, and keep watch over the prisoners. Pick four men to stay with you. You will be greatly outnumbered. If any of the prisoners disobeys any order you give, kill him immediately. Do not let them become tempted to try to overcome you and regain their freedom."

I selected Einar, Gudfred, and Hallbjorn to assist

me. I was intending to ask Asbjorn, too—I thought it would be a good idea if all of the guards were archers, as we could kill the prisoners from a distance if they should try to rise against us—but Bram, from the village, asked if he could help, so he became our fifth man.

After Bjorgolf and Bryngolf had departed with the men they'd picked to help them, the rest of us set about completing the task of securing the pirate chieftain's ship. The greatest numbers of our own dead and wounded were aboard it, for it was here that the fiercest of the close fighting had occurred. A search of the bodies scattered across its deck revealed that seven of our warriors had died during the fighting after the boarding of her—three from the *Gull*'s crew and four from the *Serpent*—and seven more had been badly wounded. Stig, to Hastein's relief, was among the latter. Though badly hurt, he still lived.

"It was their captain, Sigvald, who cut Stig down," Hastein told me, after we found him among the dead and wounded on the fore-deck. "Whatever else he may have been, the pirate was a doughty warrior. Stig had just climbed across the rail from the *Serpent*'s bow and dropped down onto the fore-deck. The pirates there had been scattered when Torvald threw the barrel among them, and we were crossing the rails as quickly as we could from both the *Gull* and the *Serpent* to press our advantage before they recovered. Sigvald charged forward, pushing through his men who were either down or falling back, to face us. I saw Stig thrust his spear at him to fend him off while he tried to find solid footing on the deck. Sigvald swung that strange axe-spear he wielded, knocking Stig's spear aside, then he chopped its blade down against his wrist, and drove its point forward through Stig's brynie and into his chest."

The wound to Stig's chest was high enough to have missed his heart and lungs. If the bleeding could be stopped and if no fever set in, he could possibly survive it. His wrist was shattered and cut half through, though. At best, he would surely lose his hand. And he had lost much blood—possibly too much. As gently as they could, Hastein and Torvald lifted him up off the deck and carried him to the bow rail, where they passed his unconscious body across into the arms of warriors waiting on the *Gull*'s fore-deck to receive our dead and wounded. Stig's head flopped back and forth limply as they did, and his face looked as pale as winter ice. I wondered if he would live out the day.

After all of our dead and wounded had been recovered, Hastein, Torvald, and the others returned to the *Gull* and the *Serpent*. By now we had bound the hands and feet of the prisoners and had lined them up sitting against the side rails of their ship, amidships, half on one side and half on the other. I set Hallbjorn to watch over them, standing in the center of the ship, an arrow nocked and ready on his bow.

I sent Bram to the bow, to secure the tow lines that were being passed aboard from the *Gull* and *Serpent*, then Einar, Gudfred, and I began the grim task of checking the bodies of the fallen pirates and killing any who still lived. As it was, we would be hard pressed to adequately care for our own wounded. We had neither the means nor the desire to also care for those of our attackers who had been badly hurt in the battle.

As we moved from body to body down the deck, I took the opportunity to search for undamaged arrows that could be retrieved. Ones that had failed to find a target and had stuck in the ship's side rails or deck were easy to recover. Those that had found their marks required more effort.

The last body I checked was lying on its side, near the base of the mast. One of my own arrows had pierced its chest. A sturdy looking longbow lay on the deck near the body. I realized that this must be the pirate's archer whose arrows had taken such a toll, felling Hrodgar, Tore, and the others.

Grabbing the body by one shoulder, I rolled it onto its back. In my mind I had pictured so deadly a foe to be a large, powerful warrior, but the archer had been a short man with a lean, wiry build. He wore neither helm nor armor. His head was topped with thick black hair, streaked with gray, cut fairly short so that it framed his face but did not hang as low as his shoulders. His close-trimmed beard was thin and wispy, and his darkly tanned face was seamed with wrinkles. He was wearing a tunic unlike any I had ever seen before: it was made of supple, tanned leather that looked to be deerskin, and had a high collar around his neck that was trimmed with fur. Besides a long knife in a scabbard on his belt, he had no weapon other than the bow that lay beside him.

I bent down and with my right hand grabbed the shaft of my arrow down low, close to the body, intending to pull it out. With luck, it would not be stuck in bone or sinew, and I would not have to cut the wound wider to free it. When I began to pull, the man gasped and opened his eyes. It startled me, and I jumped back.

He mumbled some words in a tongue I did not recognize and coughed several times. He winced when he did, and a trickle of blood leaked from one corner of his mouth.

Hallbjorn, who had been standing nearby keeping watch over the prisoners, strode over and looked down at the dying archer. "This is the one who killed Storolf, and wounded Tore? Hunh—he is a Finn."

"A what?" I asked.

"A Finn. One of the forest people. They live deep in the wilds of the lands of the Sveas and the Norse. They usually keep to themselves and do not venture away from their own lands. I wonder how he came to be one of these pirates."

The man seemed more fully awake now. He looked at the bow Hallbjorn was holding, with an arrow nocked and ready across it, then at my bow, which was in my left hand, down by my side. With much effort, he raised his right hand to his chest and tapped the arrow shaft protruding from it.

"Whose?" he asked, this time speaking in the common tongue of the north. His voice was weak, scarcely louder than a whisper, and he had a heavy accent that caused me to struggle for a moment to understand what he had said. When I did, I answered, "The arrow?"

He nodded. "It is mine," I told him.

His eyes closed. I thought—in truth, I hoped—that he had died. Killing men in battle was one thing. It did

241

not bother me, for if I did not kill them, they would do their best to kill me. But I did not like to kill the wounded. Sometimes it had to be done, but it troubled me to cut a man's throat while he lay helpless, staring into my eyes. I needed my arrow, though. A bow without arrows is just a crooked stick with a string on it.

After a few moments, the Finn opened his eyes again. "It was…good shot," he whispered.

By now Einar and Gudfred had gathered round, too. "Shall I finish him?" Gudfred asked. He was holding his sword unsheathed in his right hand. Its point was red with blood.

The archer tried to raise his hand again, but no longer had the strength. As he stared into my eyes, he crooked his finger, motioning me to come close. "Please," he whispered.

I was going to ignore him. I thought he was just begging for his life. But he inched his hand jerkily up across his chest to his neck, and began tugging at a leather cord around it. "Please," he said again, and looked at me imploringly.

I knelt beside him, reached inside the high collar of his tunic, and pulled out a small leather bag that was suspended from the cord.

"Give to my daughter," he said. Glancing over to where his bow lay on the deck, he added, "My bow I give to you."

I did not know how this man—a stranger and an enemy—expected I would find his daughter, or even if I could, that I would be willing to. I did not intend to try. And if I wanted his bow, I would take it, whether he offered it to me or not. But though an enemy, he had been greatly skilled. I respected that. "I will," I lied. It cost me nothing to give such small comfort to a dying man. I laid my bow down on the deck beside his, raised his head with my left hand, and slipped the cord bearing the small bag up over his head.

"Now?" Gudfred asked as I stood up.

Though I did not wish to cut his throat myself, this man had to die. He was an enemy, he had slain Hrodgar and Storolf, and had badly wounded Tore. I nodded. Gudfred rested his sword's point on the Finn's neck, its hilt grasped in his right fist, cupped his left hand over the pommel, and drove the blade downward. The Finn's body convulsed briefly as his blood welled up around the blade, then he kicked once and was still.

"What is in the bag?" Einar asked.

I shrugged. "I do not know."

"You should not have told him you would give it to his daughter," Gudfred said, scowling. "It is bad luck to break a promise made to a dying man. This voyage is already burdened with too much bad luck."

I did not consider the words I'd spoken to be a promise. I rolled the cord around the bag and tucked it into the pouch on my belt. I picked up my bow and the dead man's, and took his quiver, as well. I would decide later if I wished to keep them.

By now the Ravens and their men had finished with both of the pirate ships off the side of the *Gull*. The lines securing them to each other, and to the *Gull*'s hull, had been cast loose, and they had been pushed away from the side with oars. As Bjorgolf and Bryngolf led their men forward and climbed across the bows onto the fore-deck of the *Sea Steed*, Einar called to them.

"We killed many on that ship with our bows. Our arrows—will you retrieve them for us?"

Bryngolf nodded and waved his hand in assent.

I turned toward the prisoners and addressed them in a loud voice. "That ship there," I said, pointing at the *Sea Steed*. "How came your band to possess it?"

No one answered. The pirates stared back at me in sullen silence.

Gudfred strode down the line of prisoners seated along the steer-board side rail, staring intently into each man's face. Not finding whatever he was looking for, he crossed over to the other side, and continued his search. Midway down the line, he stopped in front of a man with a balding head and bushy brown beard.

"You," he said to the man seated before him. "I recognize you. You are one of Toke's men."

The man glared at him but did not answer. Gudfred glanced further down the line and pointed at a black-haired man seated two away from the first one. "And you are, also."

"You know these men?" I asked. Gudfred nodded. "That black-haired one is Toke's for certain. I know his face. He lived in the same longhouse as me for many months, while Toke was at the estate. And this one here," he said, indicating the bushy bearded man in front of him. "He went with the one-eyed man—Snorre—to Frankia. I did not know him nearly as well, but I recognize him."

I walked over and stood in front of the bald-headed

pirate. The man seated on the deck before me had been one of the warriors who had attacked the longhouse up on the Limfjord. He had helped kill Harald and the others. He had sailed with Snorre to Frankia, hoping to find and kill me there. And now he had joined these pirates, and had fought with them this day in a battle that had cost Hrodgar and too many others their lives.

"You were among the men who attacked the farm up on the Limfjord," I said. "I was there. My brother Harald was slain there. I swore an oath to kill Toke and all who helped him in that attack. I—unlike Toke—am not an oath breaker. But I will offer you this. Tell me how you became a part of this band. Tell me how these pirates came to have Toke's ship, the *Sea Steed*. Where is Toke now? What happened to him? What happened to my sister Sigrid? Tell me these things, and I promise I will kill you quickly, with as little pain as possible."

The man sneered up at me. "You will not kill me," he said. "You cannot. Your leader gave his word that we would not be harmed if we surrendered. But I will tell you what you wish to know if you free me—if you let me go."

What was it Hastein had said? *"Surrender, and I give you my word, my men will not kill you."*

"It strikes me," I told the man, "that you are in a poor position to bargain. It is true that the jarl promised that if you and these others surrendered, his men would not kill any of you. And I am one of Jarl Hastein's men. But there are many ways a man can die."

I turned to Einar and Gudfred. "He wishes to be set free. So be it."

Gudfred looked confused. To Einar I said, "Help me lift him." We grasped the man under his arms and hoisted him up onto the top strake of the ship's rail.

"What are you doing?" Gudfred asked. "What of the jarl's promise?"

"I am not going to kill this man," I answered. "I am going to release him, as he requested. I am not to blame if he cannot swim."

"Untie me!" the bald man sputtered. Einar grinned and nodded, and we flipped him over the side, into the sea. He coughed and shouted briefly, but it did not take him long to sink beneath its surface.

I stepped down the line to where the black-haired man was seated. He—and Gudfred—were staring at me in disbelief.

"And you," I said. "It would seem that because of the promise Jarl Hastein gave, I cannot kill you either, despite my own oath. But there are questions I would like you to answer. Will you tell me what I wish to know, or shall I set you free, as well?"

"I will tell you," he answered. "I will tell whatever you wish to know."

After completing their quick search for valuables aboard the *Sea Steed*, the Ravens and their men had climbed back across to the bow of the *Serpent*, released the grappling lines that had bound the two ships together, and were now using oars to push the ship away from the *Serpent*'s hull. The lines that had held Sigvald's wolf-headed ship lashed tight between the bows of the *Serpent* and the *Gull* had already been freed, and tow lines had been passed to us.

"Look," Einar said, pointing toward Oeland. "Up along the ridgeline, overlooking the shore."

I looked where he was pointing. A crowd of men and women—mostly on foot, but a few of the former were mounted on horses—lined the crest of the ridge, staring out at our ships. I wondered how long they had been watching. Had they been allies of the pirates? Were these folk, too, now our enemies?

Almost as if he had heard my thoughts, Einar murmured, "Are they friends or foes?"

Aboard the *Gull*, Hastein—who had mounted the stern deck and manned the steer-board—called out to the crew to draw their oars. Torvald, from the stern of the *Serpent*, did the same. Bjorgolf and Bryngolf led their men across from the *Serpent* onto the *Gull* where the two ships' rails were touching amidships and released the lines binding the ships together. After the rowers on both used their oars to push the ships apart, at Hastein's command the oarsmen aboard the *Gull* began backing her slowly while he pulled the steer-board over sharply. The ship gradually eased around until her stern was toward us and her bow pointing away, southward down the channel between Oeland and the mainland.

When the *Serpent* had done the same, the tow lines running back from each ship to Sigvald's were evened up, pulled snug, and tied off, and we at last were ready to get underway.

Pulling the dead weight of the towed pirate longship would be slow, heavy work for the rowers on the *Gull* and *Serpent*. Save for watching the prisoners and using our steer-board to keep the ship's bow headed straight, we aboard the captured ship had little to do. It was as good a time as any to hear Toke's man's tale, and learn what had befallen the *Sea Steed* and those who had sailed upon her.

Gudfred had gone astern to man the steer-board. Bram was in the bow, keeping an eye on the tow ropes, and Hallbjorn was still standing watch over the prisoners. Motioning for Einar to follow me, I walked over to where the black-haired man was seated on the deck, his back against the ship's rail. He watched us nervously as we approached.

"What is your name?" I asked him. On closer examination, I realized he was much younger than I had at first thought.

"Skjold," he answered.

"How long have you followed Toke?"

"Since he left."

I frowned, not understanding. "Left where?"

"When Hrorik banished Toke from his home, I left with him. I was from the village. I have been with him ever since."

When Hrorik had banished Toke. It seemed a lifetime ago. In truth, it had been less than three years. So much had happened since then. So much had changed, so many had died.

"Gudfred will want to hear this," I told Einar. "Help me lift him."

I had intended that we would grab the prisoner under his arms and drag him down the deck to the stern, but he quickly protested. "Untie my legs. Let me walk. I

248

give you my word that I will not try to escape. Where would I go?"

At the stern, we sat the black-haired man down on the edge of the raised rear deck and—despite the promise he had given—I tied his feet again. "You do not need to do that," he said. I stared at him coldly but did not answer. To Gudfred, I said, "His name is Skjold. He says he is from the village near the estate. He said he left with Toke when Hrorik banished him."

Gudfred stared at him for a time, then frowned, shook his head, and said, "I do not remember you. Who is your father?"

"Gorm."

Gudfred nodded. "I knew him." To me he said, "He was killed fighting the English on Hrorik's last raid." Turning back to Skjold, he asked, "Why did you leave your home? Why did you choose to leave with Toke, when Hrorik sent him away?"

Skjold shrugged. "I was the middle of five sons. My father's lands were not enough to provide a living for us all."

"The *Sea Steed*," I interrupted impatiently. "How did the pirates come to take her?"

"It was Toke's doing. We learned of the pirates when we passed Mon. A ship we met warned us of them. But we knew only that they were hunting the waters around Oeland. Toke did not think our company was strong enough to fight them—we have only enough men to lightly crew both ships—and he did not want to risk losing..." he glanced up at Gudfred, then at me. "He did not want to risk losing the woman."

"You mean Sigrid?" I asked. He nodded.

"Toke pulled most of the crew from the *Sea Steed* when we neared Oeland. He left only five men—just enough to sail her. I was one of them. Grimar—the man you drowned—was, too."

"Where are the other three?" Einar asked.

"They were killed in the fight with your company. They were among those slain aboard the *Sea Steed*."

"You said the *Sea Steed*'s capture was Toke's doing?" I asked.

Skjold nodded. "He told us to sail her up the channel between Oeland and the mainland. He said that if pirates were watching, they would give chase. While we drew them off, Toke would sail the *Red Eagle* past Oeland on the seaward side, out of sight of land. If there were no pirates, we were to meet along the coast, a day's sail past Oeland. If there were pirates...." He shrugged. "At least Toke and most of his men would pass safely by."

"It was a great risk for those of you who sailed on the *Sea Steed*," Gudfred said.

Skjold shrugged again. "Toke was our chieftain. The others—those who sail with him on the *Red Eagle*—were our comrades. A man who will not face risk to save his own comrades is not worthy to be called a man. And Toke promised he would reward us well, if we came through safely—if there were no pirates."

"But there were pirates," Einar said.

Skjold nodded. "Aye. There were pirates. Toke told us that if there were, and we could not outrun them, we should surrender the ship without a fight. He told us she

250

was not worth dying for."

"And that was what happened?" I asked. "The pirates pursued you, you surrendered the *Sea Steed* to them, and then you joined them?"

"I am surprised they did not just kill you," Gudfred said.

"It was a near thing at first," Skjold admitted. "But Toke had given us a plan. He told us we should ask to see the pirates' chieftain. He said we should tell him that we knew of a very valuable prize that would be coming his way soon. We were to offer to tell the chieftain all we knew of the prize, if he allowed us to join with his band and share in the taking of it. Sigvald agreed."

"What was the prize?" Einar asked. But I already knew.

"It was you," Skjold answered. "All of you. We told Sigvald that a ship would be sailing this way that had just returned from the war in Frankia. We told him of the great ransom that the King of the Franks had paid, and said that the sea chests of every man aboard the ship would be filled with silver."

Toke had not known for certain that we would pursue him. What if we had not? It had been a near thing. Would Sigvald have eventually killed Toke's five men when no rich prize appeared? Did Toke care about the danger he'd placed them in?

"Where is Toke bound?" I asked.

"To Birka. He plans to sell the woman in the slave market there. He said she will bring a very high price from the right buyer."

"The *woman* has a name," I snapped. "It is Sigrid.

And she is not a slave to be bought and sold. She is of high birth. She is my sister. Your chieftain, Toke, is her foster brother. A man who would so betray another—a woman, a member of his own family—is not worthy to be called a man," I added angrily, using Skjold's own words. He flinched and hung his head, glancing up at me nervously like a dog that has been kicked. After a few moments, I continued. "You yourself lived in her household for many months, yet helped betray her. *You* are no man. You have no honor. You are a Nithing. One gives a gift to all true men by killing such as you."

I reached behind my back and grasped the handle of my small-axe. I intended to bury its blade in this foul creature's head. But Gudfred reached out and placed his hand over mine, preventing me from drawing the axe from my belt.

"Do not," he said. "Not this way. Not now. You must honor the promise that Jarl Hastein gave these men."

Reluctantly I withdrew my hand from my weapon. But staring at Skjold, looking into his eyes, I made a promise to myself. Somehow, I thought, I will see you die.

"My sister—Sigrid," I said. "Has she been harmed?"

Skjold shook his head. "Toke would allow no one to touch her. He said that there are buyers, slave traders who sell to the Araby kingdoms far in the south, who will pay dearly for beautiful women who have never known a man. The kings and lords there place a high value on the taking of a virgin, especially those of great beauty, with hair the color of gold, or red like fire."

Einar turned his head and spat upon the deck in disgust.

"You should know," Skjold added, "that most of us did not realize what Toke intended to do, before it happened. Most of us were readying the ships to sail when he picked fifteen men, told them to arm themselves, and went up to the longhouse with them. I was among those who were left down at the ships. Then Toke and the others came back at a run, and there was fighting. We cast off as soon as he was aboard. It was done before many of us even knew he had taken the wo...had taken your sister."

"But after? None spoke against it?" Gudfred asked.

Skjold looked away. "Not to Toke. There were some of us who thought it was bad thing, who were worried about what Toke had done. I was among them. But no one spoke against it to Toke."

Skjold looked up at me. "Toke has a very great hatred of your family. Of your father, your brother, of you. He would not have listened, had anyone spoken up. It would just have made him angry. He did not take your sister only for the price she will bring when he sells her, although he believes she will prove to be a very rich prize. He took her to dishonor you, all of you—even your kin who are already dead. He thinks that if she becomes a slave, whose master uses her for his pleasure as he wishes, it would shame all of you. And he said you, more than anyone else, will know how she will suffer."

"After Birka," Einar said. "Where will Toke be

bound?"

It was a good question—one I should have thought to ask. I could not afford to let my anger and distress at what Skjold had told us cloud my thoughts.

"To Ireland," Skjold answered. "Toke has allies there."

Just then Bram came trotting down the deck from the bow. "There is a boat that has put out from the island," he said. "It is approaching the *Gull*." He glanced briefly down at Skjold, then stared longer, studying his face carefully, and added, surprise in his voice, "I know you."

"A ship?" Gudfred asked.

Bram shook his head. "A small-boat. There look to be maybe four or five men aboard it. They are waving a white flag."

It proved that the folk of Oeland were not our foes. The pirates had not been their allies. Rather, they had oppressed them cruelly. The men who had ventured out to the *Gull* in the small-boat assured Hastein we would be warmly welcomed on Oeland, and offered to lead the way to a sheltered anchorage further down the island.

By the time we reached the small cove which was our destination, a crowd of the islanders had already gathered there to greet us. Dusk was falling, but they had built bonfires on the shore, and had brought food— simple fare that could be carried easily: bread, sausages, and cheese, and most welcome of all, several small casks of ale—to share with us.

"On the morrow we will prepare a proper feast,

and give thanks to you and to the gods, who sent you in answer to our prayers," a white-haired islander named Nori told Hastein. He was a godi—a priest—and the headman of one of the small villages that were scattered across the island. Turning to face the crowd of islanders arrayed behind him, in a loud voice he cried, "Away now! We must all away, and leave these brave men to rest in peace this night. They must tend to their wounded and their dead, and no doubt they are weary after their labors this day. Let us away, and in the morning we will gather at the old fort north of here and prepare for an offering and a feast." To Hastein he said, before he walked off into the darkness, "I will return in the morning."

In truth, we were weary. My steps dragged as though I had sacks of stones tied to my feet.

The cove's shoreline was shallow and sandy, so we had pulled the bows of the three ships up onto the beach, the captured ship in between the *Gull* and the *Serpent*. Those in the two crews who were badly wounded—there were ten in all—were carried ashore and a simple open tent for them was rigged facing the fires so they could be kept warm, and so Cullain could have light by which to dress their wounds. Because Cullain was busy tending to the wounded, each of us made a cold and simple night's meal for himself from the food brought by the islanders. The decks of the *Gull* and the *Serpent* were tented to provide shelter for the rest of us who were not wounded, and many made their way there to seek sleep as soon as they had eaten.

Hastein and Torvald posted sentries in the bow and

stern of each ship, plus two to keep the prisoners under close guard, and arranged for them to be relieved at regular intervals throughout the night. "We are all weary," Hastein said. "None of us will find it easy to stay awake for long hours this night. But we must not let our guard down. The folk of Oeland have shown a friendly face to us thus far, but smiles sometimes hide treacherous intent."

After eating the light fare and washing it down with a cup of ale, I made my way toward the shelter where the wounded were arrayed, intending to look for Tore. But before I reached it, I came upon the bodies of our dead, which had been lined up off to one side of the tent. Though we had fared far better in the battle than the pirates had, our losses had been dear. Twelve of our company—eight from the *Gull*, including Hrodgar, and four from the *Serpent*—lay lifeless on the ground.

Four torches had been stuck in the sand at regular intervals along the line of bodies, and by their dim light men were tending to their fallen comrades, stripping off their clothes and armor, stiff and stained with blood, washing their bodies, and combing their hair and beards. Bram was there. The men from the village had sustained heavy losses. Bram's comrade Skuli and another man from the village named Kari, who had also sailed with us on the *Gull*, had been slain in the same fight that had taken Hrodgar's life, and a third villager, who had sailed aboard the *Serpent*, had been killed during the final fight against Sigvald's ship. Hroald, the village headman, was helping Bram clean their bodies.

Beyond them, a group of men was kneeling over

the bodies of three men. As I passed them, one looked up and called my name. It was Gudfred. He stood and stepped across the body he'd been helping remove a tunic from.

"We lost three of our men," he said, "and another is badly wounded."

Our men. It was the second time Gudfred had said that to me, speaking of the carls from the estate.

"Who are the dead?" I asked.

"Grimar, Hemming, and Baug."

Before this voyage, I could not have put names to the faces of either Grimar or Hemming. They were little more than strangers to me. Baug I knew, though only slightly. He and his brother Floki—who had confronted me in the hayfield—had been close comrades to my brother Harald, and they had assisted with my training when we had practiced fighting in a shield wall.

If the estate was mine, as I had so brashly claimed, then the deaths of these men should matter to me. But I felt nothing.

"Can I assist you with their bodies?" I asked.

One of the kneeling men turned toward me and snapped, "No! *We* are their comrades. This is for us to do."

"Floki!" Gudfred said sharply, scowling at him. Turning back to me, he murmured, "His heart is heavy with grief."

"I lost my brother, too," I said, and looked away. "I understand. If you do not need my help, I will leave you now."

At the end of the row of bodies, Einar was trying to

257

ease Hrodgar's brynie up over his shoulders. He was struggling with the task, for the death stiffness had begun to set in, plus the wound to Hrodgar's neck was so great that his head flopped about loosely whenever his body was raised.

"Let me help you," I said, and knelt across the body from him. "He was a good and brave man, and a friend to me."

None of our wounded died during the night, although from the looks of his pale visage and sunken cheeks, whether Stig—the most badly hurt—would survive was in the hands of the Norns. He still had not awakened, but that was not altogether a bad thing. Because he could not stop the wound's bleeding, Cullain had been forced during the night to cut off Stig's right hand above his shattered wrist, to create a new, clean wound that could be cauterized to stop the bleeding.

When I visited the wounded men's tent in the morning, Tore was awake, although he, too, looked very pale, and he was so weak that after we spoke briefly—he insisted I relate to him in detail how the battle had progressed, after he'd been wounded—he closed his eyes and drifted into sleep.

With the assistance of Regin, Torvald had taken it upon himself to see that a hot meal was cooked to break the night's fast. It was simple fare—boiled barley porridge—but filling, and each man was allowed to eat as much as he desired. I savored each mouthful of the nutty tasting, chewy mush, and thought that seldom had I enjoyed so satisfying a meal.

Hastein had been wandering the decks of all three ships and the beach, making a point of talking to each of our men. Eventually he made his way to where I was sitting, lazily enjoying the feeling of having a full belly and nothing to do.

"You did well in the battle yesterday," he told me. "I have heard of your deeds from more than one of our men."

I felt pleased and proud at Hastein's words, and also surprised—though pleasantly so—that others had taken the trouble to speak of me to him.

"Our attack across the bows onto Sigvald's ship would likely have failed but for the effect of your men's arrow fire. I had wondered why it took so long for the archers to support the attack, until I spoke with some of them this morning. Sigvald's archer—the Finn—came close to changing the outcome of the battle. No doubt your duel with him will find its way into the tales that seem to be growing about Strongbow."

Now I felt embarrassed. But it did not escape me that Hastein had called the archers my men.

"Gudfred—he seems a good man—told me that you also led the attack that cleared one of the pirates' ships. He said you fought like a man possessed by a berserker's fury. He claims he saw swords hit you but they did not cut, and he said he had never seen a blade strike with such swiftness as did yours. He said you left a trail of dead behind you as you cut your way from the bow to the stern of the pirates' ship."

I had no memory of swords striking me—in truth, I still could not recall the boarding of the ship and the fight that followed at all. But I did have several long bruises across my shoulders and back, and felt very stiff and sore from them.

"The warrior he described.... I know you to be very skilled with your bow, but in truth, I would not have known the man he described to be you," Hastein added.

In truth, I would not have either.

"If swords did not cut me, I am certain there was no magic to it," I told him. "The Frankish mail of which my brynie is made, and the thick jerkin I wear beneath it, no doubt are what saved me from harm."

"Hmm," Hastein replied. "You are, of course, now the captain of my archers. I fear it will be some time before Tore is fit to fight again."

"I thank you," I said. Hastein had once before asked me to command his archers. This time I did not protest.

"Now we must speak of a matter about which I am not pleased. I have learned that you and Einar killed one of the prisoners. I gave them my word that they would not be harmed if they surrendered."

I wondered if Gudfred had told Hastein of the incident. He had looked shocked by my actions. "Did you know that it was one of Toke's men?" I asked.

Hastein looked surprised. "I did not."

It was not Gudfred, then. That was a fact he would not have omitted.

"One of the pirates' longships—the one that grappled the *Serpent*'s bow, and was tied alongside Sigvald's—was the *Sea Steed*. It was one of Toke's two ships that we have been pursuing. It was the ship that Snorre sailed to Frankia."

"How did the pirates come to possess it?" Hastein asked.

"That was what I was trying to discover. Gudfred recognized two of Toke's men among the pirates who had surrendered. I was attempting to question one of them—he had been in Frankia, with Snorre—but he refused to talk. He said I could not harm him, because you had promised their safety if they surrendered. He said he would only tell me what I wished to know if I set him free."

"Which you could not do," Hastein said. "Not without my permission."

I shook my head. "Which I *would* not do. I swore an oath to slay all of the men who helped Toke kill my brother Harald and the others, up on the Limfjord."

"Hmm," Hastein murmured. "But by killing him you broke *my* promise, which I had given."

I shook my head again. "You promised the pirates that if they surrendered, neither you nor your men would kill them. Those were your words. I did not kill Toke's man. He asked to be set free, so I put him over the side. It happened that he could not swim. He drowned. *I* did not kill him. The sea did."

Hastein stared at me in silence for a long time, his face expressionless. Eventually I realized that he was struggling to keep a smile from showing. "If you made that argument before the lawgiver at a Thing," he finally said, "if a lawsuit had been brought against you over this man's death, I have grave doubts that it would keep you from being ordered to pay wergild. But it is a clever argument, nonetheless. I must remember it." Now he did smile, and shook his head. "*You* did not kill him; the sea did. And after the sea took his comrade, did the other of Toke's men talk?"

I nodded. "He did," I answered, and related what Skjold had told me. By the time I finished, Hastein's face had taken a look of cold anger.

"Toke is not a foe to be taken lightly," he said. "It was a clever move in this game we are playing to set the pirates upon us. He did not even know for certain that he was being pursued. He gambled a ship on the possibility that we were following him, and on the chance that he could use the pirates to strike at us. It was a gamble that he won. But he may come to regret it. Before, I hunted him solely for the wrong he had done to you and your folk, and for the niddingsvaark of killing the women and children in the attack up on the Limfjord, after their safety had been promised. I wished to see him brought to justice, but in truth, I was not willing to continue pursuing him indefinitely. Now it is a personal thing for me, as well as for you. I have lost good men to Toke's treachery. I will see their deaths avenged."

He shook his head slowly, and sighed. "But I fear that now we may have lost the advantage of greater numbers we held before. If we meet Toke now—if we are able to catch him—it will be a much more even fight."

The long peal of a horn sounded a warning note. With the coming of daylight, Hastein had moved the sentries inland from the ships, to form a perimeter around our camp.

"Jarl Hastein," one of the sentries called, "men are

approaching."

Eight riders made their way down the side of the distant ridge and crossed the gently sloping grassy fields that lay between it and the beach. Nori, the headman who had acted as spokesman for the Oelanders the night before, was in their lead.

Hastein and I walked over to the fire Torvald and Regin had built in front of the tent for the wounded. Besides Torvald, Gudfred and Einar were among the men gathered there. We arrayed ourselves behind Hastein as he stepped forward to meet the islanders.

"Greetings," Nori said, as he dismounted. "I hope you and your men passed a peaceful night." He glanced at the open-fronted tent and the wounded men lying inside, then beyond to the row of bodies, now draped with a tent awning taken from the captured ship to protect them from the birds. Several crows had already passed low overhead since daybreak, no doubt attracted by the smell of death.

"Have you plans yet for your dead?" Nori asked.

"It is a matter I had intended to give thought to this day," Hastein answered.

"We would join you in honoring them. And as I spoke of last night, we wish to hold a feast to give thanks to the gods, and to you and your men, for the defeat of the pirates. These"—he indicated the men who had ridden into our encampment with him—"are also headmen of villages upon this island. Let me present them to you."

After introductions had been made, Nori continued. "We have spoken among ourselves, and have decided to delay the feast until two days from now. That will give us more time to prepare for it. We also need time to select the horses for our sacrifice and to properly ready them. With your permission, may our feast not only be one of thanksgiving, but also a funeral feast to honor your slain?"

Hastein nodded—so deeply, it was almost a shallow bow. "My men and I are grateful for the honor you show our comrades."

"Good. It is settled, then," Nori said. "We will hold our sacrifice as the sun rises from the sea, two days hence. If you would join us, we would be grateful. Your men are welcome, too. Then we will cook the meat from the sacrifices during the day, and at dusk, we will feast together."

Two days hence? I knew that our men needed to rest after the battle, and our dead needed to be sent properly on their way to the next world. But how far ahead of us would Toke get in that time?

"We will burn our dead before the feast," Hastein told Nori. "It is our custom." He glanced toward the shoreline where our ships were pulled up against the beach for a moment, then turned back to Nori and added, "We will burn them in the ship we captured—the one we took from Sigvald, the pirates' captain. It will be their death ship."

Nori looked beyond Hastein toward Sigvald's ship, and his face took on a pained expression. "It is a fine ship," he said wistfully, then added, "We have no ships here upon Oeland now. We had three, but the pirates burned them when they first came."

I had noticed, in the light of day, that further down the cove was what looked to be the charred remains of a boathouse—it could not have held a ship as large as the Gull, but was long enough to have held a small longship or a knarr—and the blackened outlines of several other buildings nearby. That, I supposed, was some of the handiwork of the pirates. The sight had reminded me of Frankia, of a ruined village I had happened upon there. It was a shame we could not have kept the other two captured ships, to give to the Oelanders.

Nori continued. "We managed to save some of our small-boats by dragging them up from the shore and hiding them, but we have no ships now." He sighed heavily, and was silent for a time, as if hoping Hastein might speak. Finally he continued, "We have a boon to request of you."

I wondered if he was going to ask Hastein for Sigvald's ship—he clearly longed to have it—but he did not.

"You took prisoners, did you not? In the battle?"

"We did."

"The pirates did not make their camp upon Oeland. The entire summer they have remained nearby, but we do not know where. At first they raided us often, stealing our food and beasts whenever they could catch us unawares. After a time, they would come every few days and require us to provide them with food, in exchange for not attacking us. They called it tribute. They also stole some of our women-folk, in their first raids. We would know if they still live. And if they do, we would know where they are being held. Your prisoners will know."

"We will question them," Hastein told him.

Because Skjold had already spoken freely to us once Einar and I had convinced him that it was the prudent thing to do, he seemed the logical place to begin. Gudfred and I escorted him from the captured ship to the shore, where Hastein and the islanders were waiting. He was willing, even eager, to cooperate.

"Sigvald and his men built an encampment on the large island in the channel between Oeland and the mainland," he told us. "The same island behind which we were lying in wait for you. There is a small cove on the back side of it which provides a secure anchorage that is hidden from the channel and protected from storms. The encampment is there. And they built towers on each end of the island, from which to watch the northern and southern approaches of the channel for ships."

"The islanders say some of their women were stolen by the pirates. Are any of them on the island, at the encampment?" I asked.

Skjold nodded. "They are. There are seven of them. I heard there used to be more, but…."

"But what?" demanded one of the men who had come with Nori. He had a long, light brown beard that fell halfway to his waist, and his face was twisted by an angry scowl.

"But two of them died. That is what I heard. It was before I came—before I joined them."

"Did Sigvald leave any men to guard the

266

encampment?" Hastein asked, "Or were they all aboard the ships that attacked us?"

"He left six men on the island," Skjold answered. "To guard the women and watch over the camp."

"Will you carry us across the channel to the island?" Nori asked Hastein. "Will you help us find our women and bring them home?" He paused for a moment, then added, "We have no ships."

"Do not forget the watch towers," Skjold warned. "They will see you coming long before you reach the island."

Nori stuck his finger into his mouth, wetting it, and held it aloft. "The wind is blowing from the east, off the sea," he said. "In the morning, early, there will be fog over the water. If we cross the channel in the morning, in the fog, they will not see us."

Torvald stepped forward. "Hastein," he protested. "We do not know these waters. Sailing a ship in fog, in unknown waters, is dangerous. We could lose the *Gull* if she hits a rock and her hull is pierced."

"There will be no danger to your ship," Nori assured Hastein. "Before the pirates came, we often fished the waters off that island. Along its center, opposite Oeland, the beach is sandy and the sea offshore there is shallow and free of rocks. I will show you the way."

"We will help you," Hastein told him. "We will carry your people across to the island."

Torvald continued to protest after the Oelanders departed. "They have boats," he said. "They do not need our ship. Why must we involve ourselves with this?"

Hastein frowned. "It is but a small thing they ask us to do."

"Let these islanders deal with their own problems. I think they are still afraid of the pirates, even though there are only six of them left on the island. These men are not warriors. Did you see them? It is no wonder the pirates chose to stay here."

"I have decided, Torvald. We will help them." Hastein was beginning to sound impatient. But Torvald would not stop.

"Why must you always right others' wrongs that do not concern us? We have lost good men who came on this voyage only out of loyalty to you. This is not our concern. None of it is. It is not our fight."

I could feel my face turning red. Torvald was no longer speaking of carrying the Oelanders across the channel. And he was angry. I had never seen him speak so to Hastein. Did others among our men feel the same as he?

If Hastein noticed the meaning thinly concealed in Torvald's words, he chose to ignore it. "The pirates have been robbing ships that pass through these waters for months now. Do you not think they will have taken much wealth from them?"

Torvald's scowl gradually faded as he considered what Hastein had said. "Perhaps," he finally said.

"If there is treasure to be found in the pirates' encampment it is rightfully ours, for we defeated them," Hastein told him. "Even had the Oelanders not asked me to, I would have crossed the channel to the island to find their camp, once I learned of it. It is but a small thing to take them with us when we go, so they can search for their stolen women-folk."

10

Rauna

After the sun had passed its noon peak, we sailed the *Gull* north along the shoreline of Oeland, traveling at a leisurely pace with the sail close hauled to catch the gentle breeze blowing out of the east. Nori accompanied us to show us where we should anchor for the night. The rest of the Oelanders whom we would carry across to the island—there would be nine of them, each a man whose wife or daughter had been taken by the pirates—would join us on the morrow, before dawn.

All that day, the Oelanders had gathered brush and wood, building a great pile on the ridge above the anchorage which Nori directed us to. "In the morning, when we are ready to cross the channel, they will light it," he'd explained to Hastein. "Even through the fog, you should be able to see it for most of the crossing—for all of it, if the fog is not too thick. If you keep its light dead astern, your course will take you straight across the channel to the center of the island on which the pirates have built their camp, at a point where the beach is soft sand and the water shallow and free of rocks."

Because of the casualties suffered in the battle with the pirates—eight members of the *Gull*'s crew had been killed, and five badly wounded—Hastein had drawn ten men from the crew of the *Serpent* to help man the *Gull*. The *Serpent*'s losses had been lighter: four dead, and five, including Stig, with serious wounds. Our company, which had numbered eighty-one when we had sailed from Jutland, was now reduced to just fifty-nine warriors who were still fit to fight. As Hastein had observed, the strong advantage in numbers we had once held over Toke was being whittled away.

Most of the prisoners had been left back at our original encampment on Oeland with our wounded and the other two ships. But at my suggestion, we had brought Skjold with us.

"After we land on the island, he can lead us across it to the pirates' encampment," I'd explained to Hastein, before we had sailed north. "We will be far more likely to be able to take them by surprise if we do not have to search for it."

"Do you trust him not to try and warn those in the camp?" Hastein had asked.

"I do," I said. When I had approached him about it aboard Sigvald's ship where the prisoners were still being kept bound and under guard, Skjold had readily agreed to guide us, even though others among the pirate prisoners had given him black looks for it.

"He seems very willing to help us—and eager to please you. If you were not bound by the promise I made to the prisoners when they surrendered—if I released you from it, and gave Skjold to you to do with as you wish, would you kill him when we are through here?"

I thought it a strange question. "Why do you ask?"

"He clearly hopes to buy mercy from you with his cooperation. I am curious if your oath of vengeance will make his hope in vain."

I did not answer. I thought Hastein was misjudging

271

me, for I would have killed Skjold aboard the pirate ship the day we had taken him prisoner, had Gudfred not stopped me. Yet it was true that Skjold was trying hard to win my favor, and had I not known he had served Toke, I would have found him likeable enough.

As Nori had predicted, fog crept in across the water during the night. Although by dawn it was not so thick that I could not see the *Gull*'s bow when standing in her stern, it was dense enough that had I shot an arrow out across the water, I could not have seen where it fell. Even if the pirates kept sentries posted in the watchtowers at either end of the island—which I thought unlikely, at least during the night hours, since there were only six of them—they would not be able to see the *Gull* when we made landfall in the island's center.

The nine men who were rowed out to our ship as the night's blackness began to give way to gray all bore some sort of arms, but Torvald had been correct. The men of Oeland were not warriors. They were farmers and fishermen, peaceful folk. All had knives or seaxes in scabbards on their belts, and most carried axes, though the axe one man brought was a heavy-bladed one for splitting logs, far too clumsy to use as a weapon. Three also carried spears and one a bow, but only two of them bore shields, and there was not a sword or helm among them.

One of the village headmen who had accompanied Nori the morning before—the man with the long brown beard, who'd seemed so angry when Skjold had revealed that two of the captured women had died—was among them. It was he who had the bow. His name, I learned, was Osten. His wife had been taken by the pirates in their first raid on Oeland. He paced anxiously back and forth across the *Gull*'s deck as we rowed slowly across the channel. I could well imagine why. Even if we were successful and rescued the Oelanders' women, two of these men would not find those who had been taken from them.

Despite Nori's assurances that on the course he'd set us upon we would encounter no hazards that could damage the *Gull*, Hastein ordered her to be rowed at half speed. He stood on the fore-deck, peering ahead through the fog, while Torvald manned the steer-board in the stern. I was in the bow, too, waiting just aft of the fore-deck. Einar, Gudfred, Asbjorn, and Hallbjorn—all armed with their bows—were with me. Hastein had ordered that as soon as the *Gull* reached the island, we were to be the first ashore, to scout for enemies and stand watch as the rest of our men disembarked.

Behind us, the light of the beacon fire grew steadily dimmer, until all that could be seen of it through the fog was a pale yellow spot glowing in a shapeless wall of gray. Then even that was gone.

"How much further till we reach land?" Hastein asked Nori tensely. The old man shrugged and answered, "It is hard to say."

An annoyed expression on his face, Hastein called for Bryngolf to join him on the fore-deck. "Throw the line," he told him. "Let me know when you find the bottom."

Bryngolf pulled the heaving line—a long rope with

knots tied along it an ell's length apart, with a fist-sized stone that had a hole pierced through its center tied to its end—from where it was stowed underneath the fore-deck. Grasping the coil of rope in his left hand, he payed out ten knots worth of the line in loops into his right, then let the stone hang down from it by an ell's length. Stepping to the ship's side, he swung the stone in a circle and let it fly, the rope in his right hand slipping through his fingers as it arced out ahead of the *Gull* and splashed down into the sea.

After giving the weighted line a few moments to sink, Bryngolf glanced at Hastein and shook his head, then pulled the rope in, coiling it again in his right hand as he did, and repeated the process.

I had long lost count of how many times he had thrown the line when Bryngolf finally turned to Hastein and said, "It has struck bottom. Nine ells down."

The sea bed off the shore we were approaching proved to have a long, gentle slope to it, with shallows extending far out into the channel. Bryngolf threw the line three more times, and the count was down to six ells, before the outline of the island first showed ahead through the fog as a dark shadow against the gray. Hastein passed word back to Torvald, who slowed the cadence for the rowers even more, and we approached the unfamiliar shore at a cautious pace. But Nori's assurances proved true. When we drew close enough to see the land ahead of us clearly, a sandy beach, free of rocks, was revealed. At Torvald's command, the rowers pulled hard over the last, short stretch to the shore, driving the *Gull*'s bow almost to the water's edge before she ground to a halt, the front of her hull resting against the sandy bottom.

I dropped over the side into the shallow water and waded ashore, my four men with me—Einar and Gudfred to my right, Asbjorn and Hallbjorn on my left. We nocked arrows on our bows and crossed the beach, spreading out as we did, then moved into the trees. The fog had not penetrated there, and it had grown light enough by now to see clearly even under their shadows, for although we could not spy its shining orb, up above the fog the sun had risen.

Hastein was wasting no time. By the time we returned to the beach to report that all was clear, the gangplank had already been wrestled into position and most of the landing party was ashore. Ten men would stay with the *Gull* to guard her. The rest, with the men from Oeland, prepared to march across the island in search of the pirates' camp.

"Are there any trails?" Hastein asked Skjold. Though I did not think he would try to escape us, I was taking no chances. His hands were bound in front of him, and Bram was holding onto a short length of rope, the other end of which had been tied in a loop around Skjold's neck.

Bram looked much more a warrior now than he had when we'd departed Jutland. Although only a few of the pirates had possessed mail brynies, at my urging he had acquired one of them, stripping it and the padded jerkin to wear under it from the dead owner's body after the battle. He had also found a helm that suited him, and had returned the one he'd borrowed from me.

"None that come all the way to this shore," Skjold responded. "There is a trail that runs from the north end of the island to the south, between the two watch towers, and another that leads from that one to the encampment."

"You and your men will lead the way," Hastein told me. "Take the prisoner with you. Our main force will follow some distance back, so the noise of our passage will not be heard. As soon as you find the encampment, send word back to me. If possible, I wish to surround it before we make our presence known."

Though my four archers were wearing brynies and helms like I was, we had all left our shields aboard the *Gull*. Only Bram carried one. We would be able to move more quickly and quietly through the forest without them, and if we had to fight, we would do so with our bows.

Our initial progress was slow, for at first there was heavy undergrowth to push through. But before long we reached older woodlands, whose tall trees so heavily shaded the forest floor that it was more open, allowing us to move forward swiftly, spread out in a scouting line rather than following each other's footsteps in single file.

The island was not large. We quickly found the trails Skjold had spoken of, and it was still early morn when we reached the encampment. We crouched, hidden in the trees, and studied it. A clearing had been cut out of the forest along the shoreline of the small cove Skjold had told us of. The stumps of the trees that had once stood there still remained. The camp had no defenses—Sigvald must have felt its concealed location provided security enough. A rough-hewn log longhouse had been built from the felled trees, its roof poorly thatched with layers of cut pine and spruce branches laid across supports. It looked like it would leak badly when it rained.

Two large ship's tents had been pitched on either side of the log building. The only other structure in the camp was a small, strange looking tent that appeared to be made of animal skins sewn together and stretched around a frame of long wooden poles, which had been pitched close to the water's edge just inside the trees along one side of the clearing.

No one was visible. The only sign of life was a small fire that burned in a ring of stones in front of the skin tent.

"Where will the six be?" I whispered to Skjold. It was obvious that none of them were standing watch.

"In the longhouse. When the full company was here, some of the men slept in the tent on the right, but with so few here now, they will all be in the longhouse. It is warmer and dryer there."

Glancing again at the structure's roof, I wondered how true the latter was. "And the Oelanders' women-folk?"

"They will be in the longhouse, too."

Einar was crouched beside me. "What of the small tent, with the fire in front of it?" he asked Skjold.

"That was the Finn's. He slept there."

The Finn—the pirates' archer who had been so deadly. "He died two days past," I said. "That fire—if all are in the longhouse, who lit it?"

Just then the flap that covered the opening into the skin tent was raised, and someone stepped out. It was a female, dressed in trousers and a long tunic. She was short and slight of build.

"No doubt she lit it," Skjold responded. "She is the Finn's daughter."

I gritted my teeth. "Is there anyone else you have not told us of who is in this camp?"

Skjold looked alarmed by the angry tone he heard in my voice. "No," he said, shaking his head vigorously.

"There is no smoke coming from the draft hole in the longhouse roof," Einar observed. "Those inside must still be sleeping."

I sent Asbjorn back down the trail to tell Hastein the layout of the pirates' encampment and that they were as yet unaware of our presence. We were deep enough within the trees that there was no way the Finn girl, who had been crouching over her small fire, could have heard or seen anything, but when Asbjorn left she straightened up and stood motionless for a time, staring in our direction.

"We must silence her," Einar whispered. "And quickly. Hastein and the others will be here soon. If she hears them approaching, she may warn those in the longhouse before we can surround the camp, and they may try to flee."

Gudfred, who was crouching behind a tree on the other side of Skjold, slipped an arrow from his quiver and held it up. "If we all shoot at once..." he whispered.

I shook my head. I had never killed a woman and did not wish to do so now.

"Einar and I will move back deeper into the woods and circle around behind her. Watch for us. Once we are in position, we will come out of the trees and show ourselves to her. When we do, you and Hallbjorn should step into the clearing here, as well, so she will not run this way. Have arrows ready on your bows so she will see the danger you pose if she should try to flee, but do not shoot her. Einar and I will take her alive."

As I spoke, the girl stepped away from the fire and ducked back inside the tent. "Now," I said to Einar, and we scurried back into the depths of the forest.

Once we judged we were safely beyond hearing from the camp, we broke into a run, dodging through the trees as we circled the clearing. We would not have much time to do this. As Einar had said, Hastein and the others would reach the encampment soon.

When we could see the glint of water in the cove through gaps between the trees, we knew we had gone far enough. The skin tent had been located close to the shoreline.

"You move up along the shore, in the edge of the trees," I told Einar. "In case she tries to run that way." As he headed off, I began to creep forward, moving from tree to tree for cover, toward where I thought the tent should be. Soon I saw it, and silently crept closer. I crouched behind the trunk of a large oak tree, watching, but there was no sign of the Finn's daughter. Was she still inside the tent? If I could catch her there, she would have no chance to run away.

I stood up and took two steps forward when I heard a sound like a quiet gasp, just off to my left. It was the girl. She must have come into the forest to search for firewood—she had a bundle of sticks under one arm, and held a small-axe in her other hand. The unexpected sight of her, so close, startled me almost as much as my sudden appearance must have startled her.

"Shhh!" I said, raising my finger to my lips. "Make no sound." As I spoke the words, I realized that I did not know if she understood the common language of the north. When her father had first spoken, it had been in a tongue I did not recognize. Hopefully she, like he, also knew the common tongue.

"This encampment is surrounded," I continued. It was untrue, for Hastein had not yet arrived. "We are here to capture the pirates, or to kill them if they resist, and to free the women they stole. You will not be harmed by us if you do as I say. Do not try to warn the others or flee."

She took a tentative step toward the edge of the clearing, and I could see her looking this way and that among the trees around it. I realized she was looking for other warriors. She was trying to see if I had spoken the truth when I'd said the camp was surrounded. At least that meant she had understood what I'd said.

Suddenly she stiffened, and turned toward where the trail entered the clearing, near where I'd left Gudfred, Hallbjorn, and Bram. Her hearing was far sharper than mine. It was several moments before I, too, heard what she had—the rhythmic sound of many feet, moving at a quick pace.

Gudfred and Hallbjorn stepped out of cover, arrows laid across their bows. Gudfred was staring in my direction, toward the tent. I waved my arm back and forth to signal, but could not tell if he saw me, as I was still a ways back from the clearing among the trees.

Hastein appeared, trotting down the trail with Torvald at his side. The rest of our men were behind him in a double column. They halted, still within the shelter of the forest, when he held up his hand. He spoke briefly with Hallbjorn, who pointed across the clearing toward the skin tent. Then he turned around, gave an order to those behind him, and the warriors from the *Gull* began moving into the clearing, forming a semicircle around the longhouse.

The Finn girl—on closer examination, I saw that although short of stature, she was a young woman, not a child—stood for a few moments watching the growing ranks of warriors moving into the clearing. Then she glanced briefly at the forest behind her, and at me. She opened her arm and let the bundle of wood she'd collected drop to the ground.

Do not run, I thought, for I could tell she was considering it.

"Einar," I called.

"Here," he replied. From the sound of his voice, he was not far away.

"Come this way," I told him. "Quickly. The girl is here."

"Do not try to flee," I told her again. "I will not harm you."

I could hear Einar moving through the trees, headed in our direction. The girl looked toward the sound, fear showing now in her eyes. She glanced behind her again, toward the safety of the forest.

I fumbled at the pouch on my belt, and pulled the small leather bag from it—the one her father had given me. Holding the end of its cord which I'd wrapped around it, I let it unroll, so that the bag dangled below my hand, where she could see it clearly.

She stared at it, a stunned expression on her face, then looked up into my eyes. "How?" she asked. Like her father, she spoke with a heavy accent.

"Your father gave this to me. He asked me to give it to you. I do not break my word. Do not try to flee. I promise you that you will not be harmed."

Holding my arm out in front of me, the bag extended in offer, I moved toward her in slow, cautious steps. "Take it," I said. "You do not need to be afraid."

When I drew near, she extended her own arm and closed her hand around the bag.

"What is your name?" I asked.

"Rauna," she replied.

There are many ways one can react to danger and misfortune. The measure of a man is often revealed by how he chooses to do so. The six pirates who found themselves suddenly stranded on the small island, the rest of their comrades all either slain or taken prisoner, had elected to drink themselves into a stupor.

Einar and I walked across the clearing to where Hastein and Torvald were standing facing the closed door of the longhouse, the warriors from the *Gull* arrayed on either side of them in a line that curved around the front of the structure. Rauna followed us reluctantly, still clutching the small pouch from her father tightly in her hand. She had asked me how I had come to have it, and to have spoken with her father about her. I'd replied that I did not have time now to talk with her. As I'd hoped, her curiosity to learn more seemed to be stronger than her urge to flee.

Hallbjorn, Gudfred and Asbjorn stood beside Hastein, their bows at the ready with arrows across them. The men from Oeland were gathered in a cluster a short distance behind them.

Hastein glanced beyond me at Rauna as we approached.

"Is she one of the Oelanders' women?" he asked.

"No," I said, shaking my head. He frowned and stared at her more closely, then turned back toward the longhouse. Torvald studied her, too.

"Is she a Finn?" he asked. I nodded. I suspected it was her clothing that told him what she was. Her tunic was distinctive, and similar to her father's: it was made of supple tanned animal skins, sewn together—from their thinness, probably deerskin—and was long, coming down to her knees, with a high collar around the neck opening. Unlike her father's, her tunic had decorative woven bands sewn around the cuffs of the sleeves, the neck opening, and the bottom edge. I had not known that such garb was typical of the Finns—in truth, before a few days ago I had never even heard of the Finns at all.

"You inside the longhouse," Hastein shouted. "You are surrounded. Lay down your weapons and come out with your hands raised above your heads, where we can see them. Do not try to resist or we will kill you." To

Hallbjorn and the others he murmured, "If any of them comes out carrying a weapon, you three kill him with your bows."

We all waited, but nothing happened.

Torvald tried next, in a voice that boomed out far louder than Hastein's had. "Inside the longhouse! Lay down your weapons! Come out. Come out now. You must surrender or you will die." Again nothing happened.

I turned to Rauna. "There are six of them—six of the pirates, yes?" I asked her.

She nodded.

"Are they all inside the longhouse?"

She nodded again.

Torvald shook his head in disgust. "They are cowards. They are afraid to come out."

Rauna shook her head, and spoke in a soft voice to me. "They are probably asleep. They have been drinking ever since the night of the big fight, out on the water," she said.

Hastein turned to Bryngolf and Bjorgolf, who were standing to his right, amused looks on their faces. "Go beat on the door. Kick it in if you have to. Do whatever you must to wake them up and get them out here. Kill them if they resist."

Handing their spears to Torvald, the black-haired twins walked to the longhouse door, drawing their swords as they did. Standing on either side of it, they nodded to each other, then Bryngolf—or it may have been Bjorgolf, for in truth I could not tell them apart—began hammering on the door with the heavy iron pommel of his sword.

"Come out! Come out!" he shouted. "We have you surrounded." Then he and his brother raised their swords, holding them leveled at shoulder height ready to thrust, and crouched back against the wall on either side of the doorway.

After a few moments, the door swung open and a man wearing only trousers staggered into view, blinking and squinting his eyes against the light. A sword dangled loosely from his right hand. Seeing it, both of the Ravens stabbed their blades into the hapless pirate's bare chest, then one of them reached forward, grabbed the dying man's hair, and slung his body out of the doorway onto the ground.

"Bryngolf did not warn them they must come out unarmed," Torvald observed.

"But I did," Hastein snapped. "And it was Bjorgolf who called to them, not Bryngolf."

"Hmmn," Torvald responded. "Are you certain?"

"No," Hastein admitted.

The two brothers nodded again to each other, then lunged through the open doorway, one after the other. From inside, a woman began screaming, and then another. The men from Oeland looked alarmed. After a short time, the Ravens returned. Their swords were dripping with blood.

"They are all dead," one told Hastein. "None of them surrendered."

"It is a dangerous thing to get so drunk you cannot think," Torvald said.

Hastein spoke to Nori. "Your men can go to their

women now. There is no longer any danger."

Nori turned to the men gathered behind him and said, "Go." As the Oelanders pushed past him and rushed into the longhouse, Hastein looked over at me.

"Is she one of the pirates' women?" he asked, nodding toward Rauna.

"She is the daughter of the archer aboard Sigvald's ship," I told him. "The one who was so skilled, who shot Tore and Hrodgar and the others."

"Ah," Hastein replied. "You mean the Finn. The one you killed."

Behind me, Rauna let out a gasp.

Gudfred's jaw dropped and he shook his head in disbelief. "*This* is the Finn's daughter? And you have given her the neck pouch, as you promised you would?"

"What promise?" Hastein demanded. "What are you speaking of?"

"We found the Finn—the archer—dying on the deck of Sigvald's ship, when we were searching it and killing their wounded," Gudfred explained. "He asked whose arrow had felled him. When he learned it was Halfdan, he asked him to give a leather pouch he was wearing around his neck to his daughter. Halfdan agreed. I thought it a dangerous thing to do, to make a promise to a dying man that could not be kept. It is bad luck." He shook his head again. "But here is the daughter, and Halfdan has kept his promise. This is a strange thing, to be certain."

"What was in the bag?" Hastein asked.

I shrugged. "I do not know. I did not look."

From inside the longhouse, a man's voice sounded

286

in a wordless howl of rage and grief, then began sobbing, "Bera, Bera!"

"That is Osten's voice," Nori said. "Bera is his wife. His second wife. They were wed this spring, only weeks before the pirates came. She is just fifteen—much younger than he. Osten lost his first wife, Ingunn, two years ago. She died during childbirth, as did the child."

"From the sound of it, I fear he has lost his second wife, as well," Hastein said.

A search of the encampment revealed that the pirates' choice of the seas near Oeland as a hunting ground had proved profitable for them. One of the two ship's tents pitched beside the longhouse was filled with wares they had stolen from passing ships. There were bales of furs, bundles of tanned hides, the hair removed, three barrels filled with pots and bowls carved from soapstone, packed in straw, and another barrel containing whetstones. There were many casks of ale and wine, and—most valuable of all—a large wooden chest filled with walrus tusks, and a small one filled with chunks of amber.

Hastein sent Torvald and most of our men back across the island to fetch the *Gull* and row her around to the pirates' sheltered cove, so our new-found treasure could be loaded aboard. Torvald's mood had improved considerably. "It seems this voyage may prove a profitable one after all," he said.

A handful of us—myself, Einar, Gudfred, and the Ravens—had remained at the encampment with Hastein, to continue searching it. "Sigvald and his men must have robbed passing ships of silver, as well as these goods," Hastein said. "No doubt he has hidden it somewhere nearby—probably buried it." We questioned Skjold, but he claimed he had no knowledge of any buried treasure.

The Oelanders and their women had also remained at the encampment, waiting there for the ship to come around. Most of the women looked harshly used, and some had fresh bruises on their faces and bodies. We learned that it was the two youngest of the nine stolen women who had died: Osten's wife, who had been but fifteen years of age, and another man's daughter, even younger still. Both had been comely girls, according to Nori. Their youth and beauty had caused them to be the most frequently abused by the pirates. It had proved more than their hearts and bodies could stand.

Rauna had retreated to her tent after she had heard Hastein and Gudfred speak of her father's death, and she had not come out since.

"What do you intend to do with her?" Hastein asked me.

The question caught me by surprise. "I? Nothing." Once the pirates had been slain she had ceased being a concern to me. In truth, I had given her no further thought at all, after we'd begun searching the encampment.

"It *is* strange. Would you not agree?" he asked. "You and her father meet in battle, and you best him. Though you are an enemy and a stranger to him, before he dies he asks you to find his daughter and give her something. You agree, although you have no belief that you will ever do so. Then, just days later, you find her. I

288

do wonder what was in the pouch. I wish you had looked."

I suspected where Hastein was going with this. He saw the work of the Norns in it. I did not. He was wondering if the Norns had caused my path and that of the girl's to cross for some purpose. But no doubt the Finn had expected us to search for the pirates' encampment after the battle. He had known that if we did, we would find his daughter there. There was nothing more to it than that. It was not so strange, after all.

I shrugged. "She is not my concern," I said.

Hastein's gaze shifted to something behind me. "Ah," he replied. "Then it is also not your concern that the Oelanders appear to have plans for her."

I turned to look where he was staring. Two men— Nori and Osten—were standing in front of Rauna's tent. As I watched, Osten lifted the flap that covered the entrance into it, and started to step inside. He hastily backed away and shouted angrily, then walked over to where Rauna had piled branches of various sizes beside her fire ring. Sifting through them, he selected a stout limb the length of a man's arm, and strode back to the front of the tent.

I did not know the girl—she meant nothing at all to me—but I did not wish to see her beaten, or possibly even killed. I trotted across the clearing to the tent, Hastein following close behind.

"What is happening here?" I asked.

Osten, who was clearly very angry—his face was a dark shade of red, and his breathing was ragged—

snapped, "This is no concern of yours."

Until moments before, I would have agreed completely.

"Osten's wife was stolen by the pirates," Nori said, as if that explained what was happening.

"We know that," Hastein replied, sounding impatient.

"They killed her. They killed my wife Bera. This is one of their women. I am taking her," Osten added.

I wondered for what purpose he wanted her. To replace his wife? As a slave? To kill? "And the stick?" I asked.

"She tried to cut me just now with a knife, when I told her she was to come with me. I am going to teach her to obey."

"You will put down the stick and leave," I told him. As I spoke, I shifted my bow to my left hand, and rested my right lightly on my belt, just above where my dagger hung in its scabbard. Osten took a step back when I did.

"The pirates took his wife and killed her. He has a just claim," Nori protested.

"I am sorry your wife was taken, and that she died," I told Osten, ignoring Nori. "But this girl had nothing to do with that. And she is under my protection. It was a promise I made to her father before he died. I will not break a promise made to a dying man."

Osten was angry, but he did not have a death wish. He was but a simple farmer, not a warrior. He dropped the stick, turned, and walked off, his gait stiff and awkward from the anger in his body.

"It seems she is a concern of yours, after all,"

Hastein said, an amused expression on his face. "What do you intend to do with her now?"

"I do not know," I replied.

"You should decide quickly," he said. "The *Gull* will be here soon."

After he left, I called into the tent, "Rauna, come out. The others are gone now. We need to speak."

After a few moments, she pulled the flap aside enough so that she could peer through the gap she'd made. Seeing no one but me, she pushed it aside and stepped out. She was holding a small knife, with a narrow blade and a handle made of carved bone, in her right hand. Seeing my eyes on it, she slid it into its leather scabbard that was hanging from the belt around her waist.

"Did you speak the truth?" she asked me. "Did you make a promise to my father to protect me?"

For few moments I was silent, weighing what to say. "No," I finally said, shaking my head. "I promised only to give you the pouch."

"So you lied."

I nodded. "Yes, I lied."

"And when you made your promise to my father, you did not know who or where I was. Were your words to him a lie as well?"

"They have not proved to be. I found you, and I gave you the pouch."

From her expression she did not find my answer convincing. I did not blame her.

"What do you wish of me? What do you plan to do with me?" she asked. "And do not lie this time."

"Nothing." That was certainly true, or so I hoped. "Do you have somewhere you can go? To your people perhaps?"

"I cannot even escape this island," she said. "How do you think I can find my people?"

I sighed. "I gave you my word that if you did not warn the others or flee, you would not be harmed. I have not lied to you. Gather your things together. We will take you from the island on our ship."

"And after? What will you do with me then?"

"I do not know. We will see what can be done."

It was a good thing that the voyage from the pirates' island back to our camp on Oeland was a short one. The *Gull*'s deck was crowded with the bundles and barrels of goods we took from the pirates' encampment, plus the Oelanders and their women. Torvald grumbled at the added weight, and insisted that we discard some of our ballast stones so the ship would not ride too low in the water and be in danger of swamping if a wave should wash over her.

Rauna's possessions added considerably to the clutter on deck. The tent, even when folded up, made a sizable bundle, and the poles which had comprised its frame—which she'd insisted on bringing, though I suggested she could cut more when she needed them—were so long that the only place they could be stowed without causing a problem was on the raised rack where the longest oars were kept and the boom and sail were secured when we were not at sea. The remainder of her goods she had packed into three large leather bags, each with two straps sewn to them so they could be hauled on one's back. She did not travel lightly, and clearly did not appreciate how scarce space is aboard a ship.

"All three of these are yours?" I asked, nudging one of the leather bags with my foot. I could not imagine what one girl could possess to fill them up.

"Some of what is in them is mine. Most of it belonged to my father and my mother."

"Where is your mother?"

"She is dead."

I wondered again how she and her father had come to be a part of Sigvald's band.

I added the three bags and the bundled tent to the heap of cargo filling the center of the *Gull*'s deck and led Rauna to the stern. At Torvald's direction, the Oelanders had settled themselves in the bow, just back of the raised fore-deck. I thought it best to keep her away from them, for Osten had glowered angrily at us when we'd come aboard. "That is mine," I told her, pointing to my sea chest, which for now was pushed against the ship's side just in front of the raised stern deck. "Stay close to it. Do not wander about and get in the way."

Torvald was in the stern now, too, still fretting over the ship's balance. "Why is she aboard?" he asked.

"We cannot just leave her on the island," I answered. From the look on his face, I could see that he did not agree. "Are you going to acquire a woman on every voyage we sail on?" he grumbled.

"What did he mean?" Rauna asked, after Torvald had stomped off toward the front of the ship.

I ignored her and began removing my weapons and

armor to stow them in my sea chest. As soon as I opened it, I realized that lying in plain view inside was her father's quiver and arrows. I'd kept the arrows because I'd thought they would be matched in weight to his bow. I did not need another quiver, but I'd thought the leatherwork on this one was finely done, so I'd kept it anyway.

She stared at it for a few moments and then said, in a quiet voice, "That belonged to my father. My mother made it for him." She raised her eyes and looked at me, staring into my face. I had paid little attention to her features before. Her hair was the color of rye standing in the fields, at the end of the summer when it is dry and ready to be cut: too light to be called brown, but not pale golden either, like the color of Harald or Sigrid's hair. She had twisted it into a single long braid that hung down the center of her back. Her face had strong, high cheekbones, lightly dusted with freckles, and above them her eyes were a pale blue in color, with just a hint of gray, like the sky as evening approaches. They were glistening now with tears.

"On the island," she continued, "the man who is your leader...he said you killed my father."

I'd been wondering when she might say something about this. I was surprised she had not done so already. It made me feel very awkward, speaking with the daughter of a man I had slain.

"There was a battle out on the sea. You do know that, yes?" I asked her. She nodded.

"The pirates—the men your father was with—they attacked our ships. We fought them, and we defeated

294

them. Most of the pirates were slain in the fight. Your father was among those who were killed."

"But was it you who killed him?"

I did not want to speak of this. I sighed and said, "He killed some of my comrades. He tried to kill me. Yes, I shot the arrow that felled him."

Now let this matter be, I thought, but she would not.

"If you killed him with your bow, how could you have spoken with him?"

"After we cleared—after we captured the ship he was on, I found him lying on the deck, where he had fallen. He still lived, but he was dying. He asked me if it was I who had shot him. When I told him that I had, he asked me to give you the pouch he was wearing around his neck."

I hoped she would not want to know more about how her father had died. I did not want to tell her that Gudfred had stuck his sword through her father's throat.

"What happened to his body?"

The same that had happened to all of the pirates' dead aboard Sigvald's ship. While we were being towed behind the *Gull* and the *Serpent* toward Oeland, we had thrown them overboard.

"We put it into the sea." I told her. As I said the words, I wondered if having done so would keep his spirit bound to this world.

"What happens to your people after they die?" I asked.

Her brow wrinkled in a frown and she shook her head. "I do not understand."

295

And I did not know how to explain. Did her people die at death—was that the end of their existence—or did they have spirits that could go on to another world, as those of our folk did? The spirits of my father Hrorik and my brother Harald had gone after their deaths to Valhalla, the feast-hall of the gods, who honored brave men and great warriors by welcoming them there. My mother was there, too, taken by Hrorik to be his consort in the afterlife. The spirits of all those among our people who were not great warriors went to Hel, the land of the dead, unless their spirits became bound to this world and they became draugrs. But I did not know if the Finns had spirits that lived on after their deaths. Did all men?

"I knew he was dead," she suddenly volunteered. "His spirit came and told me, on its way to the other side."

"The other side?"

"The spirit world."

Her words gave me a sense of relief. I did not regret killing this girl's father. He had been an enemy, and would willingly have killed me. But now that she was, for at least a brief time—through no wish of my own—in my care, it would have been even more awkward than it already was if I had also condemned him to be a draugr by preventing his body from receiving a proper burial.

"You saw your father's spirit?" I asked. After his death, Harald had more than once appeared to me in dreams. But I had never seen him when awake.

"It was in the evening of the day of the fight out on the water. I was at our tent, laying wood for a fire to cook the night meal. I did not know, at the time, that there had been a fight out on the sea. I only knew that the ships had gone out in the morning to hunt, and I was expecting that they would return soon. I heard a strange noise above me, a croaking voice that seemed to be saying my name: 'Raa-naa, Raa-naa.' I looked up, and there was a raven in the tree above me. When our eyes met it nodded its head, and then flew away. In my heart I knew it was my father, and that he was telling me he had died."

"Your people become birds after they die?" It seemed a very strange belief.

She shook her head, and looked at me as if she thought me dim-witted.

"The raven allowed my father's spirit to enter its body, to get a message to me before he left this world completely and passed to the other side."

I thought it unlikely.

"Where is this place your people's spirits go to?" I asked.

She held out her hands in front of her and answered, "It is here. It is everywhere. It is all around us. We just cannot see it from this world, because it is the other side." After a moment, she added, "It is not just my people. The spirits of all things, of all men and all creatures, go there when their time in this world is finished."

The Finns, I thought, must be a simple folk to have such a belief. What of the gods? What of Valhalla? I felt certain that Harald's spirit was feasting there, not wandering unseen through the forest.

She pointed at the quiver in my sea chest and said,

"If you have that, where is my father's bow? Do you have it also? It is a famous bow among my people. My father was a great hunter."

If his skills in the woods matched his skill with a bow, I could well believe it. The bow was in the long sealskin bag I stored my own bow in. It was wide enough to hold them both.

I nodded. "Before he died, your father gave his bow to me."

She frowned. "He gave it to you?" She looked skeptical. "Is this true, or do you lie again?"

"It is true," I said, feeling annoyed. I may have spoken a few untruths when there was a reason to, but I did not like her constantly suspecting that I lied.

My answer seemed to trouble her, for she turned away and found a space nearby at the end of the line of stacked cargo filling the center of the *Gull*'s deck where she could sit, her feet tucked up beneath her, and be alone—as alone as one can be aboard a crowded ship.

The *Gull* reached our encampment on the beach of Oeland by late afternoon. While we had been gone, the hale members of the *Serpent*'s crew had been hard at work preparing for the funeral to be held on the morrow for our dead.

On orders from Nori, that morning some of the men-folk of Oeland had brought four teams of oxen to our camp. The teams had been hitched to lines attached to the bow of Sigvald's ship. As some of our men had placed cut lengths of logs in front of it for the keel to roll across and others had walked alongside, supporting the hull so that it did not tip over, it had been dragged out of the water, across the beach and fields beyond, and up the high ridge that overlooked them, to an area of level ground halfway up its side. It made a good site for a funeral pyre, high enough to look out across the land and the water beyond.

By the time we returned, the ship was already in position. The sections of logs which had been used as rollers were now propped against its sides, holding it secure, and cut brush and wood had been piled under and against the hull on all sides. The gangplank had been set in place amidships, and the sail and awnings had been arranged over the deck to tent it.

Hastein was pleased to see that the preparations were so far along. "I thank you," he told Nori, "for sending the men and the oxen to help us."

"And I you," Nori replied, "You and your men, for helping us recover our women-folk who had been taken from us. There will be joy in many households this night because of what you have done.

"I will leave you now," he said, "but I will come again before daylight, to lead you and your men to where the sacrifice will be made. It is inland, but not too far from here. The feast will be held there also."

Despite his words he did not leave, but stood rocking from one foot to the other, a look of indecision on his face.

"Yes?" Hastein asked. "Is there something more?"

"There has been much discussion among our people…," he began, then his voice trailed off. He took a deep breath and began again. "We have another boon to ask of you."

Torvald rolled his eyes. Hastein's face, which had been smiling, slowly took on a harder expression. Perhaps he expected, as I did, that Nori was going to ask that we give the folk of Oeland some of the spoils we taken from the pirates' encampment.

"What is it that you wish?" Hastein said, his voice sounding clipped.

"Your prisoners," Nori replied. "The pirates you captured. What do you intend to do with them?"

The question clearly caught Hastein by surprise. "I have not decided," he replied.

"They and their dead comrades committed many crimes against our people. They robbed us many times, and stole our women, and in the first raids, they killed some of our men-folk. These are things that should not go unpunished. Those whom you killed in the battle found the fate they deserved. But those who were taken alive should also pay. Will you give them to us?"

"You would take revenge against them?" Hastein asked.

"It is not revenge we seek," Nori replied, shaking his head. "We would mete out justice for what they have done. That is a different thing. Would you not wish to do the same in our place?"

Hastein was silent for a long time. Finally he said, "You may have them."

I was surprised by Nori's reaction. His face blanched and he gave a low gasp. I wondered if he had hoped Hastein would refuse the request. He swallowed several times, as if his throat had suddenly grown dry, then croaked, "I thank you. We will send men before nightfall to collect them." Then he turned and hurried away.

"Others of his people may wish to put these men to death, but he clearly has no taste for it," Torvald observed. "At least this takes them off of our hands."

"Hmmn," Hastein grunted in reply. He turned to me. "Do you recall what we spoke of earlier?"

I had no idea what he meant. The two of us had spoken of many things.

Seeing the confused look on my face, Hastein explained, "Your oath of vengeance. The prisoner Skjold, who has helped us in the hope of gaining mercy. If you do not wish it, I will not give him to the Oelanders with the others. I will leave his fate in your hands."

I did not answer. I did not know what to say. It was not a decision I wished to make.

"It is not easy, is it?" Hastein said, in a quiet voice. "Killing a man in battle is one thing. This is another. You must decide for this one man what I had to for all of the others. They are in our power, at our mercy. Do I let them live or send them to their deaths? They, no doubt, will feel I betrayed them and broke my word which I gave when they surrendered. But as you pointed out to me, I promised only that I and my men would not harm them."

Hastein had ordered that one of the casks of ale we had found among the wares at the pirates' camp be brought ashore, for we would drink many toasts this night to the twelve comrades whose bodies we would

301

burn on the morrow, and share many memories of them. The rest of the goods were left aboard the *Gull*, for now.

Our first night on Oeland, after washing the bodies of our fallen comrades, we had dressed them in the finest clothing we could find in each of their sea chests, and had laid each, stretched out upon his back as if asleep, upon a cloak. It was a task that was much easier to do before the death stiffness fully set in.

By now—two days after they had died—the bodies were beginning to swell and stink. Moving as quickly as possible, we lifted them by the cloaks they lay on and carried them up the ridge and onto the death ship, where we arranged them side by side along the center of the deck. Each man's armor and weapons were placed with his body, and at his feet we placed those of a pirate who had been slain in the battle. We had little else in the way of death offerings to send with them on their final voyage save the ship itself, although that admittedly was a very fine gift. At least the weapons of their slain foes and the ship captured from them would show those in Valhalla that though these men had died in the battle, they were the victors.

Einar and I helped carry Hrodgar's body, each of us grasping one of the corners of the cloak beside his feet. Hastein and Torvald held the two corners at the other end, under his head and shoulders. I thought Hastein did Hrodgar great honor by helping carrying his body, for it was not a pleasant task. Although he had been covered, as had all of the bodies, by a tent awning from Sigvald's ship, flies had found their way underneath and discovered the gaping wound in his neck. It was crawling now with maggots.

"Ugh," Torvald said. "It is a good thing we are not waiting any longer to burn them. It will take many cups of ale to remember Hrodgar as he was, instead of like this."

Hastein laid Sigvald's weapons—his helm and mail brynie, his sword, and the strange hewing spear he'd fought with—at Hrodgar's feet. I weighed placing the Finn's bow and quiver there as well, but did not. I knew it would distress the girl if her father's fine bow, and the quiver her mother had made to go with it, were burned. I should not have cared—I did not understand why I did.

"Safe voyage, old friend," Hastein said. "You were always a true comrade to me, and a brave man."

"I do not know if I could have done what he did," Torvald admitted. "Take a journey knowing beforehand that it would lead me to my death. What if he had not come?"

"No man can escape his fate," Hastein said.

As we walked back from the death ship, I told Einar about Nori's request of Hastein, and that Hastein had left Skjold's fate in my hands.

"They are coming for them before nightfall?" he exclaimed. "We have little time."

I did not understand. "Time for what?"

"You still have the rune sticks I carved, do you not? Did you bring them with you on this voyage?"

Einar had carved the sticks over the course of the first night the two of us had met. Together, we had

303

questioned Tord, the only survivor of the men Toke had sent to hunt me down after I'd escaped the attack on the longhouse up on the Limfjord. Before Einar had killed him, we had learned from Tord the names of all the men who had aided Toke in the treacherous assault that had cost the lives of my brother Harald and so many others. Einar had carved the names into two lengths of wood he had trimmed and smoothed.

"They are in my sea chest," I answered.

"Let us fetch them," he said, and broke into a trot toward the *Gull*. Over his shoulder he called, "We must question Skjold about the names while we still have time."

I caught up with him at the *Gull*. As we boarded, I noticed that Rauna had removed her things from the ship and was setting up her tent a short distance down from our campsite, on the beach.

Opening my sea chest, I dug through it until I found the two rune sticks, and handed them to Einar. As I did, I said, "But it is in my power to keep Skjold, when the Oelanders come for the others. If I did, we could question him whenever we wished."

Einar frowned. "Why would you do that? He has admitted that he has followed Toke since he was first banished by your father and left Jutland. That means he was there, that night on the Limfjord. For all you know, his blade might have helped cut down your brother Harald, or my kinsman Ulf. He probably helped kill the women and children whose safety had been promised. He joined in niddingsvaark. Why would you spare him?"

I did not have an answer. All that Einar said was true. Skjold *had* helped us, here on Oeland, and had told us much useful information about Toke's plans. But he'd done so only out of fear for his own life. He was, it seemed, a man who might do anything, betray anyone, to save himself. Why should I save him?

When Sigvald's ship had been moved, the prisoners had been taken from it and were now seated on the beach at the edge of our encampment, huddled together under the watchful gaze of three of our men. As Einar and I reached them, Hastein arrived with four more of our warriors, all fully armed. While Einar pushed his way into the group of seated prisoners and squatted down beside Skjold, Hastein pulled me aside and asked, "Well? Have you decided?"

I took a deep breath, let it out slowly, and nodded. "Yes," I said. "The Oelanders can take him, too."

"Hmmn," Hastein said. "I agree with your decision. It can be dangerous to be too merciful. If you do not kill a viper when it crosses your path, it may bite you at another time."

"Why the extra guards?" I asked, indicating the men Hastein had brought with him. Bram, I noticed, was among them, wearing his newly acquired brynie and helm.

"The Oelanders will be here soon. When these men learn they are to be taken by them, they will know—or at least suspect—what is to be their fate. We must be ready. If any try to run or to fight, we will kill them here and now."

By the time the Oelanders arrived, Einar and I were

just finishing our questioning of Skjold. One by one, Einar had read him the names carved in runes on the two sticks. There were twenty-eight of them, including Toke. For most, Skjold nodded and said, "He still lives. He still follows Toke."

Einar paused for a moment and a grim smile crossed his face before he read one of the names. "Snorre," he said.

"He is dead," Skjold answered. "You know he is dead." He glanced at me. "You killed him, in Frankia."

"Aye," Einar said. "Halfdan killed him." He slid his knife out of its scabbard and sliced, in one deep shaving, Snorre's name from the stick.

Four more times, when Einar read a name, Skjold said, "He is dead," and Einar cut the name from the sticks. All four were part of the skeleton crew who, with Skjold, had sailed the *Sea Steed* up the channel between the mainland and Oeland, while Toke had passed safely by out at sea. Three had been killed in the battle when Sigvald had attacked our ships. The fourth—Grimar— was the man Einar and I had thrown overboard and drowned.

Our sentries up on the ridge above our encampment blew a warning blast on a horn, and Torvald gave a warning shout: "Hastein, they come!" Moments later the Oelanders—there must have been close to a hundred of them, all armed with axes, knives, and other makeshift weapons, and some carrying unlit torches, as well—appeared on the crest of the ridge and marched down it, with Nori in their lead.

Einar and I stood up. "Why are they here?" Skjold

306

asked nervously. "Why so many of them, and why are they armed?"

"There is one more name on these sticks, Skjold," Einar said. "It is yours." With his knife he cut a last piece off of one of the sticks, and dropped the shaving into Skjold's lap. To me, he said, "That leaves twenty-two, including Toke, still to find and kill. Then your oath will be fulfilled."

We turned to leave. All around us, the prisoners were muttering to each other anxiously. It would not do to remain in their midst.

Skjold clutched at my sleeve. "I have helped you," he cried. "Do not let them take me. I am one of your people. I am from the village near your father's estate."

I shook him off. "You chose the path that has led you here," I told him. "You did not have to take it. You have committed many wrongs. Now you must pay for some of them."

As I walked away, I heard Bram say to him, "Skjold, is there any message you would like me to give to your family?" If Skjold answered, I did not hear it.

The Oelanders had requested of Hastein that he join in their dawn ceremony of thanks and sacrifice the following morning, and had invited the rest of our men to attend if they wished. Some, including Einar, Torvald, and Gudfred, had accompanied Hastein. I was not among those who did. The sacrifice by the folk of Oeland did not concern me, and the thought of arising yet again before dawn had no appeal. I was feeling possessed by a great weariness. The long bruises that crisscrossed my back, arms, and shoulders had grown darker and more painful over the course of the day following the battle, and my right arm and shoulder, with which I had wielded my sword during the clearing of the pirate ship—the details of which I still could not recall—felt so stiff and sore that they were painful to use.

I slept until well past daybreak. When I finally awoke I felt, if not refreshed, at least no longer exhausted.

The day of the battle, I had worn my oldest woolen tunic and trousers under my armor. It was good that I had done so. They had been far from new before, but now they were badly stained with blood that had splashed upon me during the fighting. I found a bucket aboard the *Gull*, filled it with sea water, and left them in it to soak.

My clothing was not all that was dirty and stained. My body felt filthy and smelled bad. Wrapping myself in my longest cloak against the chill morning air, and wearing only my boots underneath, I walked down the beach a ways, a clean tunic and trousers under one arm, carrying my sword in its scabbard with the other. There was no danger here—none that we knew of—but I had come to feel uncomfortable unless I had some weapon close at hand. The months of warfare and danger in Frankia had taught me that it was always the wiser course to be careful.

I did not stay in the water long, for the sea was cold. As I dried myself with my cloak and dressed, I realized that Rauna had not built a fire at her tent either yester-evening or this morning. In fact, I had not seen her at all this day. Did she have any food to cook for herself?

I stopped at her tent on the way back to the encampment and called out, "Rauna, are you in there? It is Halfdan." As soon as I said it, I realized I had never told her my name.

The flap over the tent's door shifted slightly on one side, not enough for me to see in, but I could tell that she was peeking out.

"My name is Halfdan," I told her. "I did not tell you that before."

"What do you want?"

"Do you have anything to eat? There is food at our camp, if you would like some." Cullain and Regin had prepared a large pot of boiled barley porridge for the morning meal. "It is simple, but it is hot."

She did not answer. "I am going to get food now," I told her. "Bring a bowl if you wish to have some."

When I reached the cook-fire, after stopping at the *Gull* to pick up my own bowl and spoon, I saw that Hastein and the others had returned. Hastein's tent had been pitched facing the fire, and he was seated out in front of it on one of his sea chests, eating.

Torvald had pulled his own chest beside him and was also eating, although with little enthusiasm. "There are only so many days in a row I can eat porridge," he said, "before it begins to stick in my throat. It is a good thing there will be meat at the feast tonight."

Einar, who was seated on the ground nearby with Gudfred, said, "I enjoy boiled barley for my morning meal."

Torvald held his spoon over his bowl and let its contents fall back in with a plop. He shook his head and sighed. "I would much prefer to drink barley as ale than eat it as mush."

I filled my bowl at the fire. As I turned to go and join the others, I saw what looked to be a stack of bloody horse's legs lying off to one side.

"The place of sacrifice was very strange," Einar told me, as I sat down. "It was a great stone fortress built on the edge of a cliff, very old and fallen into ruin. You will see it tonight. The feast is to be there."

"I asked Nori about it," Hastein volunteered. "He said there are many such ruins across Oeland—almost a score in all. They have all been abandoned for longer than anyone can remember. At one time, this island must have been home to many warriors. It must have been a powerful kingdom in those days. Einar told me, by the way," he added, looking at me, "of your questioning of Skjold. It was good that you did so. I did not realize Toke had so few men with him. We still have a goodly advantage of numbers—at least for now." He stared at me for a moment, then said, "You have a strange look on your face."

"There is a stack of legs by the fire. Horses' legs," I answered.

"I brought those," Torvald said. "The Oelanders gave them to me. Cullain asked for them."

"The Oelanders sacrificed two horses this morning," Einar told me. "I have never seen a horse sacrificed before. They tied their feet together and toppled them onto their sides, then cut their throats."

"And they were big, fine horses," Torvald added. "At least there will be much meat for the feast."

"But why the legs?" I asked.

Hastein answered. "Cullain is going to boil them to make a bone broth. He says it will take at least two days to make, but when it is done, drinking it will help our wounded regain their strength. He is concerned about Stig. He lost much blood and is very weak. If he does not get stronger soon, he will not heal."

Cullain walked over to the pile, picked up one of the legs, and carried it and a large iron cauldron to a nearby log that had washed up onto the beach. Using the log as a chopping block, he began to hack the leg into short lengths with an axe, tossing the pieces into the pot.

"*That* will dull the blade," Torvald said.

"Was there any sign of the prisoners?" I asked.

"Oh, yes," Gudfred answered, a grim smile on his face. "They were there. Or at least their heads were, stuck on poles at the place of sacrifice."

"Ah," Torvald said, and pointed. "Look. Here comes Halfdan's new woman."

"She is not my woman," I snapped, and turned to look. Rauna was standing at the edge of the encampment, as if fearful of entering it. She was holding a wooden bowl in her hands. Several of our men were staring at her curiously.

I stood and walked over to her. "Follow me," I told her. She said nothing, but followed, her head down so she would not have to meet the gazes of those watching.

At the fire, I took her bowl, filled it, and handed it back to her. She stared at it suspiciously. "What is this?"

she asked.

"It is barley. Boiled barley porridge. Do your people not grow barley?"

She shook her head. After a few moments, she said, "I thank you," then turned and hurried back through the camp to her tent, where she went inside, hidden from sight.

"I have never seen a Finn woman before," Gudfred commented when I returned. "She is not what I expected."

"What did you expect?" Torvald asked.

"I do not know. I have heard that the Finns live deep in the forests, and are a wild people, savages. But she is rather comely, and does not look at all like a wild savage."

"They do not look very different from us," Hastein said, "though they do not tend to be as tall. I lived for a time in Halland as a boy. I was fostered in the home of a chieftain there. He traded with the Finns each spring. They would bring furs to trade for goods they could not make for themselves. They are a simple, peaceful folk. And though they do mostly live deep in the forests, they are not savages."

"Her father was not so peaceful," Gudfred observed.

"No," Hastein agreed. "It *was* a strange thing to find a Finn fighting with Sigvald's men." To me he said, "You may not consider her your woman, but you should at least make it known that she is under your protection because of a promise you made to her father, before he died. If you do not, another may try his luck with her. If

312

our men think her an unattached woman, with no family to protect her...." He shrugged. "As Gudfred says, she *is* somewhat comely, and our men have been long away from the company of women."

"But Halfdan made no such promise to the Finn," Gudfred protested, looking surprised. "I was there. He promised only to give her the bag he wore around his neck."

Hastein looked at me and raised his eyebrows. Now I shrugged. "It seemed the easiest way to persuade Osten to leave her be."

"I wonder what was in that bag," Einar said. "I suspect it was some kind of magic charm."

"If so, it did not protect the Finn," Gudfred pointed out.

"You *did* persuade Osten to leave her be," Hastein told me, an annoyed expression on his face. "But what now? What is your plan now that she is here with us on Oeland?"

"I do not have a plan," I admitted.

"You had best come up with one. And quickly," Hastein replied.

When the sun reached its noon zenith, we marched up onto the ridge to the death ship to bid farewell to our fallen comrades. Each man brought a drinking cup with him for the toasts we would make to the dead. I carried the fine drinking horn Hastein had given me in Frankia.

The cask of ale which had been brought ashore from the *Gull* had seen hard use the night before, but was still half full. It had been carried up the hill and placed a short distance from the death ship. A small fire had been built beside it, and several unlit torches lay ready beside the fire. As each man passed the cask, he dipped his cup inside the open top and filled it with ale.

While Hastein climbed the gangplank up onto the deck, the rest of us gathered in a half circle below, facing the side of the ship. A large group of Oelanders, Nori among them, stood watching nearby.

Hastein raised his hand, signaling for silence, and began to speak.

"My comrades. My brothers—for that is what we all are now. When we began this voyage, we were not as one. We were a company in name only. But now we have fought together, and have won a great victory over a force much larger than our own. Truly, now we are all brothers in arms.

"Every victory has a price. Twelve of our company paid for our victory with their lives. We are here to honor them, and to send them on their way. This night, while we feast here on Oeland, our comrades will feast with the gods in Valhalla."

Turning slightly so he could see the twelve bodies laid out across the deck behind him, but could still be heard by those standing below, Hastein raised the silver cup he held and shouted, "To Hrodgar!" When he did, I realized that he was wearing, around his upper arm, his golden ring—the oath ring of a godi.

Lowering the cup, he continued. "He was a brave man, who valued honor more than life itself. A just man, who would not turn a blind eye to niddingsvaark. A man who lived a long and good life, and chose a warrior's death. More than once, Hrodgar has fought for me, at my side. I will miss you, my friend." Again Hastein raised his cup high, and this time we all raised ours, too, and cried out in unison, "To Hrodgar!" then drank.

As I raised my drinking horn to my lips, I whispered a private prayer to the old chieftain. "Give my greetings to my brother Harald, and to my mother, and to my father Hrorik. Tell them that one day I will hope to join them and you in Odin's great hall."

One by one, Hastein called out the names of the dead. For each, he had kind words and praises, although in truth there was not a great deal that could be said about some who had died. Skuli, for instance—Bram's friend. He was but a young man from a small village. He had no history of grand deeds to recite. But he had been willing to join the hunt for Toke. The decision had cost him his life.

I had expected the fire to be lit as soon as all the dead had been praised and drunk to, but Hastein continued to speak.

"My comrades, you may believe that the blood-price has been paid in full for our brothers who died. We ourselves took the lives of most of the pirates who attacked us, for they were no match for our courage and our blades. And the folk of Oeland have put to death those who survived the battle. But the full blood-price has not yet been paid. Let me tell you now what I have but recently learned.

"Sigvald and his band did not attack us by chance. They were but pirates, and we were clearly a formidable company. Have you not wondered why they did not just let us pass by?"

Many nodded their heads, and some muttered, "Aye."

"Sigvald was told that we would be sailing this way. He was told we were but recently returned from the war in Frankia, and that our sea chests would be filled with silver. He attacked because he believed us to be so rich a prize that the losses he would surely suffer would be well worth the treasure to be won. We sailed into a trap that had been set to kill us. Had we been lesser men, it would have succeeded. This was the work of Toke, the man we hunt. He set a very clever trap. He is a very dangerous foe. The blood of our comrades is on *his* hands."

An angry growl spread through the men listening to Hastein speak.

"This, too, I have learned," Hastein continued. "Toke sails for Birka. There he hopes to sell Sigrid, the sister of our comrade Halfdan, to slave traders. She is reputed to be a great beauty, who will be worth riches in the Araby kingdoms. And then he will sail for Ireland.

"Toke must not reach Ireland. For now, he has but twenty-one men left in his war-band. We still outnumber him by more than two-to-one. If we can catch him now, he will be ours. But in Ireland, he has strong allies. Thorgils, the greatest chieftain among the Danes and Norse who are there, will support him, as will others.

"This night we will feast. The Oelanders would honor us for our victory, and thank us for their deliverance. But on the morrow, as quickly as we can ready our ships, we will sail for Birka. On the morrow, we will take up our hunt again. And this I vow before you all. For the deaths of the twelve men we now honor, I count myself among those whom Toke has wronged. He now owes *me* a blood-debt, as well as those he owes for his past acts of treachery and murder. I *will* collect it."

Slipping the golden ring off his arm, Hastein held it aloft in his fist and shouted, "Upon this unbroken ring, I make this oath before you all: I will not give up this hunt, even if it leads me to the very edge of the world."

Our gathered warriors roared their approval. They held their cups high, and many shouted back, "To the edge of the world!" before they drank to Hastein's oath. I, too, drank, and repeated Hastein's words. But in my heart, I hoped they would not prove to be prophetic.

When Hastein finished speaking, the torches were lit and the wood stacked around the death ship set alight in multiple places. A steady breeze was blowing westward across the ridge out over the channel. It quickly whipped the points of flame into a blaze. As the fire began to engulf the ship itself, an osprey appeared high overhead and circled three times. Then it caught the wind and soared off, the smoke from the fire trailing below it. All agreed that it was a good omen. Einar suggested that the bird had been sent from Valhalla itself to guide the spirits of our comrades on their final journey.

After the burning ship had collapsed in upon itself in a shower of sparks, I walked slowly back to the camp. The others around me were in high spirits, partly from

317

the toasts we had drunk to honor our dead, and partly in anticipation of the evening's feast. Our company would be departing for it soon. The ruined fort was, Hastein explained, some distance farther up the island, and even if we left now, dusk would be falling by the time we reached it.

I realized what Hastein had told me earlier was right. If we were to leave on the morrow, I needed to decide what to do with the girl. I must speak to her now, quickly, before we left for the feast.

I did not intend to take my drinking horn with me to the feast. I would tuck my wooden spoon in my belt pouch, but Nori had assured Hastein that our hosts, the Oelanders, would provide us bowls for our food and cups to drink from. Boarding the *Gull*, I went to my sea chest to put the horn inside. When I opened it, the Finn's ornate leather quiver caught my eye.

The girl had seemed moved when she had seen it. On impulse, I emptied the arrows out and took it with me.

As in the morning, when I reached her tent she was nowhere in sight, and the flap covering the entrance was down. "Rauna," I called out. "It is Halfdan. We must speak."

I heard a rustling sound of her moving inside, but she did not answer. Sighing in exasperation, I added, "I have brought something for you. Your father's quiver."

After a few moments, she said, in a low voice which I had to strain to understand, "What is...quiver? I do not know that word."

"The leather bag to hold arrows. You said your

mother made it for your father."

She pulled the flap aside and looked out. She was on her knees, her legs tucked underneath her, just inside the door opening. She looked for a moment at the quiver in my hand, then up at my face. When she did, I could see that her cheeks were streaked with the tracks of tears. She had been weeping.

Seeing me staring, she sniffed and wiped her cheeks with her hands, then reached out and took the quiver.

"We must speak," I said again, in a softer voice this time. "My people sail on the morrow. We are leaving Oeland. We must decide what to do with you."

A look of despair washed over her face and she hung her head.

"You could stay here, on Oeland. Do you wish to do that?" It would be easiest for me if she would. I was eager to have her off my hands.

At the suggestion, she looked up at me with fear showing in her eyes and shook her head. "I am afraid of them," she whispered. I did not blame her for that.

"Where are your people?" I asked. "Where do they live?"

She pointed vaguely to the northwest. "There," she said. "Far away. Very far away."

I wondered again how she and her father had ended up here, among Sigvald's company of pirates.

"We are sailing for Birka," I told her. "Do you know Birka? Have you heard of it?"

She looked, if possible, even more fearful than before, but nodded. "I have been there. Once. With my father and mother."

That, at least, was helpful. If her people sometimes traveled to Birka, perhaps some of them would be there when we arrived. If so, I could leave her there, with someone who could help her find her way back to her home.

"Good," I told her. "Then it is settled. You will travel with us to Birka."

I had expected her to be pleased. Instead, she began trembling. Without another word, she lowered the door covering and retreated deeper into her tent.

We marched together as a company to the feast, cutting first across the grassy pastureland behind the beach, then climbing the slope beyond. When we reached its crest, I realized that what I'd thought to be a narrow ridge was far broader than I had imagined—it spanned the entire center of the island. The ground atop the ridge was rocky, far less fertile than the flat lands that lined the shore, and much of the center of the island was covered with patches of short, twisted trees.

A road of sorts—a hard-packed earthen track, wide enough for several men to ride abreast, or for large carts to travel on—ran along the edge of the crest, overlooking the wide apron of fertile pastures and fields below. We headed north along the road as the sun sank lower and lower and shadows grew long.

The sun had left the sky and the moon was not yet risen when we reached the fort. The side of the ridge fell sharply away here in a steep, sloping cliff face. A wall built of stacked stones, taller than the height of a man, began at the cliff's edge and ran for almost the length of a bow shot before curving around in a broad half circle, to meet the precipice again on the far side. As we drew closer, I could see that the fort was in disrepair. The top of the wall was jagged and uneven, and stones that had fallen from it lay along its base.

The road curved to pass across the front of the fort, where an opening was located. Presumably it had once been secured by a gate, but now it was nothing more than a wide gap in the wall. Torches had been wedged in the stones on either side to serve as beacons to guide us, and when we reached the opening, Nori was standing in it, a group of men and women gathered behind him, all singing a song of welcome. At its conclusion, they turned and led us inside.

The interior of the fort held only a flat, grassy field. Three large bonfires had been built in its center to provide light, and a long, low cook-fire had been laid in the middle of the area lit by them. While Nori addressed a long and rambling speech to Hastein, Einar and I wandered around the interior. I wondered what this place had looked like in times past. Who had built it, and where had they gone?

"In Frankia," I told Einar, "when we were out scouting for the Frankish army, I found an old, ruined fort deep in the forest. Do you not wonder, if the stones in such places could talk, what tales they might tell us?"

Einar shook his head. "No," he said, "I do not." He looked at me as if he felt it was a strange thought to have. "Come this way," he told me.

He led me to the back of the fort, along the cliff, at

the midpoint between where the long, curved wall touched its edge on either side. "This is where they held the sacrifice this morning," he said. "And it must be where they killed the prisoners, too. Look, there are their heads. I wonder where Skjold's is."

The Oelanders had built two tall tripods of long wooden poles, lashed together in a point at their top ends, with their bottom ends spread wide. The skin of a horse had been draped over each tripod so that it hung as if some gaunt, bloody ghost beast was rearing up on its hind legs. The horses' heads, which were still attached to the skins, were propped atop the tripods so they seemed to be staring out toward the distant sea.

On either side of the horse offerings, poles had been driven into the ground along the edge of the cliff, spaced so that they reached almost to the wall on either side. A human head was impaled on each pole. They, too, were facing out toward the sea. It made a grim sight. I felt glad they had not been turned the other way. I would not have liked to have their dead eyes staring at me during the feast.

Two short tables, with a bench for each, had been hauled to the fort and set up side by side, facing the cook-fire. Together, they formed the high table for the feast. Nori and three other village headmen sat at one, Nori taking the seat in the center, closest to the other table. "And you," he said to Hastein, pointing to the neighboring table, "will sit here, beside me. Please choose three of your captains to join us."

Torvald, of course, sat at Hastein's side. As the new captain of the archers, I took the place beside him.

Hastein selected Hroald, the headman from the village near the estate in Jutland, to be our fourth at the high table. I thought it a generous gesture on his part. Had the villagers not joined our company, we would not have had enough men to undertake this voyage. They'd had no duty to avenge Harald, as the men of the estate did. And they were more farmers than warriors. Yet they had come out of respect for Hrorik, my father, and for his murdered son. Now three of their eight were dead. Their honor and loyalty had cost them dearly.

I did not enjoy the feast. First Nori, then each of the other headmen at the high table felt compelled to give repeated and lengthy toasts thanking the gods for sending us to free them from the oppression the pirates had inflicted. I did not believe the gods had sent us. We had come this way for our own reasons. If the Norns had chosen to cross our threads with those of the pirates and the Oelanders, they, too had their own reasons, which we as mortal men could not see. But it was not the Oelanders' prayers that had brought us here.

I found my thoughts carrying me back time and again to my conversation that afternoon with Rauna. Why had she looked so afraid? What had occurred in Birka? Again I could not help but wonder how she and her father had come to be a part of Sigvald's pirate band.

Torvald, unlike me, was enjoying himself immensely. Although I found the horsemeat in the stew the Oelanders had prepared to be rather tough and stringy, for Torvald it was enough that it was fresh meat. And of course, the fact that there was ale—as much as we could drink—only served to cinch the feast's success in his eyes.

He nudged me with his elbow, almost knocking me off the bench. "You have a strange look on your face," he said. "You look troubled."

"It is nothing," I told him. "My thoughts are just elsewhere."

"There are times," Torvald suggested, "when it is a good thing to have no thoughts at all. You should drink more ale."

I took his advice. Later, I wished that I had not.

Many cups later—more than I could count—I was standing at the edge of the cliff, swaying dangerously, releasing the ale pressure that had built up within me. I no longer cared whether the dead eyes of the horses and executed pirates might be watching.

Nori suddenly appeared at my side. Lifting his tunic and sliding his trousers down his thighs, he too began to relieve himself.

"We offered it to each of them," he said.

"What?" I mumbled. I had no idea what he was speaking about.

"Killing the pirates. We offered each man who had a woman stolen from him the chance to kill one of these pirates. We lined them up here, and one by one, laid their necks across a log. We gave the right to strike off their heads to those who had a woman taken by them."

I did not wish to hear this. I did not know why he was telling it to me.

"There were nine," Nori continued. "Seven who had women taken, but they are now returned to them.

And two—Osten and Serck—whose women died. Four did it. They took the axe and killed a man. But the last one did not strike true. His first blow did not even kill the pirate, and it took him three blows in all to cut off his head. After that, most of the others said they did not wish to kill another man. So then Osten and Serck killed the rest of the pirates. They chopped off their heads and threw their bodies down the cliff."

I wished the old man would stop talking and leave me alone. I did not care. It was not my concern. Skjold had chosen the path he'd followed. His death was his own doing, not mine.

"Osten is not the man he once was," Nori said. The old man was a prattler. It tired me to listen to him. I pulled up my trousers and turned unsteadily to rejoin the feast.

"His anger consumes him," Nori continued. He paused for a moment, then added. "I do not know where he has gone."

I stopped and shook my head, trying to clear the ale fog from it.

"What are you saying?"

"Osten, and Serck, too. They left the feast a short time ago. I do not know where they have gone—but I am concerned."

"Why are you telling me this?" I demanded. But in my heart, I knew.

"Your jarl, your people, you have saved us," he replied. "I do not wish there to be trouble between us."

I had left my sword lying on the table at my seat. I sprinted to it, wobbling a little as I did, slung its baldric over my shoulder, then headed at a slow run toward the gate. Behind me, I heard Hastein calling, "Halfdan! Where are you going?" I did not take the time to answer.

The route back to our encampment seemed much further than it had when we'd traveled it that afternoon. My sword's scabbard kept bouncing between my legs and almost tripping me, until I finally unslung it and carried it in my left hand. And I seemed to have no wind to run with—the amount of ale I'd drunk no doubt was to blame for that. I kept having to stop, catch my breath, and walk for a time before I could run again.

The night sky was clear, but was lit by only a half moon. Once I thought I saw in the distance a figure, possibly two, far ahead on the road.

Just as I reached the point where the ridge overlooked our encampment, I heard a woman's scream from somewhere down below. There was no other woman save Rauna down there. I headed down the slope at a run, and almost immediately lost my footing and fell headlong, hitting my head on a rock and bruising my shoulder badly.

I lay stunned for a few moments, then staggered to my feet. I realized I did not know where my sword was. I had lost it in the fall.

Rauna screamed again. I headed downhill, more cautiously this time. Once I reached level ground I ran as fast as my leaden legs would carry me toward her tent.

The flap covering the door opening had been torn off. Inside, a man with black hair and a short-trimmed beard—he must have been the one Nori had called Serck—was kneeling at Rauna's head, holding her arms and keeping her pinned, helpless, on her back. Osten was squatting astride her.

I crouched and stepped through the opening into the tent. Inside, I grabbed Osten's long brown beard just below his jaw with my left hand. I jerked it hard, twisting his head back and to the side as I pulled him up off of Rauna, then I drew my dagger with my right hand and sliced the blade across his throat. As his blood sprayed out, I twisted and heaved his body out of the tent.

Behind me, Serck released Rauna and leapt to his feet. Out of the corner of my eye, I could see him sweep something up in his hand from the floor of the tent as he did. Just as I turned back to face him, he swung his arm and a heavy weight crashed against the side of my head. My knees buckled under me and I toppled over sideways. The last thing I saw as everything went black was the look of triumph on Serck's face.

11

Birka

When I next awakened we were at sea. At first, when I opened my eyes I could make out nothing. I did not know where I was, and for a moment feared I was blind. Then the gray fog that clouded my sight cleared, and above me, with an anxious look upon her face, I saw Rauna. Einar was beside her.

"He wakes," he said, then stood and hurried away.

A short time later Hastein appeared.

"We were not certain whether you would return to this world or pass on to the next," he said. "Torvald wanted to leave you on Oeland with the rest of our wounded, so Cullain could care for you. But Einar and Gudfred persuaded me to bring you along. It would be a shame they said, if we do catch Toke, for you to not be with us. And the girl has been tending to you while you have been unconscious, such as needs to be done. After the attack, we could hardly leave her on Oeland, anyway."

"Where am I?" I asked. My voice sounded like the dry croak of a raven. Hastein nodded to Rauna, and she placed her hand behind my head, raised it slightly, and held a cup to my lips. At the feel of the cool water washing over my parched throat, I closed my eyes and for a few moments thought of nothing else.

"You are aboard the *Gull*," Hastein said, when I opened my eyes again. "We are sailing for Birka. We left

Oeland yester-day, just after noon. We sailed through the night, for we have much time to make up."

"What happened?" I asked. I could remember nothing beyond the look of victory on Serck's face.

"It seems you saved the girl's life, and she saved yours," Hastein said. "The two men whose women the pirates killed—Osten and Serck were their names—attacked her. You killed Osten, but Serck struck you down. He hit you with an iron cook-pot. He was going to crush your skull with it, but Rauna slashed him across the back of his knees with a knife. He turned and swung the pot at her, but she backed away too fast and he missed. It threw him off balance—it is hard to stand when you have been hamstrung—and he fell. When he did, Rauna picked up a small-axe and split his skull with it. This girl has the heart of a warrior, for certain. Two of the sentries from our camp reached the tent just as he struck you down, and saw it all. It was over by the time the rest of us arrived from the feast. We had seen you leave in great haste, and followed. Nori told me what he had warned you of."

"Ah," I said, "I see." Although in truth, that was an exaggeration. I closed my eyes, and drifted back into sleep.

The rest of the day I passed back and forth between sleep and groggy wakefulness several times. Rauna was always there whenever I opened my eyes. She said nothing, other than to ask me, "Water?" each time I awoke. I did not speak either. My mind felt too clouded to form words.

Late in the day, I gradually became aware that the rhythm of the *Gull*'s motion had changed. I opened my eyes and saw that her sail had been lowered, and we were moving under power of her oars.

I felt more fully awake this time. I tried to sit up, but when I did, my head began spinning and I fell back. Rauna, who must have been nearby, appeared and knelt at my side. "Help me sit up," I told her.

I had been laid on a pallet made of furs and coverings which I did not recognize, and my heaviest cloak had been draped over me to keep me warm, for my boots and clothes had been removed. We were in the stern, just aft of the two rear supports of the overhead rack for the oars and boom. Two of the poles from Rauna's tent had been lashed to the supports to form a simple frame, and my second cloak had been hung over them to protect me from the sun and weather.

Behind me, stretching from the space underneath the oar rack just back of my pallet almost to the front of the ship, the center of the deck was filled with cargo: our own supplies of provisions, plus goods taken from the pirates' camp. After Rauna helped me sit up, with her assistance I eased myself back until I could lean against a bundle of furs at the end of the piled goods. Doing so left me feeling slightly breathless, and made my head pound with pain.

Hastein was alone on the stern deck, manning the steer-board. From what I could see, the rest of the crew were all manning oars. Even so, the last pair in the stern was unmanned.

Sitting up, I could just see over the rail. Off our

steer-board side, not far away, the *Serpent* was moving even with us, also under oars. Torvald stood tall in her stern. Both ships were heading toward the shore. The *Serpent*'s deck was, like that of the *Gull*, crowded with cargo. It looked as though some of our take from the pirates' store of stolen riches had been moved to her, to balance out the weight as much as possible between the two ships. Longships are not designed for carrying heavy loads of goods. The cargo they are made to carry is warriors.

"Where are my clothes?" I asked.

Rauna turned and pointed behind her. My sea chest had been moved from my rowing position to the end of the stacked cargo. "There," she said.

I was so weak she had to help me dress, which greatly embarrassed me, and again, the effort left me breathless and made my head pound. Gudfred, who was rowing at an oar opposite my pallet, watched the entire process, which made it even more humiliating. When we had finished and Rauna had helped me lean back once again against the bundle of furs to rest, he said, "Do not try to do too much too soon. A hard blow to the head, such as you received, can be a tricky thing. I knew a man once who received such a blow and seemed fine after he had awakened from it, but three days later he suddenly died. You should rest. If the blow you received does not kill you, in time you will feel better."

If his words were meant to encourage me, they did not.

After the bows of the two ships had been pulled up

against a sandy beach so we could make camp for the night, Einar helped me ashore, my arm draped over his shoulders for support. Rauna brought one of the thick fur covers—it turned out they were hers—to provide a warm, dry pad for me to stretch out on, and Gudfred carried my sea chest ashore so I would have something to lean against.

Hastein and Torvald came over while they were helping me settle myself, a short distance from where the cook-fire was being laid.

"So you live," Torvald said. "I was not at all certain you would from the way you looked, and because we could not wake you up, even the next day. The skalds will be relieved," he added.

Hastein frowned and looked at him. "What?" he asked.

"The skalds," Torvald answered. "They have been spinning such fine tales about the mighty warrior Strongbow. It would not do at all for him to be killed with a cooking pot while drunk and fighting over a woman. It would have made an ignoble end to his story."

I glared at him. If he had not encouraged me to drink so much at the feast, this might not have happened.

Trying my best to ignore Torvald, I asked Hastein, "So we are sailing for Birka? What is your plan?"

Hastein shrugged and grinned. "It is a simple one. We will sell the goods we seized at Sigvald's camp, and hopefully we will find Toke there, and kill him. And when we do, we will free your sister Sigrid, too."

"Do you really think there is any hope?" I asked. "Is he not too many days ahead of us to still be there?"

"Perhaps," Hastein admitted, "but perhaps not. Toke has gone to great trouble, and traveled a great distance, to take your sister to Birka in order to sell her there. Only in Birka will he be able to find slave traders who deal with the Araby kingdoms, where she will bring the highest price. His fortunes have taken a serious turn for the worse. Just weeks ago he was the master of a fine estate in Jutland, and numbered the folk and warriors there as his own. Now he is on the run with just a handful of men. I think the profit he hopes your sister will bring is of much importance to him."

I did not see how any of that changed the fact that Toke would have reached Birka days before we would arrive there. "But he will have had more than enough time to have sold her and be gone," I said.

"Perhaps," Hastein said again, "but perhaps not. The type of slave traders Toke seeks, the kind he needs who will pay him the price he wants, are not always present in Birka. They are traveling merchants. I think he will in wait in Birka, if need be, to get the best possible price for your sister. If luck is with us, Toke will still be in Birka, waiting for a slaver to arrive, when we reach it."

"And if he is not?"

Hastein shrugged. "Then we will sell our goods, return to Oeland to pick up our wounded, and sail back to Jutland. Our hunt will be a longer one. Winter approaches, and the voyage to Ireland, where Toke is bound, is not an easy one, even in good weather. We will take up the pursuit again in the spring."

As I pondered Hastein's words, I suddenly remembered my sword. We were halfway to Birka, and it was lying on the side of the ridge back on Oeland.

"What is it?" Hastein asked, staring at the expression on my face.

"My sword," I answered. "I lost in when I fell, running to reach Rauna's tent after I heard her screaming."

"It is in your sea chest," Hastein said. "We realized the next morning, as we were loading you aboard the *Gull*, that it was missing. Einar searched back along the path you had traveled and found it."

I took a deep breath and let it out in a long sigh of relief.

Hastein stood staring at me silently for a few moments. "There is a thing you should give some thought to," he finally said. "This is the second time that drinking too much ale has almost cost you your life." Then he turned and walked away.

Hastein's words stung. I knew what he was referring to—the time in Ruda when Snorre had first arrived at the town. I had barely escaped being gutted by him in a brawl. On that occasion, too, I had been drinking with Torvald.

A feeling of despair filled my heart. We had been so close to catching Toke. But I did not believe we would find him in Birka. I did not believe we would be in time to rescue Sigrid. I did not feel that luck was with us on this voyage.

*

Rauna had been setting up her tent near where I was sitting while Torvald and Hastein had been speaking with me. That was a thing that had changed about her. On Oeland, she had hidden herself away as much as possible, and had tried, except when absolutely necessary, to avoid me. Now she was never far away. Perhaps it was because I was so weak, and she felt indebted to me for trying to stop Osten and Serck's attack. Or perhaps she was merely frightened to be alone after the attack—or perhaps it was a bit of both.

Later that evening, after the night meal had been prepared—a simple stew made of barley and vegetables—she brought two bowls full from the cook-fire. Handing me one, she sat down beside me with the other.

We ate in silence. I found that I felt ravenous, for it had been two days since I had last eaten. I quickly emptied my bowl, and at my request, Rauna returned to the cook-fire and filled it again. But when I began to eat it, my stomach suddenly felt ill. I should not have eaten so much so fast, after having gone so long with no food at all.

After several spoonfuls, I set the bowl down on the ground beside me, and leaned back to rest. "I will finish this later," I said.

"Who is this man Toke that your leader spoke of?" Rauna suddenly asked. "You and your people are chasing him, yes?"

I nodded. "He is a very bad man," I said. "He killed

335

my brother and many others. I have sworn to avenge them."

"And he has stolen your sister, too?"

I nodded again. "Our father was a chieftain. She is high born, but he intends to sell her as a slave."

She sat staring at me, but said nothing more. I wondered what she was thinking. If, as Hastein said, her people—the Finns—were a peaceful folk, what must she think of us?

"I am in your debt," I told her, breaking the silence.

She frowned. "For what reason?"

"For my life. Serck would have killed me but for you. I consider that not a small thing."

"I did not act to save you," she said. "I was afraid for myself. I know what your kind can do to the women of my people. I have seen it. There are many bad men among your people."

After what Osten and Serck had tried to do, I did not blame her for thinking so. But she should not blame an entire folk for the acts of a few bad men. "I am in your debt," I said again. "I will not forget it. I will do all I can to help you return to your own people. In Birka we will find someone to help you."

As had happened that night on Oeland, at my mention of Birka her face took on a look of fear, and she began trembling.

"What is it?" I asked her. "What about Birka causes you fear? What happened there?"

"Do not leave me in Birka," she pleaded. "There is no one there who will help me. It is an evil place, full of evil men."

"I will not leave you in danger," I told her. "I promise you that. But you must tell me what it is you fear."

She said nothing, but sat wringing her hands and rocking back and forth.

"Rauna," I said, in a softer voice, "How did you and your father come to be a part of Sigvald's company? Was it in Birka? What happened there? I wish to help you, but I cannot if I do not know these things."

She was silent so long I did not think she was going to answer. But finally, she took a deep breath, raised her head and looked into my face, and told me the tale.

"For many years, a man—one of your people—would come to our lands to trade with my people," she began.

This surprised me. I had understood that the Finns lived deep in the hinterlands of Svealand and Gotarland. "Do you mean he was a Dane?" I asked, interrupting her.

She frowned. "What is a Dane?"

"I am a Dane. My people are Danes. We live in lands far to the west of here." It was clear she did not understand. "These are the peoples of the northlands," I told her. "Here, where we are now, is Svealand—the kingdom of the Sveas. These lands are theirs."

"No one can own the land," she protested.

Ignoring her, I continued. "West of here are the lands of the Gotars, and to the west of their kingdoms are the lands of the Danes. Beyond the Danes, across the Jutland Sea to the north, are the Norse."

She shook her head. "Do you not all speak the same

337

tongue?"

I nodded. "Yes, the common tongue of the north. What you and I are speaking now."

"And you all dress in iron, and carry many weapons, and fight, and kill. All of these peoples you speak of, they are all the same. They are all the others. *I*," she said, tapping her chest for emphasis, "am one of the people—I am *Samit*. You are one of the others."

This was going nowhere. She knew too little of the world to understand. "Continue your tale," I told her.

"The man who came each year to trade—his name was Barne—wanted furs. For them, he gave us knives, and axes, and brightly-colored cloth and beads, and other things we did not have. He was a good man. He was not evil. He taught my father, and others among our people who wished to learn it, to speak your tongue. He tried to persuade us to follow his god—he believed there was only one, which is a very foolish thing.

"Several times, he took my father with him back to Birka, where he had come from, with many furs to trade there."

"Ah," I said, "then this Barne was a Svear merchant."

Ignoring me, she continued. "When my father would return, he always had many, many goods for our people. He said Barne had taught him much about the ways of the others, and their beliefs.

"Last winter, Barne did not come. Instead, a great band of the others came to our lands. They did not come to trade. They had many weapons, and they came to rob and to kill. All who could fled deep into the forests to

338

escape them, but many were slain, and others were taken away and never seen again. Our villages were burned, and our goods were stolen."

She was as slow at telling a tale as Einar. I wondered how late in the night it would be before we got to Sigvald.

"In the spring, after the raiders had gone and our people had gathered together once again, our *noaidi* searched the other side for Barne, and found him there. He had died—he, too, had been killed by the raiders, and his spirit had left this side of the world."

Now *I* did not understand. "What is a *noaidi*?" I asked, struggling to pronounce the strange word. It was clearly of her people's language, not of the common tongue.

"A *noaidi* is a spirit traveler. His spirit can leave his body and travel to the other side, and return. It gives him great power and knowledge, to be able to see the world from both sides. Are there no *noaidis* among your people?"

I shook my head. She seemed surprised.

"What happened when your people learned Barne was dead?" I asked.

"There was much talk about what we should do. No one believed that the raiders would never come back again. Some said that we should leave, and seek new lands to live upon. But others said our people had hunted and fished these lands since time began, and our spirits, and those of our fathers and their fathers before them were bound to these lands. If we left them, when we died our spirits would be lost.

"My father said we should go to Birka, and ask the help of the others who lived there. He said when Barne had taken him to Birka, he had told him the people there had rules they lived by. If a person broke the rules and harmed another, the one who was harmed could go to a meeting of all their peoples, and ask that the wrong be made right. He said Barne had taken him to meet with the leader of the others in Birka who presided over such meetings when they were held. My father said he was a good man, like Barne was. My father told our people he would make the journey to Birka himself, and ask the leader there to help us against the evil men who had attacked us. We would take a fine gift—a bundle of the richest winter pelts of foxes and martens—to give to the leader of Birka. All of our people gave of their best furs for the gift."

This was a strange tale, to be sure. *How would it lead to Sigvald?* I wondered.

"Because the journey was so long, my mother, brother, and I traveled with my father, so he would not be alone. After many days, we reached the shores of a great lake. Birka, my father explained, was on an island out in the center of the lake. We would camp there, on the shore, and wait for a boat to pass by. My father said that was what he and Barne had done, and when a boat came, we would pay for passage to the island.

"After three days, a boat did come. There were five men in it. They were fishing. My father told them his story—why we had come to Birka—and asked them to carry us there. The men said their boat had room for only one more. So my father took the bundle of furs and went with them, and told us to wait until he returned.

"The men in the boat were evil, like the raiders had been. They had not gone far from shore when my mother saw one of them hit my father over the head, and they threw him overboard into the waters of the lake. Then they turned their boat and rowed back toward our camp.

"I had been in the woods, gathering firewood. I did not see it happen. I heard my mother scream and ran to her. I reached our camp just as the evil men's boat reached the shore. My mother told me they had killed my father. She told me to run. She picked up my brother—he was but two years of age—and ran, too. I was so frightened. I fled into the forest, as fast as I could run. My mother could not keep up. I heard her scream again, but I was too afraid to go back and help her."

Rauna hung her head and began weeping.

"It was right for you to run," I told her. "It was what your mother wanted you to do. You could not have helped her."

"You cannot know that," she said bitterly. "You were not there."

"Do you remember the man Jarl Hastein, my captain, spoke of? The evil man Toke? You asked me about him?"

She nodded.

"He and other men attacked a farm back in my homeland. They killed all of the women and children there. In the end, my brother and I were surrounded by them. My brother told me to run. He did not want me to die there with him. I did run, and I escaped, but he was killed. I know the pain that is in your heart. But you did

341

what your mother wanted you to do. You could not have helped her."

She raised her head and stared at my face, studying it. She had stopped weeping now, but her cheeks were streaked from her tears, and her breath came in sniffling gasps.

"Is this true? Or do you lie to me?"

"It is the truth. I ran because my brother asked me to. It was what he wanted for me. I could not have helped him. I could only have died as well. But now I have sworn to kill all who played a part in his death. It is why I survived."

"The men who killed my mother are already dead," she murmured.

"Tell me what happened."

"Later that day, as darkness was beginning to fall, I crept back toward our camp. I found their bodies. Because she was carrying my brother, my mother could not run fast enough to escape. They had crushed my brother's skull against the trunk of a tree and left him lying there. They had torn my mother's clothes from her, and they had, they had…." She shook her head. Her eyes were staring as if she could see her mother in her mind— what she had found that day—and there was a look of horror on her face.

"They had raped her?" I asked.

She shook her head again as if to clear it, and looked at me. "What is…raped?"

"When a man lies with a woman against her will. When he forces himself on her."

"Your people would have a word for such a thing,"

342

she said bitterly. "My people have no such word. It is not a thing that happens among us. Yes, they had raped my mother, and then killed her."

"But what of your father? Clearly he lived."

She nodded. "When the evil men threw him into the lake, the cold water woke him. But he was like you, after you were hit—he was weak and confused. He managed to swim to shore, but then fell into blackness again. I found him the next morning, lying in a bed of reeds a short distance down from our camp.

"I buried my mother and brother. I was glad my father did not see her in death. But I knew how much he had loved her. I cut off a piece of her braid, for him to remember her by. It is what was in the bag he wore around his neck—the bag he asked you to give to me. I moved our camp into the forest, where it could not be seen from the shore. And I nursed my father until his strength returned.

"My father said we must go to Birka. He said the men who had robbed him, and had killed my mother and brother, were surely from there. He said what they had done had broken the rules of the people of Birka. He told me the leader there—the man Barne had taken him to meet—was a good man, who would see that the evil men were punished.

"My father told me that there were always many very large boats—ships—at Birka, for people came there to trade from many distant lands. Barne had told him the ships came up from the south, through a narrow channel that led to the sea. My father said we would walk around the shore of the lake until we reached the channel, and there we would ask one of the ships coming from the sea to carry us to Birka.

"I begged my father not to. I was afraid. I told him that even if a boat stopped, they would just do to us what the other evil men had done. But he would not listen. He told me not all of the others were evil. He said there were many good men among them, like Barne, and like the leader of Birka, and that the good men would help us.

"It took us four days to reach the mouth of the channel. We waited there another day before a ship came up from the south. The first ship that passed did not stop when we signaled to them. After that happened, my father went into the forest and found and killed a deer. He hung its body so it could be seen from the channel, so any ship that passed would know we had meat to trade. The next ship to pass did stop. I wish it had not. My father might still be alive today if we had not gone aboard it. The captain of the ship was Sigvald."

"Sigvald?" I exclaimed. "The chieftain of the pirates? He was at Birka?"

Rauna nodded. "He had many goods aboard his ship. He had brought them to Birka to sell. He and his men had many weapons. To me they seemed much like the men who had attacked our people during the winter. They frightened me. But they did not harm us.

"My father told Sigvald why we had traveled from our own lands to Birka. He told him of the raiders, and how we had come to seek help against them. He also told Sigvald how the evil men had tricked him and robbed him and had killed my mother and brother. My

344

father told Sigvald he needed to go to Birka to tell the leader there what had happened, so he would punish the men for breaking the rules of their people. He told Sigvald he and his men could have the deer, if they would carry us there."

She fell silent. "What did Sigvald do?" I asked her. "What did he say?"

She shook her head. "It made no sense to me. At first, he just laughed. All of his men, who had gathered around to hear my father's words, laughed. Then he asked my father how well he could shoot his bow.

"I could tell my father was angry, but he was trying to hide it. He turned to me and said, 'Come, we must go.' But Sigvald said that if my father could hit a target that he named, then he and his men would take us to Birka. When my father made the shot he set for him, Sigvald nodded and smiled, and the men with him did, too.

"I am certain Sigvald knew what would happen in Birka. My father found the leader. At first he would not even speak to us, but my father reminded him that they had met before, with Barne. Barne's name made him at least listen to what my father had to say. But he gave us no help. He said what had happened in the winter, in the lands of our people, was no concern of his. He said my father had no way of knowing that the men who had robbed him, and had killed my mother and brother, were from Birka, and that even if they were, the rules my father spoke of—the rules of the people of Birka—were not for our people. He said he was sorry—I remember hearing him say that, and thinking that he lied—but there was nothing he could do to help us.

"Sigvald had gone with us to see the leader of Birka. Afterward, he told my father that the men who had killed my mother and brother could only be made to pay one way. He said my father must find them and kill them himself. Sigvald said he would help my father do this, but there would be a price. He said he needed men who were skilled with a bow. He said if my father would agree to serve him for one year, he would help him find the men who had killed my mother. After the year had ended, my father and I would be free to return to our home if we wished, and we would have riches to take with us."

"You father agreed?" I asked. She nodded. "And Sigvald helped him find the men who had killed your mother and brother?" She nodded again.

"He took us on his ship up to where our camp had been. He said that if they had been fishing in these waters that day, sooner or later they would likely come again. For two days he and his men rowed their ship along the shore there. Four times we saw small boats with men in them, fishing, and we approached them, but they were not the ones. But the fifth boat we found, on the second day, held the evil men. Sigvald rowed his ship up alongside, and one by one, my father shot them dead with his bow.

"He had never killed a man before. He had thought it would be a good thing, to kill those men. He thought there was, as Sigvald told him, a blood-price they had to pay. But he was never the same after that. And then, later, we learned the true nature of the bargain my father

346

had made. Sigvald and his men were no different than the raiders who had attacked our lands. Although he never talked to me about it, I knew that sometimes, when Sigvald took his ships out to hunt, my father killed other men, too—men who had never done him any wrong. My father was changing—he was no longer the same man he once had been. It was as if something in his spirit had died."

We sat in silence for a while. What Rauna had told me explained many things. But it left me with a problem. There would be no one in Birka who might be able to help her return to her people. I could not leave her there.

Thunder rumbled in the distance. A cold wind began blowing in off of the sea. It carried a mist that hinted of rain soon to come.

"There will be a storm this night," Rauna said, sniffing the wind. She hesitated, then added, "You can sleep in my tent—this night only. Out of the rain. I am not saying you can come to my bed. Do you understand that?"

I nodded.

She stood and walked to her tent, not looking back to see if I would follow. I rose unsteadily to my feet, gathered up the fur coverings that had formed my pallet, and staggered after her.

The following day Hastein again elected, as he had after first leaving Oeland, to sail through the night rather than stop and make camp. We had no way of knowing whether Toke was still at Birka. If good fortune had smiled on him, one or more slavers who traded with the

Araby kingdoms had been in Birka when he'd arrived, and Toke was already well on his way to Ireland by now. But Hastein did not want the desire for a hot meal and a good night's sleep ashore to delay us as long as there was still a chance fortune might smile upon us, instead— as long as there was any hope we might catch Toke at Birka.

We reached the broad mouth of the inlet leading to Birka early the following morning. The night of the feast, Nori had told Hastein how to recognize it, for before the pirates had come and burned their ships, the Oelanders had regularly traveled to Birka to trade. It was a good thing that he had spoken to Hastein about it, because the coastline we'd been passing for some time now had been an indistinguishable maze of inlets, bays, and small islands.

"You must watch for an island, located in the center of the mouth of a large bay, that has a steep rocky peak rising out of the sea in front of it, taller than the mast of a ship," he'd said. "On its seaward side, there is a great eye painted in white on the face of the peak. It is painted red in times of war. It represents the eye of Odin, the one-eyed god who sees all. It is said that the kings of the Sveas are descended from him. There is a small temple to Odin on the island behind the rock, which is maintained by the pilots who guide ships to Birka. There are always some of them on the island. You can hire one there."

"Will we need a pilot?" Hastein had asked.

Nori had nodded vigorously. "Oh yes. If you have never been to Birka, it can be a challenge to find. It is quite some distance inland from the sea. There are many small channels leading inland from the bay, but only one leads all the way to where the waters widen into the great lake where the island of Bjorko lies, in its center. Birka is there, on Bjorko. You will need a pilot to find the correct channel. And even if you did manage to find the channel without a pilot, it can be dangerous to travel through without a guide, for in some stretches there are great rocks that lie beneath its surface, that were put there by the Sveas to protect the access from the sea to Birka and the lands beyond. The channel is very narrow where the rocks are, so it can be easily blocked if need be."

The island was as Nori had described it. We had just passed a long, low-lying island when Torvald gave a shout from the stern of the *Serpent* and pointed into a bay that opened up beyond it. In the distance a gray stone pillar jutted up out of the sea. An island lay behind it. On the sheer face of the pillar was the white outline of a giant eye, taller than a man.

We lowered our sails and unshipped our oars as we neared the pillar. The narrow end of the island that lay just behind was split by a long cove that provided a sheltered harbor. At its far end, two small-boats were pulled up on the shore, and a rickety-looking wooden pier jutted out over the water. A low, square wooden building constructed of logs—presumably the temple Nori had spoken of—sat like a crown on the crest of a bald-topped hill that overlooked the cove.

When we entered the cove and rowed toward the pier, five men came out of the temple and stood watching. As we tied up our ships along either side of the pier, two of them headed down the hillside toward us.

While Hastein and Torvald walked to meet the two, the rest of us scrambled ashore to make the most of our brief stop. We were stiff and sore from so many hours aboard the cramped, crowded decks of the *Gull* and *Serpent*.

Rauna and I had spoken but little since she had told me what had happened in Birka. Once ashore, she headed with a quick pace toward a nearby tree line, where the island's forest cover grew close to the water's edge.

"Rauna!" I called. "Wait! I will come with you."

She turned back toward me and frowned. "I do not want you to come. I wish to be alone for a little while."

I understood. There is no privacy aboard a longship. Throughout the day while we were at sea, as they felt the need members of the *Gull*'s crew would drop their trousers and relieve themselves over the side or squat over a bucket. I realized how awkward the situation was for Rauna. I would not wish to be the only woman aboard a ship crowded with warriors, and have them all stare at me while I relieved myself.

"You can be alone," I said as I caught up to her. "But we do not know who is on this island. I will just wait nearby. That way you will be safe."

She considered my words for a moment, then nodded. When we reached the trees, she said, "Wait here," and walked to a patch of undergrowth growing between two large oaks, disappearing behind it.

Although my head still had a dull ache, I was

feeling more like myself. I had even felt strong enough to man an oar as we'd rowed the *Gull* into the cove, although as I'd done so, Gudfred's warning came back to me, and I'd hoped the effort would not cause me to suddenly fall over dead. It was with a sense of relief that I had shipped my oar when we'd docked.

After Rauna reemerged, we walked slowly back toward the ships. "I have been thinking much about what happened to your family in Birka," I told her. "It is good that you told me. I see now that I cannot leave you there."

"Then where will you leave me?"

"I have lands back in Denmark, on Jutland. They are my family's lands. When this voyage is over, you can come back there. You can live on my lands, and be a part of my household. You will not be back among your own people, but at least you will be safe there." I sighed. This was not a thing I wished to do. I wanted to be free of her, but I could see no other way. She would be helpless, and would soon be preyed upon, if I left her in Birka—or anywhere else, for that matter.

"What will you do with me there?" she asked warily.

Did she think I would make her a slave? Or use her as a concubine?

"Nothing," I answered. "You will be a free woman. There are a number of free men and women in the household." We were nearing the pier now. Gudfred was standing on the shore near its end, talking with Einar. I pointed at him. "Gudfred, there, is one of the carls—one of the free men—from the estate. You will be expected to work, of course. Everyone must work. But that is all."

Perhaps she would catch the eye of someone from the village, and they could take her for their wife. That would be the best solution. A villager would not expect to wed a wife with a dowry. I decided I should try to encourage Bram to get to know her.

My answer did not satisfy her. "Will I have to share your bed? Will others want me to share their beds?"

"You will be a free woman," I said again. "It will be your choice whether you share your bed with anyone. No one will force you."

"My mother was a free woman. All of my people are free. That has not protected us from the men of your kind."

"You will be safe there. I promise it. I can do nothing more for you than this. Do you wish it or not?"

By now we had reached the shore. Rauna did not answer, but put her head down and hurried away, out onto the pier to the *Gull*.

Hastein and Torvald had returned. A short, bald-headed man with a round belly and a white beard was with them. Both Hastein and Torvald had scowls on their faces.

"Reboard the ships!" Torvald called, in a booming voice. "Draw oars, and prepare to get underway. We are leaving."

The short man scampered down the pier and climbed aboard the *Gull*. As the members of our two crews filed down the narrow pier behind him, I pulled Hastein aside. "You and Torvald look angry," I said. "Is

352

there trouble? Do we not have a pilot to show us the way to Birka?"

Torvald answered. "Oh, aye, we have a pilot. It is that fat, greedy little dwarf who just boarded the *Gull*."

"Then what is the problem?" I asked.

"He is charging us ten silver pennies to guide our two ships to Birka! The regular fee the pilots here charge a ship is five pennies. But he is charging us ten, because we have two ships. He is not going to be piloting the *Serpent*! I will just be following the *Gull*."

"There is more to it than that," Hastein added. "The pilot—his name is Alf—is a nosy little man, who asks many questions but gives few answers. Had we been Norse, or Gotars, or even Vends or Franks, I do not think he would have cared. He would have taken his five pennies per ship, shown us the route to Birka, and that would have been that. But he took great interest in the fact that we are Danes. Once he realized that we are, he became very curious—too curious—about us. Where had we sailed from? How long had we been traveling? What was the purpose of our voyage? There is something about him I do not trust. Keep a close watch on him."

Nori had not been exaggerating when he'd told Hastein that Birka was quite some distance inland. The journey there took us the entire remainder of the day. At first the channel we traveled along was fairly broad. Although light, the wind was favorable, so we were at least able to cover most of the distance under sail. But during the final stretch where the channel was quite narrow, the wind shifted, and we were forced to take up our oars. Alf earned his pennies in the narrow channel, for it was there that the hidden rocks lay, and several times, at Alf's direction, we had to cut across it from one side to the other to avoid them.

Hastein had been right. Alf was a nosy little man. Whenever his attention to our course was not needed, he wandered up and down the deck, tugging at the bundles and barrels of our cargo, trying to determine their contents, all the while asking questions. The crew quickly took a dislike to him. Bryngolf snapped at him, ordering him to leave our cargo alone, but Alf merely protested that he was only trying to help us—if he knew what types of goods we had to trade, he could suggest the best merchants in Birka for them.

The light was beginning to fade and the sun was not long from passing out of the sky when we finally emerged from the channel out onto a great lake and saw, in the distance, smoke from numerous fires rising above an island that lay ahead.

Once on the lake, we were able to raise our sail and catch the wind again, heading north. Birka proved to be located toward the far end of the island Nori had called Bjorko—its southern end, facing the channel's mouth, was covered with dense woodlands and, according to Alf, uninhabited.

As we skirted Bjorko's western side, a steep, rocky hill looming over the shoreline came into view ahead. On its crest were the walls of a fortress. Pointing to it, Hastein asked Alf, "Is that part of the town?"

"The fort?" Alf asked, and shook his head. "The king keeps a large garrison at Birka, to protect it and keep the peace. It is their fort. Birka lies below and just beyond it."

After we sailed past the fort, the town came into view. Birka was not as large as Hedeby, though still a sizable town. Buildings crowded down right to the edge of a broad, curved shoreline that formed its harbor. Beyond, on the landward side, an earthen wall topped with a wooden stockade, with wooden watchtowers rising above at regular intervals, surrounded the back side of the town. The harbor itself was protected by a jetty of wooden pilings that curved in a great arc all the way across its face. A gap in the center of the jetty provided the only entrance into the harbor.

Once more lowering our sails, we rowed into Birka harbor, the *Serpent* following the *Gull*. I was at the last oar in the stern, just in front of where Hastein was standing on the raised stern deck at the steer-board. As best I could, I studied the harbor, looking over my shoulder as I rowed. Numerous piers jutted out from the shore. Many had ships tied alongside—mostly knarrs, but there was a scattering of other ships, including a few longships, among them.

By now darkness was falling, though the full blackness of the night had not yet settled upon the island. Hastein called out across the deck to Bjorgolf and Bryngolf, who were rowing the front pair, to light torches and stand in the bow, so he could better see the way. As they shipped their oars and pulled previously prepared torches from underneath the bow deck, he said to me, in a much lower voice, "Is he here? Did you see his ship?"

I shook my head. I had been looking for the *Red Eagle*—I desperately hoped it was one of the longships I saw—but the failing light was too dim for me to be able to tell. "It is too dark," I replied. "I cannot say."

Alf listened to our exchange with interest. "You are meeting someone here?" he asked.

Ignoring his question, Hastein said, "Guide us, pilot. That is what we are paying you for. Where shall we dock?"

Alf studied the darkened shoreline briefly, and then pointed to the right. "There," he said. "See that empty pier just beyond that knarr? You can tie your ships along either side. It is one of the wider piers in the harbor. It will make unloading your goods easier."

The moorage Alf directed us to lay close to the end of the harbor. Not far beyond it, the jetty of rough pilings curved to the shore at the base of the rocky hill. I wondered if it was by chance or design that Alf had sent our ships to dock below the fortress. As I stared up at its walls looming overhead, a party of warriors, carrying torches whose light glinted on their helms and armor, marched out of its gate and headed down the hill toward the town.

Alf was standing nearby. Glancing sideways at him, I saw that he, too, had been staring up at the fort. He nodded his head, then turned to Hastein. "Well, then. If you will pay me, I will be gone. My house is in the town. It will be good to sleep in my own bed this night."

When he had left, I asked Hastein, "Shall I go search along the shore and see if the *Red Eagle* is in the harbor?" I was impatient to discover whether Toke was still at Birka. We had hunted him for so long—was he finally brought to bay?

Hastein shook his head. "We will look in the morning," he replied. "If he is still at Birka this night, he will be here then as well."

My disappointment must have been evident on my face. "Halfdan," he said, "you are the captain of my archers now. And with Torvald gone to captain the *Serpent*, you are my second in command aboard the *Gull*, as well. We must take no chances. If Toke is in Birka, he may have been watching for us. He may have gained allies here, and could even now be looking for a chance to strike at us. We cannot afford to lose any more of our men. I cannot afford to lose you.

"No one is to go ashore into the town. I want a strong watch posted throughout the night. Five men, all fully armed and armored. Relieve them regularly—I need sentries who are fully awake and alert, not dozing on their feet. And tell all of our men they should sleep with their weapons close at hand. Arrange these things. I am going to the *Serpent* to see that Torvald does the same."

There was some grumbling as I made my way up the deck to the bow, repeating Hastein's orders. We had been two full days at sea, and the crew had been hoping for a hot meal, and perhaps more—in trading towns such as this, there were usually merchants who sold ale and wine by the cup, even well into the night, and there were women willing to trade their company for coin. But none even considered disobeying. The mixed crew of doubtful discipline that had begun our long journey had become a company of warriors worthy to serve a jarl.

I was just back of the fore-deck, selecting the men for the first watch—I would be among them, for I thought it unlikely that I would be able to sleep this night, with Toke possibly so near—when Einar called out, "Halfdan, men are approaching." I looked up and saw a party of men—warriors, perhaps twenty or slightly more, all armed and carrying torches—emerging from a street between two buildings just down from where our pier extended out from the shore. Although I could not be certain, they looked to be the same warriors I had seen leaving the fortress.

The Ravens, Bryngolf and Bjorgolf, who were also standing the first watch, had already donned their brynies. "Come with me," I told them, and stepped up onto the edge of the ship's top strake, then leaped onto the pier. Glancing back, I saw Hastein and Torvald climbing off of the stern of the *Serpent* onto the dock.

The Ravens and I reached the end of the pier as the column of warriors neared it. A tall, slim man with graying hair and beard who was in their lead, the only one among them not wearing a helm and bearing a shield, held up his hand and the column stopped. He took a torch from one of the warriors behind him, and holding it high walked forward until he was standing directly in front of me. "My name is Herigar," he announced. "I am captain of the king's garrison at Birka."

"My name is Halfdan," I told him.

"These are your ships?" he asked. He sounded understandably surprised.

Hastein, who had by now reached us, answered. "The ships are mine. My name is Hastings."

"Hastings." Herigar nodded as he repeated the name, and he stroked his beard with his empty hand. "And you are a Dane? You are all Danes?" he asked.

Had we spoken more, I might have believed he had guessed so from our speech. Although the Danes, Norse, Gotars, and Sveas all use the common tongue, there are some differences in the ways we speak it. But Herigar could not have placed us as Danes from the few words we had spoken. Clearly Alf had gone to him as soon as he'd left the *Gull*. But why?

"Yes," Hastein answered, "we are Danes."

Herigar seemed to be expecting Hastein to say more, for he waited a time in silence, studying him. "What is your purpose here?" he finally asked.

"This is a trading town, is it not? It is open to all— even Danes?" Hastein asked. "We are here to trade. What other purpose would we have for coming to Birka?"

"Yes," Herigar said. "What other purpose would you have? May I see the goods you carry?"

"Of course," Hastein replied.

While Hastein and Torvald escorted Herigar along the decks of the *Gull* and the *Serpent*, showing him the various bales and barrels of goods we had taken from the pirates' camp, I went to my sea chest and donned my armor and weapons in preparation for standing watch. As I was finishing, Herigar stepped back onto the pier from the *Serpent*, Hastein following behind him. Glancing back at the stern of the *Gull*, he paused when he saw me, then walked back along the pier until he was close enough to speak.

"You have armed yourself since I arrived," he said to me. "Why have you done so?"

"I am standing the first watch aboard our ship this night," I replied.

"You do not need armed guards standing watch through the night here," Herigar said, turning to Hastein. "My men and I keep the peace in Birka."

"I am by nature a cautious man," Hastein said in reply. "I am certain Birka is well guarded by you and your men, but I have always found it wise to place my greatest trust in myself and my own men."

Herigar again stared at Hastein for a long time without speaking. Hastein returned his gaze, neither speaking nor blinking. It was Herigar who finally blinked and looked away. It clearly annoyed him that he had.

"We are not accustomed here to see merchants who bring their goods aboard a longship. Such are designed for war, and are poorly suited for carrying cargo," he said.

Hastein shrugged his shoulders again. "These are the ships I own. And I am not accustomed, when I come to a town to trade, to be met by an armed force. Do you greet all who come to Birka to trade in this fashion? "

Herigar shook his head. "No," he admitted, "I do not. But merchants who trade here do not generally bring a war-band to do so. I, too, am a cautious man."

Again there was an uncomfortably long silence between them. This time it was Hastein who broke it.

"Is there anything more you need of us?"

"Yes," Herigar said. "Since you have come to Birka to trade, you must pay the king's landing tax. All merchants who come must pay it. It is the price for entry to our market, and for the right to trade here. You may pay me now. Four aurars of silver for each ship—a mark in all, for both."

"The king must have his due," Hastein said.

After Herigar and his guard had left, Hastein called Torvald and me to the stern of the *Gull* to hold council. The Ravens, plus Einar and Gudfred, gathered with us.

"We must be very watchful this night. There is more to Herigar's visit than meets the eye," Hastein said.

"Do you not think it is just what he said?" Torvald asked. "Between our two ships we do have many warriors. It does not make us look like merchants. Surely he was just being cautious."

Hastein shook his head. "That may have been a part of it. But it was significant to him that we are Danes."

"Clearly Alf went to him as soon as he left the *Gull*," I pointed out. "He, too, found it of great interest that we are Danes. It is as if they all are watching for Danes to arrive."

"That is how it strikes me, too," Hastein said. "But why? Has Toke somehow set Herigar and his men against us, as he did with Sigvald?"

"Sigvald was a pirate," Torvald protested. "Herigar is a captain serving the Svear king. The Sveas and Danes are not at war. Surely Herigar would not risk provoking

361

King Horik, and starting one, by attacking Danish ships for no cause."

"I do not know. What you say should be true," Hastein replied. "But there is something beyond what we can see that is afoot here. We must be very careful."

After standing the first watch I tried to sleep, but although I felt weary, my efforts did not meet with success. As I had anticipated, the thought that Toke might be near—that on the morrow, we might find him—kept me feeling tense and wakeful, and now, due to the strange visit by Herigar and his men, I was also concerned that we might be in danger from them, as well. By the beginning of the third watch—the last before the morn arrived—I conceded that I would find no rest this night, and was back in the bow of the *Gull*, standing guard again. Bram and Gudfred, plus Hallbjorn and another of Hastein's men named Harek, were manning the watch with me.

A dense fog had settled upon the town and harbor during the night. Standing on the raised fore-deck, I could barely see past the end of the pier to which we were moored. The first row of buildings in the town, a short distance beyond, was no longer visible at all.

I was staring into the gray wall of nothingness, considering whether I should post some of our sentries farther forward, on the shore, when out of the corner of my eye I saw something creeping along the pier behind me. It startled me, and I raised my bow—I had been holding it strung, with an arrow nocked on the string, for some time now, for the fog was making me uneasy—as I spun around to see what it was.

I heard a gasp, then a frightened voice said, "It is me!" barely louder than a whisper. It was Rauna.

"What are you doing?" I hissed, also whispering. I felt angry, for I could well have killed her.

"I need to go ashore," she said.

"No one is to go ashore," I told her. "Those are Jarl Hastein's orders."

"I *need* to go ashore," she said again. "Please. I will not go far. I will not be long."

It was a bad time for her modesty to assert itself. I almost told her no. Instead I sighed and said, "Very well. Wait a moment. I will come to the end of the pier and watch for you. You must not go far."

When we reached the end of the pier, I told her, "You must stay close. The fog is very thick. Do not go so far that I cannot see you, and you cannot see me. Now hurry!"

She walked a short distance down the shore. I could still see her, but only dimly. She fumbled with her clothing and squatted down. After a few moments, she stood up again, but she did not return. She seemed frozen. Then suddenly she dropped into a low crouch, crept forward into the fog, and was gone.

If I could have put my hands upon her at that moment, I would have shaken her until her teeth rattled. Where had she gone, and why?

I knelt and held my bow at the ready while I pondered what to do. I had not decided—in truth, I felt befuddled by her unexpected actions—when she appeared again out of the fog, directly in front of me, moving quickly in a low crouch. As she drew near she raised a finger to her lips, warning me to be silent, then tugged my arm as she reached me, pulling me back down the pier toward the ships.

After we had gone a short distance, I whispered, "What were you doing?"

"I heard sounds," she explained. "Iron on iron. And voices whispering."

I remembered that on the pirates' island, she'd seemed to have unusually keen hearing. She had heard Hastein and his men approaching well before I had, even though she'd been further away.

"There are many men, wearing iron, hiding back between the buildings," she continued. "Many men."

"Did they see you?" I asked.

She shook her head. "I do not think they saw anything, but if they did, I was down on my hands and knees—they will think they saw a dog."

Climbing back aboard the *Gull*, I whispered to the others on watch, "Warriors are gathering between the buildings. We are in danger of attack. Bram, go warn the watch aboard the *Serpent*, and tell them to rouse her crew. But tell them to do so quietly. Harek, wake our men and tell them to arm themselves. Gudfred and Hallbjorn, keep watch here, and have your bows ready. Everyone must be silent—warn those you wake, Harek, to make no sound. The warriors gathering in the town must not realize we are aware of them. I am going to wake Hastein."

Rauna followed me as I trotted back to the stern. Hastein was stretched out on the stern deck, wrapped in a thick cloak. We had not tented the *Gull*'s deck for shelter because of Hastein's fear that Herigar might mean us harm. He was sleeping so soundly that I had to shake his shoulder hard, and whisper his name over and over, to awaken him. When I finally did, he sat up with a start, but was clearly still groggy.

"Hastein," I told him, "warriors are gathering between the buildings on the edge of the waterfront. I fear we are to be attacked."

He shook his head, trying to clear it. "How many?" he asked. "Was Herigar with them?"

"I do not know. I did not see them. Rauna did. But she said there are many of them."

He frowned, clearly wondering how it was that Rauna had seen them, but did not waste time asking. "We must warn the *Serpent*," he said.

"I have already done so. I sent Bram to warn them, and to tell them to rouse their crew. Harek is waking our men aboard the *Gull*, and telling them to arm themselves."

Behind us, all along the deck of the *Gull*, muffled sounds and shadowy movements in the dark and fog indicated that the crew was rising.

"Good," Hastein said. "I must arm myself. Go back to the bow and resume watch. I will be there soon."

As I turned to leave, I saw Rauna huddled on the deck beside my sea chest, squatting with her arms wrapped around her knees. She looked frightened. "There is likely to be fighting," I told her. "Go to the stacked cargo at this end of the ship, in the center of the deck, and make a space for yourself in it. Stay low, and

365

cover yourself so you cannot be seen. I must go."

She did not move. "Hurry!" I said. "You are not safe here." After a moment I added, "And I thank you. You did well."

By the time I reached the bow, many of the *Gull*'s crew had already gathered there, some still pulling on their brynies or adjusting the straps of their helms. "Have you seen anything?" I asked Gudfred.

He shook his head. "No, but in this fog, that means little."

I needed all of our archers with me. "Asbjorn, Einar," I whispered to the men gathered just back of the fore-deck, "Where are you?"

"Here. Here." Their voices came from somewhere within the crowd of men in front of me.

"To me. Bring your bows." Spying Bjorgolf and Bryngolf among the men who were already armed and ready, I waved to them and said, "You come, too."

As soon as they had all joined me up on the fore-deck, I explained my plan. "We archers will form a line across the pier. Hallbjorn, go now across to the *Serpent*, and tell them we need the archers in her crew to join us, also. Bjorgolf, Bryngolf, I need you to gather men and form a shield wall behind us. When they come, we will shoot a volley at them, two if we have time. Then you must open the wall long enough for us to fall back behind you. Quickly—let us go! We do not know how soon they will attack."

We were already on the pier, forming the two lines across it—the archers even with the fronts of the ships, the shield wall a short distance behind—when Hastein

366

and Torvald arrived. "What are you doing? What is happening here?" Hastein said gruffly.

When I had explained, he nodded and said, "It is good. Well done."

"After we retreat through the shield wall," I added, "the archers will move to the fore-decks of the *Gull* and *Serpent*. The attackers will not be able to reach us there,"—because of the curve of the hulls, the ends of the ships in both the bow and stern did not abut the pier—"but we will be able to shoot our arrows into their ranks from either side."

Hastein nodded again. "Good," he said. "I have no doubt they outnumber us—perhaps greatly. But they can only attack down this pier, which gives us an advantage. We must bleed them when they come."

"We can use the cargo," Torvald suggested, "to build a wall across the pier. If we fight from behind it, our position will be stronger still."

"Do it," Hastein told him. "But take no more than ten men with you. I want the rest here, with me, at the shield wall."

Torvald's planned wall was not yet built—he and his men were still wrestling barrels and bales of furs from the decks of the two ships onto the dock—when the Sveas made their move. But the five archers from the crew of the *Serpent* had joined Einar, Gudfred, Hallbjorn, Asbjorn and me, to form a line of archers ten strong stretched across the wooden pier. We were waiting with arrows at ready on our bows, straining to hear or see anything in the dense fog that hid the shore.

"I think I hear something," Einar whispered. He

was standing beside me, on my right. After a moment, Gudfred, who was on my left, said, "Aye, I do too." And then, just beyond the end of the pier, the shadowy forms of warriors, moving forward in a crouch behind their shields, appeared out of the fog.

The need for silence was past. "Draw!" I cried, and as one we raised our bows, drawing our arrows back as we did. We could see only dim shapes, making it impossible to aim carefully, but I locked my gaze on one and said, "Loose!"

As soon as my right hand released its hold on the string, I reached down to the quiver hanging at my right hip, clawed another arrow from it, and slapped it across my bow, fitting its nock onto the string. On either side, the others did the same.

Beyond the end of the pier, on the shore, our arrows struck. Dull thuds and sounds of splintering wood meant that some had hit shields, but screams of pain told us that others had found their targets.

"Draw!" I shouted. "Loose!"

Again our shafts sped down the length of the pier and into the shadowy shapes in the fog. They were no longer bunched in a close line. I could make out gaps, and men were milling about in confusion. As yet, they were still too surprised and disarrayed by our unexpected missile fire to rally and attack. Their confusion gave us time to strike them again.

"Draw! Loose!" and a third volley sped on its way.

From somewhere back in the wall of fog, a voice—it sounded like Herigar—shouted, "Forward! Charge them! Cut them down!"

As men surged forward out of the fog and ran down the pier, their feet thudding on its wooden planks, their voices howling angry battle cries, I shouted, "Back! Fall back!"

Behind us, every other man in the front rank of the shield wall stepped in front of the man to his right. I turned and ran back through one of the gaps, as the other archers did the same.

"Close the wall!" Hastein ordered. "Ready! Front rank down! Lower spears!"

The front rank of the shield wall knelt and extended their spears forward at a low angle, bracing the butts of the shafts against the surface of the pier. The second rank pressed close behind them, shields overlapping, their spears extended out chest-high above the kneeling men. The third rank had slung their shields across their backs and were holding their spears high in both hands, ready to thrust them over the shoulders of the warriors in front of them, should any of the enemy battle their way close to the line through the thicket of stabbing blades.

The Sveas had courage. They threw themselves against the spears, trying to swat them aside with their shields and swords. I watched for but a moment, then cried, "Archers—to the fore-decks."

Einar and Gudfred had already made their way to where the side of the *Gull* was lashed against the pier and had climbed aboard her, and now they were running up her deck toward the bow. I followed them at a fast trot, Asbjorn and Hallbjorn beside me, as the archers from the *Serpent* headed for their ship.

Even before we reached the fore-decks and hit them

with our arrow fire from either side, the Sveas' attack was wavering. When our arrows, shot from almost point blank range, began to fell them, they broke and ran. Some retreated cautiously, backing down the pier with shields raised and weapons ready, in case our shield wall charged, but others turned and ran. I put an arrow in the middle of the back of one who did. He may have been fleeing for now, but that did not mean he would not attack again later.

Silence settled over the pier, broken only by the groans of wounded men. I did not know how many of our attackers we had felled on the shore with our initial three volleys, but scattered along the pier I counted nine down with arrows in their bodies, and in front of the shield wall, four warriors wounded in the brief melee there were dragging themselves back down the dock, leaving broad smears of blood across its planks. Gudfred shot one and killed him, but when he did, Hastein called out, "Let them leave," so we held our fire as the other three crawled away.

None of our warriors had taken even a minor wound. It had been a one-sided fight.

We readied ourselves for a second attack, but none came. "They are waiting for daylight," Gudfred said. "For the fog to burn away." His words would prove to be true.

While we waited and watched, Torvald and his men completed their barricade of cargo across the pier. When another attack came, we would no longer have the advantage of surprise. But our attackers would still have only the width of the pier to approach us and fight in, and our archers could still fire into them from the ships' bows on either side—plus now the warriors in our shield wall would have a makeshift stockade to protect them, as well. I thought we still held the upper hand.

By now the sun had risen above the fog and was beginning to melt it away. I had joined Hastein and Torvald at the center of the barricade across the pier. We could not yet see clear sky overhead, nor all the way to the far side of the harbor, and the fortress above was still completely hidden by low clouds that wreathed the top half of the rocky hill. But the buildings along the shore, beyond the end of the pier, were visible now.

Torvald pointed toward an open space between two of them where a road through the town ended at the harbor's edge. "They come," he said.

A group of warriors, in a tight wedge formation with shields overlapped, marched slowly toward the end of the pier. They were too few in numbers to be an attack, and were waving a white flag attached to the shaft of a spear overhead.

When they reached the edge of the pier, a voice— Herigar's—called out, "May we approach without being fired upon?"

"Let us see what they have to say," Hastein muttered, and shouted back, "You may approach."

They stopped a spear's cast away from the cargo barricade, far enough down the pier so that our archers in the ships' bows would not have lines of fire into their flanks.

"You and your men fight well, Dane," Herigar said, when they had stopped. "I respect you for that. But though you have won the first skirmish, this is a battle you cannot win."

Hastein said nothing. After a few moments, Herigar continued. "Even now, archers are moving into position on the hillside above you." I glanced up at the hill. Men carrying bows were carefully making their way down its steep slope. They were a considerable distance away, as far as a long arrow shot. It was much too far for them to be able to shoot with any accuracy, but they could still lob arrows down onto us, and some, no doubt, would find targets.

"My garrison numbers many more men than you have," Herigar said. "You have bloodied us. I will grant you that. And if we must fight this to the end, I have no doubt that I will lose more of my men. But in the end, we will overrun you. And I make this promise: if we must fight this to the end, we will offer no mercy. In the end, you will all die. Lay down your weapons now, surrender to us, and we will not take your lives. It is your only chance."

"That is not much of an offer," Torvald observed.

"No," Hastein agreed. He shouted back, "After your treacherous attack on us, we have little cause to trust that you will honor any promises you make. We may be in a bad position here, as you say. It may even be our fate to die here. But it may not. That is something no man can predict. In any case, when I die, it will be with my arms unbound. We will not surrender."

"You are a fine one to speak of treachery, Dane," Herigar answered. "Did you think we do not know why you are here? We have blocked the entrance to the harbor. A ship is anchored across it, and chained to the posts on either side. The rest of your fleet, when it arrives, will not be able to get in. No one will rescue you. And your two ships will not be able to escape. If you do not surrender now, we will attack—and you will die."

"What is he saying?" Torvald muttered. "He makes no sense."

"None of this has ever made sense," Hastein said. "Wait!" he called.

"You will surrender?" Herigar asked.

"No," Hastein replied. "But before you attack, we should talk. You are seeing enemies where there are none. There is no fleet coming. There is only us—only our two ships. And we came to Birka in peace—we mean you no harm. We are not your enemies. We do not know why you see us as such. Think on it. What if you are making a mistake? You are sending your men to fight and die for no reason. And it will not be a small matter, between our king and yours, if you kill two shiploads of Danes for no cause."

Hastein's words were followed by a long silence. Finally Herigar responded.

"If you are lying, you will gain nothing by this. But you are trapped here, and cannot escape. We need not rush to kill you. We will talk."

It took a little while to arrange the terms of a truce between us. In exchange for delaying his attack, Herigar first wanted hostages, but Hastein would give him none. He asked to be allowed to retrieve the bodies of his dead and wounded from the pier, which Hastein granted.

373

Neither side trusted the other, and treachery was alleged by both. In the end, Herigar agreed to hold off his attack only until the sun reached its noon zenith. He and Hastein would meet at the end of the pier, each accompanied by just one man. No one would bear arms or wear armor.

Hastein chose me to accompany him. "We are here in Birka only because of Toke," he explained. "And I cannot help but wonder if Herigar's belief that we are enemies is a seed Toke somehow planted. If so, there is no one more a part of all of this than you."

We walked down the pier to where Herigar and his chosen man stood waiting. I suspected Herigar had chosen his companion solely on the basis of his physical strength. He was stocky, with a low, heavy brow, a chest the size of a barrel, and massive arms. He looked like the spawn of a cave troll—and like he could rip a man's head from his body with his bare hands. Clearly Herigar believed we might break the truce and use our meeting as a chance to try to kill or capture him—at least I hoped that was why he had chosen his guardian, and not because he planned treachery himself. Hastein and I together would be no match against this troll-man, without weapons.

When we reached the pier's end, Herigar cocked his head and looked up. "The sun crosses the sky, Dane," he said. "Speak. I do not know what you hope to convince me of, but your time to try is passing."

Hastein seemed, for the first time since I had met him, to be at a loss for words. It was a bad time for that to happen. Finally he drew in a deep breath and let it out

374

slowly, then asked, "Can you tell me, Herigar, why you believe we are your enemies?"

I did not think it a strong beginning. Neither did Herigar. He rolled his eyes and said, "This is why you asked for a truce? Do you think me simple minded? You and your men are not merchants. You did not sail all the way across the Austmarr, from Denmark to Birka, to trade the goods aboard your ships. You could have traded them at Hedeby, and been back home in your own beds within a few days' time."

It was so simple a truth that I had not seen it.

"It is true," Hastein said, after a few moments, "That when we left Jutland, the purpose of our voyage was not trade."

A triumphant look filled Herigar's face. "Then you lied to me, when you said you had come here to trade. And when you said your name is Hastings. Is it not true that your name is Hastein, and that you are a powerful jarl in the kingdom of the Danes?"

Hastein's surprise showed on his face. He and I exchanged quick glances. Surely this could have come only from Toke.

Herigar continued. "That struck home, did it not? I see it on your faces. So you lied when you said you came here to trade, you lied about your name, and you concealed that you are a powerful leader among the Danes. And yet you accuse *me* of treachery?"

Hastein shook his head. "I have my reasons for hiding my name," he said. "They have nothing to do with you, or with your town. And I *am* a jarl over northern Jutland—it is true. That I did not choose to announce that fact is my own business. But we did come in part to trade, though that was not our original intent. We acquired the goods you saw well into our voyage—at Oeland. And as we were bound for Birka anyway, we thought to sell them here."

Herigar waved his hand at Hastein's words, as if brushing away a fly. "You acquired your trade goods at Oeland? You have many bales of furs. When did Oeland become a center for the fur trade? You are lying again, Dane. You are here on behalf of Anund. Your plan was to sneak into Birka disguised as merchants, and hold the harbor's entrance so the rest of his ships could enter. With the harbor closed, he will have to attack by land and face the town's walls. But if you let him into the harbor, Birka's soft underbelly will be exposed. Do you think I do not see this?"

"Anund?" Hastein said. "I know no Anund. Is that not the name of one of the kings of the Sveas?"

"Your time is up, Dane," Herigar snapped. He wheeled, his cloak swirling around him as he did, and began walking away in long strides. "Come!" he called over his shoulder to his companion, who was backing away, watching us warily.

"Wait!" I cried. I had to know. "Was a man named Toke here? Was it he who told you we came to attack Birka?"

Herigar stopped. He stood still, his back to us, as if weighing my words.

"We came here hunting him," I continued. "That is why we are here in Birka. It is the only reason. He murdered my brother. He stole my sister, and brought her here to Birka to sell her into slavery. She has golden hair. Her name is Sigrid. Is she here?"

Herigar half turned and stared over his shoulder at me. *Come back,* I thought. *Listen to us.* But then he continued on, without looking back again. Watching him leave, I felt all of the hope inside of me draining away.

We waited all day for the attack to come, but it did not. Not long after Herigar stormed away, a longship crowded with warriors rowed across the harbor and anchored just out of bowshot, between our ships and the harbor's entrance. Beyond it, the ship blocking the entrance was pulled to one side, and a second longship rowed out of the harbor, raised its sail, and headed away toward the south.

Later in the afternoon, a smaller ship—a knarr— was rowed out and tied up alongside the anchored longship. Its decks were piled with wood, and several small barrels were stacked together in its stern. Torvald pointed at them. "Those will be filled with oil," he said. "They are going to send a fire-ship against us."

Waiting and waiting and waiting is a hard thing, when you expect at the end of the wait to die.

As the day wore on and no attack came, all but those standing watch in the ships' bows and at the barricade removed their helms. I unstrung my bow, for I did not want its limbs to take a set from being strung too long. Bryngolf and Bjorgolf used a pair of scissors to trim each other's hair and beards. "We want to look our best when we enter the feast hall of the gods," they explained.

Torvald passed the time carrying all of the longest oars to the sterns of the *Serpent* and the *Gull*. He also filled every bucket on the two ships with water from the harbor, and lined them up in the rear of the ships. "When they send the fire ship at us," he explained, "if we can hold it off long enough, it will burn down to the water and sink. I do not fear dying from steel, but I do not wish to burn to death. It is a bad way to go."

Hastein opened a fresh barrel of the smoked herring we had purchased on Mon, and insisted that all eat to keep up their strength. The sight and smell of food reminded me of Rauna. I realized I had not seen her since the night before.

Fetching a water skin from my sea chest, I filled it from the big cask in front of the *Gull*'s mast. Carrying it and two of the smoked herring in my hands, I walked along the stacked cargo back of the mast, calling out softly, "Rauna. Rauna, where are you?"

She had made a space between two bales of furs, and had stretched one of her own furs from her bedding above the opening. She was well hidden—I had no idea where she was until she pushed the skin aside and stood up. I noticed that she held her small-axe—the one she had killed Serck with—in her right hand.

"I have brought you some food," I said, and handed her the herring and water skin. She stuck the axe handle through her belt and took them from me, quickly raising one of the fish to her mouth and chewing at it hungrily.

What will happen to you, I wondered as I watched her eat, *when the Gull is overrun?* I hoped Torvald's plan would be successful at fending off the fire ship.

An idea occurred to me. "I will be back soon," I told her, and hurried back to my sea chest. Digging down to the bottom of it, I found my gold torque and the small leather bag of silver coins I had brought on the voyage.

Returning to Rauna, I handed her the torque and told her, "Put this on your arm." She frowned and looked puzzled, but did as I asked. I passed her the bag and said, "These are silver coins. They are very valuable. Keep them with you. Hide the bag inside of your tunic, if you can."

"I do not understand," she said.

"Listen to me very carefully," I told her. 'You must remember what I am telling you. The Sveas—the warriors here in Birka—are going to attack our ships again. Eventually they will win. You must stay hidden here until the fighting is over. Afterward, they will search the ship. They will find you. When they do, this is what you must say.

"You must tell them that you are the wife of the son of a great chieftain in Denmark. The chieftain's name was Hrorik Strong-Axe. Say the name."

She struggled with it. I repeated it again for her, and she said, "Rorik?"

"That is close enough," I said. "Remember it. And tell them that your husband's name is Halfdan, and that he is a famous warrior who is called Strongbow. The name was given to him by Ragnar Logbrod. Remember that, also."

"Why can you not tell them these things?" she asked.

"Because I will be dead."

A long silence followed. Finally she said, in a quiet voice, "You wish me to be your wife?"

"If you say you are my wife," I explained, "it may save your life. I wish that. It may keep you from being harmed. The men who are attacking us are members of the Svear king's own war-band. They will be men of honor. They will kill us because they believe we are their enemies, but they will not kill or dishonor the wife of a fallen foe." At least I hoped they would not. It was Rauna's only chance.

Despite the Sveas' preparations, the night passed without incident. By morning, we all were weary from lack of sleep, and from watching so long for an attack that did not come. Hastein in particular looked haggard. The fact that we were trapped, and he could think of no way for us to escape, was weighing heavily on him.

Just past noon, the longship we had seen leaving Birka the day before returned. A short time later, Herigar approached the end of the pier, accompanied by a single warrior who waved a white flag of truce.

"Come," Hastein said to me. "Let us see what he wants now."

When we reached him, Herigar told us, "I sent a ship down the channel to the sea, and for some distance beyond. They saw no sign of a fleet."

Hastein said nothing. He just stared at Herigar, a weary expression on his face.

"I am responsible for the protection of this town. For all of its folk," Herigar continued. "Their safety has been entrusted to me. I do not take lightly threats against them."

"We were never a threat," Hastein said.

"You said you knew nothing of Anund. When were you last in the court of King Horik of the Danes?"

"I attended a council there in the spring. Many chieftains of the Danes did also. Afterward, we carried war against the Franks. King Horik took a fleet against the town of Hamburg and burned it. My men and I sailed with a second fleet against western Frankia. We returned to Denmark less than a month ago. I have not seen Horik, nor been to his court, since the spring. We left Jutland on this voyage only days after we returned."

Herigar let out a long sigh. "For many years, King Bjorn shared his rule over the Sveas with his younger brother, Anund," he said. "But Anund is an ambitious man. He grew tired of sharing power. He tried to incite the people against Bjorn, by telling them that the gods were turning away from the Sveas because Bjorn had allowed the worship of the White Christ to be practiced in Svealand. He said we must purge our kingdom of the foreign god, and all who worship him, to regain the good graces of the gods.

"Matters came to a head at midsummer. There has been a drought lasting for months now that began in the spring. Because of it, the harvest this year will be small. Many took it as a sign that what Anund had been saying is true. Some of those whom Anund swayed came to Birka. They burned the Christian's church King Bjorn had allowed to be built here, and killed its priests. Only one, a Frank named Gautbert, escaped their fury. I helped him hide, and to make his way safely back to Frankia.

"King Bjorn was enraged, and banished Anund from Svealand. He fled to the court of King Horik. We know that he has been seeking to raise a fleet there, to support his return and help him capture the throne. When he comes, he will strike at Birka first, for it is the gateway into the kingdom."

"And you thought, merely because we are Danes, that we were the vanguard of Anund's attack?" Hastein asked incredulously.

"Not *merely* because you are Danes. You and your men are not merchants—that is clear. As I pointed out before, the goods you have brought could far more easily have been traded in Hedeby. Then there is the matter of your name. You told me it was Hastings, but while he was piloting your ship, Alf heard men address you as Hastein. And you are a jarl—a powerful leader among the Danes. A man such as that might well join Anund in a bid to capture the Svear throne."

"How did you know Hastein was a jarl?" I asked.

"Ah," Herigar said. "Yes—that is the other part of this. There was a man—also a Dane—who came to Birka before you."

"Did you also suspect *him* to be in league with Anund?" Hastein asked. There was a bitter tone in his voice. He and I both knew who this Dane had been.

Herigar shook his head. "He came in but a single ship, and even that was undermanned. But I questioned him to learn if he knew about Anund and his plans."

And from your questions, he no doubt learned that

Anund had been banished, and had fled to Denmark seeking support for his return, I thought.

Herigar continued. "He told me he did not know anything for certain, but he said there was a jarl, a frequent visitor at Horik's court, who was a great adventurer and Viking. If any in Denmark were likely to join with Anund, he would almost certainly be among them. He told me this jarl was named Hastein."

"The name of the man who told you this—it was Toke, was it not?" I asked.

Herigar nodded. "It was."

"I did not tell you my true name because we are hunting Toke," Hastein said bitterly. "He is a clever and dangerous foe. I did not want him to realize, if he was still in Birka, that we had arrived here, too." He sighed. "Toke plays men against each other like they were pieces in a game of hnefatafl. At Oeland, he told pirates that we were carrying much silver on our ships, so they would attack us."

"I have heard there is a strong band of pirates at Oeland," Herigar said. "I have urged King Bjorn to send a force to clear them out."

"There is no need," Hastein told him. "They are all dead now. The goods we carry—the goods we brought to trade here in Birka—we took from their camp, after we defeated them. Toke—where is he now?"

"He is gone," Herigar said. My heart sank.

Herigar let out a long sigh. "It seems," he said, "That this Toke has indeed played me against you. I acted out of concern for the safety of Birka and its folk, but…." He shook his head and sighed again. "I am thankful that at least none of your men died as a result of my error. It weighs heavily enough on me that some of my own men have died due to my mistake of judgment."

He hesitated, then extended his hand to Hastein. "It is much to request, I know. But I ask your forgiveness for how you and your men have been treated here at Birka, and offer my hand in friendship."

I thought it a generous gesture for Herigar to say he had been in the wrong.

Hastein reached out and clasped wrists with Herigar. "I accept your friendship, and will value it. As to what has happened between us here, had I been in your place, I might well have done the same."

"What of my sister Sigrid?" I asked.

Herigar looked uncomfortable. "Birka's market is one of the largest in the north for the slave trade," he said. "It is not a thing I am proud of. I, myself, follow the White Christ. I believe it is wrong for men to buy and sell each other. It is wrong to make men into property. The Son of God taught that we should strive to treat others as we would have them treat us. When I became one of his followers, I freed all of my own slaves. But the slave trade brings much wealth through Birka, and the king's tax upon it is something he has no interest in giving up."

I did not care about Birka's market, or the king's tax. I did not care what Herigar believed. "What of my sister?" I asked again.

"After he arrived in Birka, Toke let it be known that he had a woman of rare value and beauty to sell. She was of noble birth, he claimed, and had never been known by a man."

"When you heard a woman of noble birth was to be sold, you made no effort to stop it?" I asked.

Herigar shook his head. "She was not Svear. Selling her broke no laws of our land." He continued. "There were, at the time, three traders here in Birka who travel down the rivers of the eastern road. Buyers for the slave markets of the Araby kingdoms at its far end pay high prices for fair-skinned women with golden or red hair. Such are greatly valued as concubines by the nobles there. One of the traders even had an Araby buyer with him, who had made the long journey up the eastern road to see our lands.

"For three days Toke plied the three with tales of the beauty of this woman, but he would not let any of them see her. Then, on the fourth day, he offered her for sale. It was in a ship's tent he had set up upon the shore. By now rumors about this woman had spread throughout Birka, and many wished to attend the sale just to see her. But only those who showed Toke they possessed at least enough to meet his minimum price, the amount at which he would open bidding—a full mark of silver—were allowed into the tent. The three eastern road traders and the Arab of course all attended, as did several other merchants from the town. I attended, too, out of curiosity. Toke could hardly have barred me from entering.

"Toke provided us all with wine and ale and food. No doubt he hoped that drink might help loosen the purse strings of the buyers. While we waited, he had your sister examined. There is a crone who works for the slavers here in Birka. When it is claimed that a female slave has never been with a man—a thing that makes her of greater value—she inspects them, for a fee. The crone came out and told us it was as Toke had said—the woman had never known a man.

"Then Toke brought her into the tent, with a cloak wrapped around her, and stood her in front of us. He jerked the cloak away, and left her standing there naked for all to see. He allowed any who wished to stand near her, to walk around her, to examine her closely. Only actually touching her was forbidden.

"All that he had said was true. Your sister is a woman of rare beauty. For that alone, she would have brought a high price. But it was more than just her beauty that excited the traders, and drove them to bid higher and higher against each other. Most women in such circumstances would have been weeping, or shaking with fear. But your sister shed not a single tear, and the only thing that showed in her eyes and on her face was anger, and hatred for us all. The traders all agreed that the nobles who would bid on her, down in the Araby kingdoms at the far end of the eastern road, would pay a fortune for the sport of breaking such a woman to their will.

"In the end, it was the trader who had brought the buyer with him up from the south who won her. Together, they offered three and a half marks of silver for her. It is an unheard of amount for a single slave."

"You said Toke has already gone. My sister...Sigrid?" I asked, although in my heart, I already knew the answer.

Herigar shook his head. "The trader who bought her left Birka the day before you arrived. By now he and his Arab companion may already be upon the eastern road."

12

How Dangerous Can It Be?

Before he left us, Herigar requested that Hastein discourage any of our men from entering the town. "I know now, of course, that you are not a threat," he explained. "But for several days the folk of this town have believed, as did I, that you were part of an attack on Birka, and on them. They have lived in fear these past days, and fear often breeds anger. Though you are not allied with Anund—and I will make certain that is widely known—still, you are Danes. The folk here expect that someday soon Anund *will* come with a force of Danes to attack Birka. I do not wish there to be any trouble between your men and the townsfolk. I will send merchants here to look at your goods and trade with you."

He did more than that. Herigar seemed truly remorseful for what had occurred. Toward evening, a cart arrived carrying three kegs of ale, four roasted suckling pigs, plus baskets filled with sausages, bread, and cheeses. It was a feast extended as an offering of peace. By evening's end, our men were drinking toasts to his generosity and good will. All were in good spirits, for we had fought and beaten a stronger adversary without any losses of our own, had escaped what for a time had seemed a certain death, and now looked to profit, as well, by selling the goods stolen by Sigvald's band during their months of piracy.

All were in good spirits save me. Toke had fled, and Sigrid was lost.

"Do not be discouraged," Hastein told me. "For now, Toke has escaped us. But we know where he is bound. I give you my word—in the spring, we will follow him to Ireland. By then, those of our company who are wounded will once more be hale, and after spending a winter at ease in their homes, the rest of my men, including Svein, will be eager to join us."

I did not answer.

"I am sorry about your sister, Sigrid," Hastein continued. "But she is gone. There is no way now that we can find her. Her fate has been set by the Norns, and the paths of her life and yours will not cross again. You must accept that."

I knew what Hastein said was true. But I could not drive from my mind the image of Sigrid, standing alone, naked and helpless before a group of slavers bidding against each other to purchase her. I could not drive from my mind the images of what would happen to her after the slaver who had bought her sold her again.

Later that night, while the rest of the crew were drinking toasts to Herigar with the fine ale he had provided, Rauna came to where I was sitting, alone in the dark on the deck of the *Gull*, my back against my sea chest. I wanted to be alone with my thoughts, and wished she would go away.

"The man you were hunting—the bad man—he is gone from Birka, yes?" she asked.

I nodded.

"Your sister—he sold her to be a slave, as you

feared?"

I nodded again, and turned my head away, willing her to go and leave me alone.

"And the men who bought her have taken her away?"

"Yes," I said, sighing heavily. "They have taken her away."

"My father was a very great hunter—the greatest among all of our people. He taught me much. I am in *your* debt. You saved me twice. I am very good at tracking. I will help you follow these men and find your sister."

It was a kindness so unexpected that it clutched at my heart, and for a few moments I was unable to speak. I looked at her, kneeling in front of me, and said, "I thank you. But they have taken her across the sea. I do not know where she is. I cannot help her. No one can."

The merchants promised by Herigar appeared the next morning. They were a surly lot. Torvald, whom Hastein had put in charge of the negotiations, quickly became angry at the prices they offered for our various goods. He had envisioned the prizes captured from Sigvald's camp bringing in far more wealth. When one merchant's offer for a bale of furs provoked him into a shouted tirade of curses and insults about the man's parentage, Hastein took over the bargaining.

"Is this the best offer you will make for these?" he demanded.

"It is the best offer I will make to a Dane," the man sneered.

"We have ten such bales. Will you take them all for the same price each?"

The merchant, a fat man with beady eyes, was clearly surprised. "Aye, I will," he replied.

"Then they are yours. Give me the silver—do not try to short weigh me on it—and take them."

Hastein walked along the pier where the rest of the goods were stacked, and quickly found buyers for them. The Birka merchants smirked at each other, for the prices Hastein accepted would allow them to make generous profits when they resold the goods.

Einar and I had been watching the negotiations. Hastein walked over to us, a disgusted look on his face. "They are little better than robbers," he said. "But whatever we take for these goods will be profit, as we paid nothing for them. I wish to be done with this and be gone. I am eager to see the last of Birka, and we have a long journey ahead of us before we reach Jutland again. Winter fast approaches, and I would have us off the sea. I will not sell the walrus tusks or amber here, though. Their value is too great to throw away. We will take them back with us, and sell them for a fair price in Hedeby."

That evening, after the merchants had left and the goods that had crowded our decks were gone, we were readying the *Gull* and the *Serpent* for departure on the morrow. Torvald sent men to gather discarded ballast stones that were scattered along the shore so he could rebalance the ships. He had had to remove many from inside the bottoms of the hulls of the *Gull* and *Serpent* before they had sailed from Oeland, to compensate for the weight of the goods we'd taken from the pirates' camp.

Herigar—for once not accompanied by an armed guard—walked down the dock to our ships. A tall man with blond hair and beard was with him. In his stature and build he much resembled Hastein, though he looked to be somewhat younger.

Assuming Herigar had come to say his farewells, Hastein and Torvald met him on the pier between the two ships. I joined them, as did many others of our company, including Einar and Gudfred. Although we had once thought him a foe, and would have killed him if we'd had the chance, now all had come to view the captain of Birka's garrison with great respect.

"So you are leaving Birka?" Herigar asked.

Hastein nodded. "Aye. At first light we sail for Oeland. We left some of our company recovering there from wounds, after our battle with the pirates. Then from Oeland, it will be back to Jutland, and our homes."

"I wish you a safe and speedy journey." Turning to me, Herigar indicated the man with him and said, "This is Rurik. He has only recently arrived in Birka, although I knew his father years before. He has traveled the eastern road. He has information that may be of interest to you."

"Herigar has told me that your sister was sold to a slave trader," Rurik said, "and that he has left Birka, headed for the eastern road."

"Yes," I said. "That is true."

"They will be sailing for Aldeigjuborg. It is at the

392

northern end of the eastern road, and lies almost due east from Birka, across the Austmarr. Once they cross the sea, they will enter a long, narrow bay, and must sail to its far end. A river empties into the bay there. The river is not long, and leads to a great lake, much like the lake Birka is located on. Another, much longer river empties into this lake on its southern shore. Aldeigjuborg is there, on that river."

"How long a journey is it?" I asked.

He studied the *Gull* and *Serpent* briefly. "In fast ships such as these, even if you have only modest winds, you can reach the end of the bay in three days' time, sailing without stopping. With stronger winds, the journey will be briefer than that."

"The men who bought your sister are not sailing in a longship," Herigar volunteered. "They are in a knarr. They are carrying many female slaves in addition to her, plus other cargo. They cannot sail nearly as swiftly as these ships can. And they may not sail straight through. If they break their journey for the night, once they reach the bay on the far side of the Austmarr…."

"Hastein!" I cried, turning to face him. "It is possible we can catch them!"

He shook his head. "It is too long a chance, Halfdan. They left Birka five days ago. Even if their ship is slower than ours, too much time has passed. By now they surely will have reached Aldeigjuborg, or at the very least be nearing it. They almost certainly will have already departed down the eastern road by the time we could get there. I am truly sorry, but that is a journey I am not willing to take."

"They may not leave Aldeigjuborg so soon," Rurik said. "The eastern road is very long and very dangerous. They will not travel it alone. There is safety in numbers. They will surely wait until other merchants are ready to make the journey, as well. And they cannot travel the road in a knarr. They will need a ship—or more likely several ships, if they are bringing many slaves and much cargo—with shallower drafts and more oars than a knarr, for they will be traveling upriver for the first part of the journey and may often have to row, and there are several portages where the ships must be dragged over land. It will take them some time to prepare for this journey. They will not leave Aldeigjuborg quickly. There is even a chance, with winter so near, that they may bide there until spring. Many of the eastern road merchants make their homes there."

"We do not know the way," Hastein protested, sounding exasperated.

"I can guide you," Rurik offered. "I am seeking passage to Aldeigjuborg, for my kinfolk are there, and I have been very long away."

"Surely this is a journey the Norns wish us to take," I pleaded. "They would not have provided us with a guide, and a chance to find Sigrid, if that were not so. She is my family," I added. "The only family I have left."

Hastein scanned the faces of the men who had gathered around, watching and listening. "We sailed on this voyage to hunt Toke," he told them." That is why all of you came. If we do this, it will only be because we all agree to it. I will not make this decision alone."

"We should do this thing," Gudfred said. "Hrorik

Strong-Axe was our chieftain. Sigrid is his only daughter. If there is a chance to save her, we should try. We should do this for Hrorik, for Sigrid—and for Halfdan."

"Aye, aye," the men from the estate and the village cried, all voicing their approval.

"Torvald?" Hastein asked.

"What of our comrades back on Oeland?"

"I will get word to them that you have been delayed," Herigar said.

Torvald looked from side to side, into the faces of Hastein's men. Bryngolf, Hallbjorn, and the others nodded to him. "Halfdan is our comrade," Torvald said, shrugging his shoulders. "We should do this thing."

Hastein waited, but no one spoke against it. "Then it is decided," he said, but did not sound pleased.

Turning to Herigar, he asked, "What is the name of this slaver we are seeking, and how many men does he have?"

"His name is Hugliek," Herigar replied. "He has fifteen warriors who help him sail the knarr and protect his goods. And there is the Arab buyer, also. He has two warriors of his own people with him as guards."

Hastein sighed and shrugged his shoulders. "We have sailed the length of the Austmarr, and have faced pirates and the garrison of Birka," he said resignedly. "Compared to that, this is but a short journey, and we will only be dealing with a small party of merchants. How dangerous can it be?"

Maps

THE SEA VOYAGE: DANISH WATERS

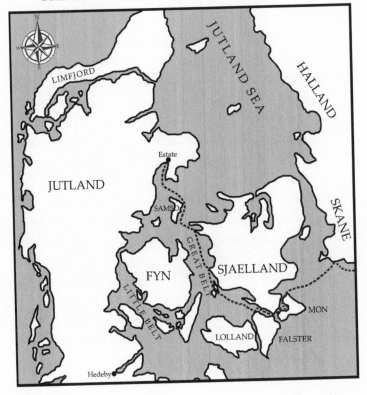

THE SEA VOYAGE: THE AUSTMARR

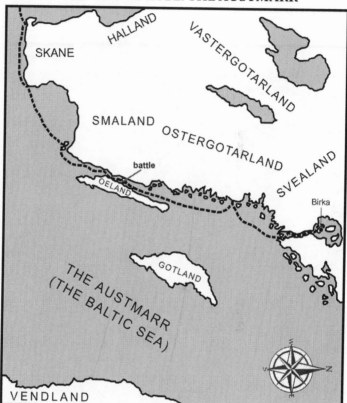

Diagrams of Sea Battle

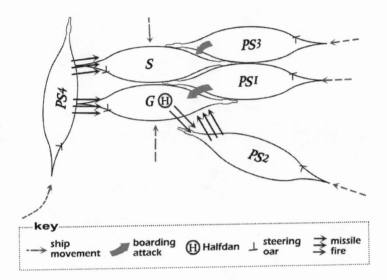

key

→ ship movement | ⬗ boarding attack | Ⓗ Halfdan | ⊥ steering oar | ⇶ missile fire

1. Pirate ships 1, 2, and 3 block the channel, and Pirate Ship 1, Sigvald's ship, rows close to the *Gull* and *Serpent*. Sigvald demands payment of a toll to allow Hastein's ships to pass. Hastein refuses, and the battle begins.

2. The *Gull* and *Serpent* are lashed together into a fighting platform. Pirate ship 1 rows between their bows, grapples both, and her crew tries to board the *Gull*. Pirate Ship 3 grapples the *Serpent* and her crew tries to board, while missile fire from Pirate Ship 2 is directed at the *Gull's* defenders, in her bow. Pirate Ship 4 directs missile fire at the *Gull* and *Serpent* from off of their sterns.

3. From atop the *Gull's* water cask, Halfdan (H) and Tore shoot at Pirate Ship 2, killing a number of its crew, until return fire drives them into cover. Hrodgar takes command of the defense of the sterns of the *Gull* and *Serpent*.

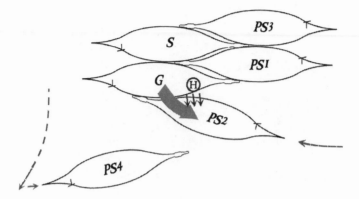

4. Pirate Ship 2 moves further down along the side of the *Gull.* Halfdan and the other archers, who have moved under cover to the *Gull*'s side, launch surprise volley fire and kill most of the warriors in the bow of Pirate Ship 2,

5. A boarding party, led by Hastein and Torvald, grapples Pirate Ship 2, pulls it to the side of the *Gull,* boards it, and with support from the archers, clears the ship.

6. Pirate Ship 4 backs clear of the sterns of the *Gull* and *Serpent* and heads toward Pirate Ship 2.

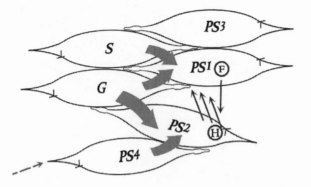

7. Boarding attacks are launched from the bows of the *Gull* and the *Serpent* against Pirate Ship 1, but initially are beaten back. Halfdan and the other archers, who are supposed to support the attack with arrow fire from the stern of Pirate Ship 2, are pinned down by fire from the Finn archer (F) aboard Pirate Ship 1.

8. After the Finn archer is killed, Halfdan and the archers fire volleys into the defenders on the bow of Pirate Ship 1, and Hastein and Stig lead their men onto her, pushing the defenders back.

9. Pirate Ship 4 grapples Pirate Ship 2 and her crew boards to attack the archers and retake the ship. Hrodgar leads a counterattack from the *Gull*, but is killed.

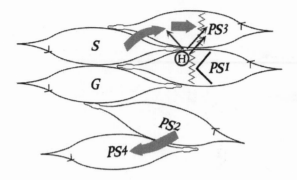

10. Led by Halfdan, the archers aboard Pirate Ship 2 and the warriors who came with Hrodgar from the *Gull* drive back the attackers from Pirate Ship 4, then board their ship and clear it.

11. Aboard Pirate Ship 1, the pirates have fallen back to just before the mast, where they form a wedge battle line and are holding off Hastein's shield wall.

12. Halfdan, Einar, Asbjorn, and Hallbjorn cross to the bow of Pirate Ship 1 and shoot into the defenders in the bow of Pirate Ship 3, the *Sea Steed.* Gudfred leads a boarding attack from the *Serpent* onto Pirate Ship 3, then with supporting fire from Halfdan and his archers on Pirate Ship 1, clears the ship.

13. Aboard Pirate Ship 1, Sigvald is killed by arrow fire, and the rest of the pirates surrender.

Glossary

Aldeigjuborg: The Viking peoples' name for the settlement of Staraja Ladoga, located on the River Volkhov off the southern end of Lake Ladoga. Staraja Ladoga was an important trading center during the 8th and 9th centuries, and was the northern end of the two trade routes known as the eastern road that led down through Russia along several of its rivers to the Black and Caspian Seas.

aurar: Literally "ounces" (singular: eyrir); a Viking era measurement of both weight and value of silver. Eight aurar equaled one mark.

Austmarr: The "East Sea," a term used by Viking era Scandinavian peoples to refer to the Baltic Sea in northern Europe. The Baltic was also called the "Eastern Lake," the "Eastway," or the "Easterway," although the latter two terms were sometimes used to refer to not only the Baltic Sea itself, but also the lands bordering it.

baldric: A belt or strap, usually made of leather, worn over the shoulder, from which a sword's scabbard would hang, typically positioned at the opposite hip. Wearing a sword on a baldric, instead of attaching the scabbard to a belt at the waist, had the advantage that the scabbarded sword could more quickly and easily be removed.

berserker: Warriors in Viking age Scandinavian society who were noted for their exceptional fierceness and fearlessness in battle, and for their moody, difficult dispositions in periods of peace.

Birka: A town located on the island of Bjorko on Lake Malaren in Sweden. By virtue of its location near the eastern end of the Baltic Sea, Birka was an important trading center serving the eastern road, two long trade routes running down several rivers through the lands of modern Russia, eventually reaching the Black and Caspian Seas. Using the eastern road, Viking merchants were able to trade directly with the Byzantine and Muslim Caliphate Empires.

bracer: A long cuff of leather worn by archers on the wrist area of the arm they hold their bow with, to protect against the slap of the bowstring when the bow is shot.

braces: On a square-rigged ship, the lines attached to the ends of the yard, used to rotate it and the sail around the mast.

brynie: A shirt of mail armor, made of thousands of small iron or steel rings linked together into a flexible garment.

butt: A backstop, usually made of rolled and compressed hay, used for archery target practice.

byre: A barn or animal shed. In Viking era Scandinavia, a farm's animal byre was usually connected to the main longhouse, or hall, in which the inhabitants of the farm lived.

carl: A free man in Viking-age Scandinavian society.

common tongue: The proto-Germanic language now known as Old Norse, which during the Viking era was spoken across Scandinavia. According to some of the older sagas, it was also spoken by the Anglo-Saxons in England, who had migrated from their Scandinavian homelands several centuries earlier, although by the later centuries of the Viking era the language in England had evolved into Old English.

Danevirke: A great earthen wall built across the base of the Jutland peninsula of Denmark, from coast to coast, to protect the Danish lands from invasion by the Franks.

denier: A Frankish silver coin, first introduced as a standard measure of currency by Charlemagne. Deniers were roughly equivalent in size and value to English silver pennies of the time, in that it took 240 of each to make one pound.

draugr: The walking dead; a dead person who is not at rest and roams in the night.

eastern road: Trade routes used by the Vikings that traveled down through what is now Russia, on the Volga and Lovat-Dnieper River systems, allowing Scandinavian merchants to trade directly with the Byzantine Empire and the Muslim Caliphate.

ell: A length of measurement based on the distance from the tip of the middle finger to the elbow, about eighteen inches.

Falster: A Danish island located below Sjaelland and just west of the island of Mon.

felag: The agreement made among members of a ship's crew prior to a voyage which covered, among other things, how any profit from the voyage would be divided.

Finn:
The name commonly used during the Viking era to describe the Sami peoples of northern Scandinavia. The Sami, sometimes also called Lapps by outsiders, lived a hunter-gatherer lifestyle in areas of the lands that are now Norway, Sweden, Finland, and Russia.

fletching:
The three feathers at the back of an arrow used to stabilize its flight.

Frankia:
Also called Francia; the land of the Franks, roughly corresponding to most of modern France, Belgium, the Netherlands, and western Germany. By A.D. 845, the former Frankish Empire had split into three kingdoms: West Frankia, roughly corresponding to modern France; the Eastern Frankish Kingdom, stretching from the Rhine River eastward through the lands now comprising modern Germany; and the short-lived Middle Kingdom, which stretched from Frisia in the north to the Mediterranean coast of modern France, and also included parts of northern Italy.

godi:
A priest in pagan Viking age Scandinavian society. The position of godi was usually held by a chieftain, and typically a godi would preside not only over religious festivals and sacrifices, but also over a Thing, or regional assembly. A godi could also administer oaths, which were usually sworn on a special ring of iron or sometimes gold.

Gotar: One of the two main tribal groups that inhabited much of the lands composing modern Sweden. Although the lands of the Vastergotars and the Ostergotars were separate, independent kingdoms before and during the early part of the Viking era, the more powerful Svear kingdom to the east became dominant by the latter part of the tenth century, and during the latter centuries of the Viking period Svear kings ruled both peoples and lands.

great belt: The channel between the Danish islands of Sjaelland and Fyn.

Halland: A province or region along the west coast of modern Sweden, which during the Viking era was considered to be part of Denmark.

Hedeby: The largest town in ninth-century Denmark, and a major Viking age trading center. Hedeby was located near the base of the Jutland peninsula on its eastern side, on a fjord jutting inland from the coast.

house carl: A warrior in the personal service of a chieftain or nobleman, who lives in the chieftain's longhouse.

Huginn:	According to Viking mythology, one of two ravens who would keep Odin, the chieftain of the gods, informed of all that occurred across the worlds of gods and men. The name Huginn meant "thought." Odin's other raven was named Muninn, meaning "memory."
i-viking:	To go raiding.
jarl:	A very high-ranking chieftain in Viking-age Scandinavian society, who ruled over a large area of land on behalf of the king. The word and concept "jarl" is the origin of the English "earl."
Jutland:	The peninsula that forms the mainland of modern and ancient Denmark, named after the Jutes, one of the ancient Danish tribes.
Jutland Sea:	The sea to the north and east of the Jutland peninsula, separating it from Norway.
knarr:	A general-purpose ship used in Viking-age Scandinavia for trade and other commercial uses. Though of similar construction to longships, knarrs tended to be shorter and broader, had higher sides, and were designed to be propelled primarily by sail, although they could be rowed and typically had three to five oars per side.

Limfjord: A long fjord that runs completely across the northern tip of the Jutland peninsula in Denmark, providing a protected passage during the Viking period between the Scandinavian lands and the North Sea.

longship: The long, narrow ship used for war by the peoples of Viking-age Scandinavia. Longships had shallow drafts, allowing them to be beached or to travel up rivers, and were designed to be propelled swiftly by either sail or by rowing. They were sometimes also called dragonships, because many longships had carved heads of dragons or other beasts decorating the stem post at the bow of the ship.

mark: A measurement of silver by weight, roughly equivalent to eight ounces.

mast-fish: The large, heavy wooden brace on the deck of a longship which supports and braces the ship's mast.

Mon: A Danish island located to the south of Sjaelland, which has high cliffs facing east over the Baltic sea.

niddingsvaark: Work of infamy; the dishonorable acts of a Nithing.

Nithing: Also Nidding; one who is not considered a person because he has no honor. Nithing is the root word from which the word "nothing" evolved.

nock: The notch cut in the rear of an arrow, into which the bowstring is placed to shoot it. When an arrow is seated on the bowstring it is "nocked." Also, the name of the notches cut into the tips of a bow's limbs, in which the bowstring is secured to the bow.

nor: A brackish lake or lagoon connected to the sea by a channel.

Norns: Three ancient sisters who, according to pagan Scandinavian belief, sat together at the base of the world-tree and wove the fates of all men and of the world itself on their looms.

Norse: The Scandinavians who lived in the area of modern Norway. During the mid-ninth century, large portions of the Norse lands were at least nominally ruled by the Danish kings. Non-Scandinavians sometimes used the term Norsemen, or Northmen, to describe any Viking raiders from the Scandinavian lands.

Odin: The Scandinavian god of death, war, wisdom, and poetry; the chieftain of the gods.

Oeland: The island of Oland, located just off the coast of Sweden. Although before the Viking era and during its early years the inhabitants of Oland were considered a separate people or tribe, referred to in several early Anglo-Saxon sources as the Eowans, by the latter centuries of the Viking Age they were subjects of the Svear kingdom.

Ostergotarland: The land of the Ostergotars; the lands in central Sweden which were the traditional homelands of the Ostrogoths.

reef: To make the surface of a sail smaller so that it will catch less wind.

reefing lines: On the sails of Viking ships, rows of rope lines spaced across the sail horizontally, which could be used to tie up sections of the sail in order to reef, or shorten it.

Ruda: The Viking's name for Rouen, a Frankish town near the mouth of the Seine River.

runes: The alphabet used for writing in the ancient Scandinavian and Germanic languages. Runic letters, comprised of combinations of simple, straight strokes, were easy to carve into stone or wood.

Samso: One of the northernmost of the Danish islands, located roughly nine miles off the eastern coast of Jutland.

scot: A tax or duty, usually in the form of military service, owed to the king.

seax: Also saxe; a single-edged knife, often quite large, widely used as a weapon and tool in the Scandinavian, Germanic, and Anglo-Saxon cultures.

sheets: On a square-rigged ship, the lines attached to the bottom corners of the sail.

Sjaelland: The largest of the Danish islands, and the homeland, during the Viking era, of the Danish kings.

skald: A poet.

Skane: The southwestern region of modern Sweden. During the Viking era, both Skane and Halland, the coastal region directly above Skane, were considered part of Denmark.

steer-board: The device used to steer Viking ships, serving a purpose similar to a rudder. Although conventional rudders are typically mounted centered on the stern of a ship, the steer-board, or steering oar, on Viking ships was mounted on the right side of the ship, close to the stern. The modern word "starboard" for the right side of a ship is derived from the use of a steer-board on the right side of Viking ships.

stem post: On a Viking longship, the heavy timbers attached to either end of the keel which curved up to create the bow and stern of the ship, and to which the strakes, or planks of the ship's hull, were attached.

strake: One of the planks used to form the hull of a Viking ship. The strakes were thin—often no more than an inch thick—and the hull was constructed by overlapping the strakes and riveting them together, rather than by nailing planks butted side by side against a frame, the other common method of constructing a wooden hull.

Svear: One of the two main Scandinavian tribes or peoples who inhabited the area of modern Sweden. The kingdom of the Sveas was located in what is now eastern Sweden.

Thing: A regional assembly held periodically in Viking age Scandinavian countries where citizens of an area could present suits to be decided by vote, according to law. Lawsuits heard at Things were the forerunner and origin of what became, centuries later in English culture, the concept of trial by a jury of peers.

Thor: The pagan Scandinavian god of thunder and fertile harvests, of strength, honor and oaths, and the mightiest warrior among the Scandinavian gods.

413

thrall: A slave in Viking-age Scandinavian society.

Valhalla: The great feast hall of Odin, chief of the Vikings' gods.

Vends: What the Viking era Scandinavians called the Wends, a collective name given to various pagan Slavic tribes that inhabited the southern coast of the Baltic Sea, in the areas of modern day Germany and Poland. Wendish towns were frequent targets of Viking raids in the Baltic, and the Wends in turn often raided up into the Danish islands.

wergild: The amount that must be paid to make recompense for killing a man.

White Christ: The Vikings' name for the Christian god, believed to have originally been a derogatory term implying cowardice because he allowed himself to be captured and killed without fighting back against his captors.

yard: On a square-rigged ship, the boom to which the top edge of the sail is attached.

Historical Notes

This installment of Halfdan's adventures in *The Strongbow Saga* is bracketed at either end by actual historical events of the ninth century. During the year 845 A.D., the Danes launched a two-pronged attack against the Frankish kingdoms to their south. One prong was an assault up the Seine River by a fleet of 120 ships—the campaign which forms the historical background for *Dragons from the Sea* and *The Road to Vengeance*, books two and three of *The Strongbow Saga*. As *The Long Hunt* begins, Halfdan and his comrades, including Jarl Hastein, have just returned to Denmark from that campaign in Frankia.

In the second prong of the Danes' 845 attack against the Franks, another Danish fleet, led by King Horik himself, sailed up the Elbe River and attacked the Frankish town of Hamburg. According to a report of the attack in the Frankish source *History of the Archbishops of Hamburg-Bremen* by Adam of Bremen, the Viking army burned the town, destroying it—a marked contrast to the Danes' treatment of Paris after capturing it. Although we cannot know why King Horik treated Hamburg so harshly, one possible reason may be that it was the location from which the Franks had previously launched two unsuccessful invasions of Jutland—the first led by the Frankish emperor Charles the Great, or Charlemagne, and the second by his son, Louis. It may well be that Horik intended the destruction of Hamburg to be an object lesson for the Franks, in retribution for their earlier attempts to invade and conquer the Danish mainland.

Also in 845, or not long thereafter—the existing historical records do not specify the exact date—turmoil was occurring in the Kingdom of the Sveas, located in what today is eastern Sweden. Prior to this time, Svealand had been jointly ruled by two brothers, Bjorn and Anund. But around the year 845, according to the Frankish source *The Life of Anskar* by Bishop Rimbert, the brothers had a falling out, Anund was expelled from the kingdom, and fled to Denmark, leaving his brother Bjorn as the sole Svear king. In Denmark, Anund sought supporters to help him regain the throne by promising to lead them to Birka and allowing them to pillage it. He eventually was able to secure the support of enough Danes to return to Svealand with a fleet of twenty-one Danish ships, plus eleven of this own. In the end, though, Anund agreed to accept a ransom from Birka's citizens, and the town was spared. It is these events in which Halfdan and his comrades become tangentially involved at the end of *The Long Hunt*.

In trying to provide readers of *The Strongbow Saga* with a historically accurate portrayal of the period and of the Vikings' culture, I draw upon a wide range of sources, including reported archaeological findings, contemporary accounts such as the various Frankish chronicles and the Anglo-Saxon Chronicle, and the old Viking sagas. The latter were not reduced to written form until the twelfth and thirteenth centuries—after the end of the Viking period—and thus are considered by some historians to be of dubious historical value. I personally believe that such attitudes ignore the fact that the sagas were originally a form of oral literature, and as such would have been passed down from generation to generation by professional storytellers with considerable accuracy. While some of the sagas seem clearly to have been fanciful tales created solely for the purpose of entertainment, others are strongly based in actual historical facts and the lives of actual people. Two saga sources I drew heavily on while writing this book were *Egil's Saga*, which covers events occurring over a period from the mid-ninth century through the end of the tenth, and the *Heimskringla*, a compilation drawing on numerous Viking era sagas, tales, and poems to tell the history of the kings of Norway, which was written down in the thirteenth century by Snorre Sturlason, an Icelandic skald and writer.

When Halfdan buries some of the wealth he won in Frankia before setting out on the voyage across the Austmarr, he is doing what apparently was a common method of protecting one's wealth during a time when banks did not exist. Numerous Viking era hoards have been found buried in Scandinavia, as well as in England, which was heavily settled by the Vikings. The practice is supported not only by archeological finds, but also by saga accounts. For instance, in *Egil's Saga*, toward the end of his life the title character buries the considerable wealth won over his lifetime in a wilderness location in Iceland, afterwards killing the slaves who helped him bury it. *Egil's Saga*—or more specifically, a description of a feast contained in that work—was also the source for the practice of providing female drinking-horn partners to honored guests at a feast, as Jarl Arinbjorn does in the story at the feast he holds for Hastein on the island of Mon.

The funeral on Oeland, in which the bodies of the slain members of Hastein's company, including the chieftain Hrodgar, are cremated on a longship dragged up onto land and burned, is inspired by a famous account, written in the tenth century by an Arab traveler named Ibn Fadlan, of the funeral of a Viking chieftain which he witnessed in what is now Russia.

When Sigrid is sold into slavery in Birka, a historical issue I faced was what price she might have brought to Toke. Although silver coins were widely used in Viking era Scandinavia, for the most part the coinage had no standardized, generally accepted value—their worth and value in commerce was determined by the weight of silver contained in them. Some common measurements of silver did exist. A mark equaled roughly one-half pound of silver. One mark contained eight aurar (singular eyrir), or ounces, or twenty-four ortogar (singular ortug), each weighing roughly one-third of an ounce. The weight of a silver penny could vary. In England, Norway, and Sweden, 240 pennies typically equaled a mark, but in Jutland, 288 pennies did—and then there was the problem that pennies were not always struck to precise weight, or sometimes were shaved by unscrupulous merchants, making them lighter in weight than they were supposed to be. Thus a scale and set of verified weights would have been indispensable to a Viking era merchant.

The price Sigrid is ultimately sold for, four marks of silver, was suggested to me by a passage in the Laxdaela Saga, in which a chieftain named Hoskuld purchases a female slave from a slave trader known as Gilli the Russian, and pays three marks for her—a price described as three times the normal price for a female concubine. In that story, the slave proved to be the daughter of an Irish king, stolen some years earlier in a raid, although Hoskuld was not aware of that fact when he bought her. I reasoned that Sigrid might command an even higher price because of her noble birth, virginity, defiant courage, and the market in which she would ultimately be resold.

The Island of Mon, Ragnar Logbrod, and His Sons

The character of Jarl Arinbjorn, who rules over Mon for the King of the Danes, is my fictional creation, as is the fact that he and his men serve as the eyes of the Danish realm in the south, watching for attack. However, Mon's location—situated just south of Sjaelland, which was the largest of the Danish islands and the seat of the Danish kings, and on the western edge of the open Baltic Sea—coupled with the fact that its eastern coastline boasts tall cliffs looking out over the sea which are the highest land in all of Denmark, suggested to me, for the purposes of the story, that Mon's cliffs might well have served as a location from which to watch for attackers approaching Denmark by sea, from the south or east. During the Viking era, Mon and other Danish islands were certainly more than once the targets of Wendish raiders coming from those directions.

In the story, Hastein purchases provisions for his two ships while on Mon, including smoke-preserved herring. During the Middle Ages, the town of Stege, located on the nor in central Mon, was the center of a thriving herring fishery, and of significant trade in herring. I thought it reasonable that the inhabitants of Mon might have already been curing and trading herring on a smaller scale by the mid-ninth century when *The Strongbow Saga* is set.

While researching Mon for this story, I encountered an intriguing assertion that the last independent king of Mon was Hemming, a son of Sigvard Snake-eye, a son of Ragnar Logbrod who is also sometimes called Sigurd Snake-in-the eye. Unfortunately the assertion contained no attribution as to its source, and also claimed that Hemming purportedly ruled Mon in the early 800s. For a variety of reasons, I find the statement somewhat suspect. First, for Hemming to have ruled in the early 800s, it would place Sigvald as having lived in the 700s, and second, because Mon is so much smaller than Sjaelland, the seat of the Danish kings, and is separated from the larger island by a channel less than a mile in width, I find it unlikely that Mon would have been an independent kingdom as late as the early ninth century. However, the passage did inspire me to make Sigurd a character in the story, having been fostered with Jarl Arinbjorn by his father, Ragnar Logbrod. Sending a son to be raised in the household of another chieftain was not uncommon among the higher classes of Viking era

Scandinavian society. Doing so not only tended to cement alliances between families, but also would serve to protect a family line, in that at least one male member would not be among those killed if an enemy attacked and wiped out a chieftain's household.

The above-mentioned reference to Sigvard and Hemming also highlights a problem when attempting to find historical evidence of the life and exploits of the legendary Viking leader Ragnar Lodbrod—also sometimes called Lothbrok or Lodbrok—and his progeny. Because there is little concrete historical evidence of any kind concerning Ragnar, and because he figures in some sagas and poems from the period which clearly are largely fictional creations, some historians doubt that Ragnar existed at all. However, Bjorn Ironsides, one of his sons, was without doubt an actual Viking leader during the mid-ninth century, about whom there are several mentions in both Frankish and Irish sources. Ivar the Boneless, sometimes also called Ingvar, is another son of Ragnar who is both a semi-legendary figure and a historical one who figures prominently in the history of the Vikings in Ireland and England during the latter decades of the ninth century. Accordingly it seems likely that the historical Ragnar would have been a Viking leader in the early to mid-ninth century, and thus could well have been the leader of the Viking fleet that captured Paris in 845, who was—according to the Frankish *Annals of Xanten*—named Ragnar.

For the purposes of the story in *The Strongbow Saga*, I have drawn some details about Ragnar and his sons from the *Saga of Ragnar Lodbrok*. Although that work is without a doubt one of the old sagas which is more fiction than fact, nevertheless it does provide a source for some of the legends which grew up about Ragnar and were popular tales during the Viking era. According to *Saga of Ragnar Lodbrok*, Sigurd Snake-in-the eye was Ragnar's youngest son by his second wife, Kraka, who was also the mother of Bjorn and Ivar. The same saga was my source for Ragnar having two older sons, Agnar and Eric, by his first wife Thora, and for the tale of their deaths while trying to conquer the Svear kingdom, as Sigurd relates to Halfdan.

Sea Voyages and Piracy

The sea voyage east in pursuit of Toke posed a number of research challenges, not the least of which was determining what the Viking era Scandinavians would have called the Baltic Sea. Some sources indicate that it was sometimes called the Eastern Lake, but passages in both the *Heimskringla* and the *Ynglinga Saga* refer to it as the Austmarr, or Eastern Sea—the name I chose to use in the story. The Austmarr would not have been considered by Viking era Scandinavians to have included the waters around northern Jutland and the Danish islands; those were called the Jutland Sea in the north, and the Great Belt and Little Belt in the south, between the islands.

I used several sources to estimate sailing times between destinations for the story. Ninth century written records from the court of King Alfred of Wessex in England—commonly known today as Alfred the Great—

include accounts by two different merchants, Wulfstan and Ottar, who sailed and traded in the Baltic, that recite the lands and peoples passed on their voyages, as well as sailing times between various destinations. Another source I drew upon was the excellent website for the Viking Ship Museum at Roskilde in Denmark. The museum has constructed a number of replicas of vessels of different sizes and types from the Viking period, and has tested and sailed them extensively. Its website includes information about the vessels' rowing and sailing speeds, which I used when writing this story.

In the story, for most of the voyage Hastein's two ships stop each night, and their crews make camp upon the shore. While the Vikings without question at times took lengthy sea voyages on which they sailed straight through, day and night, until they reached their destination, from accounts of voyages in numerous sagas, it appears that where possible—and particularly when sailing through Scandinavian waters—they often broke their journey at night. There are several reasons for them to have done so. Longships—the type of ship used for war and raiding—had shallow hulls and open decks with no shelter whatsoever. Although the sagas indicate that when at anchor, tent-like shelters were often rigged over the decks of longships, using awnings and possibly the sail, such shelters would not have been feasible while the ship was underway. And aboard the open, exposed deck of a longship while at sea there would have been no way to cook a meal for its relatively large crew. Thus for the crew to be able to sleep in any kind of comfort out of the weather, and for them to be able to have a hot meal, it would have been necessary to anchor or beach the ships for the night.

While computing sailing times using the ship speeds determined by the Viking Ship Museum and comparing them to the sailing times reported by the ninth century merchants Wulfstan and Ottar, I realized that it seemed probable that on their voyages, the latter took few, if any, breaks for the night between destinations. A possible reason could have been a fear of pirates. Most merchants would have sailed a knarr, or similar vessel, rather than a longship, for knarrs had deeper, broader hulls in proportion to their length than longships, and would have been able to more securely transport large amounts of cargo. However, compared to a longship a knarr would have a relatively small crew, making it much more susceptible to attack and capture.

Pirates were a common risk in the Baltic Sea. A vivid example is found in Rimbert's *Life of Anskar*, which relates how, in the year 839, the Christian monk and missionary Anskar undertook a journey from Hedeby to Birka. However, the merchants with whom he had taken passage were attacked by pirates, who took the ship and all the goods it contained—including forty books Anskar and his companions had been carrying to use in their mission. The crew and passengers were put ashore, and Anskar was forced to continue his journey to Birka over land. To lessen the possibility of such attacks, some merchants probably chose to pursue a more tiring and strenuous, but safer, course by sailing far out to sea, day and night, between destinations.

The Viking-era Scandinavians, incidentally, would not have considered their raiding to be piracy, although the victims of their raids—the Franks, English, and Irish—often referred to the Vikings as pirates. In the Vikings' warrior culture—as in many warrior cultures throughout history—raiding another tribe, people, or land in order to steal their possessions was considered an honorable and legitimate means of acquiring wealth. However, the Scandinavians would have considered sea-going bandits who indiscriminately robbed any passing ship to have been pirates.

The Island of Oland

In the above-mentioned account by the ninth century merchant Wulfstan of his voyages across the Baltic Sea, among the lands he mentions passing is Eowland, the land of the Eowans. He is referring to the long island off the coast of Sweden known today as Oland, and which is called Oeland in the story. Although later in the Viking era, Oland was absorbed into the Kingdom of the Sveas, during the mid-ninth century it was still considered an independent land and its population a separate people from the nearby Sveas, as were a number of other islands in the Baltic, including Bornholm—known in the Viking era as Burgundaholmr, the island of the Burgundians, which today is part of Denmark—and Gotland, which is now a part of Sweden.

While researching my way east across the Baltic, in order to be able to write about the company's sea voyage, I discovered that Oland has a fascinating, although enigmatic, history, which I chose to draw on

425

for the purposes of this story. Approximately eighty-five miles long and ten miles wide, Oland contains the ruins of nineteen large stone forts, built between 300 and 600 A.D. The forts were all abandoned between 600 and 700 A.D. and fell into disrepair, but during the eleventh century some were rebuilt and were used during the rest of the Viking era and into the Middle Ages. A number of Viking-era buried treasure hoards have also been found on Oland, and there are several stone ship settings, marking the sites of Viking age burials.

Archaeologists and historians do not know who built the forts, other than the obvious—persons who lived on Oland during the time of their construction. But the answers to questions such as what was the nature of the culture and community existing there at the time, was it a militarily powerful kingdom, and why the forts were ultimately all abandoned around the same time remain unknown.

One fort—Eketorp—has been the subject of extensive archaeological excavation, and has since been reconstructed. The rebuilt fort, which today operates as a living history museum, provides graphic visual evidence of the imposing military might that must have characterized the culture of the Oland fort builders at the height of their power.

The feast on Oeland during the story takes place in the ruined fort now known as Barby, or Barby Borg. Although all of the other forts on the island are circular ring forts, and many contain the ruins of interior buildings, Barby consists of a semicircular wall enclosing an open space overlooking a steep cliff-side. The sacrifice of horses by the Oelanders in the story is based on a theory developed after a large number of horse bones were discovered in a nearby pit during excavations at Eketorp.

My characterization of the population of Oland as having become, by the mid-ninth century, a somewhat meek folk with little ability to defend themselves against armed intruders such as Sigvald's pirate band is my fictional creation for the purpose of the story, although it was inspired by the mystery of the abandoned network of forts on the island.

The Sea Battle

The old sagas contain numerous accounts of sea battles fought between naval forces during the Viking era, and I have long intended to work such a battle—an iconic aspect of the Viking period—into Halfdan's story in *The Strongbow Saga*. As preparation for writing the battle scene in *The Long Hunt*, I reviewed numerous saga accounts of such battles, including those in the *Heimskringla*, *Egil's Saga*, and *The Saga of the Jomsvikings*.

Common elements found in many Viking era sea battles included the practice by the weaker defending side—and on occasion both sides—where they would lash their ships together to create a single large floating platform from which to fight. As a passage in the *Heimskringla*, describing the battle of Solskel won by King Harald Fairhair of Norway, states: "[I]t was then the custom when they fought on ships to lash the ships together and fight on the stems"—i.e., in the bow and stern of the ships.

Early phases of such battles generally consisted of heavy missile fire back and forth: shooting arrows, throwing spears, and, in many descriptions, also throwing stones. The latter would almost certainly have been ballast stones pulled out of the bottoms of the ships' hulls for use as improvised missile weapons.

Eventually, attempts to board the enemy's ships would occur, for Viking sea battles were ultimately decided by brutal, close-quarters hand-to-hand combat. Based on the various saga accounts, it was not uncommon for boarding attempts to be beaten back, often repeatedly, but in the end, battles were decided when a ship was "cleared"—i.e., all of its defenders were either slain or so badly wounded they could no longer fight.

The *Heimskringla* contains a very vivid account of the famous battle of Svold, in which King Olav Trygvason of Norway, while sailing separate from his main fleet with only three warships, was ambushed by a much larger fleet composed of a mix of Danish ships led by King Svein Forkbeard of Denmark, Swedish ships led by King Olav of the Sveas, and followers of Eric the Jarl, a Norwegian nobleman who was a sworn enemy of Trygvason. During that battle, an archery duel between two skilled bowmen occurred, which inspired the duel during the sea battle in *The Long Hunt* between Halfdan and the Finn archer on Sigvald's ship. One of the two dueling archers in the battle of Svold, who fought from the ship of Eric the Jarl and who bested a famed archer aboard Trygvason's ship, was described as "an outstanding bowman...who was called Finn and who was said by some to be a Finn." That description planted the seed in my mind which led to the characters of Rauna and her father becoming part of the story.

The tactic Halfdan uses to defeat the Finn archer—having Asbjorn, Gudfred, and Einar shoot at the Finn's shield bearer, to cause him to flinch and expose the Finn to Halfdan's shot—was inspired by an account of a battle in the *Heimskringla* that occurred when a large force of Wends, raiding up the western coast of Sweden, attacked a town in Vastergotarland. During the battle, a skilled Wendish archer was killing a man with every arrow he shot. The Wend was protected from enemy fire by two shield bearers, but a father and son pair of archers, among the defenders of the town, killed him. The father shot at one of the shield bearers, causing him to pull his shield away to protect himself just long enough for the son to be able to shoot an arrow into the Wendish archer's head.

Sigvald's unusual armor and weapon are inspired by several different saga sources. Mail shirts, or brynies, were quite expensive and fairly rare during the early centuries of the Viking era. The typical mail armor worn during that period would have been a shirt with short sleeves, coming down at most to the elbow, and a relatively short skirt which covered only part of the thighs. More comprehensive mail armor did exist, however. King Harald Hardrada of Norway had a special mail shirt which was so long that his men nicknamed it "Emma," perhaps because its length was the same as a woman's dress. I envisioned Sigvald's long brynie as being a somewhat similar garment.

Sigvald's axe-spear does not match any actual weapon found from the period. However, there are descriptions in several sagas of heavy "hewing spears" of unknown design, and in *Egil's Saga*, at one point the title character and his brother both fight in a battle armed with unusual, heavy spear-like weapons called, in the English translations of the saga, "halberds." The translator must have been unable to discern an exact meaning for the original Old Norse description of the weapon, for a halberd is a long-handled pole axe that was developed centuries later during the Middle Ages. However, I chose to arm Sigvald with a somewhat similar, though far shorter, weapon—a spear with an axe-like blade on its shaft, which could be used for both stabbing and hewing.

The Sami

The ancestors of the Sami people—also called Lapps, although not by the Sami themselves—were a people of Finno-Ugrian ethnic origin, who reached Scandinavia as early as 10,000 B.C., long before the Germanic tribes who became the Viking peoples reached the same lands. By around 800 B.C., possibly earlier, they had split into two distinct cultures: the Finns and the Sami.

The Finns were concentrated mostly in the lands which today comprise southern Finland, plus Estonia and western Russia, particularly the area around Lake Ladoga. By the Viking Age, the Sami populated a broad swath of land across Scandinavia, including parts of modern day Norway, central Sweden, and Finland.

During the Viking era, the Sami lived a simple hunter-gatherer existence and engaged in seasonal migrations, moving to coastal and lake regions in the summer, when fishing played a major role in their food production, and deeper into the forests in winter, when hunting—particularly the hunting of reindeer—became their primary source of food, as well as a means of acquiring furs to be used as trade goods. By the Viking period, it had apparently become common for the Sami to gather in relatively large winter villages, although in summer months they may have more often lived in smaller, family-based groups. While migrating and during summer months, the Sami often lived in tents made from animal skins that looked remarkably like the tipis of North American Plains Indian tribes. Although known today as herders of reindeer, the Sami of the Viking period merely hunted the deer—they did not domesticate and begin herding them until the late 1500s.

The Sami were, rather confusingly, called "Finns" by the Viking era Scandinavians, or sometimes "Skridfinns," which translates roughly into "Ski" and "Finn"—during the winter months, the Sami traveled and hunted on a primitive form of ski. Both archaeological and saga evidence reflect that the Sami engaged in trade with the Viking era Scandinavians, exchanging furs for goods they did not produce. However, saga sources, as well as the account told by Norwegian merchant Ottar to King Alfred of Wessex, also reflect that some Scandinavian chieftains regularly extracted "tribute," paid in furs, from the more peaceful

Sami, and both Viking sagas and Sami legends tell of occasional raiding expeditions against the Sami.

Knowledge of the old Sami religion is spotty at best, for the Scandinavian peoples of the Middle Ages and later forced the Sami to convert to Christianity and did their best to stamp out all vestiges of their former beliefs. Apparently their gods were closely connected with different aspects of nature, and they believed in two parallel realms of reality: the physical world and the spirit world. The Sami's shamans, called noaidi, were men and women who possessed the power to enter into trance states and travel back and forth between the two worlds.

Sweden and Birka

During the Viking Age, the lands which constitute modern-day Sweden were not a single country or kingdom. Both Skane, the region comprising the southwestern coast, and Halland, just above Skane, were considered Danish lands. The ancient homelands of the Goth tribes—Vastergotarland and Ostergotarland, collectively known as Gotarland—stretched from the western coast above Halland across central Sweden. To the northeast was Svealand, the Kingdom of the Sveas.

Between 1,000 and 300 B.C., waves of Germanic peoples migrated out of Scandinavia and into eastern Europe, establishing new homelands there. The Goth tribes—the Goths, Ostrogoths, and Visigoths, as they were known to the Romans—conquered and settled vast regions, at their peak controlling lands ranging from the Baltic to the Black Sea. But in the late fourth century, the

Huns invaded the Goths' lands from the east, and drove them and other Germanic tribes westward into the Roman Empire, precipitating its collapse.

By the beginning of the Viking Age, the original Scandinavian homelands from which the various Goth tribes had migrated hundreds of years earlier were still identified by name. Although they were collectively considered a single people, the Gotars—or Geats, as they were known to the Anglo-Saxon English—in the early Viking era, two distinct Gotar kingdoms at least nominally still existed: Ostergotarland and Vastergotarland. But as independent kingdoms, they figure almost not at all into the history of the Viking era, and well before the end of the period, the lands and peoples of the Ostergotars, and parts of Vastergotarland, had fallen under the rule of the Sveas.

The town of Birka, located on the island of Bjorko in Lake Malaren, within the kingdom of the Sveas, was an important trading center in the early centuries of the Viking era. It was flourishing by 800 A.D., but was abandoned around 970, possibly because subsiding water levels in Lake Malaren made access from the sea more difficult.

Archaeological examinations have provided much evidence about Viking Birka. The town faced a natural harbor which may have been surrounded by a man-made barricade of pilings, and was protected on its landward side by an earthen wall, probably topped by a wooden stockade. A fort, built atop a rocky hill, overlooked the town, and was apparently manned by a garrison of warriors provided by the Svear king.

According to Adam of Bremen in the *History of the Archbishops of Hamburg-Bremen*, the channel leading from the sea to Lake Malaren and Birka had hidden obstacles of boulders which had been placed there to make access more difficult for the unwary. Building on that description for the purpose of the story in *The Long Hunt*, I created the fictional island and temple to Odin where pilots wait to guide ships up the channel.

The Frankish monk and missionary Anskar reached Birka in 839 A.D. after a perilous journey from Hedeby in Denmark. With the permission of Bjorn, one of the kings of the Sveas, he founded a Christian church in Birka, and converted many of its inhabitants, including Herigar—sometimes also spelled Hergeier in Frankish sources—who is described by Adam of Bremen as the king's prefect in Birka. After two years, Anskar returned to Frankia to become Bishop of Hamburg, but the church flourished under the care of the priests he left behind until 845, when an uprising occurred against the Christians in Birka, and one of the priests there, named Nithard, was slain. Another priest, Gautbert, escaped with the help of Herigar, who is repeatedly described in Frankish sources as a good man. The attack on the Christians in Birka is attributed by Adam of Bremen to instigation by Anund, the brother of King Bjorn who was subsequently expelled from Svealand.

Within the kingdoms of Viking-era Scandinavia, there was no general taxation of the populace by the kings. The primary means of raising revenue were raiding other lands and collecting tribute from peoples who had submitted to the superior might of a given king. The king was entitled to call upon his own people for service in times of need, and kings did sometimes collect specialized tolls or taxes, particularly in relation to towns. Although I have thus far found no explicit references to a tax on merchants who traded in Birka, in Norway a tax called the landaurar was assessed on merchants and travelers landing in the kingdom from abroad. Given that the Svear king maintained a fort and garrison at Birka to protect it, I think it likely that he, too, would have imposed some similar sort of tax to help defray that expense. I have based the amount of the landing tax which Herigar assesses against Hastein—four aurars of silver per ship—on the Norwegian landaurar, which equaled five aurar when established in the late ninth century.

Readers who would like to learn more about the Viking peoples, culture, and history, and the world in which *The Strongbow Saga* is set are urged to visit www.strongbowsaga.com, an educational website dedicated to the Vikings and their age. Those seeking news about the *Strongbow Saga* series or wishing to discuss the story with the author or other fans are encouraged to visit my website, www.judsonroberts.com.

Acknowledgements

It has been a long and winding journey to reach publication of *The Long Hunt*, the fourth installment of Halfdan's adventures in *The Strongbow Saga*. The first three books of the series, *Viking Warrior*, *Dragons from the Sea*, and *The Road to Vengeance*, were originally published by HarperCollins Publishers between 2006 and 2008. Many mistakes were made which I will not go into here, but their ultimate result was that after publishing book 3, HarperCollins cancelled the series.

Not being someone who is prone to give up without a fight, I regained the rights to the series from HarperCollins, and with the help of my wife, Jeanette, formed my own publishing company, Northman Books Inc. Together we republished new editions of books 1 through 3 over the course of 2010 and 2011. Once the series was alive and kicking again, I began work on book 4, *The Long Hunt*.

Work on the book was interrupted when, in early 2012, Jeanette and I realized a long-held dream and moved from Houston, Texas to a small farm on the eastern edge of the Cascade Mountains near Eugene, Oregon. The change from being a city-dweller to small-scale farming on our own homestead has been a wonderful, transformative experience, but on a farm the work is never done. Learning our new life caused me to fall far behind in my writing, although in the long run it has greatly enriched the story in *The Strongbow Saga*. Being surrounded by the beauty and majesty of nature, having daily encounters with wildlife, and living a life that is closely tied to the rhythms of the seasons has without question given me a deeper empathy and understanding of life in a simpler time. But when 2012 ended and there was still no new installment of Halfdan's story, I made a vow to myself and to the loyal fans of the series that the next book would come out in 2013.

It could not have happened without Jeanette. Many, many days while I worked at my desk, she single-handedly managed our farm: cutting and storing hay by hand, tending to our garden, caring for the animals, as well as taking care of the myriad chores that exist within every home. I am blessed to have her as my partner in every aspect of our lives.

Republishing a preexisting book is a very different undertaking from creating one from scratch. Whatever issues I had with HarperCollins, I was fortunate to have had wonderful editors there, whose input greatly enhanced books 1 through 3. After I completed writing *The Long Hunt*, four volunteer editors read my efforts and gave me their suggestions and feedback, and they, too, helped the finished book become a better product. My thanks go out to my wife Jeanette, who has a strong feel for the integrity, flow, and emotional impact of stories; to her daughter Laura Beyers, a professional technical writer and editor who helped identify several scenes where the emotional reactions and motivations of characters could be more clearly manifested; to Alexa Linden, a long-time fan of the series who has often corresponded with me about it, who sometimes seems to know the characters almost better than I do, and helped me keep them true to themselves; and to Luc Reid, a friend and author who helped me focus on the structure and plot arcs of the story.

Layla Milholen was the copy editor for *The Long Hunt*, and I am in awe of the thorough job she did polishing away its rough edges.

Luc Reid deserves special thanks. He has been a part of *The Strongbow Saga* since its very beginning in 2001, when he gave me editorial feedback on my first efforts at putting Halfdan's tale into words. He has played a major role in the republication of books 1 through 3, and not only acted as one of the editors for *The Long Hunt*, but also transformed my rough sketches into the maps and diagrams that are contained in the book, created its cover, and set up the format for the print edition of the book. He is a good friend, a man of numerous talents, and a true comrade. Thank you, Luc.

When writing, I draw inspiration from many sources. Two bits of phrasing in the story I borrowed from songwriters. In chapter one, Halfdan recalls Genevieve's final words when they parted in Paris. The phrase "shelter my love from wind and wave" is from the song "Nostalgia" by Emily Barker. And in chapter eleven, when Hastein tells Herigar that "when I die, it will be with my arms unbound," his words are taken from the song "This Is Why We Fight" by The Decemberists.

Last but far from least, I would like to thank all of the loyal fans of the series, including those who have recommended it to their friends and family, creating a word-of-mouth demand that has kept it alive, and who have so often told me how much they enjoy the story and long for more. My thanks to those who have taken the trouble to contact me and tell me that some aspect of Halfdan's story touched or moved them, and to those who have written to thank me for bringing to light aspects of their ancestors and heritage. All of you have helped keep my own faith in this journey alive. You are why I write.

Judson Roberts
December 2013

Made in the USA
Lexington, KY
02 February 2014